For Norman and Gwen
Best wishes
John R Knaggs
The Alamo – San Antonio, Texas
Oct. 1, 2005

This book is dedicated
to the memory of my beloved mother,
Samantha, whose support, understanding and
editing formed the basis for the
quality of the book.

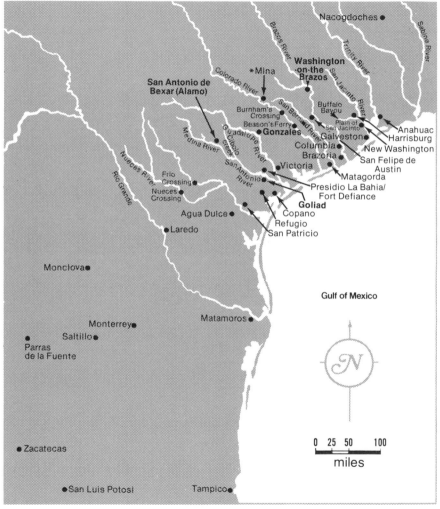

Nacogdoches ●

Washington-on-the-Brazos

＊Mina

San Antonio de Bexar (Alamo)

Burnham's Crossing

Beason's Ferry

Gonzales

Buffalo Bayou

Plain of San Jacinto

Galveston ●

Anahuac

Harrisburg

New Washington

Columbia

Brazoria ●

San Felipe de Austin

Victoria ●

Matagorda

Presidio La Bahia/ Fort Defiance

Goliad

Frio Crossing ●

Nueces Crossing ●

Agua Dulce ●

Copano

Refugio

San Patricio

●Laredo

Monclova ●●

Gulf of Mexico

Monterrey ●

Matamoros ●

●

Saltillo ●

Parras de la Fuente

● Zacatecas

N

0 25 50   100

miles

●San Luis Potosi

Tampico ●

＊Now known as Bastrop

The above map of a portion of Texas and northern
Mexico contains the major points of reference for
the political and military action described in this
book.

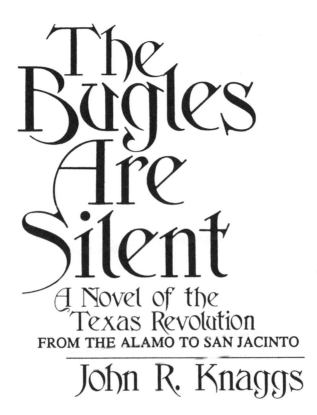

The Bugles Are Silent

A Novel of the Texas Revolution
FROM THE ALAMO TO SAN JACINTO

John R. Knaggs

COVER BY DON COLLINS

Sunridge Publishing Co.
1800 West 46th Street
Austin, Tx. 78756

FIRST EDITION - SEPTEMBER 1977
SECOND EDITION - MARCH 1978
THIRD EDITION - NOVEMBER 1984
FOURTH EDITION - AUGUST 1986
FIFTH PRINTING - JULY 1989
SIXTH PRINTING - AUGUST 1992
SEVENTH PRINTING - MAY 1995
EIGHTH PRINTING - FEBRUARY 1996
NINTH PRINTING - SEPTEMBER 1996
TENTH PRINTING - JUNE 1997
ELEVENTH PRINTING - JUNE 1998
TWELFTH PRINTING - OCTOBER 1999
THIRTEENTH PRINTING - NOVEMBER 2001
FOURTEENTH PRINTING - APRIL 2003
FIFTEENTH PRINTING - APRIL 2005

Published By

Sunridge Publishing Co.
4707 Sinclair Ave.
Austin, TX 78756

Library of Congress Cataloging in Publication Data

Knaggs, John R   1934-
    The bugles are silent.

        1. Texas — History — Revolution, 1835-1836 — Fiction.
I. Title.

PZ4K677Bu [PS3561.N27]   813'.5'4   77-22775
ISBN 1-881825-02-7

Printed and bound in the United States of America.

Foreword

Every American generation sooner or later comes back to the story of the Texas war for independence, for whatever the problems and pressures of the present, this is a story that will never die.

It has all the elements that have fascinated human beings through the ages: a struggle between peoples, a struggle for land, for ideals, for freedom — a clash of cultures that was inevitable upon this continent, and which was decisive for the history of the continent, however we may look back on it today. It was a struggle in which good and decent and courageous men and women were caught up on each side, along with the rash, the evil, and the bold. It was a rush of events that even strong men could not control, which only may appear fore-ordained in retrospect. It is a story that must be told and retold, so long as men are men.

Nothing can transcend the stark drama of the Alamo, the grim defiance of warriors against fire and steel and death, or the Greek tragedy of Goliad, played out not by the stars but against the flaws of human character. The retreat of Sam Houston's army, the trial of one man's will and courage against the hinge of fate, the sudden, explosive reversal of fortune at San Jacinto, all these were, are, and will remain high human drama until the end of time.

Above all, the Texas Revolution was a human drama. Its great men were just that, men, not mythic figures acting out roles to assure their immortality. They were heroes who had known failure and despair, who got drunk, made mistakes, suffered now from pride and arrogance, now from rashness or folly — and it is easier, perhaps, for us to understand their folly than their awesome bravery when the chips were down, the string played out.

There were no "marble" figures at the Alamo, and no cardboard characters at Buffalo Bayou. These were Americans and Mexicans as complex as any people struggling against fate today, facing an explosive reality grimmer than those most generations face.

Texas, Texans, and to a vast extent, all Americans alive today are what we are because of what happened in the year 1836. Had things gone otherwise, had those men and women behaved differently, there might easily be no North American Republic stretching from sea to shining sea.

Yet, strangely, less is known about the bloody Texas Revolution than any decisive conflict of modern times. The armies carried along no historians. We have little, if any, indisputable proof of what was said, done, or not done, at command conferences or on the walls of the Alamo. The accounts we have are often conflicting, in every case embellished by self-service or legend. The Texians of that time, as one of them wrote long afterward, were given to action, but not to writing about it.

Of the thousand-odd Texians at San Jacinto, not one bothered to write a comprehensive account until decades had passed. Meanwhile, the leaders had become political and even personal enemies, usually more interested in damaging reputations of their rivals than setting history straight. And Santa Anna, to the end of his long and incredible career, continued to write self-serving explanations to justify the conduct of his Texas campaign.

To the historian, these accounts of the high leaders are not so important, or so useful, as the bits and pieces gleaned from other sources. Letters of "little" people as well as great, odd bits of factual evidence here and there, a casual recorded fact — all these add up to recreate the reality of that year of blood and soil that decided the eventual fate of this continent.

And it is largely upon this sort of evidence that John Knaggs has built his novel.

Long before I saw it, I was aware of the thoroughness, even the stubbornness of his painstaking research — asking questions to which the historian really had no answer, pursuing his own solutions. He delved into the people of 1836, Texan and Mexican, trying to discover how they lived, thought, and felt, how they perceived their world, to tell their story in *their* terms, not his or ours.

He considered unrecorded data about the conditions of weather and state of the moon — because the plans, battles, and destinies of the Texas Revolution were designed by mud and moonlight, and forage and fordage — myriad "little things" the average historical novelist forgets.

He read the letters of Houston, Bowie, Almonte, and Santa Anna, not only to measure what each said, but to get the measure of each man revealed by how he said it.

And out of all this he has written a novel which portrays as none yet has the vital struggle for the soil and soul of Texas from each side.

The events are real; they happened. The big names, the high leaders, all lived and did these things. But the very human men and women, the fictional characters around whom Knaggs has weaved his story, letting us see and feel it through their eyes and emotions — I believe that they lived, too, in some fashion in those years. It all *could* have happened. For fiction portrays reality as well as "history", if it is based on human fact.

That is what gives this novel its reality, its style, and its importance.

San Antonio, TX   5 May 1977   T. R. Fehrenbach

Preface

If Thomas Paine had been a Texan in mid-1835, he probably would have written that "these are the times that confuse men's souls."

About 20,000 colonists were considering a revolution against Mexico, a nation of more than seven million people, with no natural buffer to impede the flow of Mexican soldiers.

Most colonists would have been satisfied if Texas could become a separate state in the Republic of Mexico under liberal provisions of the 1824 Mexican Federal Constitution. But the Texas territory had been combined with Coahuila into one sprawling state of Northern Mexico, its distant capital alternating between Saltillo and Monclova.

Stephen F. Austin, "The Father of Texas" and leader of the Peace Party, had been imprisoned in Mexico City for more than a year and in his absence, no unifying leadership had emerged. War Party leaders advocated declaring independence and creating a republic. Their view finally prevailed after a disastrous attempt at separate state government.

Ethnic animosity existed, but this revolution was by no means a simple case of Anglos vs. Mexicans. Its root cause was an extension of the ideological conflict that had been raging for years throughout Mexico between Federalist and Centralist political factions. This clash, plus regional loyalty and practical considerations, divided communities in Texas and families of Anglo and Spanish name.

Those Texans of Spanish name who opposed Mexico were known as "Tejanos." Among them was Lorenzo de Zavala, architect of the 1824 Constitution and a staunch Federalist who became a bitter enemy of the Centralist faction that ultimately included the opportunistic dictator, Antonio Lopez de Santa Anna. Zavala resigned high office in the Mexican government to promote the revolution, signed the Declaration of Independence and was named the first vice president of the Republic of Texas.

Other prominent Tejano leaders included Juan Seguin, J. Antonio Navarro and Francisco Ruiz, father of the alcalde (mayor) of San Antonio de Bexar during Santa Anna's occupation of that old settlement.

In picturesque San Antonio de Bexar, citizens of varied ethnic background had lived in harmony for years, but in the new Anglo-dominated settlements, animosity developed over many issues, including the policy of Roman Catholicism as the national religion.

In fairness to the Mexican position, it should be borne in mind that the Catholic tradition in sparsely-settled Coahuila and Texas extended far beyond the religion itself. The only semblance of order and civilization in the 1700s and early 1800s was provided by a few presidios and the Spanish missions operated by Franciscan priests.

Following Mexican independence, many of the elaborate mission compounds were used as forts and staging areas, the most famous being San Antonio de Valero, the Alamo.

Many Texas leaders had hailed the ascendency of Santa Anna in 1833, believing he would uphold the 1824 Constitution. But in 1835, as he rapidly created a military dictatorship, their sentiment changed to fear and rebellion. In September of 1835 when Austin returned from imprisonment, he was finally convinced that war was the only solution, and the first shot of the revolution was fired a few weeks later at Gonzales. Volunteers from America streamed into Texas to join the insurgents, keying the determination of Santa Anna to conduct a campaign for total victory.

A thread running through the whole cloth was the consuming ambition of some Texas leaders — particularly Sam Houston, Jim Bowie and William Barret Travis — to control this vast land they had grown to love.

This novel attempts to provide insight into both sides of the conflict, recreating the fast-breaking events and extraordinary circumstances that led to resolution of hostilities at the San Jacinto Battleground.

Every effort was made to authenticate historical events, though accounts vary on many details. Fictional characters include Captain Alvarez, Lieutenant Calderón, Bozita, Rosa Elena Tristán, and the Arredondo, Gates and Hargrove families. All locations are authentic with the exception of Houston's cabin and the Hargrove Plantation, which is a fictional substitute for the Jared Groce Plantation.

John R. Knaggs   Austin, Texas

"As I walked through the low door . . . and came into the darkling light of the ancient fortress . . . I looked first for the place where Travis drew the line . . . It is a line that not all the piety nor wit of research will ever blot out. It is a Grand Canyon cut into the bedrock of human emotions and heroical impulse.

"For hundreds of thousands of Texans and others who could not cite a single authenticated word spoken in the Alamo or a single authenticated act performed . . . the gesture and the challenge made by William Barret Travis are a living reality . . . Nobody forgets the line. It is drawn too deep and straight." — *J. Frank Dobie* — From *"The Line That Travis Drew," In the Shadow of History*

"Measured by its results, San Jacinto was one of the decisive battles of the world. The freedom of Texas from Mexico won here led to annexation and to the Mexican War, resulting in the acquisition by the United States of the States of Texas, New Mexico, Arizona, Nevada, California, Utah, and parts of Colorado, Wyoming, Kansas and Oklahoma. Almost one-third of the present area of the American nation, nearly a million square miles of territory, changed sovereignty."
— carved in the stone base of the San Jacinto monument near Houston.

Part I:

To The Alamo

Chapter 1

ON a cold, blustery day in February of 1836, Sam Houston rode alone to his cabin nestled among pecan, willow, and sprawling oak trees near a shallow creek in Central Texas.

Once inside, he removed his buckskin outfit, complete with beads and moccasins which, though unpopular among some of his friends and a subject of ridicule for his detractors, remained a vital link to his continuing rapport with the Cherokees. No matter what he wore, as he neared his forty-third birthday, Houston was an imposing figure at six-foot-four and two hundred and thirty-five pounds.

Having wrapped a quilt around his muscular body, he brushed wavy brown hair from his high forehead. With a damp towel, he wiped the dust from his face, dominated by searching blue eyes and a resolute mouth.

Though weary from a long day's journey, he felt relieved as he relaxed before the warmth of a field-stone fireplace, satisfied that his negotiations with Cherokee leaders in East Texas had been successful. If that powerful tribe would remain peaceful, a total effort could be concentrated against Mexican forces that were sure to come from the south. A two-front war, Houston believed, would be disastrous to Texan hopes for achieving independence from Mexico.

Houston was commander-in-chief of the Texas army, serving under a provisional state government of the Republic of Mexico, established under the Mexican Federal Constitution of 1824. General Antonio Lopez de Santa Anna, president of Mexico, had destroyed the Federal system and refused to recognize the Texan government, created the previous November.

Frustrated to find the governor, Henry Smith, was unable to control the council which often undermined Houston's plans, favoring the views of Colonel James W. Fannin, Houston had undertaken the Cherokee mission as a respite from the political turmoil. He believed the only solution was for the convention scheduled March 1 at Washington-on-the-Brazos to declare independence and create a stable new government around which Texans would rally to fight.

Though Houston had been elected a delegate to the forthcoming convention, his thoughts that afternoon were consumed by the military situation. Rumors had been filtering from the south that a large Mexican army was being assembled under the command of Santa Anna himself.

Houston was awaiting intelligence reports from Colonel Edward Burleson, one of his few trusted field officers, and Lieutenant Jason Gates, a dependable young courier and scout. After changing into cotton pantaloons and a frayed black frock coat, Houston ate an early supper of beef stew and thick bread, brought by a neighbor. As he resettled by the fire, Gates arrived.

"Must be the worst winter we've had, General," Jason said, placing his felt hat on a rack of deer horns mounted on the wall.

"There's nothing wrong with you that some stew and coffee won't cure," Houston said. "Take your time."

Jason swept the sandy-brown hair from his tired face that, at the moment, appeared older than his twenty-two years. After answering Houston's call for volunteers, he had soon become the general's favorite among the young officers.

While Jason was eating, Burleson arrived. He was among a handful of seasoned Texan military leaders in whom Houston had confidence. Burleson had received the surrender of General Martín P. Cós, Santa Anna's brother-in-law, at San Antonio de Bexar the previous December following the determined Texan attack led by Ben Milam, who was killed and later given a full Masonic ceremony.

A native of North Carolina, Burleson had arrived in Texas in 1830, receiving title to land in Stephen F. Austin's second colony near Mina. At forty-three, he was in top physical condition, a tall, steadfast individual with strong religious convictions, who could appear to be shy when sensing he was not in total command of a situation.

"Still not drinking whiskey, Ed?" Houston asked, as Burleson refused the jug and poured himself a cup of coffee. "You earned yourself quite a victory over at San Antonio. I haven't heard much about it, so tell us how you defeated Cós."

"I may as well level with you, Sam," he sighed. "I didn't lead the attack or participate in the combat. I tried to prevent the men from assaulting Bexar."

"What happened?"

"As you recall, Stephen Austin had original command of that army. He tried to organize an assault on the settlement, but the company commanders wouldn't support him. After Stephen departed for the convention, the men voted me their commander. Since they hadn't supported Austin, I was cautious. I hadn't enough scouting information to convince me we could whip Cós without heavy losses.

"I had advised the men we should sustain the siege or consider disbanding. They were milling around, some preparing to leave, when Milam took his rifle, drew a line in the sand, shouting 'Who will go with old Ben Milam into San Antonio?' They were like a herd of longhorns spooked by lightning. First thing you know hundreds were shouting and clamoring for a fight. When I realized they were determined to attack, I instructed Neill to provide artillery support and I organized the reserves. Milam led them into fierce house-to-house combat in the settlement where he was killed at the Veramendi place. Cós soon decided to capitulate and you already know the terms I made—retire south of the Rio Grande never to return. Cós left for Laredo with all his troops, meaning there is not a single solitary Mexican soldier remaining in Texas."

"The battle of Bexar was a signal victory," Houston said, standing near the fire, "but I'm afraid it was also the harbinger for a war we're unprepared to fight."

"The victory cut our forces three ways," Burleson said. "No sooner had I negotiated the capitulation with Cós than our soldiers of fortune cooked up that wild goose chase to Matamoros. They said it was there for the taking, and away they went. Others, like myself, retired to our farms and families. Neill has only eighty effective men left to man the garrisons near San Fernando Church and the old mission."

"Which old mission?" asked Houston, pacing the floor slowly.

"He chose the Alamo. Neill said that for artillery purposes in guarding the settlement, the Alamo is more favorable than Concepción which is too far from the settlement."

"Well," Houston interrupted, "it's a moot point. I sent Bowie to San Antonio with orders to abandon the garrisons and remove the artillery."

"Sir," Jason said, "I have new information. There's sickness in Colonel Neill's family and he's gone to help out. Before he left, he decided to abandon the garrison near the church and moved all the men and artillery into the Alamo. When Colonel Bowie arrived, Colonel Neill convinced him that the Alamo shouldn't be abandoned since we had twenty-four artillery pieces, eighteen operational, and no way to transport them. Then Colonel Travis arrived with a small contingent under orders from Governor Smith to reinforce the Alamo, and he agreed with them that the Alamo must be defended."

"You say that Smith sent Travis?" Houston asked.

"That's correct, General," Jason said, shuffling through notes from his saddle bag. "Before Colonel Neill departed, he designated Colonel Travis as his successor, commanding the regulars. The volunteers wouldn't accept Colonel Travis, voting Colonel Bowie as their commander."

Houston cursed as Burleson stared over his cup of coffee. "Son, are you telling us that Travis and Bowie share the command of the Alamo garrison?" asked Burleson.

5

"Yes, sir, Colonel."

Houston stood by the fire, shaking his head. No planning, no organization, no discipline. Now, he thought, we also have the ultimate mistake in a military operation — a joint command — and a joint command of a garrison that should be abandoned.

"Have they developed any unified strategy?" Burleson asked.

"No, sir. Soon after Colonel Neill departed, Colonel Bowie was prepared to help Colonel Travis fortify the old Alamo mission, but found that no reinforcements were forthcoming except those few brought by Colonel Travis. Colonel Bowie got drunk one night and released several prisoners from jail, which upset Colonel Travis. When Colonel Bowie said he would lead an ambush on Santa Anna south of Bexar since they didn't have enough men to defend the old mission, Colonel Travis was more than upset, he was furious. He removed his men from the Alamo to the Medina River until Colonel Bowie sobered up and apologized."

"At least they're together again," Burleson chuckled.

"Bowie has been drinking heavily since his wife and children died," Houston said, "but I know him and that wasn't drunk talk about an ambush. It makes more sense than waiting in that old mission to be wiped out. Bowie is a gut fighter, but he's a shrewd man."

"Colonel Travis wants to command the Alamo garrison as a strict military operation," Jason said, "but he can't with more than half the men loyal to Colonel Bowie."

"Do they agree on anything?" Burleson asked.

"Well, yes, sir," Jason said, "they agree that Santa Anna himself will lead an assault on San Antonio to vindicate family honor since General Cós is his brother-in-law. Colonel Bowie says that since Santa Anna traveled that route with the Spanish army years ago, he'll return the same way."

"Moving a large army overland in winter would be quite a feat," Houston said. "Makes more sense for him to choose a coastal invasion, landing at Copano with a probable first attack at Goliad."

Jason placed two more logs inside the gray stone fireplace. Logically, he agreed with Houston, but a gnawing feeling brought back clearly his recent conversation with Bowie. He handed Houston a map that Bowie had marked for him, detailing the overland routes available to Santa Anna from the Rio Grande to San Antonio de Bexar and Goliad. Houston studied the map of the area south of San Antonio leading to the Rio Grande.

"There's not a single settlement in that country," Houston said. "There can't be much winter grass. How can Santa Anna move an army across that terrain in the winter?"

"Colonel Bowie says Santa Anna can drive an army harder than any man who ever lived," Jason said. "He says that the Mexican government would have to contract with another country to transport a large army by ship. His Mexican friends tell Colonel Bowie the army is being assembled in Saltillo, whereas if Santa Anna were planning a coastal invasion, the assembly point would probably be Veracruz or Tampico."

"If Bowie attempted an ambush," Burleson said, "and failed, Travis would be left without enough men to stand guard around that lonely old mission. It seems to me that the wise course is to consolidate our forces from the Alamo and Goliad. The questions are where and when. What does Fannin think?"

"As you know," Jason said, "Colonel Fannin is the only field officer with formal military training. He seems jealous of Colonels Bowie and Travis and, I suspect, of you also, General. His scouts can't find evidence of enemy activity between Goliad and the Rio Grande. He believes the Mexicans will mount an attack against Goliad this spring because we have more troops there than at the Alamo and Goliad protects the coast. He's convinced Santa Anna won't expose his troops to this weather. He doesn't believe in Bowie's idea of an ambush because there's too much danger of losing valuable men and such tactics rule out the use of artillery."

"What would convince Fannin that he should take his men to Bexar?" Houston asked.

"I don't think he would abandon Goliad unless there was hard evidence that a large Mexican force was moving against Bexar. He's well-fortified in Presidio La Bahia, which he calls Fort Defiance, with four hundred well-trained men, adequate provisions and ammunition. With the political situation so confused, he might defy an order from you."

Houston toyed with the jug of whiskey. "I won't be able to gather any volunteers until after the convention. If there's a main force Mexican attack mounted against the Alamo, the only hope would be Fannin. If Fannin's right, I'll have time to gather and train enough troops to reinforce both garrisons. But if Bowie's right, there's no way the Alamo and Goliad can be defended properly."

"I hate to say it, Sam," Burleson said, "but I believe Bowie's theory about Santa Anna. He could lay siege on the Alamo even before Fannin could arrive with his men, even assuming Fannin would agree to reinforce the Alamo."

"In that case, Ed, we've simply run out of time."

"Is there no way, sir," Jason asked Houston, "that we can raise two or three hundred volunteers for the Alamo?"

"I point no finger at any individual," Houston said, "but I believe the people have lost confidence in the government. They answered the call for the siege of San Antonio to protect their lives and property, and afterward believed the war was won. But lately, what with the bickering between the governor and council which has severed lines of authority, they won't respond again until the enemy is on the scene.

Unfortunately, that'll be too late for the southern garrisons. We'll be forced to fight from the interior. If there's another answer, I wish to God I knew it."

"There's no other answer," Burleson said. "The provisional state government is a disaster. My only hope is that a republic can be created with responsible leadership, before the enemy arrives. Unfortunately for Bowie and Travis, the new volunteer units from Alabama and New Orleans reported off the boat to Fannin."

"Fannin almost assumed the role of commander-in-chief," Houston said. "However, he's in for a rude awakening from the next convention, because I have the votes to be named commander-in-chief of all men under arms in Texas. Then there will be no question of military authority." Houston sat down to write an order to Fannin. "This is about all I can do now," he said. "Fannin may disregard this order, but when you deliver it, Jason, I want you to inform him that General Houston is confident he will be named commander-in-chief at the convention. He will understand what that means."

Burleson read the order which stated simply that Fannin should reinforce the Alamo garrison "as soon as possible" upon learning of a major Mexican assault force moving toward San Antonio. "After you deliver this order," Houston said to Jason, "ride over to San Antonio for late intelligence, then report back to me."

"General," Jason asked, "if Santa Anna brings five thousand men to Texas, what chance do we have?"

As he sipped whiskey from a tin cup, Houston relaxed. "I'm not sure I can answer your question so you'll understand. What we can't measure is the resolve of our people bearing arms, the resolve of our non-combatants who must sacrifice to support our army, and perhaps more importantly, the resolve of the Mexican soldiers. No matter how determined Santa Anna may be, I can only hope that his soldiers won't be entirely dedicated to a war on soil they don't know or love. Bugles and bright flags are inspiring, but loneliness and empty stomachs will destroy an army as surely as weapons."

Burleson soon departed and Jason retired to an adjoining room for a welcome night's rest. Houston remained by the fire.

In addition to the perplexing problem with Fannin, Houston found himself commander-in-chief of a small, undisciplined army composed largely of volunteers whose loyalty was often pledged only to individual field commanders whom they elected. There were no uniforms nor pay for the men. Other than weapons owned by volunteers for hunting and defending their homes against Indian raids, the only ordnance consisted of weapons and ammunition captured from Mexican garrisons. Among the foot soldiers, there were teen-aged volunteers, and there had been one veteran of the American Revolution, Stephen Williams, who was seventy-five when he participated in the Texan siege of San Antonio.

8

Despite adversity, Houston remained determined to press his ability and experience to the utmost. When he had first ventured into Texas in 1832, the challenge and opportunity captivated this headstrong soldier of fortune, seeking a new avenue to political leadership. Houston had seen a vast, sparsely-settled country, blessed by abundant water and fertile soil in the northern and eastern areas. Though there were only about twenty thousand Anglo colonists in Texas, most of them seemed to be prospering by growing cotton, corn, sugar, and various grains and vegetables. Cattle and hogs were in such abundance that fat beeves brought only eight to ten dollars each and fat hogs from three and one-half to five dollars each. Sheep and goats prospered on the western ranges and edible wildlife was abundant throughout the territory. It was a challenging, invigorating country that had captured the imagination of the restless Houston. Upon completing that first tour of Texas, he had reported to President Jackson the enormous potential of the territory which he estimated would someday support millions of people.

After settling in Nacogdoches, where he built up a law practice while courting Anna Raquet, Houston had found himself in demand to participate in the swirling political events leading toward hostilities. He became a member of the War Party, but often urged caution on the basis that the Texans were not prepared. As War Party leaders, including Fannin, Travis, and his friend Bowie, pressed pell mell toward war, Houston began scouring maps and all other relevant information that would enhance his ability as a military leader.

A turbulent and paradoxical man, Houston had already achieved more than most of his ambitious contemporaries might have dreamed of attaining. He had fought under Jackson in the War of 1812, winning the admiration and lifelong friendship of Old Hickory by displaying raw courage in battle. Tennesseeans had declared him a hero, with the field officers subsequently electing him major general.

With a booming voice and magnetic personality, he had entered politics, easily winning election and re-election to Congress before being elected governor. During a campaign for re-election in which he was considered a sure bet, Houston married Eliza Allen from a prominent Tennessee family. A few weeks later Eliza left Houston and he resigned as governor, refusing to explain the reason for the marital break-up. Mysteriously, he disappeared among the Cherokees with whom he had lived for three years as a teen-ager. His bewildered friends were left with no means to defend him.

His Indian friends accepted him as a citizen of the Cherokee nation from which he took an Indian wife, Tiana. But the restless man from Tennessee was tormented during those three years. He had received a name of affection and respect from the Cherokees, "The Raven," but because of his frequent drinking sprees, they also called him "The Big Drunk."

9

When he re-emerged in Anglo affairs as an Indian agent, largely with the help of President Jackson, he offered no explanation for his broken marriage nor his preference for living with the Cherokees. He maintained his close ties to Jackson, conferring with his aging mentor in Washington or at Jackson's Tennessee plantation, The Hermitage.

After viewing the potential in Texas, Houston had vowed to become a leader of the new republic. Before his self-inflicted political demise in Tennessee, Houston had been discussed as a future presidential candidate. That ambition still sparkled in his heart, but the route would be vastly changed. A republic and eventual statehood were in Houston's plans for Texas. Those goals would require time, and all the resources that could be mustered inside and outside Texas, but his ties to President Jackson were widely known, enhancing the aura of importance that surrounded Houston.

On that lonely night in Central Texas before the smoldering fire, Houston visualized Jackson in the White House, wishing to help the Texans, but with his hands tied by a treaty with Mexico and the opposition of wary abolitionists, who viewed the Texas territory as another potential slave state. Though Houston wanted Texas to become a state in the union, he never mentioned the subject, particularly with widespread if tenuous support finally having developed for creating a republic after months of haggling over whether to remain in the Republic of Mexico.

Of late, Houston had displayed a maturity in contrast to those earlier turbulent years. He had finally recognized his worst enemy stalked from within, a brooding personality with a short-fused temper. He had reduced his consumption of alcohol to the extent "The Big Drunk" nickname was no longer bandied about, and he had managed to control his temper. He still cursed, but only when provoked.

He had rapidly won respect among seasoned Texas leaders such as Bowie and Burleson, who recognized his strategic planning ability, linked to considerable political acumen. His numerous critics, on the other hand, viewed him as a rebounding opportunist, trying to convert military fame into high political office, possibly as an agent for President Jackson. Yet, none doubted his word, though he was prone to search ahead and temporize, while carefully weighing contingencies. Pressing him for a commitment could be a difficult task, indeed.

Recognizing the complexity of the military problem he faced, he truly believed he was the only individual on the scene capable of meeting the challenge. What weighed so heavily on his mind that night was the lack of time to solidify the political situation while preparing for military action. If only he had two months to build an army, Houston thought, he might defeat Santa Anna even outnumbered by two to one. Though confident that he would receive the authority to function properly as commander-in-chief, gnawing doubts remained in his mind about leadership for the new government.

The previous convention had bypassed the logical choice, Austin, for governor in favor of Henry Smith, who was outspoken in his disdain for any and all people with Spanish names. Smith had upset Houston by making caustic remarks about his friend Bowie allegedly being too close to "Mexkins" because of Bowie's marriage to the late Ursula Veramendi. If that sort of thinking should dominate the forthcoming convention, Houston thought, a skilled statesman on the Texan side, Lorenzo de Zavala, might be ignored. Houston was convinced Zavala's experience in drafting the Mexican Federal Constitution of 1824 must be brought to bear if the Texans were to produce a sound constitution for their new republic.

We're sitting on a powder keg with a short fuse burning, Houston thought. Without a popular political leader, the convention might collapse in bickering or it might produce some flimsy government no better than we've had. It's imperative for that convention to present a strong framework of government that the people will support. Zavala must play a prominent role. "There are no miracles on the horizon," he murmured to himself.

Chapter 2

EARLY the next morning, Jason rode home to Gonzales, that sprightly settlement near the green waters of the Guadalupe River. He informed his family that he would soon be off again to Goliad, San Antonio, and back to report to Houston. Though he was totally dedicated to Texas independence and was loyal to Houston, Jason served under threat of being disinherited by his father. Ben Gates shared the view of many other successful colonists that an agreement might yet be reached with Mexico to avoid further hostilities. Five years before, Ben had brought his family from Kentucky to Gonzales where he operated a farm, general store and livery stable. The family included his wife, Martha, who kept books for the business, and Sandra, who was seventeen. Jason had worked closely with his father, enjoying a strong relationship before fighting had erupted.

In October, Ben had restrained Jason from joining the Gonzales rebels who defied a Mexican force sent to capture the town's cannon. Shortly after that encounter, Jason had told his father that he was joining the army, no matter what his father might say or do. His mother had intervened to prevent an open break between father and son, and she quietly welcomed Jason's courier assignments that provided cooling off periods.

After Ben said the blessing over lunch, he looked at Jason. "Son, I can't stop you . . . but why must we have war to keep our land and our families together?"

"Dad, Mr. Austin tried hard to convince Santa Anna to change some things. Now, our leaders believe Santa Anna is a worse tyrant than Bustamante. They believe he's going to invade our country with a large force. We have no choice but to fight."

"We have the choice to return to Kentucky while you're still alive," Ben said.

Martha winced. She wanted to cry, but held back tears.

"No land, no money, no anything is worth losing you," Ben said. "These leaders can't expect us to sit by and wait for Santa Anna to kill our youth and ravage our land."

"Dad, please, we're getting right back to where we were before. I believe we have to fight. You don't. But please, Dad, try to understand that I would never be happy if we left now. You've worked hard. You love your family and this land. So do I, and because I love our family and this land, I have to fight."

"How," Ben asked, "has Houston convinced you we can ever win against all the resources of Mexico? There aren't more than twenty thousand colonists in Texas and there are about eight million people in Mexico."

"You're right about numbers, Dad. In fact, there are probably more Indians in Texas than colonists, but I'll reveal the secret for our forthcoming victory," he said, smiling over his coffee cup. "Santa Anna can't stand cold weather."

Jason soon excused himself, saddled up, and rode toward Goliad. When he arrived the following day, he rode slowly by Mission Espiritu Santo in order not to startle guards stationed between there and the presidio on the hill. As he approached Presidio La Bahia, or Fort Defiance, he marvelled at the huge compound with its high, thick walls. The guards challenged Jason, but they permitted him to enter the compound where he was escorted to Fannin's office. Jason took a seat while Fannin read the order from Houston. To Jason, Fannin was a problem simply because he had opposed Houston, whom Jason admired more than any other Texas leader. Fannin often had reminded groups of Texan political leaders that he was the only man with West Point training, implying Houston was incapable of leading the army. Though only thirty-two, Fannin had impressed Texans with his military prowess, having fought at Gonzales, and during the Texan siege of Bexar. On neither occasion, Fannin would point out, was Houston in combat, though Houston had been in Bexar briefly early in the siege.

After accepting a cup of coffee, Jason came directly to the point. "I thought you'd be interested, sir, in knowing that General Houston expects to be named commander-in-chief when the new government is formed."

Fannin frowned, reviewing carefully each word in the brief order. "At this time," he said, "Houston should be more concerned with the military situation than with politics. I thought he'd be raising volunteer units to reinforce this garrison and the Alamo."

"Sir, I believe he considers an enemy attack imminent."

"That's merely a hunch of Bowie's, nothing more. If one reviews the strategic situation carefully, the conclusion is that an overland movement of any size can't be accomplished in winter. In the first place there isn't adequate grass to feed the animals necessary to transport a large force. If an attack is imminent, it'll be here, not at San Antonio, and the enemy will land at Copano. I remind you that General Cós brought his force by sea."

13

"Sir, Colonel Bowie claims to have intelligence that Santa Anna assembled an army at Saltillo. That would almost surely mean an overland movement."

Fannin slammed down Houston's orders. "Young man, I have no intention of arguing the point with you. I refuse to move my troops to the Alamo on the basis of Bowie's hunch or questionable information from some of his untrustworthy friends. I also feel no burning responsibility to honor any of Houston's orders, particularly since his own friend, Bowie, ignored his order to abandon the Alamo. Further, you may as well know that many of us aren't pleased with Houston's recent conduct. He came to this area, uninvited, to speak against the Matamoros campaign that had been authorized by the council. The council is certainly more representative of the people than is the governor, and Houston had no business injecting himself into that situation. We could've captured Matamoros, a strategic location that Santa Anna may now use as a staging area."

"Be that as it may, sir, the problem now is that the Alamo garrison only has about one hundred and fifty combatants. You have four hundred, and if the enemy plans to concentrate on the Alamo, we should consolidate our forces with all dispatch."

Fannin's eyes grew cold. "I command a force adequate to defend this fortress, a genuine fortress, against an enemy force five times our number. Bowie and Travis insist on trying to fortify that old fallen-down mission compound without enough men to defend an area one third that size. Further, I consider Goliad to be a more strategic location for the defense of Texas than San Antonio."

When Fannin paused, gazing out the window, Jason prepared to leave. Finally, Fannin turned to face the disappointed young courier. "You may inform Bowie and Travis that I'll consider reinforcing the Alamo, but the intelligence on the enemy must be certain. I can assure you, young man, that when you place yourself in the polished boots of Santa Anna, you'll see that he's certain to strike at Goliad."

After hurriedly eating a meal of venison and cornbread, Jason spurred his horse to full gallop for a rapid journey to San Antonio de Bexar. The following day, he heard the long, melancholy peals of bells from San Fernando Church and one of the missions down the San Antonio River. When he rode toward the Alamo, he saw the tricolor flag of 1824 and a flag of the New Orleans volunteers flying smartly in the crisp north breeze. The 1824 flag was emblematic of the Mexican Federal Constitution under which the Texans took up arms and established their disastrous provisional state government. Since independence had not been declared, the 1824 flag was still flown, but the impasse between the governor and council had prompted the Alamo defenders to take sides. Their decision had been to honor allegiance to Governor Smith and to express their sentiment for independence at the forthcoming convention.

14

The guards recognized Jason but challenged him, in compliance with strict orders from Colonel William Barret Travis that no one would enter the compound without being identified. When told that Bowie should not be disturbed, Jason reported to Travis in his planning room on the west wall of the Alamo compound. At twenty-six, Travis was the youngest major commander in the Texan army. Like Houston, he had come to Texas after an unhappy marriage which he would not discuss with anyone. After that separation, he had practiced law and been a lay preacher in Alabama until 1832 when he came to Texas, establishing a law practice at Anahuac. Travis had moved to San Felipe de Austin where he became a successful attorney, closely associated with Judge Williamson, Austin, and Governor Smith.

However, in the summer of 1835, Travis had become the most unpopular man in Texas for leading a wildcat raid on the Mexican garrison at Anahuac. Since no organized Texan group had sanctioned the attack, the legal basis was indeed vague. When hostilities had broken out a few months later, Travis was vindicated. A tall, trim man with reddish-brown hair and blue eyes, Travis had a reputation as a favorite among women for his chivalrous manners and bright conversation. At festivities in San Felipe, he was known as a fun-loving dandy, who often contracted for musicians at balls which he attended in coat and vest with bright pantaloons and pumps, instead of traditional buckskin and boots.

In the Alamo, he was hard-pressed to maintain support among seasoned frontiersmen who found his youth, intense personality, and strident command posture none to their liking. They related more to the mature, personable Bowie, whose reputation as a fighter far exceeded that of Travis. When most of the volunteers had voted for Bowie as their commander, Travis had considered relinquishing his share of the command to Bowie, recognizing the frivolity of a joint command. However, he had determined to maintain the share of command bestowed upon him by the departed Colonel Neill.

"Should we wait for Colonel Bowie?" Jason asked Travis.

"No, he needs some rest. I want to speak to you alone for a moment. I want you to convey certain sensitive matters to General Houston. Tell him that the command situation has become impossible; no, not impossible, but critical. Bowie's in no condition to command, yet he insists on trying. In addition to his illness, he injured a shoulder trying to mount an artillery piece."

"Colonel Travis, perhaps you should put that in writing to General Houston."

"No, I'm not going to cry about this in a formal dispatch to Houston. Simply convey the status. Here's a formal request for reinforcements. What can you tell me about our chances for more troops?"

"Colonel, there are no troops available at the moment for this garrison."

Travis banged his fist on the table, and he glared at Jason. "Why in God's world won't Fannin bring his troops to the Alamo?"

"Frankly, Colonel Travis, Colonel Fannin's been just about as independent as you and Colonel Bowie. General Houston has ordered him to reinforce the Alamo, but he told me he wouldn't embark from Goliad without firm intelligence about enemy activity here."

"The settlement's full of rumors that Santa Anna is en route. Some of Bowie's men say he's coming toward the Rio Grande at this time. Isn't General Houston assembling troops?"

"Volunteers are hard to find in the colonies. General Houston hopes that Santa Anna will be delayed by weather. The general needs time to recruit and train an army, plus the fact that he's a delegate to the convention."

Travis remained tense. After pacing the room rapidly, he paused to face Jason. "If no troops are available, what about provisions? Due to Bowie, we can't secure adequate supplies. Bowie's known and respected in the settlement. When he talked about leading ambushes and long scouting expeditions, he dried up our sources of supply and credit for this garrison. No one in Bexar believed this mission could be defended without him and his men. Now, it's too late, with the enemy en route and Bowie in pitiful condition."

"I don't know that I can offer any hope, Colonel. Fear has gripped the settlers. They're more concerned about supplies for their own families than in supporting the military effort."

After reviewing a map of the territory between San Antonio and the Rio Grande River, Travis dispatched an aide to find Bowie. When Jason had last been in the Alamo, Bowie was coughing profusely, but he was still Jim Bowie, the enigmatic gut fighter who was fluent in English, Spanish, and French, the gambling frontiersman who had accumulated — and some said lost — a fortune greater than any other Texan. At forty-one, the onetime logger from Louisiana was fifteen years older than Travis, one of many reasons for friction between the two. Jason had viewed the joint command between Bowie and Travis as utterly impossible. Bowie was known to brood over a battle plan quietly, often invoking the assistance of a large amount of whiskey, but he could move with fearful decisiveness, night or day, to carry out his plan. His views on military operations were not to be found in any textbooks at West Point.

Travis, though not formally trained, insisted on a strict military operation. He had a short temper and a confident air about him that prompted shouting matches between him and Bowie. At one unsettling stage in their joint command of the Alamo, the only item they could agree upon was to meet solely on a private basis in order to prevent any further confusion and dissension within the garrison.

When Jason saw the gaunt figure entering the planning room, he was shocked. Bowie must have lost at least twenty pounds since he last saw him, Jason thought, and his once bright eyes were now dimmed by the effects of an extended siege of fever and congestion in his chest.

"I want Sam to know a few things," Bowie said, looking directly at Jason. "The hardest thing in the world is to judge oneself. I may have been right about attempting an ambush of Santa Anna, but it doesn't matter now. I can't lead an operation outside or inside these walls. Maybe the Lord will take me before any more fights; I didn't think I would make it through last night."

"Colonel Bowie," Jason said, "I can assure you General Houston maintains the highest regard for you and he believed there was merit in your idea of an ambush. I heard him say so."

"Well, it's out of the question now," Bowie said. "I'd wanted to try the Nueces or Frio crossings, but I'm the only one who could've led that kind of operation. Travis, here's a formal letter, relinquishing my share of the command. I want you to hold the news for a few days in order for me to talk to some of my men. Otherwise, you may have another election on your hands and another joint commander."

Travis paused a moment, scanning the letter. "I appreciate your forthright action for the cause of unity in this garrison, Jim. My friends call me 'Will,' and my good friends call me 'Buck.' "

"I prefer calling you 'Travis.' Now, I have one other condition not spelled out in my letter. Will you stop barking orders at these men? Some are old enough to be your father. My men don't know anything about the military, but they can fight like wounded mountain lions. We can put up a damn strong defense here if they spend their time warming for combat with the enemy rather than worrying about you ordering them around."

He may be sick, Jason thought, but he sure has a spark or two left in him. Jason expected Travis and Bowie to launch into another of their spirited arguments, but Travis had become pensive, and for the first time since Jason had known him, the intense young leader broke into a wide smile. "Perhaps I've been a bit high-handed, at times," Travis said. "I apologize."

Bowie smiled weakly. "Now that all this back-slapping is over, let's have some whiskey and talk about what needs to be done."

Thus, the full command of the Alamo garrison passed into the hands of a fine young horseman, a lieutenant colonel of cavalry, who must mobilize artillery and riflemen to convert an old mission into a fortress.

Though Bowie coughed deeply a few times, he seemed relieved, carrying the conversation to Travis about deployment of men and artillery batteries in anticipation of an attacking force. Bowie and Travis agreed on most details before Bowie asked Jason about reinforcements. The answer did not deter Bowie. "In that case," he said,

"I have some ideas about obtaining provisions, but we need more troops. I fear for the cause of independence if we lose this garrison. Santa Anna will attack here. Can't they understand that this is the most important garrison in Texas? If we kill or capture Santa Anna, we win everything!"

"I'm afraid it's too late," Travis said. "Fannin's the only hope and he probably won't come. We have less than one hundred and fifty effective men. We should have at least five hundred to defend this place properly."

They were interrupted by an aide who informed them that David Crockett had arrived in the settlement, had made a short speech, and was en route to the Alamo with sixteen men from Tennessee. Riding into the Alamo compound, Crockett and his men made an impressive appearance, carrying their long rifles sheathed in decorated buckskin covers. The veteran frontiersman was within six months of his fiftieth birthday, but he was trim in his buckskin outfit covering his stocky, six-foot frame.

Several Alamo defenders called on Crockett for a speech, and the tall Tennesseean responded, remaining in the saddle. "I told the people in Tennessee that if they didn't want me in Congress any longer they could go to hell, and I was going to Texas. After leaving Tennessee, I figured I didn't have to make any more speeches," he drawled, "and if you fellows need speechmakers more than you need fighters, you're in real trouble." Amid applause and laughter, Crockett dismounted, waving his coonskin hat. As the excitement subsided, Crockett quietly asked Bowie where they might find a jug of whiskey. Before they walked away, Crockett whispered to Travis that he had heard Santa Anna was en route to San Antonio with five thousand men. "What will be our strength?"

"With your courageous volunteers," Travis replied, "we have one hundred and fifty effective men, depending on sick call."

"Lead me to your whiskey," Crockett said to Bowie, shaking his head.

As they walked away, Travis placed his arm on Jason's shoulder. "You know, this is a place old Brit Bailey would have loved."

"I don't believe I've heard of him," Jason said.

"I was in my law office in San Felipe one afternoon, drawing up papers for a land transaction, when this weathered old character stomped in, demanding that I prepare his will immediately. He dropped five dollars on my desk, so I began writing. Well, old Brit Bailey wanted a standard will until he came to dictating terms for his funeral. He stared at me and said: 'I never bowed to no man in my life, and I won't bow in death. I want to be buried standing up.' Therefore, I wrote that stipulation into his will and sure enough, he was buried standing up in his coffin."

"You mean a hole was dug straight down in the ground?"

"That's right," Travis laughed. "Old Brit had some friends about as ornery as he, and they thought it was quite a tribute. So they dug the hole, and down went old Brit, feet first."

Travis' spirits had been buoyed immensely by Bowie's relinquishing his command, plus the excitement created by the sudden appearance of the legendary Crockett. Since Travis had come to the Alamo, he had lived, day by day, under stress and uncertainty. This had been a banner day compared with most of the tedious, frustrating days of the preceding weeks.

Jason prepared to depart. "Colonel Travis, I suppose I'd better head back to report to General Houston."

"Tell every soul you see, including the general, we need men and provisions with all dispatch."

As Jason left the Alamo, warmer air was blowing from the west bringing a chilling drizzle. In the damp twilight, he lost a trail to a farm where he had planned to spend the night. The best cover he could find was a sprawling live oak tree under which he tied his horse and slept until dawn. When he resumed his journey, the weather remained cold and drizzling, but he spurred his horse repeatedly and arrived at Houston's cabin before noon.

On the door, Jason found a note signed by Houston, who had departed for a meeting in Gonzales. Jason left his report and Travis' message inside and mounted for the last leg to Gonzales, shuddering from chills and fever. When he arrived at home, his mother took one look at his pale, drawn face before ordering him to bed. Jason had caught pneumonia.

Chapter 3

WHILE the Texans had temporized in confusion, General Antonio Lopez de Santa Anna had been designing a campaign to strike before the rebels were prepared. In September, he had dispatched his brother-in-law, General Cós, to Texas with an army in excess of five hundred to require the feisty Texans to pay duties demanded by Santa Anna. Cós had found the atmosphere hostile, filled with Federalist rhetoric and threats of war. After Cós had dispersed the Legislature of Coahuila and Texas, and Mexican forces had failed in an attempt to remove a cannon at Gonzales, the Texans girded for a major engagement.

When Santa Anna had learned that Cós could not repulse the rebels who were laying siege on San Antonio de Bexar, the mercurial Mexican president dashed to San Luis Potosi, in Central Mexico, to take command of the Army of Operations which he organized in incredible haste.

From San Luis Potosi, he issued a withering assortment of orders, including the designation of Saltillo, a picturesque old town nestled in the mountains sixty miles west of Monterrey, as a major staging area where six thousand troops would soon be assembled. From Saltillo, he planned to lead the vanguard over more than two hundred torturous miles of unsettled semi-desert country to San Antonio de Bexar.

Upon learning of Cós' surrender to Burleson, Santa Anna had sent a blistering note to his brother-in-law, who was informed at Laredo on Christmas Day of 1835 that he could forget about the treaty not to return to Texas. Cós' forces would join the Army of Operations under Santa Anna.

A native of Jalapa, Mexico, Santa Anna was the son of middle class Mexican parents of pure Spanish blood. Nearing his forty-second birthday, he counted a quarter century of military experience and was destined to fight in more battles than Napoleon and George Washington combined.

He had remained in the Spanish army through years of conflict with Mexican patriots, finally changing sides when he perceived the

Spaniards would not prevail. After vaulting into prominence, he had become a national hero by leading the Mexican army that defeated an invading Spanish force at Tampico in 1829, eight years after Mexico had won her independence. "The Hero of Tampico" had threaded his way through the labyrinth of military-clergy politics to attain the presidency in 1833 with the support of Zavala, who believed then that Santa Anna was dedicated to Federalist principles. After Santa Anna threw in with the Centralists, creating a dictatorship, Zavala withdrew his support, opting for the uphill struggle toward a new republic in Texas.

Santa Anna was a rare blend of military leader, political dictator and a vain, lonely man who needed new challenges to keep his mind active and alert. Trim and of medium height, he dressed immaculately and carried himself in a confident, military manner at all times. Women found him strikingly handsome, and when on military campaigns far from his family, he found time to return the attentions bestowed upon him by admiring young ladies.

Articulate and persuasive, he was accustomed to having his way. His determined pursuit of political dissidents had made him the undisputed dictator of Mexico, south of the Rio Grande. He viewed the Texan uprising as another regional, but more serious, challenge that must be destroyed with all dispatch.

In Saltillo Santa Anna had studied the maps of Texas carefully, charting reliable new intelligence that reported the rebel strength at the Alamo and Goliad. His strategy vindicated the thinking of Bowie more than Fannin. His forces would strike at both Texan garrisons, with General Urrea assigned to lead a thousand men down the Rio Grande to Matamoros where he would cross the river for a sweep to Goliad. Santa Anna would lead a vanguard of fifteen hundred men to San Antonio de Bexar in order to contain the Alamo garrison. Some thirty-five hundred additional troops, including units transporting the heavy artillery, would reinforce the vanguard at San Antonio.

After departing Saltillo, winter weather and rugged desert terrain created burdens for the Army of Operations as it advanced for the two-pronged invasion across the Rio Grande. As he had expected, Santa Anna met no resistance from the enemy as he drove the army relentlessly across barren prairies and twisting arroyos and creeks. Other than occasional patches of mesquite and prickly pear, or *tasajuillo* cactus with its curved thorns, there was nothing to break the monotony of the terrain or to protect the men from the biting north winds howling into their faces. Moving into the teeth of a dry norther, the soldiers coaxed burros and oxen to continue pulling pack wagons and gun carriages.

At a campsite near the Nueces River, about eighty-five miles south of San Antonio de Bexar, Santa Anna sat in his elaborate field tent and reviewed plans with Colonel Almonte, his most trusted aide.

Almonte reported that by his new estimates, the Texans probably had no more than seven hundred men under arms throughout the entire province. Their scout from San Antonio placed the rebel force there to be between one hundred twenty-five and one hundred fifty.

"Even if they should decide to consolidate all their troops in the Alamo," Santa Anna said, "I will have more than adequate strength to destroy this rebellion. If General Urrea maneuvers near Goliad on schedule, our victory at San Antonio will be easily attained. We will lay siege on the Alamo and there will be no reinforcements for the rebels."

Outside Santa Anna's tent, it was almost dark at the campsite where Captain Carlos Alvarez and Lieutenant Juan Calderón brought their plates of dried meat, beans and tortillas near a warm fire of mesquite limbs.

Carlos, a friendly, balding farmer from Saltillo, whose weathered dark brown face was deeply lined from a lifetime of hard work in the sun, had organized a militia unit in Saltillo that was then ordered to join the Army of Operations. Juan, a disciple of Santa Anna, had enlisted shortly after entering law practice in Mexico City. A handsome young bachelor of pure Spanish blood, he was much lighter complexioned than his friend from Saltillo. His rather long hair was always neatly combed and he carried himself in the same confident manner of his beloved leader. Juan's father had been among the first shrewd aristocrats in Mexico City to align with Santa Anna, and an army commission for Juan had been available for the asking.

Carlos and Juan had become friends during the tedious journey from Saltillo to the Nueces River. Their blue and white uniforms were soiled and scratched, but their spirits were high.

"This land is not so far from Saltillo, but it is vastly different," Carlos said. "I recall it well from that campaign years ago."

"What in the world are those creatures?" Juan asked, pointing to some strange, hairy animals, rooting and grunting in a dusty arroyo.

"Those are *javelinas*, wild hogs," Carlos said. "I wish His Excellency had not forbidden hunting. A young *javelina* makes a tasty meal."

"And I wish this weather would warm up a bit," Juan said.

"You should welcome the cold," Carlos said. "The rattlesnakes are asleep. You see those heavy reeds, the *sachahuista*, out there? There is no greater fear than to walk among those reeds when they are dry and to hear a rattlesnake sound his warning. It is as if there are a hundred snakes around you."

"I have heard that mountain lions infest this country as well."

"They will not attack people, but they hunt game here if they can't find it in the Sierra Madres. The first time I heard one scream at night I thought it was a woman. They are strange creatures, probably the hardest of all to track down."

22

"Well, I'm not interested in tracking animals. I'm ready to track down the rebels at San Antonio de Bexar. His Excellency is carrying out a brilliant plan that should catch the rebels completely by surprise."

Carlos tossed a branch of dry mesquite at the fire. "I have listened to all that has been said at the briefings; I do not like the plan. I believe we are going to San Antonio de Bexar because Santa Anna knows this territory and because his brother-in-law was dishonored there. Our scouts say the enemy is much stronger at Goliad, far to the east of Bexar. I think we should attack their stronger garrison first."

"Carlos, you're talking nonsense. You cannot question the judgment of His Excellency, a military genius. Besides, you must agree San Antonio de Bexar is a strategic location with more garrison space available, and probably more artillery and ammunition to be captured."

"You have ready arguments, Juan. All I can tell you is that I know from other battles how commanders lose sight of their real objectives. I believe Santa Anna has chosen this route and battleground more from his personal desire to avenge the defeat of General Cós than on the true military situation."

"But General Cós was caught in an unfortunate situation. That will not happen to us."

"Juan, I came on this campaign only because I was ordered to organize the militia in Saltillo. I am not one who falls at the feet of Santa Anna."

"Carlos, Carlos, let's not argue. I happen to have brought along something which fights this cold weather better than any logs on a fire." Juan produced a bottle of mescal, the biting forerunner of tequila, and Carlos laughed.

"My friend Juan, you are indeed a bright young man from the City of Mexico. You brought mescal for a journey in the winter while I brought only light wine. We may disagree on the military situation, but in this case, you are the better man."

They drank half the bottle of mescal as the fire burned slowly into embers beneath the twisting shadows of the oak trees, along the lonely Nueces River. "And what will you do after this campaign?" Carlos asked.

"With our success, I will be in demand in the military, but I intend to pursue a career in law or diplomacy. And what about you, old soldier?"

"Old? I am only forty, but for one fresh out of school, that must sound old. My sole desire is to return to Saltillo where I have a farm and family. The people at Parras de la Fuente have promised to teach me to grow grapes for wine, which could make me somewhat prosperous. In any case, if I can return home, I will be happy. I hope this is my last campaign."

"Carlos, don't you have a strong feeling of loyalty for Mexico? Don't you want to crush these rebels and secure this land forever for our country?"

"Juan, you are not a farmer or rancher. Haven't you noticed how sparsely settled this country remains? Why have war when so much land is here for people to farm, to run cattle, or to raise sheep and goats? Of course, I am loyal to Mexico or I would not be here. How strongly I feel, I cannot say."

"But these rebels have refused to accept the Supreme Government under Santa Anna," Juan said. "He has given them opportunities to comply with reasonable government policies, but they have defied him by creating a state government under the Constitution he no longer recognizes."

"I know little of politics. I had been told the *empressario*, Austin, is an honorable man."

"No one questions the integrity of Austin, who made many attempts to avert war. But other colonizers, such as Ben Milam, Jim Bowie, and a professional agitator called Travis, have spent their time stirring up trouble rather than tending to their business, forcing Austin to accept their views. Their military commander, a man named Houston, is said to be more concerned with the welfare of the Cherokee Indians than the Anglo settlers."

"Juan, where in the world did you learn all this information?"

"Directly from His Excellency and Colonel Almonte. Since Colonel Almonte and I are among the few officers who speak and write English, I often translate newspapers and other material for His Excellency."

"How will the rebels deploy their troops?"

"Bowie and Travis command the Alamo garrison, if you can call it such, with a meager force of one hundred and fifty men. A man named Fannin, a trained military leader, commands the garrison at Goliad, in the Presidio La Bahia, with about four hundred men. Our scouts have been unable to track down Houston, who may be assembling troops to reinforce those two garrisons. That is one of the reasons His Excellency chose to make a lightning move across the desert. After we lay siege on the Alamo, and General Urrea contains the Goliad area, Houston will be hard-pressed to provide any relief."

"You know much more about these rebels than I," Carlos said. "I only know that they are fighting for their land, and they may be in no mood to surrender, no matter what their strength may be."

"But Carlos, we have a fully-equipped army to overcome a band of poorly-organized settlers and green volunteers from America. They have won a few skirmishes, but they have yet to meet a real army. These arrogant fools have defied the authority of the Supreme Government and must be punished. His Excellency is convinced that the victory at Bexar will be the most important of the campaign."

24

"And what if Houston is not captured at Bexar?"

"Lorenzo de Zavala concerns Santa Anna more than Houston in terms of influencing more people to fight. Houston is not an effective political leader, because many of the colonists do not trust him. Apparently, he is not leading the army either, since Milam and a man named Burleson forced General Cós to capitulate. Milam was killed, but Burleson, like Houston, has not been located."

"I regret that I was not assigned to General Urrea," Carlos said, after taking another swig of the warm liquid.

Juan almost gagged. "How can you say that? One finds honor and glory in serving with the Napoleon of the West. There is no finer general alive."

"Juan, there is more to being a general than leading men to victory in battle. I have heard from friends that Santa Anna permitted wanton killing during his campaign against the Federalists at Zacatecas last year. Those people were our countrymen, as are the people in Texas."

Juan frowned, gazing into the fire. Carlos could not follow the ideological conflict between the Federalist and Centralist political factions, a conflict that had pitted Urrea, governor of the northern state of Durango and proponent of Federalist principles, against Santa Anna. Almonte, confidant to Santa Anna, had argued earlier to give Urrea, the most competent commander available, major responsibility in the Army of Operations to avoid further friction.

Santa Anna had reluctantly agreed to assign Urrea to the Goliad area, but his allocation of troops in Texas was indicative of his determination to have the signal victory under his own belt. Five thousand troops went to San Antonio with its paltry one hundred and fifty rebels while Urrea took only one thousand men toward Goliad to confront at least four hundred enemy troops.

"I do not wish to argue politics with you, Carlos," Juan said. "General Urrea is an outstanding commander, but I would simply point out that His Excellency is bringing stability to our country after years of turmoil. After this campaign is completed, he will be hailed throughout the world for unifying all of Mexico. Our countrymen respond to what they can see in Santa Anna rather than to Zavala's vague ideas. The fact that José Urrea has joined our army should convince you this is the proper course for our country."

Carlos didn't respond. It had been twenty-three years since his first campaign as a dedicated seventeen-year-old officer. First in the Spanish army, and then in the struggle for independence, Carlos had found himself away fighting when he needed to be with his wife, Estella, who somehow had managed to maintain their farm and raise their children. Like many of his countrymen, he had believed the fighting was over in 1821 when Mexico won her independence, so that the continuing turmoil from the military juntas baffled the simple farmer. He only knew he could never trust Santa Anna, who had fought so long on the Spanish side he had barely made his flamboyant defection to the Mexican side in time.

He turned to Juan. "I do not question our scouting reports now, but I wonder if the enemy will have reinforcements at San Antonio before we arrive?"

"So much the better, Carlos. The more they have at San Antonio the more we will kill — and our campaign will be much easier."

"You said 'kill,' Juan. You mean kill or capture, do you not?"

Feeling the effect of the mescal, Juan wanted to end the conversation, but he had developed a strong sense of camaraderie toward the farmer from Saltillo.

"Carlos, His Excellency offers only two choices to the rebels — surrender or death. Bowie and Travis have openly defied the authority of the Supreme Government. If they will surrender the Alamo garrison, we might imprison them. But if they choose to fight, they will all be killed."

Carlos was also feeling effects from the mescal. His words came slowly and carefully as the fire burned down into ashes and the camp grew dark and silent. "I believe in taking prisoners. I cannot kill a wounded or unarmed man in cold blood."

"Carlos, you must, if necessary. They will kill us if they can. You know that."

"I have talked to friends who fought in this territory, and have not heard of any executions of our men after they were captured."

"That is not the point, Carlos. These people are defying authority. That is treason and the punishment is death. We must have order, no matter what is required."

"I must think about that, Juan, and we must get some sleep."

26

Chapter 4

AS they departed the Nueces area, some of the soldiers who had traveled both roads complained that the artillery could better be transported over the road from Laredo. But Santa Anna had chosen the upper route, which had been used twenty-three years previously by a Spanish army unit in which he had been a young lieutenant. He also chose a campsite on the Medina River near the spot where he had been cited for bravery in a bloody battle of that campaign against a poorly-organized band of rebel settlers and soldiers of fortune. Repeating that success had been foremost in his mind since leaving Saltillo.

At the Medina campsite, a drenching rain spoiled any hopes Santa Anna had entertained of surprising the rebels. As his troop dried clothes and cleaned weapons, he rode to a ridge three miles southwest of San Antonio de Bexar from where he surveyed the settlement area through his field glass. It was dominated by five majestic mission compounds, with only the Alamo in the immediate vicinity of the settlement, just east of the San Antonio River. The other missions were downstream, ending with San Francisco de Espada farthest from the settlement. San Fernando Church towered over the downtown commerce area where two large plazas provided a friendly, uncluttered atmosphere for several stores and shops. Most houses were one-story adobe or thatched huts, but to the west, a few wealthy citizens owned fine Spanish colonial homes of field-stone and heavy timber.

Cottonwood and pecan trees bordered the gentle, narrow San Antonio River that twisted its way through the settlement east to the Alamo. Townspeople debated whether the old mission took its common name from the Spanish word for cottonwood (*alamo*) or whether a Spanish cavalry troop from Alamo del Parras had named the abandoned mission when it was garrisoned in the early 1800s.

In either case, Mission San Antonio de Valero, founded in 1718, was locally known as "the Alamo" long before Colonel James Clinton Neill chose it as a suitable fortress in which to mount the eighteen cannons captured from General Cós.

Santa Anna, surveying the busy and sprawling settlement, surmised it must be more populous than the four thousand reported. His face tautened as he saw, flowing briskly in the breeze above the Alamo, the Mexican tricolor flag of red, white and green with 1824 inscribed in black on the white bar. He sneered at those numerals that reminded him of the bitter internal conflict in Mexico over the Constitution that provided a decentralized form of government similar to that of the United States.

"They are all going to die," he murmured to himself, scanning distant figures atop the high walls surrounding the Alamo compound, "and that despicable flag will be burned over their bodies."

Advance scouts reported that all Texan combatants, alerted by ringing church bells, had retired to the Alamo, leaving the settlement to Santa Anna uncontested. Because of its dominant Spanish and Mexican influence, he had no intention of sacking the settlement or punishing its non-combatants, a mistake committed by the Spanish army in 1813. If a spirit of cooperation could be established and maintained with local officials, he would guarantee that the picturesque settlement would not be disrupted.

With bugles sounding and banners waving, the vanguard of the Army of Operations established its sovereignty over San Antonio de Bexar. Santa Anna dispatched Colonel Batres to find the alcalde, or mayor, to secure a suitable building for his quarters and command post. Acquiring a one-story adobe house with stone patio and courtyard, Santa Anna designated a planning room and sat down to discuss policy matters with Almonte.

If ever there were contrasting individuals who worked well together, Santa Anna and Almonte were that pair. Almonte had a quiet, almost stoic, personality. Mystery shrouded his parenthood, but most people believed him to be the son of a patriot priest, José Maria Morelos, and an Indian woman. In 1834 he had made an extensive tour of Texas and filed a comprehensive report with the Mexican government. As editor of an influential newspaper that opposed Bustamante, he had found a new leader in the ascending Santa Anna, who appreciated his unstinting loyalty and unusual abilities. At thirty-three, Colonel Almonte remained Santa Anna's closest advisor on military and political matters.

"The siege is in effect, Your Excellency," Almonte said. "Scouts to the east report no enemy activity on the road to Goliad. The first phase of your plan is successful."

"I knew the rebels would not be prepared. I defy Houston to come out of hiding with whatever reserves he can muster. Is there still no report of his whereabouts?"

"None. There are many defectors and agents available to us in the southern areas of the province, but I suspect Houston will concentrate his efforts in the Anglo areas, such as San Felipe de Austin and

28

Nacogdoches. Our intelligence reports indicate there are few rebels from those areas in the garrisons here and at Goliad. For some reason, those colonists have not yet taken up arms."

"All the more reason to pursue my plan here. I will remove the backbone from the rebel movement before the arms and legs are moving. Now, I would like to confer with the alcalde."

"Your Excellency, you should know that the father of the alcalde has chosen to join the rebels. He is a delegate to their next convention."

"Almonte, since the alcalde has not fled, I assume he has the presence of mind to perceive his political standing and his future belong with the Supreme Government, not with Zavala and the rebels."

"Very well. Also, Your Excellency, I want to request that you assign Lieutenant Juan Calderón to your staff. Administrative work will be increased and I need some assistance."

Santa Anna recalled the early political support he had received from Juan's father, the prominent Señor Calderón of Mexico City. "An excellent idea," he said. "Summon young Calderón immediately."

When Juan reported to the planning room, he was pleased to be offered a seat and a glass of wine. "I have decided," said Santa Anna, "that you will become a personal aide of mine, reporting only to me and Colonel Almonte. I have observed you closely and I believe you have the potential to develop into an outstanding military leader, but you must learn strategy and organization."

"Your Excellency, I am deeply honored. I assure you that I shall perform to the utmost of my capability." Juan was surprised and elated, seeing this as a rare opportunity to gain valuable military experience, and perhaps more importantly, to become closely associated with His Excellency. "I do wonder why you chose me, sir."

"I believe you have the most potential among the younger officers. I became an officer at a younger age than you. I had to fight my way forward against enemies on the field and enemies within our own political leadership who could not foresee the destiny of Mexico. After this campaign is completed, we shall have stability throughout our nation. I will need loyal, intelligent young men to maintain that stability, and to build. There will be opportunities to serve abroad, if you should desire. But for now, you must keep your head and heart in this campaign." Santa Anna walked to a window from which he viewed the Alamo. "I detest the arrogance of these rebels. They are small in number, but they are dangerous because they can influence people in the United States of the North. It is imperative that this revolt be crushed, as soon as possible."

"Your Excellency, surely you do not anticipate an invasion by the United States of the North?"

"No, I do not anticipate an invasion, but the political climate in America as regards Mexico is important. Stephen Austin is even now in America seeking support. Sam Houston, however, who could pose a more dangerous problem as a close friend of President Jackson, remains in Texas. I believe the rebels have failed to utilize what meager talent they possess."

"Since Houston is not here or at Goliad, where can he be? They have no other concentrations of troops."

"You have just committed your first mistake in your new position," Santa Anna smiled. "You cannot assume there are no more concentrations of enemy troops. All we know for certain is what they have here and at Goliad."

Almonte returned to the planning room, informing Santa Anna that the alcalde would soon arrive.

"What is your latest estimate as to when we will achieve maximum troop strength?" Santa Anna asked Almonte.

"Weather permitting, full strength of five thousand will be achieved in eleven or twelve days."

"And what of the heavy artillery?"

"Again, with decent weather, no longer than twelve days. With rain and high creeks, fifteen or sixteen days."

Santa Anna smiled. "Remember, Almonte, how so many of those faint hearts said we could not assemble and transport such forces in winter? I have proved them wrong again. Now, the siege lines should be tightened each day as we receive reinforcements. When the artillery arrives, I want bombardment of the Alamo around the clock. This will wear them down. If they become tired and run low on provisions, they should want to surrender, knowing their situation is hopeless."

"On that point, Your Excellency," Juan asked, "if they should surrender without firing a shot, would you consider sparing them?"

"That is a difficult question. Unusual circumstances could change matters, but we have a written policy by the Supreme Government to treat most of these rebels as traitors. If the rebels in the Alamo choose to fight, they will all be killed. On the other hand, if they should choose to surrender the Alamo, saving us men and valuable ammunition, I might spare them. I will soon extend to them an opportunity to surrender at discretion."

Ramón Caro, Santa Anna's soft-spoken personal secretary, interrupted to announce the arrival of Francisco Ruiz, alcalde of San Antonio de Bexar, and Fermín Arredondo, a prominent merchant. As Juan departed, Santa Anna welcomed them into his planning room.

"Señor Alcalde," Santa Anna said, motioning for them to take seats, "you honored me with your prompt attention to my housing needs, and Señor Arredondo, your generous offer of terms for provisions for the army will not be forgotten."

30

Ruiz and Arredondo were cautious, courtly men who had friends and family on both sides of the war enveloping Texas. Arredondo had witnessed with pangs of conflict his close friends J. Antonio Navarro and Jim Bowie insist on war, joining the Texan cause, while others like himself, whose business depended on commerce from the interior of Mexico, remained loyal to the Supreme Government.

"Your Excellency," Arredondo said, "Señor Ruiz has yielded to me the honor of inviting you to your first dinner of the campaign in San Antonio de Bexar. He will be there tonight, but he insists that my table is the best in Bexar."

Ruiz smiled, openly uneasy in the presence of Santa Anna, but the Mexican general replied at once. After long days of desert travel, eating the mediocre field kitchen fare, the mere thought of a well-prepared dinner in gracious company was compelling. "But of course I accept," he smiled.

"And Colonel Almonte," Arredondo said, "we would be honored if you would also join us."

"With much pleasure," Almonte replied.

Santa Anna insisted that Arredondo and Ruiz have a glass of wine. As they chatted, Ruiz relaxed, assuming Santa Anna respected his continued loyalty, even as his father, with Navarro and the Yale-educated Samuel Maverick, went as delegates to pledge independence at the Texan convention. His and Arredondo's "courageous stand of neutrality," as Bowie mocked it, required dealing with whomever controlled the settlement, a rather delicate position in 1835-36, control having changed four times in eight months.

Arredondo also was impressed by the handsome, well-groomed president of Mexico, sharing with him that caste camaraderie of pure Spanish blood which remained strong throughout Mexico despite the bitter aftermath of the war with Spain. This relieved Arredondo's conscience, gnawing him since his recent refusal to grant provisions on credit to Colonel Travis, believing the Texan cause was hopeless. Moreover, Arredondo was proud of all legacies of Spanish rule, including the picturesque mission compounds, and resented the Anglo colonists who lacked appreciation for the Catholic tradition.

Although many citizens had fled, fearing a repeat of the atrocities committed in 1813 by the Spanish army, Ruiz and Arredondo departed convinced that Santa Anna, as commander-in-chief, was a man with whom they could deal in order to preserve their community and their positions.

Santa Anna dressed carefully for the evening in white silk trousers, fitted tightly into spotless black boots with silver spurs. His dark blue coat with large gold epaulets was buttoned closely to his chest, and his array of elaborate medals had been polished that afternoon. Caro drove him and Almonte by carriage to the sprawling two-story home of the wealthy merchant.

Arredondo greeted his guests and introduced them to his wife before adding, "My daughter, Corina, will soon join us. She is always a little late." Pausing in the drawing room before Francisco Ruiz and his wife arrived, Santa Anna was complimenting the Señora when he spied Corina gliding down the narrow, winding staircase. She carried herself with a maturity and confidence beyond her twenty-one years. He read the Spanish heritage in her light complexion and soft brown hair, while she drew her thin, firm mouth from her father and the warm, hazel eyes from her mother. She wore a striking green silk dress that clung tightly to her slender body. Upon being introduced to Santa Anna, she surprised him with her calm, direct manner.

By candlelight, they sat down at the ornate mahogany dinner table to enjoy the best the Arredondo family could offer. The table was set on exquisite linen with imported china and crystal, the fine silverware coming from Taxco, near Mexico City. Two long silver platters held partridge baked in wine, tender strips of broiled beef, called *carne asada*, and *cabrito*, young goat barbecued slowly over a pit of mesquite coals. Servants also brought guacamole salad, rice, small boiled onions sautéed in butter, thick dinner rolls with *guajillo* honey, and steadily replenished glasses of fine Spanish wine.

"We would appreciate," Arredondo said, "learning firsthand from His Excellency what is the mood of Mexico in terms of commerce and the future."

Finishing a delicious bite of partridge, Santa Anna placed his fork gently on his plate. "I would say that this is a time of great challenge. The entire well-being of our nation is involved in this revolution, which tests again my ability to consolidate our empire."

"In all honesty," Corina said, "I find it surprising to see Your Excellency leading an army of thousands to conquer so few insurgents."

"Numbers here are not significant," Santa Anna said. "This campaign could prove to be pivotal for Mexico. I have agents in the American capital who tell me President Jackson wants this territory to become part of the United States of the North. I must remind you the American minister to Mexico, Mr. Poinsett, attempted twice to purchase Texas soon after we won our independence. I am convinced that Sam Houston is an agent for President Jackson; they have fought together, they are close friends, and they want to deliver this territory to the United States. If they should be successful, their next desire would be California and all the land inbetween. In the fifteen years since we won our independence, we have endured internal conflict and foreign threats, but I have no intention of conceding our land to the Americans, the French, or anyone else."

"Your Excellency, do you believe President Jackson is involved in this uprising?" Arredondo asked.

"No, not at present; he would have moved, but for the slavery issue. These Texan colonists want slavery, but the political situation forbids the admission of more slave territories as states. Of course, this situation could change."

Corina leaned slightly toward Santa Anna. "If your campaign is successful this winter, do you believe the Americans will try at some later date to conquer this land?"

"No. Though the greedy Americans look with longing to the south and west, they are weary from their wars with the British and the Indians. I must successfully conclude this campaign to protect the legitimate interests of Mexico, discouraging any American desires for future aggression. The Mexican empire must remain the largest on this continent, larger than any in Europe, save Russia. This is our destiny, and I defy the United States to intercede!"

"The great conqueror Napoleon must have spoken words similar to those," Corina smiled.

"It so happens," Santa Anna said, "that I am a true admirer of Napoleon. I have been called 'The Napoleon of the West,' a term I must say I appreciate more than 'The Eagle.' "

"Ah, but Your Excellency," Ruiz said, "that term 'The Eagle' is most appropriate for your advance to San Antonio de Bexar. You flew in faster than the insurgents expected." Santa Anna smiled, lifting his third glass of wine.

"Since you are an admirer of Napoleon," Corina said, "I trust you adhere to the principles of military leadership and honor that he upheld?"

"What do you mean?"

"Only that an adversary without adequate means for defense should be given an opportunity for an honorable surrender."

Almonte almost dropped his glass of wine. At best, Santa Anna would give Corina a severe tongue-lashing, he thought, or accuse her father of sedition. Arredondo frowned at his daughter, always too sincere, too direct. Why in God's name had she confronted the dictator of their land? He had started to admonish her when he caught Santa Anna's amused smile. Toying with his glass of wine, the general leaned toward Corina. "I am told that you and your family know Jim Bowie. Is that true?"

"Yes," Corina replied. "We knew the Bowies well, but the family is gone. Only Jim remains."

"Jim Bowie married the daughter of Governor Veramendi," Ruiz said. "She and their two children, along with her father and mother, perished in Monclavo during the cholera epidemic of 1833."

"But, of course," Santa Anna said. "I am the godfather of Ursula Veramendi. Pardon my asking questions, but I sometimes need to refresh my memory. What kind of man is Bowie?"

Ruiz spoke softly. "He was one of our most outstanding citizens until he lost his wife and children. He was here and in my home on numerous occasions. I am told he made a fortune trading in slaves with the French pirate, Jean Lafitte, and there is talk that he found a silver mine north of here, but no one knows for certain."

"He is a fighter, a strong-willed fighter," Arredondo said. "That is why he has led successful skirmishes, and why he is now a leader of many men in the old mission. Even men who have not fought with him before know him by reputation, and they will follow his leadership."

"You both missed the most important thing about Jim Bowie," Corina said. "He is, above all, a vibrant human being, who fights hard against what he thinks is wrong and defends what he believes is right. Furthermore, he has a special appeal for me as a man of prestige who is gentle and kind to all people."

"He is, indeed, an interesting man," Ruiz said, "but I understand he has taken ill, vastly reducing his ability to lead his men."

"And what of that freebooter, David Crockett?" asked Santa Anna. "He has no land nor family in this territory. Why is he here?"

"He has led fifteen or sixteen men into this garrison of insurgents," Ruiz said. "They brought long rifles that are said to be amazingly accurate. Of their motives, I cannot say."

"You see," Santa Anna said, "why I am so concerned about these American politicians. Crockett and Houston have both represented Tennessee, Jackson's state, in the American Congress. I am certain they want this territory to join the United States."

"Disregarding their motives," Arredondo said, "I must say to Your Excellency that I know the roster of those men in the old mission. They represent all sections of America, in addition to people from Mexico and Europe. An annihilation of that garrison might create martyrs throughout the world."

"My dear Arredondo," Santa Anna replied, "you are a gracious host, but a most naive man. I have devoted my life to bringing order to Mexico. These traitors are declared enemies of the nation, defying the authority of the Supreme Government and militating under a flag we cannot recognize as representing a legitimate government. Furthermore, their comrades are preparing to declare independence, but lack the resources necessary to sustain a republic; therefore, this can be nothing more than a cloaked bid for eventual statehood. I have no choice but to destroy their rebellion and restore order to this territory, which is, I remind you, nothing more nor less than a province of the Republic of Mexico.

"After this campaign is completed, I shall institute a policy of limited immigration, restricting Texas colonies to people from south of the Rio Bravo, or Rio Grande, as you people call it. The crucial mistake of the past has been allowing Americans to secure land for practically nothing. These perfidious foreigners are not content with receiving land for farming or raising cattle. They are scheming and speculating with land companies, financed by greedy American interests in the Eastern United States. These Anglo colonists have defied their benefactors, therefore they have forfeited their right to remain in this territory."

"Well," Ruiz said, returning to familiar ground, "I suspect the battle preparation in the old mission will be directed by Travis, now that Bowie has been taken ill."

Santa Anna paused, fork in hand, to question anyone at the table. "And what of this young man, Travis?"

"A competent attorney, I am told," Ruiz responded, "but one who deals too much in notes and credit. He also has a short temper."

"I would think at twenty-six he is too young to be a commander," Arredondo said.

"Youth is no barrier to command ability," Santa Anna said, "but he must be an impetuous, irresponsible person — that attack he led on our Anahuac garrison last year was patently illegal. Even his own countrymen denounced it as such."

"Travis has a reputation of being a 'regular,' adhering more to principles of military discipline than Jim Bowie," Ruiz said. "They also say he is an eloquent speaker who can inspire men to fight."

"I found it incredible," Santa Anna smiled, "when I was informed that Bowie and Travis held a joint command. Never in the annals of military history has there been a joint command in a successful operation. This defies a fundamental principle of military organization — but that is among the many foolish courses of action these rebels have chosen."

Corina's beautiful face showed a deep sense of concern. "You speak only in military terms. Cannot you consider the human beings involved? With your superior force, you should offer the small Alamo garrison some honorable terms for surrender."

"Corina," her father snapped, "you must not confront His Excellency. You owe him an apology."

Corina sat silently, as her mother promptly summoned servants to bring pastry, coffee and fine French brandy. Santa Anna gently swirled the brandy in his glass. "Corina, I will make you a promise. I will offer them the opportunity to surrender on one condition — that you show me the gardens."

Before he could raise his hand in protest, Arredondo saw his daughter excusing herself from the table to join Santa Anna. Permitting her to take a stroll without a chaperon was abhorrent to Arredondo, but he felt powerless to intervene.

Corina and Santa Anna stepped into the pleasantly cool, crisp evening. Following the high stone walls of the courtyard, they strolled in soft shadows near a frescoed tile fountain bathed in pale moonlight. Corina pulled her white shawl tightly against her body and did not resist when Santa Anna slid his arm gently around her shoulder. As they approached a long arbor filled with twisting mustang-grape vines, Corina broke the silence. "You have seen the gardens, my share of the bargain. What terms of surrender will you offer?"

Santa Anna smiled, shaking his head. "You have spoken of nothing but those traitors in the old mission. Have you no other interests? Tell me about yourself. I cannot believe that such a beautiful young woman is not married or betrothed."

"I was betrothed, but my fiancé died when the plague swept this country. I was in New Orleans with relatives at the time. I did not even know he was ill. I loved him deeply."

"I am sorry, Corina, but you are too beautiful to mourn forever. You must look ahead to a happy life."

She gazed across the courtyard. "I must apologize to you now. I regret that I was so direct at the dinner table."

"I will accept your apology on one condition — that you give me a kiss."

Corina was startled. She looked into his eyes to determine if he were only joking and he returned her look with a wry, fanciful smile. "Oh, I don't think I should . . ." she said as he pulled her to him for a gentle kiss. At first she did not resist, but as he prolonged the kiss, she clenched his arms to pull away. Instead of continuing to hold her tightly, he released her and she sighed, "I . . . we should not have done that."

"It was much more exciting than the dinner conversation," he said, leaving the arbor to view the prairie to the south. "Ah, look over there. Look at all those campfires from our newly-arrived troops."

"How many troops do you have?"

"I will not tell. You might run to the old mission to inform Jim Bowie."

"I suppose I deserved that."

"And I must return you to your parents. Will you have dinner with me tomorrow night?"

"I will ask Father's permission, but only on one condition, that you will not kiss me again."

"And I deserved that," he smiled.

When she came inside, her father was playing three-card monte with Ruiz and Almonte. He frowned when his daughter privately relayed Santa Anna's invitation.

"He is a married man," Arredondo protested, "and he must be twice your age. He has no right to ask you to dinner. Besides, La Dueña is ill. It is out of the question."

"He is the president of Mexico," she said, "and commander-in-chief of the army. He is the only person who can save Jim Bowie. And what of your friends Juan Seguin and Gregorio Esparza? The mere chance to save those men should compel us to try anything."

"Corina, you place too much trust in people. I do not believe Santa Anna has any mercy in his heart."

"Then why are you helping his army? I know you are doing business with him."

"This war has confused our lives, my dear."

"Confused, Father, or corrupted?"

"Corina, I will not tolerate that! I am not about to risk a lifetime of achievement for anyone outside our family. Do you understand?"

Corina gazed out the window toward the dark outline of the Alamo walls in the moonlight. "I understand how you feel, Father, but please understand that I must do all I can to save them. I cannot live with myself if I do not try."

Arredondo studied his daughter, whom he loved dearly, and tried to speak, but the words would not come. He walked slowly across the room to the card table and summoned Almonte. "Colonel, my daughter would like to accept a gracious invitation from His Excellency for dinner tomorrow night. I trust that upon our acceptance, you will serve as escort and chaperon throughout the evening."

"With great pleasure, sir," Almonte said.

As the game of monte continued at the Arredondo home, Juan and Carlos entered a large, crowded cantina a few blocks away. The cantina was filled with Mexican officers, since most enlisted men could not afford the cost and contented themselves with wine or warm beer at their campsites.

"Now, we can forget the military situation for a while," Juan said, lifting a glass of wine.

Carlos joined the toast. "I agree, but I hope that Santa Anna will soon order an attack. At present, we have the greater strength, but each day we wait gives them time for reinforcements."

"Frankly, Carlos, I believe Santa Anna wants them to be reinforced. We have a confined area here. A few more men for the enemy will not make any difference. We can starve them out."

"Enough, Juan. We were going to forget the military situation. Besides, here comes some entertainment."

Guitarists and dancers eased onto a narrow stage at the rear of the cantina. A stunning young girl danced gracefully, but forcefully, to a spirited rendition of a familiar Mexican ballad. She wore a flowing knee-length skirt, her low-cut white blouse secured by a bright red sash. With her long black hair tied tightly behind her head, she flashed dark eyes at the cheering audience as she swirled through the dance.

After the music ended, she went by the tables, stopping to ask Juan and Carlos if they wanted more to drink. "I cannot believe," Juan said, "that such a fine dancer must wait tables."

"When the cantina is busy, all of us must work," she replied impatiently, tapping a sandal-clad foot on the floor.

"You dance beautifully," Juan said, introducing Carlos and himself.

37

"My name is Bozita, and I am in a hurry. More wine, or not?"

"Would you like another glass, Carlos?"

"No, thank you," Carlos said. "I have some duties to complete tonight. I will see you in the morning, Juan. Good night."

Juan looked at Bozita. "Will you not join me for a glass of wine?"

"No, I cannot. Perhaps later."

Juan watched her swish from table to table, balancing the tray carefully on one hand. Half of the men in the cantina invited her to join their tables, but she declined, relentlessly filling orders and breaking only for her turn on stage.

Growing hazy with wine, Juan found Bozita more and more appealing. He had known beautiful young girls in Mexico City, but none with such spark and intensity. She gave total concentration to her provocative dancing and was still able to convert immediately into the most efficient, detached waitress in the crowded cantina.

It was almost midnight before the Mexican officers began drifting out. Juan, flushed with wine, was in high spirits when Bozita sat down next to him with a small glass of mescal and a slice of lime.

"That is not easy for a man to drink," Juan said. "I did not expect to see a young lady trying it."

"It is late and I have had nothing to drink. Besides, I like mescal and I am not a young lady."

"At any rate, you are the most attractive woman I have seen since I left home."

"You are full of wine. Any woman would look good to you."

"That is not true. I watched you dancing and working the tables; you do both gracefully."

"Well, I am also tired. Since your army arrived, I have worked twice as hard as before. With the Texans, there was not as much business. There were not as many, and some farmers did not drink at all. And then there was Jim Bowie and some of his people who drank all the time."

"What kind of man is this Bowie?"

"There are two men — the one before his family died in the plague and the one after. The first one was fine; we all liked him. The second is not so fine. He drinks too much. He starts fights, and with that big knife he carries, he is dangerous."

"Aren't you pleased that we have restored order?"

"I really do not care."

"You mean you have no loyalty to Mexico?"

"I have loyalty to myself. I will say the Mexican officers usually behave better than some of Bowie's men. Judge Seguin had more faith in the other commander, Travis, to keep order in the streets."

"And what is your opinion of Travis?"

"A tall, handsome man who dresses well. Courteous. He appears to be much younger than Jim Bowie. I have heard that Bowie is sick and Travis now may be the sole commander. Now, I would like another drink if you will buy it for me."

Juan ordered a mescal, but hesitated to pay the high price asked by the bartender. "That is more than they charge in the City of Mexico for the finest mescal. How can you ask such a price?"

The bartender glared at Bozita, who shrugged her shoulders. "You have to pay extra if you want me to sit here," she said. "If you do not want me here, I will leave."

Juan placed the money in the bartender's hand. The cantina was almost dark and empty, but instead of feeling romantic as he had earlier, he was nettled. "I have never been to a place with an extra charge for speaking to a waitress."

"You have not been here before."

"I am sorry if I appeared angry. It is not the money, but the principle involved. I only wanted to be friendly and share a conversation with you."

"What is principle? This is the way we do business. I work here and none of my time is free. Do you understand that?"

"Yes, I understand, but you seem to be bitter. You are young and beautiful. You should not be that way."

"You are a young fool. Go find a girl of your kind. Good night, Lieutenant." She tossed down the last of her mescal and disappeared behind the bar, leaving Juan alone in the quiet cantina.

Chapter 5

THE following morning, Santa Anna reviewed field reports on his siege of the Alamo plus new intelligence reports on the Texan leaders.

"I find these latest reports entirely inadequate," he snapped at Almonte and Juan. "What I want to know is the whereabouts of Sam Houston and Lorenzo de Zavala. I cannot believe that in their desperate military situation, they would concern themselves with another convention. What can it accomplish? They can meet and draw up papers and listen to Zavala make another of his endless speeches, but that will not secure them any more troops and ammunition."

"Houston is reputed to be a shrewd man," Almonte said. "He may be gathering troops somewhere that our scouts cannot determine."

"Perhaps so," Santa Anna said. "I want a special reward offered for accurate information on their whereabouts. Houston may remain hidden for a period of time, but Zavala cannot resist the temptation to speak out. When he does, I want to know where he is. Then I will silence that despicable traitor."

"Perhaps I should not speak to the point, Your Excellency," Juan said, "but I would assume Zavala could not effectively rally Anglos for this uprising."

"You are welcome to speak, Lieutenant," Santa Anna said, "and you are partially correct about Zavala. While most Anglos probably will not listen to him, he is a dangerous influence on Mexicans who should support our government. Among several blunders committed by my distinguished brother-in-law was his failure to have Zavala and this insolent Travis placed in chains last year. Zavala may be a charlatan, a traitor, and a curse on our nation, but he is an eloquent speaker and writer. I regret deeply that I· am among the Mexican leaders who placed him in prominent government positions; such a background lends prestige to his lies and manipulations."

"Your Excellency," Juan asked, "how did Zavala maneuver himself into the presidency of the Constitutional Convention of 1824?"

"By doing exactly that: maneuvering. Now that I recall that convention, and the unrealistic document that it produced, I am not so sure that Zavala cannot influence Anglos as well as Mexicans. He is a misguided politician, with his vague ideas about democracy, but he has a lofty determination about him that appeals to gullible people."

"I also wonder about Antonio Navarro," Almonte said.

"I believe him to be an honorable gentleman," Santa Anna said, "but I am afraid that Zavala and that erratic young firebrand Juan Seguin have convinced him to rebel. Like Zavala, his prominence in previous government service, plus the respect he commands, make him, even among Anglos, a formidable adversary."

"I noticed," Almonte said, "that you avoided the subject of these traitors yesterday and at dinner last night."

"Only out of respect for Ruiz. I find it most distasteful that his father is en route to that ill-fated convention where the insurgent leaders in effect will be signing their names away to a firing squad. I did not care to embarrass Francisco at dinner last night. He must know his father is committing suicide if he signs that so-called declaration of independence, and so has prepared himself for the inevitable. This is all the more reason to respect Francisco and to reward his cooperation in the future."

"Shall I instruct our agents to make special effort to arrest these other traitors?" Almonte asked.

"Yes," Santa Anna said, frowning and pacing the floor. "This is all most distasteful. I cannot understand how these men, who had earned respect in our government, can now turn their backs on their own people. Yes, have special orders, with appropriate rewards, issued for the death or capture of Seguin and Navarro as well."

"Since Ruiz's father is a delegate to the convention, should we not include him in the order?" asked Almonte.

"No, I do not think that is wise."

"Then, sir, does that mean you will spare him?" Juan asked.

"No, but I do not want to upset the alcalde at this time. Besides, Zavala is much more important; I would rather hang him today than Austin or Houston."

At dinner that night, Santa Anna could not match the Arredondo meal, but he did provide a surprise for Corina. He had a barrel of live fish transported from Matamoros for his favorite dish, *ceviche*, a raw fish cocktail in a marinade of delicious oils and spices.

As they were finishing the meal, Santa Anna glanced at his watch and asked Almonte, "Is it not time for my meeting with General Castrillón?"

"I do not recall a meeting with General Castrillón."

"Normally, you are most efficient, Almonte, but you have forgotten my request to bring General Castrillón here for a conference tonight."

"But Your Excellency, Caro and Calderón have been dismissed for the night. There is no one available to seek General Castrillón. As a matter of fact, I have no idea where he may be at this hour."

"That is your concern, Almonte. I must see him tonight, and you should be on your way."

"Your Excellency, I have absolutely no recollection of your request. Surely, Caro would have logged it on the daily calendar."

"Almonte, you and Caro have been working too hard. Perhaps you should take some time off tomorrow, but tonight I must confer with General Castrillón. That is an order, Colonel."

"If you will excuse me," Almonte sighed to Corina, "I shall return at the earliest possible moment."

Corina was more amused than concerned as the loyal aide departed, leaving her alone with His Excellency. "Is this how you conduct matters of state in the capital?"

"Almonte was a bit careless," Santa Anna smiled. "I am confident he will not repeat such a mistake. Now, Corina, will you join me for a stroll through the plaza?"

They walked along a path where cottonwood and pecan trees cast long shadows over the shrubs and flowers. Soft strains of zither and guitar music bore the lilting melodies of "La Paloma" and "Adelita" into the starlit plaza.

She caught Santa Anna by surprise when she asked if she might address him by his first name. He paused by a pecan tree, gazing across the plaza. "Since I became president, you are the only woman to ask me that question. A few have assumed the privilege; others would not dare. To you, the answer is 'yes.' "

"Antonio, I am aware I was rude last night, and I apologize, but I have been so concerned that there would be unwarranted bloodshed."

"You should be thankful that you have no family or loved ones to be involved in the fighting."

"I suppose I should, but I pray that bloodshed can be avoided."

"Then, are you in love with Jim Bowie?"

"I cannot say. I think the answer is 'no' in the sense that one falls in love to marry. But I felt pity for him after he lost his wife and children, for he loved them so much. Ursula and I were close friends, and somehow I feel an obligation to help her beloved husband."

"I find it difficult to believe that this slave-trading instigator of duels could inspire love or admiration in someone so delicate. You have refused to recognize his faults."

"He remains a fine, genuine human being. Of course he has faults, but he has been an outstanding citizen, and both Anglos and Mexicans hold him in high esteem."

As Santa Anna started to respond, a thundering volley of cannon fire roared through the night as the Mexican batteries renewed their bombardment of the Alamo. Corina recoiled against Santa Anna, who held her tightly for a moment. When he tried to kiss her, she pulled away, pointing to the tower of San Fernando Church. "Why has that red flag been placed on our church?"

"I ordered it displayed there, Corina, after I did what you wanted me to do — offer the rebels an opportunity to surrender."

"What was their response?"

"Their response was a cannon shot, from their largest artillery piece. I am told that the insolent Travis himself fired the fuse. Then I ordered the flag placed so all the rebels can see it."

"Does that flag mean no quarter?"

"Yes."

"Can you not make them another offer?"

"Perhaps, but I will not tolerate further such insolence."

"What were your terms?"

"A surrender at discretion."

"Which means?"

"It means that after they surrender, I will determine what their fate may be."

"But they have not dealt with you directly before. Can you not offer them terms before they surrender?"

"I am not authorized to conduct such negotiations with traitors."

"But Father says that you have all the power at your command."

"My dear, that is not true. Mexico is a republic with a full system of government, although it is true that my countrymen have bestowed extraordinary responsibility in my hands, more so than has President Jackson, who often seems to let Congress run the American government."

"But I have listened to Lorenzo de Zavala speak eloquently for the Federal Constitution of 1824."

"Corina, you are beautiful, but hopelessly naive. Zavala would have you believe that the American form of government is ideal for Mexico — this is a fantasy. When our people, including those in this province, recognize that a strong central government is necessary for Mexico, we will have peace and stabililty throughout our land."

"What of Señor Navarro and Francisco's father? They are among our most prominent citizens."

"They have been deluded by Zavala. You may be sure that I will not leave this province before I silence Zavala forever. But let us not spoil the evening with a political discussion. Let us talk of more pleasant things."

"Antonio, I will not be rude, nor will I speak again of Dr. Zavala, but I must request — or beg — that you remove that terrible flag from our church and offer some terms to those poor souls in the mission."

"Corina, I obviously feel a strong affection for you, but you have intruded far into matters of state."

43

He slid his arm around her as he had done the previous night, but she eased away. "Antonio, if you can show no mercy for those men, I cannot permit myself even the slightest affection for you. I felt something for you last night, but I will not be a pawn on your chessboard. I know I cannot be the queen."

Santa Anna had never been confronted by a woman, or a man for that matter, who could divert him from his objective so carefully and persistently. He gazed across the plaza, past the scattered buildings, to the Alamo, dimly lit by a few fires and torches inside its compound.

"I regret that the situation may be hopeless as far as the Alamo is concerned," he said, "but Bowie has relinquished his share of the command to this impetuous young fool. With my honor and that of Mexico at stake, I cannot permit 'Mr.' Travis — for he certainly is no colonel — unusual concessions, especially after today's flagrant display of arrogance. Corina, you must be realistic. Your father and most of his friends are loyal to Mexico. I can be of vast assistance to your father, and I intend to be if a spirit of cooperation continues to exist."

Santa Anna slid his arm around Corina and she again pulled away as footsteps approached from the house. Almonte turned the corner to announce that General Castrillón awaited Santa Anna at his planning room.

"Almonte," Santa Anna snapped, "your efficiency has returned rapidly."

"At your service, Your Excellency. And at your service, Señorita Arredondo. I must now return you to your home lest your father become concerned."

As Almonte went ahead, Santa Anna pulled Corina close to him. "When may I see you again?" he whispered.

"When you remove that flag and offer terms for a surrender."

While Santa Anna consulted with General Castrillón, Juan and Carlos sat drinking a few blocks away at the cantina.

Juan proposed a toast: "To the glorious victory we will soon achieve for His Excellency and the Supreme Government." But Carlos refused to join him, toying with his glass of wine as he stared at the table. "What is wrong, old soldier?" Juan asked.

"I am afraid your glorious victory will not come so easy. Santa Anna made the rebels even more desperate by placing that flag on the San Fernando Church. They will fight like demons now that they do not expect to survive. Santa Anna is wrong. We should offer terms for a surrender, and if that fails, we should assault the fortress. But they should know we will take prisoners."

"Carlos, the rebels left His Excellency no choice. Since they insulted him, they do not deserve any mercy."

"Juan, you are unseasoned in war. I would much rather fight a large group of trained men in an organized army on a battlefield under recognized rules of war than confront a few desperate men entrenched in a fortification. If we overcome their artillery and rifles, they will fight to the death with pistols and knives. Do you understand?"

"Yes, but you know we have more men and artillery. We can use our artillery to destroy the walls, rendering the rebels vulnerable inside the compound."

"Remember, Juan, our British muskets have nowhere near the range of the rifles possessed by the enemy. In order to create breaches in the walls of the Alamo, we must establish batteries within their rifle range. That is a risky task indeed."

"Are you saying those squirrel hunters have superior military rifles?"

"Yes, and you have forgotten also that the rebels have eighteen cannons mounted for use, more firepower than I imagined they could possibly have."

"But a few cannonballs cannot repulse our attack columns."

"Juan, you should spend more time talking to veterans of combat here. These rebels are resourceful. When we assault that fortress, they will spray us unmercifully with those shotguns they call cannons."

"What do you mean, 'spray'?"

"They will fire grapeshot and canisters, which will be like shotguns spraying jagged bits of metal. They will not fire cannonballs."

"I thought grapeshot was similar to musket balls."

"They do not have that variety. Instead they have stripped this settlement of all its old horseshoes, files and nails. From that they have made their grapeshot, and I fear it will be deadly at close range."

"Carlos, you are a veteran soldier, but you worry too much. I am convinced His Excellency will prepare a superb battle plan. Surely we can overcome that small force without losing many men."

"No matter what you say, Juan, an assault on that old mission, against men who will fight to the death, will be harder, much harder, than Santa Anna contemplates."

Despite the concerns voiced by Carlos, Juan was anticipating the impending battle, his first experience as a part of a combat operation. "Carlos, what is the most exciting, the most thrilling aspect of a battle?"

"I have never found combat to be thrilling."

"Well, what do you feel?"

"I feel fear. That is the first enemy to overcome."

"And what is the most important thing in your mind?"

"Not to become confused. With cannonade, musket fire and men shouting, the noise can get so loud you cannot hear orders or bugle calls. In such instances, close organization of the troops is most important. If they become confused, they may be routed."

"How will you prepare your men for this assault?"

"They will know who to follow should I fall. I am studying the terrain carefully, and if the enemy fire becomes intense, as I expect, we will use arroyos and irrigation ditches rather than die in the open areas."

"I wish I could be with your column in battle."

"Be thankful for the position you hold. You will be alive after the battle, and I may not."

"I had not thought of that. I wish you would not speak in such gloomy terms."

"I apologize, Juan, but I have no desire for glory or land grants in this territory. I only want to complete my duty and return home. If I should die, my children will suffer greatly. I worry about that each day and night."

"I will wager you a glass of wine, and I will buy it now, that you will not be killed."

"No, thank you, Juan. Two is all for me. I must retire."

As Carlos departed, Juan ordered another glass of wine. Bozita had been cool toward him all evening, but when she brought the wine, he invited her to join him.

"It is early. There is too much business now. Perhaps later."

As she swished by the adjoining table, a swarthy, middle-aged captain grabbed her around the waist, pulling her to him. She tried to free herself, but he tightened his hold. Juan sprang from his chair and twisted the captain's arm, pulling it from Bozita's waist.

"You are out of place, Lieutenant," the captain snapped.

"And you are a discredit to the Army of Operations," Juan said.

The captain tried to slap Juan's cheek, but Juan dodged the blow and struck the captain with a hard right cross to the jaw, sending him sprawling across a table. Other officers restrained the two, and the captain, on being escorted from the cantina, shouted at Juan, "You will hear from me about this!"

Juan returned to his table where he slumped into a chair, wondering what the consequences might be for striking a superior officer. Bozita sat down beside him with a small glass of mescal. "Will you be in trouble?"

"I suppose I will know tomorrow."

"It was a foolish gesture."

"I thought he was hurting you. Besides, I do not want to see him or anyone else holding you."

"You have no idea how many men have held me."

"I want to see you more, Bozita, and to hold you."

"I told you last night it is foolish. I have no family, no home worthy of the name. There is nothing for us. You know that."

"I know no such thing. I know I would strike another man if he hurt you. And I know that I want to hold you so very much."

46

"Yes, you want to hold me. They all want to hold me. For a price you can hold me."

"You do not sell your body. You are only trying to hurt me."

Bozita set down the small glass. She started to speak, but merely sighed and walked briskly away from the table.

Early the next morning, Almonte summoned Juan into a small staff room adjoining Santa Anna's planning room. "This is a serious charge brought against you by the captain."

"I did not instigate the altercation," Juan said, after reading the charge. "As a gentleman, I interceded in behalf of a defenseless woman who was the victim of an indiscretion committed by this captain."

"I am certain there are two sides to the question," Almonte said. "The important thing is that you not be the subject of such questionable conduct again. Since you are a member of His Excellency's staff, your reputation is my responsibility. I will make certain the captain realizes this was an unfortunate misunderstanding, unworthy of concern to His Excellency."

"Thank you very much, Colonel."

"However, I must confine you to quarters until after the resolution of hostilities. I regret taking this action, Lieutenant, but this is a serious charge and I must be careful not to impair my relationship with the other officers."

Juan winced, thinking of the nights to be spent alone in his quarters. "Very well, Colonel. I consider this to be harsh punishment, but I accept it in view of the circumstances."

Though usually bored with personnel matters, Almonte respected Juan and hesitated before dismissing him. "I suspect you had a bit too much to drink last night."

"No, sir."

"Then are you somewhat infatuated with this barmaid?"

"I suppose so. I have never felt quite like this about a girl before."

"Bear in mind, Lieutenant, who you are and what you are."

That night after supper, Carlos made his way to the smoke-filled cantina. At first he couldn't find Bozita, but finally she emerged from a large table in a far corner with a tray full of empty glasses. He motioned to her and she came to his table.

"Is he in trouble?" she asked.

"Yes, he asked me to tell you he is confined to quarters until after hostilities are resolved."

"You mean he cannot leave his quarters at all? Must he live in a tent?"

"No. He is a personal aide to General Santa Anna. As such, he lives in the house where Santa Anna and Colonel Almonte are quartered."

"He must be more important than an ordinary lieutenant."

"His father is much more important than an ordinary citizen of Mexico. He is a close political supporter of Santa Anna, so Juan has been given a special opportunity to serve on His Excellency's staff."

"Will he be in the battle?"

"No, he will not be in the assault forces."

"Then he has little to be concerned about."

"But he is concerned about you. He asked me to tell you he does not regret defending you."

"Believe me," Bozita sighed, "I have done nothing to encourage such a foolish gesture on his part. I am a *mestizo*, more like you, Captain, and I cannot understand why he pays so much attention to me. There can be no love between us."

"The fact that you are half Indian will not discourage Juan. He is an unusual young man."

"He only wants to have my body."

"You are wrong. He has shown he is willing to sacrifice for you."

"It cannot be, but thank you for coming by," she said.

Nettled by Corina's steadfast position, Santa Anna had turned elsewhere to find romance. Parental objections on the behalf of one particularly attractive girl, however, prompted a ruse whereby Santa Anna's proposal of marriage was accepted, and then formalized by one of his cronies, disguised as a priest. Apparently unaware that Santa Anna had a wife and children, the bride lived with him until he dispatched her to San Luis Potosi where she ultimately bore him a son. The settlement buzzed with the scandal.

Indignant upon learning of the affair, Juan confronted Almonte. "I did not participate, nor do I approve," Almonte said, "but there was nothing I could do about it. He arranged everything among a few of his cronies and it was done in utmost haste."

"It makes a mockery of his moral leadership," Juan said. "Has he no respect for the church? I cannot believe he would do such a thing."

"It is done," Almonte said, "and the wise course is for you not to discuss it further with anyone."

Almonte and Juan logged data on the newly-arrived reinforcements, including their weapons and ammunition, supplies and means to transport artillery and baggage wagons. Almonte was pleased with the army's progress except for the reports that heavy artillery would be further delayed due to swollen rivers and creeks.

Santa Anna strode into the room with a wrinkled map on which he had marked several times. "I have decided to test the preparations made by Mr. Travis." Spreading the map on a table, Santa Anna outlined a plan placing artillery in and near La Villita, a complex of small houses and huts along the west side of the river. "By placing these batteries near the Alamo, we can tear apart the west and south walls. I am sending a contingent of infantry to draw their fire while I personally supervise establishing the batteries."

Santa Anna chose to test the south side of the Alamo defense, it being the only part of the compound not enclosed by high walls. Travis had assigned Crockett to that area, counting on the accuracy of the Tennessee riflemen to repulse any infantry attack. As additional support, three cannons were mounted atop the Alamo chapel.

At mid-morning, Santa Anna dispatched his forces, some two hundred strong, toward La Villita. As they moved into close range of the Alamo, Travis climbed the chapel, saber in hand. He had cautioned artillery batteries and riflemen to await his signal. Since Carlos' unit had been assigned to the reserves, the veteran officer from Saltillo climbed atop a house in La Villita to watch the skirmish. It seemed that Travis and the Texans were asleep, as they allowed the Mexican soldiers to advance within two hundred yards of the Alamo. Then Travis waved his saber and shouted "fire!" The Texan batteries and riflemen fired as one into the onrushing Mexicans, many of whom fell beneath the slashing spray of hot metal and rapid rifle fire, most of Crockett's men having more than one rifle at their stations.

Captains Blair, Carey and Dickinson soon had their artillery pieces reloaded and firing. Gregorio Esparza, one of Seguin's men and a fine artilleryman, raced to the southwest battery to help reload that huge eighteen-pounder, the Texans' largest artillery piece. Confined to his bed with a high fever, Bowie knew from the concentration of fire that a general engagement was not in progress. Moreover, he knew from the sound of the artillery and rifle shots that the firepower generated by the Alamo defenders was three or four times that of the Mexican forces.

After those first withering rounds, the Mexican soldiers fell back. They sallied forth a few times during the next two hours, but never penetrated far enough to cut down any of the shouting Alamo defenders. When the skirmish ended, Travis was exultant to find no casualties, while the enemy had sustained several losses.

As he descended from the house in La Villita, Carlos shook his head. "Now," he said to Juan, "do you understand the danger behind those high walls?"

Juan's face was flushed with anger and disappointment. "It was a hastily conceived plan, Carlos. I am confident His Excellency will be more cautious in planning the final assault."

"What you saw today will be repeated unless we have equally heavy artillery."

"There may be other means. They cannot survive without food and water."

"We cannot cut off these supplies; they have a well and there are many cattle in their corral."

"I am confident His Excellency will devise a proper plan."

Inside the Alamo, Travis savored the cheering and shouting that followed the Texan victory. As the excitement subsided, he invited

Crockett to his planning room. "I'm convinced," Travis said, "that we can repulse an attacking force up to a thousand men. With two hundred more riflemen, we could hold out forever."

"When we concentrate our firepower in one area, we can repulse heavy attacks," Crockett said, "but if they move more artillery into range, and attack from all four sides, there's no way we can keep them out. Can't you try once more for reinforcements?"

"Yes," Travis said, pointing to a map. "I'll send a report of the skirmish to General Houston with another request for help, and dispatch my friend Bonham to plead our case with Fannin once again."

"Tell him not to be too long-winded. We're running out of time."

James Butler Bonham soon reported to Travis. At twenty-nine, this lifelong friend of Travis and fellow-attorney shared with him a reputation as a fine horseman, the ideal man for a daring mission through the Mexican siege lines.

"James, you'd better button yourself close to that horse, and veer away from the Goliad road for some distance. I'm sure Santa Anna has that area under surveillance."

"I'll leave under cover of darkness."

"Plead the case, James. We must have help from Fannin."

The Texans spent the next few days strengthening the Alamo walls, supervised by Green B. Jameson, an engineer who had learned how to construct support platforms for artillery from the departed Colonel Neill. Jameson, a Kentuckian who had practiced law in San Felipe de Austin, found his work challenging as he constantly bolstered the walls with dirt to withstand the cannonade.

In the early morning hours of March 1, Travis awakened to shouting in Alamo Plaza. Leaping to his feet with shotgun in hand, he raced outside his room to find that a thirty-two member contingent from Gonzales had sneaked through the Mexican lines to reinforce the Alamo. Captain Albert Martin extended his hand to Travis. "There aren't many of us," Martin said, "but we all brought weapons, ammunition and a little food."

"God bless you," Travis said. "I'd about given up hope for receiving any help."

Travis invited Martin to his planning room where he produced a bottle of brandy. "How did you make it through their lines?"

"We found a dry creekbed. We had to crawl quite a ways after hearing Mexican guard units on both sides. I suppose there was enough cover from trees and darkness. The worst enemy I saw was a skunk. If that rascal had cut loose in the creekbed, I guarantee you we'd never have made it."

Travis smiled. If Bonham is successful, he thought, we can hold Santa Anna here in San Antonio de Bexar until Houston brings an army to drive him back across the Rio Grande.

Chapter 6

SEVERAL hours before the thirty-two men from Gonzales arrived in the Alamo, Houston had ridden into Washington-on-the-Brazos where delegates were gathering for the convention that would declare independence and create a republic.

On convention eve, the small settlement bustled with people and rumors. Everyone wanted to discuss the news, particularly about the Alamo where many of the delegates had friends or relatives. Since the War Party had swept the election, there was no question about the sentiment for creating a new government. However, delegates were sharply divided over whether to postpone the convention to gather reinforcements for their besieged compatriots in the Alamo.

Houston had thought through the Alamo situation from every conceivable angle. It always came back to Fannin, for Fannin's troops were prepared for combat. If this untrained, undisciplined little group of men tried to slice their way into the Alamo, the result would be disastrous. Yet, the highly-charged emotional atmosphere caused Houston to approach the situation cautiously.

The most practical argument for an immediate declaration of independence and organization of a new government was Austin's report that recognition from the United States was out of the question until a stable government was formed and functioning properly. Most delegates knew the cause of Texan independence was hopeless without eventual support from the United States. But with friends and relatives in peril at the Alamo, some delegates were in no mood to consider such practical matters. Copies of Travis' letter of February 24 were in circulation, addressed not only to the people of Texas, but to "all Americans in the world." About Santa Anna's demand for surrender at discretion, Travis wrote:

> *I have answered the demand with a cannon shot and our flag still waves proudly from the walls. I shall never surrender or retreat. Then, I call on you in the name of liberty, of patriotism and everything dear to the American character, to come to our aid with all dispatch . . . If this*

*call is neglected, I am determined to sustain myself as long as possible
and die like a soldier who never forgets what is due to his own honor
and that of his country. VICTORY OR DEATH.*

Houston reminded himself that these delegates represented the
vanguard of the War Party, which held Travis in the highest esteem
for his daring raid on the Mexican garrison at Anahuac the previous
summer, a raid that had lit the revolutionary fuse. Determining the
situation was indeed tenuous, Houston listened, spoke of contingencies, but avoided direct comments on the Alamo situation.

Houston's only private conversation that night was with Zavala,
who, at forty-six, had a longer record of public service than any other
delegate. After serving in the Mexican Constituent Congress and the
Mexican Senate, he had been elected governor. He then participated
in the uprising that resulted in the election of Vincente Guerrero as
president of Mexico, who named Zavala minister of the treasury.
Later appointed minister to France by Santa Anna, he remained in
Paris until he became convinced Santa Anna was destroying the Federal Constitution of 1824 in order to establish a dictatorship.

Receiving land in Texas, Zavala settled on Buffalo Bayou near the
town of Harrisburg. An intense intellectual with a competitive nature,
Zavala was deeply concerned about the propaganda aspects of the
Texan revolution. As he sat down with Houston in a far corner of a
tavern, he loosened his wide tie and pulled some newspaper clippings
from a pocket of his black frock coat.

"Sam, the thrust of the Mexican propaganda campaign is against
the 'perfidious foreigners, illegal invaders from the United States who
are aiding a few Texas traitors conducting a war without a legitimate
government,' and so on. This can be effective. Though tyrants and
scoundrels, Santa Anna and José Tornel, his secretary of war and
marine, are indeed crafty with this particular rhetoric."

"Then you consider it essential that we form a complete new government here and now?"

"Yes, Sam, otherwise we'll appear before the world as renegades
and pirates. Our provisional state government was ill-conceived, and
burdened by mediocre leadership."

"You know I agree, Lorenzo, but if I read the mood of this convention, it's clamoring for a fight at the Alamo, rather than worrying
about enemy propaganda and the legal ramifications. If Fannin had
reinforced the Alamo, Travis would not be calling for help, but I've
not been able to establish military authority. I can't fault these men
for wanting to reinforce the Alamo, but we must create a functional
government or we'll see our cause perish from confusion and bank-
ruptcy, even if we survive the invasion by Santa Anna."

"The gravest mistakes," Zavala said, "are often made by people
with noble motivations. This is one of those terrible situations in

which the head and heart cannot be together. Though a military dictatorship rules Mexico, that government is recognized as legitimate. We must confront their despotism with a legitimate republic."

"I intend to speak to the point tomorrow at the proper time," Houston said. "I trust you'll be prepared to support my position?"

"Yes."

In cold, crisp weather the following morning, the delegates assembled in Independence Hall — Noah Byar's gunsmith shop, a long one-story, oak structure with high ceilings. Sixty-three delegates had been elected, but as Houston stood inside the doorway, clad in buckskin and boots, he estimated less than fifty had assembled. Among those yet to arrive were Samuel Maverick of San Antonio, one of two representatives of the Alamo garrison, and John J. Linn and Juan Antonio Padilla, both of Victoria, delayed by Urrea's advance.

Houston had hoped that Maverick in particular would arrive to convince the delegates the Alamo defenders wanted the convention to declare independence and create a republic, rather than attempt a meager reinforcement mission. He had faith in the attorney's powers of persuasion, but communications were uncertain and Maverick had reported to the wrong location. His absence, Houston surmised, might make the opening session more difficult.

Though Texas was a sparsely settled frontier territory, the delegation was not without legal and political experience. Several delegates had served in their respective state legislatures and a few, including Houston, had served in Congress. Zavala and Navarro had lifelong experience in public affairs.

George C. Childress called the convention to order. At thirty-two, Childress had earned his reputation as a hard-hitting editor of the Nashville *Banner*, crusading steadfastly for constitutional liberties and, after a visit to Texas, for the Texan cause. Houston and the other convention leaders had agreed Childress was most qualified for the pressing task of drafting a declaration of independence and they favored Richard Ellis for president of the convention.

At forty-five, the studious Ellis, a native of Virginia and friend of Stephen F. Austin, was no stranger to parliamentary procedure, having served in the constitutional conventions of both Alabama and Arkansas. After being elected convention president, he appointed a five-member committee, with Childress as chairman, to draft a declaration of independence. Ellis then opened the floor for discussion.

A grim delegate arose to move that the convention be adjourned, but Ellis had already recognized another delegate with an entirely different matter on his mind. "I contend," he said, "that we ought to put our cards on the table. We have endured religious persecution in our country. The Mexicans have forced us to be Catholic. I say that in declaring our independence, we should ban the Catholic church from Texas forever!"

The hall fell silent. Zavala, Navarro, and Ruiz were embarrassed and, along with several other delegates, somewhat stunned by the injection of this volatile issue. Adjusting his wide black bow tie, Ellis searched quietly in the pockets of his frock coat for a note he had received from Childress, urging that the religious issue not be discussed until the following day when a draft would be submitted.

Sensing an unusual opportunity, Houston asked to be recognized, and rose to speak. "Now, sir," he began, "I submit to you that two wrongs never make a right. If you will review the Declaration of Independence and the Constitution of the United States, you will find that what is truly important is freedom, including the guaranteed freedom to worship the Almighty in any manner one may choose. I do not believe for one minute that the Good Lord cares whether I worship in the Catholic church or Methodist or Baptist or by myself in a wide open prairie. He wants us to worship and to be tolerant of one another. I see no harm in expressing our concern about religious persecution in the bill of particulars, but we would make a mockery of our dedication to liberty if we were to ban any church . . . I know how some of you feel about this, but I believe we must be unstinting in our dedication to freedom or we shall recreate the same path of oppression that we seek to change." Some of the delegates applauded. Others studied Houston carefully, well aware that oratory was one of his most effective weapons and wondering where he was headed.

"Now, gentlemen," he continued, "everyone here ought to be reminded that we are not declaring against what 'the Mexicans' have done. To this day, most of us in this room are Mexican citizens. We are here to declare against the tyranny of a dictator whose despotism ignores the rights, needs, and desires of the people it governs. I venture to say that the highest prices on heads Santa Anna wishes to silence forever are not on the heads of Travis or Bowie, or Austin or Houston, but on the heads of these gentlemen here — Zavala, Navarro, and Ruiz. Gentlemen, they are with us because they are men of high principle, dedicated to liberty! And let us not forget the valor and dedication of Captain Seguin and many others of Spanish name who are in the field, fighting with us for liberty. Gentlemen, we owe these patriots a round of applause!" Led by Houston, a warm round of applause broke out with a few whoops of "Hear, Hear" resounding around the hall. Houston sensed the timing was perfect to pre-empt the Alamo issue.

"Gentlemen, most of you know Colonels Travis and Bowie. I certainly am not commissioned to speak for them, but I have known them as resolute patriots, I have served with them under arms, and if there is one thing I can reaffirm to you today," he said, raising his voice, "they are men of the highest principle, dedicated to liberty even at the sacrifice of their lives!" Shouts and cheers accompanied a loud wave of applause throughout the convention hall.

"I can say to you without equivocation that William Barret Travis and Jim Bowie want a free, independent republic! The Alamo defenders have elected Samuel Maverick to represent them here at this convention. Unfortunately, he has not arrived, but I am sure as the sun will rise tomorrow that he is en route with all dispatch. And I will wager any person here one hundred dollars that he will vote for a declaration of independence and a new constitution!" Another round of warm applause folowed that statement.

"It is, in my judgment, only fair and proper for us to continue this convention in order for the Alamo garrison to be fully represented. Therefore, I will conclude my remarks by moving that the committee, appointed by President Ellis to draft a declaration of independence, proceed immediately, and that we rely on those gentlemen to present us with a comprehensive bill of particulars that we can accept or amend as we so choose." Warm, steady applause engulfed the hall as Houston sat down and Zavala rose to make a seconding speech.

"Mr. President, an eminent Roman statesman once said . . ."

Thomas Jefferson Rusk, a thirty-two-year-old firebrand who anticipated being named secretary of war in the new government, interrupted, saying, "Dr. Zavala, the issue is not dead Roman statesmen, but live enemy soldiers!" Zavala was nettled, but Navarro and Ruiz joined the laughter, welcoming a break in the tension-filled session. Zavala stood his ground, nodding slightly toward Rusk.

As laughter subsided, Zavala spoke again. "A salient point has been raised by General Rusk, dramatizing the desperate military situation in which we find ourselves. However, gentlemen, I believe we must recognize, or admit, that our first serious attempt at self-government was indeed a failure. We constructed that government and its collapse has contributed in no small measure to the terrible situation enveloping our compatriots at the Alamo. Therefore, I submit to you that we have a grave responsibility here, one that we cannot fail to fulfill.

"Colonel Travis writes that the Lord is on our side. I pray that he is, gentlemen, for time is certainly not on our side. If the Alamo falls, the tyrant will soon sweep our settlements, and believe me, I know well the vindictive nature of Santa Anna. Our towns and homes will be burned, our bridges destroyed, and worst of all, our people will be forced to flee from their country.

"Gentlemen, our task is to establish a sound, stable government that the world will soon recognize! No sovereign nation will consider recognizing our government unless it possesses a strong structure and representative features that will earn the respect and support of all our people.

"Let us not haggle over trivial details in the declaration, and I suggest we all agree to work each and every night until the critical task of drafting provisions for the new government is completed. Let us aim our time and energy in that direction and not expend ourselves in non-essential endeavors . . . I wish to second the motion made by General Houston."

The two speeches combined to create a salutory, sobering effect on the delegates. No one spoke against Houston's motion which was adopted without a dissenting vote, though three delegates chose to abstain.

When they adjourned for lunch, Houston walked out with Zavala. The tall military commander and the cultured statesman shared a pensive mood as they strolled across the gentle knoll toward the swirling Brazos River, winding its way through the settlement.

"After I spoke with you last night, Lorenzo, I met with some of my compadres. I told them you're the most qualified man for president of the Republic of Texas, but it's not in the cards."

"I appreciate your confidence in me, though I'd suspected that a Spanish name, with previous ties to Santa Anna, wouldn't suit the first president. I would hope that honor would be yours."

"That's not in the cards either. You know I want to be president, but I have no choice but to pursue this war to the exclusion of politics. If I defeat Santa Anna, the people will elect me their president."

"And well they should."

"It appears then as though the delegates will name David Burnet or Samuel Carson president until hostilities are ended. Regardless of which they name, we want you for vice-president, if you'll serve."

"I'll serve in any capacity I can."

"Agreed, then. Now, if I'm subsequently a candidate for president, I want you to run for vice-president."

"Agreed."

"I must leave in a few days. I trust you to help draft a sound, strong Constitution."

"My name is first among the signers of the Mexican Federal Constitution of 1824, which I believed would provide stability for Mexico and protect its people from the ravages of military dictatorship. I trust that sort of document is what we want for our republic."

"In the mold, yes, along with the U.S. Constitution."

"They are, of course, quite similar. We'll have no major problems drafting such a document, but you know it'll take time."

"Of course, and I can't stay here for the proceedings. As soon as the declaration is adopted and I'm renamed commander-in-chief, I must start gathering troops. If Fannin ever decides to reinforce the Alamo, there may yet be time for me to organize a third force. Frankly, I'm surprised Santa Anna hasn't already attacked."

"It well may be, Sam, that in his zeal to occupy San Antonio de Bexar, he arrived with the vanguard far in advance of his major forces and larger cannons. Heavy rains could've prevented his reinforcements from arriving on schedule."

56

"You've known Santa Anna for years. What are his strengths and weaknesses?"

"In a political sense, his strength is his ability to assess a confused situation and to strike rapidly for whatever he wants to achieve. Some of his military campaigns have been marked by the same rapid, often unexpected, strikes. Thus, his countrymen refer to him as 'The Eagle,' and we must admit he moved at least part of an army into Texas more rapidly than we anticipated. So long as he has the upper hand, he'll dominate any situation, military or political. Though he uses opium to calm his nerves, he's prone to make impulsive decisions if he becomes impatient or intimidated."

"How does he react to pressure?"

"If you can ever surprise him with highly unusual circumstances, he may panic."

"I understand he hates you."

"Yes, I suppose he does. He cannot understand how strongly some of us believe that we must protect our country from dictatorship. I've never wanted to admit that I hated any person, but I must say I dislike Santa Anna intensely. I consider him to be an unbridled charlatan, a military despot whose only guiding principles are those that serve him, not the people of Mexico. But I will say that if Santa Anna did not exist, the military would create one in his mold."

"Well," Houston sighed, tossing a branch on the ground, "he has us in an uphill military campaign to say the least. My best estimate is they now have us outnumbered about seven to one."

"If the Alamo can somehow be held, that should raise morale throughout the colonies."

"If the Alamo is held, Lorenzo, it will be a miracle."

On the following day, Childress presented the convention with a long, powerfully-worded bill of particulars emphasizing the failure of Mexico to uphold its Federal Constitution of 1824. "The Mexican government, by its colonization laws, invited and induced the Anglo American population of Texas to colonize its wilderness under the pledged faith of a written constitution, that they should continue to enjoy that constitutional liberty and republican government to which they have been habituated in the land of their birth, the United States of America."

Well aware of the Protestant fervor among the delegates, Childress pounded the religious issue, but stopped short of calling for a ban on the Catholic church. Childress then castigated Santa Anna "who, having overturned the constitution of his country, now offers as the cruel alternative either to abandon our homes, acquired by so many privations, or submit to the most intolerable of all tyranny, the combined despotism of the sword and the priesthood."

The document bore down on denial of trial by jury, failure to establish a system of public education, the extended imprisonment of

57

Stephen F. Austin for no just cause, "piratical attacks upon our commerce," and various alleged abuses by the military dictatorship.

In closing, the Childress draft stated that "the necessity of self-preservation, therefore, now decrees our eternal political separation.

"We therefore, the delegates with plenary powers, of the people of Texas . . . do hereby resolve and declare that our political connection with the Mexican Nation has forever ended; and that the people of Texas do now constitute a free, sovereign and independent republic . . . and conscious of the rectitude of our intentions, we fearlessly and confidently commit the issue to the decision of the Supreme Arbiter of the destinies of nations."

Delegates arose, cheering and applauding their approval. After Ellis called for order, they unanimously adopted the draft by Childress. No one seemed to care that Houston had pleaded the previous day for the arrival of Maverick, representing the Alamo garrison, to consider the document. Maverick and a few other late-arriving delegates were permitted to sign the document, but they were absent on the historic signing of March 2, 1836.

Houston signed the document on his forty-third birthday, registering his third change of citizenship in seven years, counting American, Cherokee, Mexican and Texan. Among the fifty-nine delegates who ultimately signed the declaration, only two were natives of Texas, Navarro and Ruiz, who were born in San Antonio de Bexar. They varied in age from Dr. Junius Mottley of Goliad, youngest at twenty-four, to Collin McKinney of Red River, a seventy-year-old surveyor. Most of the delegates were landowners who had worked hard to develop their stake in Texas, and so were willing to place their names on the line to protect their interests. Here was the leadership core that supported the campaign against General Cós, that produced Travis and Bowie for the Alamo, and that solicited support from the United States.

Since the delegates were strongly oriented to the American form of government, they emulated it in preparing the Texas Constitution, with one major change — a president was prohibited from succeeding himself after serving a single three-year term, although he could serve again after a three-year absence.

Houston, who had won many a political point in late night discussions over tin cups of whiskey, was not pleased with the impending selection of Burnet for interim president, favoring Carson, who also had served in the U.S. Congress. While Houston and Burnet shared an affinity for Indians, their personality differences were acute, causing Houston to anticipate serious problems down the road.

At forty-seven, Burnet was a stern, straight-laced individual who dressed and conducted himself in an austere manner. A onetime judge, this native of New Jersey found Houston's modus operandi none to his liking. He had complained recently that Houston's schemes were more the product of a jug of whiskey than any sound reasoning. When one of Houston's friends reported that remark, Houston cursed Burnet before terming him "an old hog thief," which was far worse than the cursing.

Though he remained sensitive to criticism, Houston had learned to ignore the ineffectual and to dismiss others with a biting remark. Since Burnet was widely known for his own sensitivity to criticism, Houston hoped that Zavala would serve as a steadying influence. To this end, Houston had reluctantly compromised on Burnet for president with the condition that Zavala would be named vice-president and Rusk, secretary of war. That last position was crucial to Houston who considered Rusk more important to achieving success in the field than the support of Burnet. After all, he concluded, there was little Burnet could do to help the army as the new republic would have precious few funds. The army would remain dependent on whatever provisions it could gather while hoping Austin could secure more tangible support in the United States.

Chapter 7

EVEN before the delegates had assembled, Bonham had arrived at Goliad in a downpour carrying Travis' urgent appeal to Fannin for reinforcements. In Presidio La Bahia, the Texan commander read the request.

"I've already attempted to reinforce the Alamo garrison," Fannin said, pouring coffee for the intense Bonham, who had refused food. "I started a march with three hundred men a few days ago, but a wagon broke down, among other problems."

"My God, sir, couldn't you have continued? The Alamo situation absolutely demands that you bring reinforcements. Travis can't hold out much longer without help."

"It wasn't entirely my decision to turn back," Fannin said. "Recognizing the gravity of the situation at the Alamo, I called a council of war. The officers pointed out again that if we abandon this fortress, or leave it with such a small force that it can't be defended, we are exposing the entire coastal area to Mexican assault. With those logistical problems I mentioned, it all added up to what I believe to be a wise decision — occupy Fort Defiance with a force that can sustain this position."

"But sir, you are, by this failure to act, placing certain doom on the Alamo garrison. There may yet be time to consolidate your force with ours, and we could hold the Alamo until Houston gathers a large army."

"I've never trusted Houston," Fannin said. "He walked out as governor of Tennessee to become a Cherokee, and then, with our country under threat of invasion, he walks off to the Cherokees again. We're fighting Mexicans, not Cherokees."

"Sir, the Cherokee treaty was essential to protect the northern settlements while we conduct war in the south. Whatever the reasons for his recent activities, he'll probably be named commander-in-chief of the army after independence is declared. But we simply don't have time to concern ourselves with Houston. Your forces and ours are all that matter."

"Bonham, you're a bright young man, but you must understand the strategic situation. General Urrea is maneuvering in this area with a large force. If my men were caught in open combat between here and San Antonio, we would be wiped out or forced to surrender. It's too late to consolidate our forces. I suggest that you remain here. I could use a man of your ability and your chances of survival would be much greater."

"Is your decision final, Colonel Fannin?"

"Yes, Bonham, it is."

"Then I'll report the result of my mission to Travis or die in the attempt."

"You, sir, are a fool."

Instead of returning directly to San Antonio de Bexar, Bonham swung north to Gonzales, seeking reinforcements. Finding the settlement almost deserted of men, he was preparing to depart when he met a former courier for Travis, who told him the enemy siege lines had been tightened. The courier said he had attempted to return to the Alamo two days previously, but Mexican cavalry, riding the outer perimeter of the siege lines, had chased him for miles. He urged Bonham to remain in Gonzales, but the boyhood friend of Travis bade him farewell and rode on.

On the morning of March 3, Bonham reined up just beyond the perimeter of the eastern siege lines. At first, he thought he might have to wait until nightfall, but soon the Mexican cavalry changed guard, momentarily leaving an open path. Since the cavalrymen carried only sabers and pistols with short range, he dashed through the gap within fifty yards of the startled cavalrymen, arriving at the Alamo unscathed.

Entering Travis' planning room, Bonham flung his hat onto a table. "I bring bad news, Buck. Fannin started over here with three hundred men, had some equipment problems, called a council of war, and turned back. Now, he knows General Urrea is moving toward Goliad with a large force so he's keeping all his forces there."

Travis frowned, slowly pacing the floor. "So be it," he sighed, "but don't spread this around the garrison. It would be terrible for morale. Perhaps we'll hear from Houston."

"Doubtful. He's gone to Washington-on-the-Brazos. Besides, Fannin doesn't think Houston has any troops under arms."

"Then all we can do is hang on and hope," Travis said. "I'll send another report to the convention."

On the night of March 3, Travis wrote a long, detailed report of the siege, reaffirming his determination to fight to the death, if necessary. For the first time, the resolute young commander felt truly helpless. He knew time was running out rapidly, yet he must hide his own concern from those lonely men who had manned the walls throughout the siege.

As he awaited the courier, Travis' thoughts turned to loved ones. After writing a warm letter to his fiancée, Rebecca Cummings, he penned a note to his friend, David Ayers, who had custody of his son, Charles, at Montville, a tiny community near Washington-on-the-Brazos:

Take care of my little boy. If the country should be saved, I may make him a splendid fortune; but if the country should be lost, and I should perish, he will have nothing but the proud recollection that he is the son of a man who died for his country.

Men gathered around the courier with their own letters, for while no one mentioned such things, most felt this might be their last opportunity to communicate with the outside world. Amid cheers, the courier slipped away into the night.

On the afternoon of March 4, Santa Anna called a meeting of his general staff. He rarely called such meetings, but he believed the time for battle was drawing near, and he wanted to weld support of his staff to that idea and discuss details. He decided on an open discussion in which he would lead them along his line of thinking. As they gathered in his planning room, Santa Anna ordered Juan to post on a wall the large drawing of the Alamo compound. He handed a pointer to his brother-in-law.

"Since General Cós occupied this compound recently," Santa Anna said, "I have asked him to describe it for us in such a manner as to be instructive for our forthcoming attack."

Cós felt the strong cross pressures. He knew Santa Anna was frustrated by the siege and ready for battle. Yet General Castrillón had made a convincing argument to him privately that the only sensible course was to await the arrival of heavy artillery.

Cós painfully recalled the confrontation with Santa Anna after his forced march to join the Army of Operations. "You miserable wretch," Santa Anna had said, "I ordered you to arrest the traitors Zavala and Travis. I ordered you to take Bexar and hold it. You may yet redeem yourself and the honor of this family when we return to Bexar. Do not fail!"

"But Antonio," he had protested, "I signed a capitulation agreement not to take up arms again in Texas."

"Return to Texas with me now as a general, or I will have you stripped of rank and you can march in disgrace as a foot soldier to the City of Mexico."

Cós tapped the pointer on the drawing. "The enclosed compound exceeds five acres, with about half in the plaza between the west wall and the barracks, hospital and chapel. This plaza is indefensible, once we penetrate the walls. The rebels are using the areas inside the east walls as cattle corrals. These areas are likewise indefensible, once our men are inside the compound. The barracks northwest of the chapel, however, are two-story and of thick stone construction. It will be most difficult to drive the enemy from this area where they will probably retreat for a last stand."

"What of their artillery?" asked Castrillón.

"In a moment, please, General. Let me point out the enemy has had ample time to fortify all exterior walls from the inside with vast amounts of dirt. I fear those walls will be most difficult to breach, except the north wall, which has been slightly shattered by our artillery. I estimate they have seventeen or eighteen artillery pieces that are operational — an enormous amount of firepower. If we assault the enemy before reducing the walls, I fear we will suffer tremendously high casualties from the artillery."

"You speak as though that old mission is impregnable," Almonte said.

"Certainly not, but there will be a high price to pay to conquer those walls, unless we delay the assault until our twelve-pounders arrive. We could then blast holes through the protective barriers all around the compound."

"And when might those cannons arrive?" asked General Ramirez y Sesma, the cavalry commander.

"In perhaps three or four days," Almonte said. "The weather has delayed them."

"But this appears to be the weakest point in their entire fortification," said Colonel Duque, pointing to the area between the one-story barracks on the south wall and the chapel. "There is no high wall in that area. Why could we not concentrate our forces there and quickly break into the compound?"

"I will answer that question," Santa Anna snapped. "You should recall the skirmish of February 25, Colonel, when we tried to concentrate a strong force in that area. They are not fools. They have artillery trained to protect that apparent weakness and their men with the long rifles are stationed there. We will, indeed, pay a price for taking this fort, but it will be worth every drop of blood to demonstrate the determination of the Supreme Government to destroy this rebellion. Now, gentlemen, it's obvious to me there is a difference of opinion about when to assault the Alamo. Speak up!"

Castrillón argued for delaying the assault until after the arrival of the larger artillery pieces, contending available artillery was incapable of breaching the walls. Knowing Santa Anna couldn't now direct his wrath on him, Cós, along with two colonels, agreed with Castrillón.

Santa Anna, Almonte, and Ramirez y Sesma, however, argued for an immediate assault. Three other officers offered no opinion, leaving the question open. Frustrated, Santa Anna asked if there were other matters to be considered.

Almonte caught His Excellency off guard by reopening a divisive issue. "I have heard repeatedly concern expressed about the policy of no quarter for prisoners. I must say that I disagree with that policy on moral and philosophical grounds, besides its being against the teachings of the church."

"My dear Colonel," said Ramirez y Sesma, "the fact of the matter is that precedent exists for such a policy and the Supreme Government, not only through His Excellency, but through General Tornel, has enunciated this policy for the appropriate reasons."

Castrillón, a veteran of many military campaigns, gave Ramirez y Sesma a harsh glance as he rose to speak. "Gentlemen, I have carefully read General Tornel's statement, and I find nothing in it that would extend a blanket policy of no quarter. The true fact of the matter, General Ramirez y Sesma, is that the order spells out that those to be treated as pirates are those who are invading this territory to assist the rebels under arms. There is nothing in the order that applies to Mexican citizens of this territory who have taken up arms."

"Are we to concern ourselves," asked Ramirez y Sesma, "whether a rebel is a pirate from the United States of the North or a rebel who has lived in Gonzales? I submit that both have defied the Supreme Government and should be put to the sword."

"I disagree," said General Arago, chief of staff. "There are several Tejanos in the Alamo garrison — they are certainly citizens of this province. Travis and Bowie are also citizens, and I am told the Gonzales reinforcements are citizens of that community. If you follow General Tornel's order, any of those men could be spared, if captured. If you follow the laws of God and humanity, no prisoner should be executed."

Shaken by the unexpectedly strong challenge, Santa Anna hurriedly intervened. "This meeting was called to discuss an assault plan, not to argue religion and philosophy. May I remind you, gentlemen, that my battlefield experience extends beyond that of any of you. Each situation is unique, and in this war, it is expedient, perhaps critical, to impress upon the enemy that we will not tolerate their defiance, or this uprising will assume proportions far beyond what you might imagine. The policy of no quarter for insurgents was effective in spreading fear when I came to this territory twenty-three years ago. Although I have pursued a policy of mercy toward non-combatants, those who take up arms will not be guaranteed the same. I believe it appropriate now to take a vote on this matter."

Santa Anna had his clear majority, but Arago and Castrillón, plus the independent-thinking Almonte, all voted loudly in opposition. "When the blood red flag was first raised on the church," Arago said, "I believed it was a ploy to frighten the enemy. If this is to be absolute policy, then I must resign as chief of staff. I will not be a party to wanton butchery."

64

Confronted by such substantial opposition, Santa Anna thought rapidly. "General Arago, you have a long, distinguished record of service. The Army of Operations is indebted to you for your splendid service during this campaign. It disturbs me greatly to be branded a butcher, and I assure you that I pursue only those policies I believe to be consistent with the goals and objectives of the Supreme Government."

Sensing that emotions had calmed a bit, Santa Anna developed the threads for a clever ruse. "Since this question has, indeed, caused deep concern, I will propose a new plan. I shall offer generous terms of surrender to the Alamo garrison, and grant a forty-eight hour cease fire for the rebels to consider these terms, guaranteeing their lives be spared. In your concern about this matter, Almonte, will you deliver the new terms?"

As Almonte nodded approval, Santa Anna faced Arago. "General, in light of such a generous offer, will you not agree to remain in service with the Army of Operations?" Arago nodded slowly, not thinking through the contingencies within the broad strokes of Santa Anna's sudden policy change.

Upon adjourning the meeting, Santa Anna invited them to return at eight o'clock for dinner. While Santa Anna called Ramirez y Sesma aside, Juan spoke to Almonte. "I cannot understand," Juan said, "why you feel so strongly about this matter of not taking prisoners."

"Have you ever seen a man die?"

"No, sir."

"Seeing men die is one thing. Seeing them die in cold blood is quite another."

"Joaquin," Santa Anna whispered to Ramirez y Sesma, "you must carry out a special mission for me tonight and you must not discuss it with anyone. Agreed?" The cavalry commander nodded.

"Shortly after Almonte returns from delivering my terms, I want you to send a few of your best horsemen close by the Alamo to draw enemy fire, but instruct them not to return the fire. Make certain it is done within minutes after Almonte delivers my surrender terms. That is all."

Santa Anna drew up a long proposal for the Alamo defenders, including what he had outlined in the meeting, plus an offer to remove the non-combatants, without fear of reprisal, to the settlement at any time during the forty-eight hour cease fire. If the Texans chose not to surrender, they could make their sentiments known by firing weapons or by simply allowing the forty-eight hours to expire.

Shortly after Almonte delivered the terms under a truce flag, he rejoined Santa Anna in the planning room. Soon, they heard a few scattered rifle shots from the Alamo. "Their insolence is constant," Santa Anna said. "I believed those terms, that guaranteed their lives, might have been appealing."

"Can we be certain that rifle fire was a formal reply? Previously, they fired their eighteen-pound artillery piece."

"Of course that was their reply. All our units have been instructed to maintain a peaceful posture while you delivered terms and until such time as the enemy replied."

"Very well," Almonte said. "Shall I instruct our artillery batteries to resume firing?"

"No. I believe it wise to permit all our units to rest until I order the assault."

That evening, Santa Anna was a charming host, engaging his fellow officers in lively conversation. Prior to the first toast, he announced casually that generous new terms had been delivered to the Alamo, but they had been summarily refused. "Colonel Almonte will verify this, if there are any questions," he said. When no one spoke, Santa Anna motioned to his waiters to begin serving the meal. "Now, let us enjoy a fine meal with, of all things, Spanish wine by way of New Orleans. The Spaniards will not trade with Mexico, and the New Orleans volunteers are fighting us here in Texas." The officers laughed and Santa Anna instructed his waiters to keep the wine flowing so long as a glass could hold it.

As the dinner party broke up, Santa Anna detained General Amador. "I am told, General Amador, that you have traveled extensively by ship and you know the ways of the weather."

"I have observed weather closely. Mariners determine many interesting things from their studies of the sun, moon and stars."

"Then, could you tell me how long the moon will remain in the sky tonight?"

"Yes, there was a full moon only a few nights ago. The moon will remain in the sky until well past dawn."

"And tomorrow night?"

"About the same, I would say."

"Do you expect bad weather tomorrow or the next day?"

"I would expect the weather to remain clear for at least a day or two, but Your Excellency knows this country is subject to sudden northers, wet or dry, and also to rain from the Gulf of Mexico."

"At this time of year, a norther would be more likely."

"True, but it will not be long before rain will come frequently, particularly in the country east of here."

"Thank you, General, and have a good night's rest."

When Travis received the new surrender terms, he had taken the envelope to his planning room to read the contents carefully. He heard a few rifle shots from the north wall, but paid little attention to the short volleys that had been commonplace during the siege. Surprised by the new terms, but determined as ever not to surrender, Travis' first impulse was to send an immediate reply by firing the eighteen-pounder at Santa Anna's headquarters. But think of your men, he told himself. "I have the power to make this decision," Travis murmured to himself, "but the responsibility is too grave."

Rejecting an immediate reply, he next thought to call the entire garrison together, explain the terms, and take a vote. But recalling the bitter experience of the earlier vote that had given him and Bowie their joint command, he rejected that idea, and considered calling a council of war. He remembered, however, that Fannin's council of war had determined to abandon their march to reinforce the Alamo. I must counsel only with those in whose judgment I place the highest trust, he thought. He invited only three, Bonham, Bowie and Crockett. Bonham was Travis' faithful friend, but also a calm, clear thinker under pressure; Bowie was knowledgeable and Travis needed his help to solidify support; Crockett also had his following, as well as being the oldest and perhaps wisest among the Alamo leadership.

Travis had never met Crockett before the flamboyant Tennesseean rode into San Antonio de Bexar two weeks before the arrival of Santa Anna. He had thought Crockett to be a mediocre politician and frontier raconteur, but soon had been impressed upon hearing Crockett address a crowd: "Fellow citizens, I am among you. I have come to your country, though not, I hope, through any selfish motive whatever. I shall identify myself with your interests, and all the honor that I desire is that of defending, as a high private, in common with my fellow citizens, the liberties of our common country."

And high private he had been. Bowie and Travis tried to bestow the title of colonel on him, but he refused, saying he had an agreement to "coordinate the military activities of the Tennessee volunteers, not command anyone." But Travis, who had come to admire Crockett, often addressed him as "colonel." Crockett had spun many a fine yarn about his adventures, and he issued challenges for long, loud fiddling matches, but he also had worked hard, fought hard, and contributed sound advice for difficult decisions made during the siege.

Since Bowie was bedridden, they met in his room. After explaining the provisions of Santa Anna's new offer, Travis paused without comment. Finally, Crockett spoke. "Then, gentlemen, we have three choices — surrender, attempt an escape, or fight to the death. Take the first, surrender. If this is a bona fide offer, these are generous terms. But can we trust Santa Anna? And while my boys are mighty disappointed that we have so few combatants in this place, I believe they would rather fight than crawl out on their bellies."

"I recall," said Bowie, "Navarro talking about the inhumane treatment Santa Anna sanctioned when he was a young officer here years ago. From what I've heard about his campaign in Zacatecas last year, he hasn't changed. I suspect this is nothing more than sweet-smelling bait to get us to surrender, then be executed."

"Even if it's not a trick," Bonham said, "and we surrendered, we would be treated like dogs. We would be forced to leave Texas at any rate; the only real choices, in my opinion, are to fight or try to escape."

"You fellows leave me out of the escape argument," Bowie said with a weak smile.

"There is no real argument there," Crockett said. "A few might escape at night, but a mass attempt, night or day, would surely be spotted and we would be cut down in the open. I'd rather fight in the open, but with the odds we face, it's out of the question."

After a long pause, Travis broke the silence. "Gentlemen, the decision appears to be evident."

"Travis," Crockett said, "I believe you ought to offer the men the opportunity to attempt escape before the cease fire ends."

"Fair enough," Travis said. "If no reinforcements arrive tomorrow, I will call a meeting of the entire garrison tomorrow night and explain the situation."

"In that case," Bowie said, "I believe the four of us had better do some talking with our compadres. I'll sound out Esparza and Fuentes among the Tejanos, plus Jameson and a few other Anglos. I suggest we be selective in discussing this situation; otherwise, we could have a spooked up herd on our hands."

"Agreed," said Crockett, "but Jim, you really don't have any business staying here in your condition. Why not leave tomorrow with the other non-combatants so you can receive some better medical treatment?"

"I joined in your decision to fight. So long as I can squeeze a trigger, I am a combatant."

Crockett had brought along a jug of whiskey. When Travis and Bonham departed, he was saddened to notice that Bowie could no longer lift the jug. Crockett poured whiskey into a tin cup and Bowie drank it slowly, breathing hard.

As Travis and Bonham walked through the barren plaza, they were approached by Antonio Fuentes of Bexar, a friend of Bowie's. "Three of us have a plan to ambush Santa Anna," Fuentes said. "We are sick of his blasphemy and threats."

"And what is the plan?" asked Travis.

"It's simple, but it might work. We wait until about two o'clock in the morning, when there are fewer guards and most of those are sleepy. We swim the river from right over there to near Soledad Street where we can move in the shadows from house to house until we reach his headquarters. If one of us, only one, can find him, you know what happens."

"I cannot order or sanction such a mission," Travis said. "Their siege lines are drawn so tightly, I doubt you could get through."

"I know every foot of that area, Colonel Travis. I know that by swimming the river quietly, our chances are good of slipping into the settlement unseen."

68

"For Heaven's sake, Fuentes, don't you realize Santa Anna's headquarters must be heavily guarded?" Travis asked.

"But think of the result, if we are successful."

Travis frowned. "I can't dismiss the idea, but I know these tactics are more in the nature of what Bowie would entertain. I will strike a bargain with you, Fuentes. If your friend Bowie agrees the plan may work, I have no objection, but you must wait until tomorrow night."

"Agreed," Fuentes smiled.

He found Bowie propped up in his bed, sipping whiskey from a tin cup, and gazing out a window across the open prairie bathed in moonlight. "That's a Comanche moon, Fuentes," he said. "It's perfect for their kind of night attack. They catch you asleep and drop you with their arrows while you can't even see them. That moon will be too bright all night to try an ambush. You wouldn't get twenty yards outside the walls before being detected. No cover."

Fuentes was crestfallen, but accepted the invitation to join Bowie and Crockett for their second round from the jug. When they discussed the cease fire and surrender terms, Fuentes laughed. "The last man on earth I would trust is Santa Anna," he said.

After breakfast on March 5, Santa Anna had Juan summon a doctor from the nearby hospital. "Doctor, I would appreciate your opinion," Santa Anna said. "At what time of night, or early morning, would you say a person is sleeping most soundly?"

"That depends on when he retires."

"Well, suppose he retired at ten or eleven at night?"

"In that case, at about three or four in the morning he probably would be most deeply in slumber."

"Thank you very much, doctor."

Santa Anna then summoned Almonte, Caro and Juan into his planning room. Pacing the floor, he spoke rapidly, rarely completing a sentence, until Almonte interrupted, suggesting that he take a break since Caro could not record the flow of broken sentences. Santa Anna retired briefly to his bedroom where he took five grains of opium. "I have never seen him so nervous," Almonte whispered to Juan. "He must have completed the battle plan."

When Santa Anna returned, he began pouring out details for storming the Alamo. "The time for battle has arrived; we will attack before dawn tomorrow. Since the enemy cannot possibly defend a five-acre compound with only two hundred combatants, we will assault from all directions. We should concentrate on the north wall, but without letting the enemy train all their fire at any one area.

"I want all men in the assault forces in bed by sundown, and awakened at midnight. Assemble them at one o'clock in the morning, but the cavalry need not saddle up until three o'clock. The cavalry under General Ramirez y Sesma will prevent enemy escape and assure that our infantrymen attack with the utmost valor. The four attack columns will be led by General Cós, myself as a reserve commander for that column: Colonel Duque, with General Castrillón in reserve; Colonel Romero with Colonel Salas as back-up; and Colonel Morales with Colonel Minon in reserve."

Reviewing various reports, he ordered allocations per column, including troops, scaling ladders, crowbars and axes, plus the order that no soldier carry a blanket or overcoat since this might impede his movements. The allocation of cartridges was skimpy as well since each soldier would have a bayonet, the only weapon Santa Anna considered critical for storming the Alamo.

"The order to attack," he said, walking to the window where he could view the Alamo, "will be sounded by buglers upon my signal at four o'clock in the morning. Now, Caro, put all this in writing for General Amador to distribute. Notify him that he is to join me and Colonel Amat with the reserves at the north command post no later than three o'clock in the morning. Then, notify all field commanders to assemble here at two o'clock this afternoon for their briefing session."

When the officers gathered in the planning room, Caro and Juan gave each several sheets of paper, a goose quill and inkwell. The familiar drawing of the Alamo compound was posted on the wall. Santa Anna stood before the drawing with a pointer held casually in both hands at his beltline. "Gentlemen, we have laid siege on the old mission for twelve days. Our men have performed well, but I fear their morale will falter if we temporize any longer. Furthermore, we must be aware of the danger of unnecessary delays in this area. Spring rains will soon sweep the land, creating enormous logistical problems, particularly in the eastern areas where we may expect the enemy to make a stand. Therefore, I have determined the time for battle has arrived."

Savoring the tension he felt building in the room, Santa Anna moved a few paces to his right so all the officers could view the drawing of the Alamo compound. Tapping his pointer on the outlines of the outer walls, he explained his plan. "You have all complained about the enemy's superior artillery and resourceful use of grapeshot. You have seen their long rifles cut down our men, who were helpless to return their fire from such distant range. Therefore, gentlemen, my plan is to virtually neutralize those enemy advantages with the element of surprise, and our superior troop strength."

Castrillón was on the edge of his chair after that last statement. "How, may I inquire of Your Excellency, can we storm a fortification, with look-outs on the walls, not to mention pickets outside, and hope for any element of surprise?"

"We will attack at four o'clock in the morning," Santa Anna said, pointing to the open areas beyond the perimeter of the outer walls. "At that time, there will be adequate moonlight for our men to cross the ditches and place scaling ladders on the walls. The enemy garrison should be fast asleep, assuming we surprise their pickets outside the walls. But even if alerted, the rebels will be half asleep and unaccustomed to sighting their weapons in moonlight."

A murmur swept the room. The officers were intrigued by this unique plan presented by Santa Anna, who was enjoying himself immensely.

"The most important items in this assault," he continued, "will be scaling ladders and bayonets. Once our men are over those walls, the bayonets carried by our superior forces will rapidly achieve a complete victory! I assume this plan meets with the approval of you gentlemen, including those who have advocated delaying the assault until our larger artillery arrives. Are there questions?"

"Yes," said Castrillón, "this plan precludes use of our artillery, relying entirely on the element of surprise and the ability to scale the walls. With only that one breach in the north wall, I question whether we can easily enter the compound."

"Of course, it may not be easy," Santa Anna said. "Success will depend on strict silence until our troops are within musketshot range of the walls. When they reach that position, my signal will be given and our men will storm the fortress. This is a far superior plan to any that would have the enemy await us in broad daylight. Are there other questions?"

When no one spoke, Santa Anna motioned to General Amador. "Splendid, now you will receive your orders." As Amador distributed the orders, Santa Anna continued, "As you can see by these orders, our assault should succeed using less than two thousand men. However, I will use the reserves, if necessary. Tell your men in forthright terms that this is a battle to defend the Supreme Government and our national honor against traitors and foreigners who would steal this land from our beloved Mexico. Stress that their individual courage will be awarded by the Legion of Honor, with a medal and a grant of land in this province. Tell them they must fight to avenge their fallen comrades, who died here last December and during this siege. Read them the names of the men lost from their units. Bear in mind, gentlemen, that revenge is a powerful emotion! When they cross those walls, they must be prepared to fight to the death — and well they should since they will each have a bayonet and the enemy will have few, if any."

Santa Anna scanned the faces in the room for signs of doubt or protest. Only Castrillón appeared uneasy, but the veteran commander raised no further questions. "I suggest," Santa Anna said, returning to the center of the room, "that you retire to your respective positions. Remember, deliver a strong speech to your units before sundown. Those soldiers who wish to pray at San Fernando Church should do so before your speech, but they must all be bedded down at sunset. God and liberty, gentlemen!''

As the officers departed, Juan asked Almonte if he might be excused to visit his friend Captain Alvarez, whose unit had been assigned to an attack column. "Your confinement is not ended until tomorrow," Almonte said. "However, you have performed your duties well. Permission granted if you will not visit the cantina."

"Agreed, and thank you, Colonel." Juan had grown to admire Almonte's calm, steady demeanor, exemplified in Almonte's forthright stand against Santa Anna's policy of no quarter. Behind that stoic facade of efficiency and detachment, Juan surmised, is a man of sensitivity and strong moral conviction. Already revolted at Santa Anna's bogus marriage, Juan reconsidered the opposition to the no quarter policy and took another stern look at the hero of the ruling class of Mexico.

Juan was delighted to leave the general staff atmosphere and seek out his friend from Saltillo. They ate an early supper at Carlos' campsite where the men were busy securing scaling ladders and other equipment for the assault.

"I have questioned some actions of His Excellency during the siege," Juan said, "but his battle plan is brilliant. Do you agree?''

"No. I know he wants to make it difficult for the enemy to fire on us. But we should attack at dusk or daylight when it is as difficult to sight weapons and our men would be rested. Under his plan, they will be weary, bedded down too early, and awakened, if they are asleep, before they have had adequate rest."

"But Carlos, it will give us the element of surprise. The rebels will be fast asleep when we attack, so they will be less effective fighters, besides the problems with sighting their weapons before daylight."

"Have you read each and every word of those orders?''
"Yes, I have."

"Well, young friend Juan, it is going to be cold tonight and my men are forbidden to carry blankets or overcoats. They must lie on the cold ground for at least an hour. That is heartless, but Santa Anna has never cared about the welfare of his men on the line. He only cares about the generals and colonels who have helped him to power.''

"Being bitter will not help you fight a battle."

"I will say one more thing about this so-called battle plan. Those enemy riflemen will drop us all if we march toward the walls in columns. If we attacked rapidly in one large unit at the north wall, where the breach exists, we would win the battle in a matter of minutes. But our attack columns will give the rebels easy targets. It is a stupid battle plan, Juan, stupid. Let us not discuss it further. Are you going to see Bozita tonight?''

"No, I am forbidden until tomorrow, after the battle. You did speak to her for me?''

72

"Yes."

"And did she appear the least bit interested in me?"

"I believe she is more interested than she will admit, but she is a difficult person to understand. She reminds me of Estella, before we were married. She was a clerk in her father's store in Saltillo. From the moment I saw her, I wanted her as my wife, but she paid no attention to me, always managing to busy herself elsewhere. Finally, about the tenth time I had visited the store, I strode up beside her and asked, 'Will you be my wife?' She just stared at me, so I said, 'Think about it, and I will return to talk about it.' I waited four days, returned and we talked about it. The following month we were married."

Juan smiled. "But I still do not understand why Bozita shows so little emotion at all."

"I suspect there is a sensitive girl behind all that disdain. She is not ashamed of being *mestizo*, but something else leads her to the guise of a cold, hard person."

"If things go well tomorrow, I intend to see her, and perhaps solve this mystery. Then, we can celebrate together."

"Perhaps. For now, may I make a request of you?"

"Of course."

"If I am killed tomorrow, will you see that my wife receives proceeds from the sale of land I would be awarded for this campaign?"

"Yes, but I expect to be with you at the cantina tomorrow night. The Lord be with you through the battle."

At sundown, Carlos strolled up Potrero Street, across the Plaza de las Islas Canarias, to the San Fernando Church. Lighting a candle, he knelt to pray for a fight with valor and without the loss of many lives. As he walked toward his campsite, he decided to stop at the cantina. The romance between Juan and Bozita had taken him back twenty years to the delirious days of his own courtship. The memory brought a welcome respite from his anxiety over the upcoming battle.

Only a handful of officers were in the cantina. When Bozita came to his table, he knew he must hurry, and he tried to think what might make his point most effectively. "I spoke with Juan this afternoon and he asked about you."

She shrugged, asking for his order.

"I am going into battle in the morning, perhaps to die. May I make a simple request of you that you can fulfill in one minute?"

"I suppose so. Your order will not take but a minute since it is so quiet tonight."

"No, this is not an order. Just a request for you to think about something. Will you do that?"

"All right."

"For just a moment, Bozita, pretend that you are not here, but some place that you really enjoy, your favorite place. Now, tell me the truth, would you be happier if Juan Calderón were at your side?"

As he had caught Estella off guard twenty years ago with his sudden marriage proposal, he found Bozita taken aback for the first time. She hesitated and smiled faintly. Finally, she laughed and said, "For an old farmer from Saltillo, you are clever and fast with the words."

"I must leave now, Bozita. May I make another request?"

"All right."

"Do not be harsh with him. He cares more about you than he understands or rather more than you have allowed him to understand."

"Carlos, I could care for him, but you know it will not work."

"I know of no such thing. He is a strong-willed young man, who will not turn back once he knows where he is going."

"I have felt a little lonely since he has been confined. How would I feel if I became his woman, and then he left me here when he returned to his home?"

"I must leave. Promise me you will not treat him harshly."

"I promise, and I will pray for your safety."

Carlos returned to his campsite, but like hundreds of his comrades, he could not sleep at that early hour. Gazing at the stars, he recalled his childhood, courtship and marriage. How he loved Saltillo and the rugged country surrounding that beautiful old town. Then he thought of Estella and their five children, on weekend trips to Monterrey, that exciting city where he took his produce to sell. How deeply he loved his family and how much he missed Estella now, so steadfast and efficient during the day, yet so tender and lovely at night. Santa Anna's order came less than five hours before time to depart, leaving him only a few moments to dash home and bid farewell to his family and Estella, holding back tears for the benefit of the children. It was all so vivid now, as though it happened yesterday, or perhaps it was the longing in his heart that made that picture so dominate his mind.

74

Chapter 8

DURING the late afternoon of March 5, Travis toured the Alamo compound with Green Jameson, engineer in charge of directing fortification of the old mission. Jameson pointed out the heavy earthen embankments reinforcing the high walls to withstand cannonballs and give riflemen easily accessible walkways into the compound. The parapets and platforms were constructed to reduce danger for the men firing over the walls. But Jameson's most imaginative work lay at the roofless chapel where he had built wood structures to support artillery batteries above the abandoned place of worship. With Captain Dickinson, Jameson had devised support structures for mounting the eighteen operational cannons, to be calibrated for maximum effectiveness. Throughout the compound, Jameson's work was obviously outstanding.

"It's only on the north wall that we're vulnerable," Jameson said. "The enemy batteries fired yesterday from such close range that the wall couldn't help but be breached. It's miraculous that we have no greater damage."

"I'm more than satisfied, Jameson. Without you, we wouldn't have a fortress."

As they strolled near the breached north wall, they heard shouts and cheers from a Mexican camp somewhere along Potrero Street, echoed a few minutes later from behind the north Mexican battery and then from another camp to the south near Alameda Street. I wonder, Travis thought, if that *cabron* will break the cease fire? But none of the camps assembled for battle. "They must have passed around some mescal," Jameson said. Travis smiled, keeping a wary eye on the Mexican batteries, which remained silent.

Travis had called a meeting of the entire garrison for shortly past sundown. Most of the non-combatants had departed for the settlement, except Captain Dickinson's young wife, Sue, who chose to remain with their child, Gregorio Esparza's wife and children, and many of the sick, including Bowie. As the non-combatants streamed from the Alamo into the settlement, Santa Anna had each questioned

75

as to Travis' plans, but none could say other than there was to be a meeting after sundown.

By torchlight, the Alamo garrison gathered in the plaza of the compound. As Travis walked slowly from his planning room, he was still uncertain what to say, other than to present the facts and make a strong appeal for all to remain and fight. He considered the many dispatches he had sent pleading for help, and decided to incorporate the thrust of them into a speech, to be made more direct and personal. Plead the case, counselor, he told himself. Plead the case for all to remain and fight to the death.

He saw Esparza and Fuentes walking past the chapel. I must not forget the Tejanos, he thought. I'll ask Fuentes to translate. Indeed, the handful of Tejanos needed some encouragement. Though despair knew no name in the Alamo, these men had endured some slurs from a few late-arriving Anglos who had cursed all "Mexkins." These Tejanos had joined the Anglo insurgents at the prompting of the popular firebrand, Juan Seguin, and J. Antonio Navarro, their patrician father figure. They had taken up arms for the Federalist form of government within the Republic of Mexico. In a few short months, that cause had melded into the movement for independence, which meant the Anglos would rule the land. They knew the Mexican Army considered them the worst traitors of all. They had betrayed their native people, joining the hated "Norteamericanos, who sought to steal this country from Mexico, the rightful owner."

With Seguin and Navarro absent, the Tejanos related only to Bowie, who had been a loyal friend and benefactor, but he was on his death bed, barely able to speak. As the garrison assembled, they gathered near Bowie, who had been carried to the plaza on his cot.

When Travis appeared before the men, he realized he uncharacteristically had forgotten his hat. With his tousled, reddish-brown hair blowing gently in the crisp evening breeze, he stepped forward to speak. "Men, I called you together because I feel compelled to inform you that our situation is grave, indeed. No help will be forthcoming from Colonel Fannin, and I have received no word from General Houston, who apparently has no troops under his command at this time.

"Santa Anna has offered new surrender terms, which I consider to be nothing more than a rotten trick. If the tyrant truly desired our honorable surrender, that blood-red flag would not remain hanging from the church! Santa Anna has committed blasphemy by raising that massacre symbol on a sacred place of worship . . . and if we should surrender, we would be put to the sword by that ruthless dictator! I shall never surrender or retreat!" A wave of cheers followed that pledge.

Travis had been pacing before the men, speaking in sharp tones. He paused, lowering his voice. "Men, the Lord is on the side of the brave who will stand and fight against tyranny. We bear witness to the miracle of sustaining cannonade and bombardment for twelve days without the loss of a single man. The Lord is on our side! And may God grant that all Texans will stand firm, as you have stood throughout this siege. Your high-souled courage will infuse the fire to liberate our country from the bondage of military despotism. You have served in the brave manner that characterizes the patriot, who is willing to die in defense of his country's liberty and his own honor. You have served in a manner that will endear you to your country-men forever. I feel a strong sense of pride, having the privilege of serving as your commandant. Some of you are much older than I, some much younger — in fact, too young to be here fighting. You have come from all over the United States and even from Europe. And from our beloved Texas! Let me say that the thirty-two volunteers from Gonzales displayed extraordinary courage when you refused to turn back after our grave situation was apparent to you. From a dark night of despair, you emerged to rekindle our spirits, renewing faith in our noble cause and our determination to defend the Alamo!" A wave of cheers followed that tribute to the Gonzales volunteers.

"From San Antonio de Bexar, these brave Tejanos have friends and loved ones within sight across the river, safe in the settlement, yet you remain here, in the Alamo, fighting for liberty!" Another round of cheers filled the night air.

Travis, an accomplished trial lawyer, sensed he was winning the case. He would put spurs to the mount. "Yes, we are fighting for liberty, and we must keep the faith! I know Houston, Thomas Jefferson Rusk and Sam Maverick! I know Zavala, Navarro and Ruiz, the elder!" Pointing his finger at the garrison, Travis shouted, "There is no doubt in my mind that our compatriots have declared independence! We are free men!" Cheers and whoops resounded throughout the plaza as many of the men waved their rifles in the air. "Therefore, let us not fight under false banners. I say we should lower the 1824 tricolor tonight, and burn it!"

Santa Anna was stationed at his command post north of the Alamo, slightly beyond range of Texan weapons. Hearing the shouting, he stormed out of his tent with a field glass to observe the ghostly sight of a long, thin shadow dancing on the walls of the barracks, dimly-lighted by an orange glow from the torches. "You do not believe those fools would attempt an attack?" he asked Almonte.

"With their meager force, it is out of the question."

"Then why are they shouting and cheering? Could they have received reinforcements?"

"That also is out of the question. We control all possible points of entry for a force of any size."

His curiosity piqued, Santa Anna watched the Alamo as Travis' figure continued to cast its shadow on the barrack walls.

"We are free men, and we are all Texans, united by our unstinting devotion to liberty and the destiny of our country. And men, we are the first line of defense! If we do not fight to the last breath, the colonies will be ravaged and our country lost forever. The eyes of our countrymen are upon us! We must hold our ground!" By this time, most of the men were shouting approval at the end of every sentence, but a few were beginning to hang on each word carefully, sensing this was no ordinary harangue from their not-so-popular commander.

"It is said that an army travels on its stomach. You have suffered through these long, lonely days of siege without coffee, sugar or salt . . . but you are the salt of the earth! You have endured each privation and withstood every disappointment in order to fulfill your duty time and time again. I am confident that this determined valor and desperate courage, heretofore displayed by you, will not fail you in the final struggle! And although you may be sacrificed to the vengeance of a blood-thirsty tyrant, the victory will cost him so dearly, that it will be far worse for him than a defeat. Now, I call on you, in the name of liberty, of patriotism, and everything dear to the Texan character, to prepare yourselves to die like soldiers, who never forget what is due their own honor and that of their country. Victory or death!"

Travis had been pacing briskly before the men, shouting every word. As the cheering subsided, he paused to face them and spoke in a lower tone. "Men, the end of the siege is near. I have made my decision, but I cannot order you to lay down your lives. Those who do wish to escape should leave now, under cover of darkness," he said, slowly unsheathing his sword. Drawing a deep breath, he traced a long line in the dust with his sword, then raised his head and shouted: "Those who will fight to the death, step across this line and join me!"

Some of the men were stunned. Until now, they had refused to admit to themselves the hopelessness of their situation. They were weary, crestfallen men, far from home with little to gain in this unlikely confrontation. And now, this intense young commander, with whom their friend Bowie had clashed so often in the past, was asking them to step across a line into certain death.

While they hesitated, Bowie motioned two of his men, an Anglo friend and a Tejano comrade, to carry him across the line on his cot. As Bowie had chosen to live, so did he choose to die. As they carried Bowie across the line, Fuentes gave a hurried translation. *"Si no quiere combate, vaya en la noche, ahora! Si quiere combate, sin rendirse, muchachos, vamos con Colonel Travis!"* All the Tejanos crossed the line, and all of the men formerly under Bowie's command moved en masse to join Travis, except Moses Rose. Within seconds after Bowie's gesture, Crockett ambled across the line, his Tennessee volunteers not far behind.

Most of the men under Travis' original command promptly followed with Bonham leading the way, but a few wavered. Travis had hit them too hard and fast, giving them such a narrow choice. Finally, they came to a man, leaving only Rose on the other side of the line.

Louis "Moses" Rose, a native of France, had served in Napoleon's army before coming to Texas in 1826, to settle in the Nacogdoches area where he had worked as a day laborer in sawmills and as a teamster. At fifty-one, he recalled decades of military service and hard work with little to savor for his sacrifice and toil. Although respected as a dedicated soldier, he was not prepared to lay down his life, thus he refused the challenge from Travis.

In the early evening on the plaza of the Alamo, Rose remained a silent, solitary figure, bathed in the glancing shadows of the torchlight. When loud hissing and grumbling rose, Travis raised a hand. "It's his decision. Leave him be." Rose assembled his few belongings, climbed over the east wall behind the chapel, and disappeared into the night.

In the wake of Travis' fiery speech, a strong sense of camaraderie engulfed the garrison. For the first time since he had become their commander, Travis felt he was their spiritual as well as military leader, a necessary distinction since he considered morale equally important to ordnance and provisions. For the final defense of the Alamo, he had instilled a visceral fighting spirit that would prove to be his signal contribution. "Get some rest, men," he said in a relaxed voice. "All officers report to my planning room."

Since Bowie had been returned to his room with a coughing spasm, Travis invited Esparza and Fuentes, though they were not officers. Proud of the newly-molded solidarity, including the Tejano commitment, he wanted to maintain it, and recognized Bowie's support had been vital.

Emotionally exhausted by his demanding speech, Travis opened the planning session with important announcements though his voice sounded almost bored. "Since Colonel Bowie is incapacitated and David Crockett doesn't accept the rank we have offered him, I'm hereby designating Captain Baugh to assume command, should I be killed or incapacitated. In the event the enemy penetrates the plaza, making our fort indefensible, I believe that Major Evans, master of ordnance, should set fire to the powder depot. Any objections?"

"A question," said Captain Dickinson. "When you say 'penetrate,' how many do you mean? If the enemy can't put four hundred soldiers within these walls, we can hold the fort."

"The problem," Travis said, "is that Major Evans can't stop the battle to count enemy soldiers. I believe the proper order is for him to determine if he believes the fort is being overrun, and if so, set fire to the powder depot. Agreed?" No one objected. "Now, should Captain Dickinson be killed or incapacitated, because our artillery batteries are so diversely located, the command should fall into zones. I leave the designation of zones to Captain Dickinson, consulting with Blair, Carey, Esparza, and Bonham."

Crockett, though still a "high private," always attended sessions with the officers since he was in charge of the Tennesseeans. The veteran frontiersman had been impressed by Travis' emotional speech, thinking the youthful commander had hit the motivating points with masterful timing. He was further impressed with the key details Travis projected into the plan of battle.

"Now," Travis said, "we must utilize every pinch of powder and each piece of metal. Santa Anna is a disciple of Napoleon, therefore he'll attack with columns, probably from all directions. However, their muskets aren't accurate over seventy-five or eighty yards, while most of our riflemen have more than one hundred yards in range. So first drop the ladder bearers when they get into range — that's essential. If their attack columns are too large for riflemen alone to repulse, you artillery commanders use common sense. Calibrate your pieces for extremely close range, using only grapeshot and canisters. You can't miss; it's just a question of how many you drop per shot. Remember, first priority is to drop the ladder bearers."

Travis glanced at Crockett, whose compadres were proud of their marksmanship. "All riflemen should be instructed to aim for the chest or stomach. None of this fancy firing for the head. A wounded enemy soldier, out of action, is as good as dead, so make sure each rifle shot counts from those walls. If they pour inside our walls, Lord help us. All we can do is fall back into the various barracks and the chapel. Trying to fight in the plaza would be suicide. Any questions?"

"That sounds just fine," Crockett said. "I would like to suggest that riflemen aim for officers as their second priority. They wear epaulets on their shoulders. You all know that, but when combat starts, it's hard to remember too much and if you've got just one or two things in mind as far as sighting that rifle and firing, it's a hell of a lot easier. And the more officers we drop, the more confusion we create for the enemy. Now, the big man himself, Santa Anna, wears fancy stuff like the other generals, but you can recognize him by the high plumed hat he wears. If that shows up in rifle range, make sure you drop him. That could change the whole picture."

"Colonel Crockett, I appreciate your comments," Travis said. "And since Colonel Crockett has injected such cogent, forthright comments into our final battle planning, I feel compelled to designate him third in command of the garrison, behind Captain Baugh. Is there objection, other than from Colonel Crockett?" The officers laughed while Crockett smiled.

After the meeting was adjourned, Baugh asked Travis if the pickets should be ordered back to their positions and if a cannon shot should be fired to signify the Texans would not surrender. "Negative on both, Baugh. We'll let the cease fire run out naturally, so everyone can get some rest. The pickets can sleep in the compound tonight. Let's have just you, myself and a couple of other officers alternate a watch through the night. That should be sufficient."

As he walked outside his planning room into the plaza, Travis noticed the moon was rising. He asked Esparza and Fuentes to make certain each Tejano understood the details of the battle plan. Both had been impressed by Travis' speech though their command of English was insufficient to comprehend all that he said. As Travis departed, handshakes were warm. *"Sin rendirse, muchachos,"* Travis said.

"Don't worry," Fuentes replied, "none of us will surrender."

After receiving Dr. Pollard's report, Travis counted on having about one hundred and eighty-five combatants for the battle, if no more men were lost to sickness. At best, he thought, shaking his head, we will be outnumbered by ten to one. At worst, fifteen to one.

After strolling around the moonlit plaza, Travis decided to pay Bowie a visit. When he arrived in his room, Bowie was wrapped in a blanket, apparently asleep. Travis started to leave as Bowie raised himself slightly, his gaunt face barely visible in the sparse light from a single candle at his bedside. "Sorry, Travis, I had to pour down almost half a jug to warm up after a run of chills. Your speech was so damned long, I almost froze out there."

"Perhaps it could've been shorter, but I wanted them to understand the scope of the situation."

"Forget it. Pour us a drink," Bowie said, pointing to a bottle of cognac. "I liked the way you worked in the declaration of independence and burning the flag of 1824. You know why? Because that bastard Santa Anna will lose a fancy trophy."

Travis laughed, relaxing for the first time that day. The cognac was tasty, and Bowie, incredibly, was regaining the strength to continue the conversation. "Travis, that was a wise stroke, bringing in the declaration of independence. That raised the men's spirits more than I anticipated. I wonder how the convention is going? You and I worked and fought to kindle that fire of independence and here we sit, miles away, with no knowledge of what they're doing."

"I imagine Houston and Zavala are dominating the proceedings," Travis said, "with Houston working harder behind the scenes than anyone. He's a political jackrabbit at conventions. I only wish he had recruited some men for us, rather than spend that valuable time with the Cherokees. I remember Austin being upset about Houston's conduct a few times last fall during the siege on Cós."

"You and Austin never have understood Sam. He's slow to react to the military situation in Texas, since his best fighting experience was with well-organized units under General Jackson. Our army has been impossible to manage, lacking training and a unified political authority behind it."

"Perhaps so, but there seemed to be less grumbling when Austin was in command."

"We all love Stephen Austin, but he had no business being commander-in-chief last year. Stephen is a cultured gentleman, and a statesman, but certainly no military man. Burleson, Fannin and I were moving around the Bexar area with uncoordinated units, and there was no strategic planning that Stephen could convince us would work. Remember some of the orders he issued? They were so vague, they were useless. Whereas Houston, with enough time and with competent organizers like Burleson, Rusk and Seguin, might've developed an army adequate to contest Santa Anna. He at least would've prevented such foolishness as that attempt to invade Matamoros."

"I noticed you didn't mention the name 'Travis' among the competent military organizers."

"All right, Travis, I'll say it. For what you've had to work with, you've done a hell of a fine job. This is a well-organized garrison, cocked and primed for combat."

"I appreciate that, Jim, and I appreciate the support you gave me tonight. But I can't agree with you on Houston as commander-in-chief. As a politician, I have a high regard for him, but he certainly has let us down here. He doesn't think it wise to fight from fortifications, but with enemy troops far outnumbering ours, where are we supposed to fight? I'd rather see Houston as president of the republic than commander-in-chief of the army."

"I'd rather see him as both," Bowie said, "except that would be falling into the trap the Mexicans are in. Nevertheless, in my opinion, Houston is our most effective politician and our strongest military leader. And remember, Sam didn't want us to fight here. He believed we should consolidate our forces in the interior of the country, on friendlier ground."

"And I remember," Travis countered, "it was you who agreed with Colonel Neill not to abandon the Alamo, believing so strongly in the strategic importance of this area."

"Of course. I've disagreed with Sam from time to time, but what I'm trying to drive home to you is that he has more valuable command experience and strategic planning ability than any of us. And since we're confronted by a vastly superior invading force, I favor his being commander-in-chief rather than being president of the republic. I only hope they provide a strong government in support; this governor-council was a disaster."

"On that we agree," Travis said. "I could see early on that the system was breaking down. I trust our delegates will devise a system similar to the United States government — at least that seemed to be the prevailing sentiment. Yet another reason to prefer Houston as president is his closeness to President Jackson who could help us gain recognition and support from the United States."

82

"I can't argue with that, but there isn't going to be a republic unless the war is won. At any rate, who would you have for military leader? Not Fannin."

"Certainly not! I blame Fannin much more than Houston for our miserable situation here. His vacillation is inexcusable. I believe he wanted all along to stay at Goliad, hoping to defeat General Urrea and thus gain some credit. Had he come here, others would receive the credit, if credit were due."

"Travis, that's a hell of a thing to say about a man. He may have had problems other than those Bonham reported."

"If so, he should've notified me in writing. I consider his inaction reprehensible, bordering on treason!"

"Calm down, Travis. Losing your temper won't solve anything. Pour us another drink."

In his most candid moments, Travis had admitted to himself the only realistic hope for the Alamo garrison lay in the hands of Fannin, not Houston. But Houston's disdain for defending fortifications had annoyed Travis, who believed the Texans must be prepared to fight from defensive positions. His conviction had not changed, and his bitterness toward Fannin was intense, since Fannin had refused to comply with what seemed to Travis an obvious strategy.

"In any case, who's your choice for commander-in-chief?" Bowie asked again.

"Edward Burleson. He's experienced and dependable."

"No question about that, but Ed isn't the type leader to defeat Santa Anna against these odds. Ed is a hunter, not a trapper, and Sam can be both. A skillful trapper knows he must be patient, clever, cunning, and maybe just plain lucky, or he'll never see anything but the tracks of his prey. To me, that's Sam Houston."

"You speak as though we've been defeated already. Jim, I'm still holding out some hope that if we repulse their initial assaults, inflicting heavy casualties, they'll grow disorganized and quit."

"You have to hold out hope, but Santa Anna won't leave Bexar without our blood on his hands. He has too damned many troops to be denied a victory. Make him pay dearly for the victory, but don't deceive yourself about blunting their assault."

"I know it seems hopeless, but you should've seen the enthusiasm at our planning session. Besides, Santa Anna might wander into range. If we could drop him, their army would retreat in confusion."

"Not much hope there. Since he became a general, and especially dictator, they say he stays well out of range until the contested area is secured. Then he comes riding in to make his royal appearance."

"If you were in his place, Jim, how would you hit us? And when?"

"I'd concentrate all my forces to hit the north wall, at the breach point. That would render ineffective most of the Alamo artillery batteries in other areas. Initial casualties might be heavy, but once inside that wall, the battle would be all over in a matter of minutes. When? I'd strike at night under that Comanche moon."

"You don't think he would hit us at night?"

"Well, I wouldn't trust his cease fire to the end of the deadline, but I doubt he would strike at night. I suspect he might hit us shortly after dawn, or sometime during the day tomorrow. But I wouldn't trust that cease fire deadline, if I were you."

"We'll be prepared. I'm permitting all but myself and a few other officers to sleep all night, so the men will be well rested tomorrow. They were weary tonight."

"I know, and I can't blame them. I recall Crockett saying once, 'We may as well march out and die in the open. I don't like being penned up.' A lot of those men feel the same way. And remember when I wanted to lead an ambush attempt on Santa Anna south of here? Did you think I was drunk?"

"Well, you had annoyed me by releasing those prisoners from jail when you were drunk, so I was in no mood to listen. I'm familiar with some of the river crossings to the south and I couldn't believe both major routes could be covered without leaving the Alamo undermanned."

"Travis, get down off your high horse. We're only talking, not defending ourselves in court. The Alamo is undermanned now, anyway. My thought then was to stop the big, long rattlesnake winding his way into our country by hitting him one swift lick in the head before he could coil and strike. I've dreamed of killing that bastard Santa Anna in his fancy plumed hat. Along the Nueces where the trees and vines are thick, it would be easy. One might even live to tell about it.

"You see, Travis, I never had the hope you did that Fannin would reinforce this garrison. I came to know Fannin well during our siege on Cós. I don't question his integrity, as you have, but I know his weaknesses. That West Point training makes him sound like a competent commander, but he can't make up his mind. When I learned the size of the force Santa Anna had assembled south of the Rio Grande, I knew the only realistic way to stop him was by ambush. Only this cursed disease kept me from heading south with Fuentes and a few others."

"Dreaming and talking about that," Travis said, "will only make you bitter."

"About all I can do is dream," Bowie said. "That one about Santa Anna recurs each night. I've never lost my love for this land and I know Santa Anna will try to drive every last Anglo settler from Texas."

"Do you think this war could've been avoided?"

"Not after Santa Anna came to power. I'm not saying Austin was wrong in trying to negotiate. He had to try and separate statehood might have prevented war. But Santa Anna was determined to make himself dictator, which meant reducing the states to provinces. That, he has now accomplished, except for Texas."

"I suppose Veramendi would've been on our side?"

"Sure, he was a strong Federalist and a follower of Zavala. Lord, how I miss him and my Ursula. You know, Travis, the happiest days of my life — the only truly happy days of my life — were spent with her. I settled down to a style of life I'd never known. Instead of roaming the coast night and day, trading in slaves, or risking my neck with my brother Rezin searching for lost mines, I learned the life of the landed gentry from Veramendi. Life was gentle, pleasant. We had long, leisurely meals, listened to music from Spanish harps and zithers. Ursula was the most beautiful woman I ever saw. All the land, slaves and money in the world could never replace her."

At one time, Bowie was thought to be the wealthiest Anglo in Texas. But he had been known to trade hard and fast, and the loss of his family possibly had taken the keen edge from this once astute entrepreneur. It was speculated that Bowie had suffered large financial setbacks.

Intrigued by the stories, Travis decided to venture onward. "You mentioned Rezin. Did you two find that silver mine in the San Saba Canyon?"

Bowie laughed. "I believe the Comanches had concealed the shaft. They fought like wounded *javelinas* when we drew near where the map showed the mine to be. Hell no, we never found the mine! But we've enjoyed all the speculation."

Travis laughed and poured another round of cognac. After a moment, Bowie continued. "Now that you've pumped me dry, Travis, I want to ask you a question. How did you gain custody of your son?"

"Custody of Charles was simply the one condition of my divorce on which I wouldn't budge an inch. If we ever fight our way out of here, I'll marry Rebecca Cummings of Mill Creek, near San Felipe. She's made my life complete, and I know she'll make a wonderful mother for my little Charles."

"You're fortunate, Travis, to have a child. I regret losing mine, even more now that things are drawing to a close."

"For Heaven's sake, Jim, don't be depressed. We may make it."

"You may, if a military miracle occurs, but I can't. My chest feels as though someone has a rope around it, and now and then pulls it tighter and tighter. I can't take much more."

"Have another glass of cognac. That will help."

The severe pains in Bowie's chest would not abate, but the cognac made them bearable. "Fuentes tells me you can speak some Spanish, Travis. That was news to me. You should've used some in your speech tonight."

"I'm not that good, and I didn't want to stumble as I spoke."

"Stumble? You sounded like a preacher who knows his gospel. I thought you were going to fire the eighteen-pounder and lead a charge into Bexar with the Lord at your side."

Travis laughed. "I bet you never knew I was a Methodist lay preacher in Alabama and couldn't find a single, solitary Bible in San Felipe."

"Now, don't give me all that preacher talk, Travis. I know too many of your friends who say you're faster with the women and a deck of cards than any other young blade in the colonies."

"Well, a man has to have diversions, but Rebecca's the only one now. As for gambling, I never was much at anything except monte, which is more luck than skill."

"You've had your share of luck, Travis. I thought you were through after that Anahuac raid last year, but you were dealt right back in."

"Did I catch hell for that! Some said I should issue a public apology, but I wasn't about to apologize for something for which I was proud."

"Where did you learn Spanish?"

"When I was secretary of the *ayuntamiento* at San Felipe, I had to learn some Spanish, though I told our delegates to castigate the Mexican government for requiring us to transact our affairs in Spanish. I thought that was wrong, but I did enjoy learning it."

"I hope you've developed more respect for our citizens of Spanish name. You had a reputation here as being a lackey for Governor Smith, the champion of white man over all."

"I still respect Henry Smith, but he tried to convince me this was a race war, Anglo vs. Mexican, and that certainly isn't true. With Austin gone, I think Zavala is our most eloquent spokesman, and a man of unquestioned integrity."

"Here in San Antonio, everyone, Anglos, Mexicans, Spaniards, *mestizos*, Indians, whatever, were dedicated to enjoying life together. That spirit can prevail throughout Texas if the leadership works together to make it happen."

"You must be in a better mood, Jim. I wish I could agree, but I believe the war will divide the people, unless Santa Anna is stopped here. The Anglo animosity toward people of Spanish name will spread by leaps and bounds. I know, because San Felipe was becoming that way when I departed."

"Perhaps you're right. Sometimes war punishes those who least deserve it."

Travis was tired, and one more drink would make him too sleepy to make the rounds again. He arose from his chair, placing his glass next to the bottle of cognac. Bowie leaned forward. "I have only one pistol and a couple of big blades. I'd be much obliged if you'd loan me your pistol. I expect some unfriendly visitors."

86

Travis laid his pistol on the table next to Bowie's bed where the two knives and the other pistol were neatly arranged. "Good night, Jim."

"Give 'em hell, Buck."

From the top of the Alamo chapel, Travis scanned the settlement and prairies in all directions. There was no sign of activity, not even the customary fires at the enemy guard posts. In the cold night air, standing alone above the abandoned place of worship, the weary young commander prayed one last time. Satisfied that a pre-dawn attack was highly unlikely, he relaxed, waiting to be relieved by Captain Baugh.

Baugh joined him and reported three more officers had volunteered to maintain a watch; Travis could sleep the night. Bone-weary, he curled up on his cot, fully clothed, without removing his high boots. He soon fell asleep, his long sword and double-barreled shotgun resting against his bed. That indomitable spirit had never allowed him to accept the finality of an impending defeat, but time had run out on William Barret Travis.

Chapter 9

WHILE Travis slept, Santa Anna paced his tent in a waspish mood. No one had given a plausible explanation for the shouting and cheering from the Alamo that had pierced the night air a few hours before. If the rebels had decided to fight, why didn't they fire their big cannon? Why all those torches? Could that young fool Travis be planning some surprise maneuver? "Calderón, bring General Cós! Hurry!"

Cós, like most of those Mexicans designated for the assault, could not sleep early in the evening. The gnawing anticipation of combat had deprived him of sleep for three fitful hours, and he had just dozed off when Juan awakened him. He hurriedly donned his coat and pulled on his boots, cursing his distinguished brother-in-law. "We have been through this plan time and again! What now?"

"I am not certain," Juan said. "All I know is His Excellency has been in a scalding frame of mind ever since the rally in the old mission."

"Has there been any enemy activity observed since then?"

"None."

"Then what can I say or do?"

When he appeared before Santa Anna and Almonte, the bleary-eyed Cós requested a drink of mescal, but His Excellency would order only coffee. "Now, Martín," Santa Anna said, "I want you to recount exactly what led to the arrest order for young Travis. And tell me about his military activity here during the rebel siege against your army."

"Very well, Antonio," Cós sighed, having reported all this in detail before. "I issued an order last year for his arrest after he led an illegal operation against our garrison at Anahuac. Travis had taken command of a small group of firebrands, who found a boat and cannon, whereupon they surprised Captain Tenorio, our commander, by landing their little mob without warning.

"Captain Tenorio wisely avoided bloodshed by capitulating to this mob, knowing that Travis' occupation of the settlement would not be approved by the Anglo colonists. Eventually, most of Travis' countrymen denounced his attack as devious and illegal."

"Devious and illegal," Santa Anna snapped, "but daring and successful. Proceed."

"During the enemy siege of Bexar, Travis was a minor officer, a captain, but a favorite of Colonel Austin who commanded the rebels during part of the siege. Austin sent him to intercept a large *caballada*, about three hundred horses, that I had dispatched to Laredo. With a superior force, Travis overran our contingent somewhere between the Frio and Nueces. My men were forced to capitulate."

"When did Travis attack?"

"At night, taking our small camp by surprise."

Surprise attacks, Santa Anna thought as he paced the earthen floor of his tent, are the mark of this unlikely adversary. Holding a candle near a drawing of the Alamo compound, he studied it carefully, before facing Cós. "If you were Travis, what would you do?"

The coffee had helped Cós bring his mind into sharper focus. He asked for another cup, sensing the onset of one of Santa Anna's piercing probes that would require his utmost attention. Judging Santa Anna's mood, Almonte wondered if he might alter the attack plan at this late hour. "You reported, Antonio," Cós said, "that the rebels had refused to surrender. This narrows their choices to fighting or attempting an escape."

"Yes, of course, Martín, but what would you do if you were the rebel commander?"

"That's a difficult question. If I chose to fight, I would remain in the compound. They lack the troops to fight outside the walls."

An obvious answer, Santa Anna thought, and worthless. "Almonte?"

"The rebels might attempt an escape during the night, believing darkness would hamper our pursuit. However, it is more likely they are determined to defend the old mission."

Having implemented his own ruse, Santa Anna now suspected Travis of some trickery. Almonte's suggestion of a possible escape attempt appeared most logical. If Travis was leaving the cease fire in effect to lead a surprise escape attempt in the pre-dawn hours, he will be in for a rude surprise himself, Santa Anna surmised, visualizing the assault lines soon to be assembled in all directions. But no matter, either the rebels will become easy victims while they attempt an escape before I order the assault, or they will die in the compound.

Convinced he was prepared for any contingency, Santa Anna dismissed the officers. He fell asleep on his field cot after instructing Almonte to awaken him no later than three o'clock. Dame Fortune had dealt an ironic hand, indeed. Both sides reached critical command decisions on March 5, yet neither guessed the nature or timing of his adversary's choice. A strange hand was about to be played out, matching the ingenuity of two highly contrasting individuals. But although Santa Anna and Travis contrasted in many ways, there were striking similarities. Both were hyperactive, and their boundless energy had carried them into more endeavors, including gambling and affairs with numerous women, than most of their contemporaries could match. They were fastidious in dress and grooming, and meticulous in preparing for battle. Both commanders were astute in using psychology to motivate their men. But the overriding factor in the visceral emotional pitch that gripped Mexicans and Texans was that both felt deeply this area was part of their homeland.

Among settlements in Texas, only San Antonio de Bexar appealed to Santa Anna and his men. The Spanish-Mexican heritage and population gave it an appearance and flavor similar to cities in the interior of Mexico. The rebels in the old mission were trying to steal their land and those traitors must be put to the sword.

Bowie and his Tejano friends were citizens of San Antonio, and the nucleus of the Alamo garrison came from the original Texan force that had taken the city from General Cós. They had paid a price, including the loss of their popular leader, Ben Milam, and they had no intention of surrendering this soil. The volunteers from Gonzales had often traded in San Antonio, and had friends and relatives there. They had responded to Travis' plea with the fervent desire to stop Santa Anna before he reached their nearby settlement.

The confrontation had become a clash of cultures, of political ideology, and finally, of nations. Travis had convinced the Alamo defenders they were fighting for their liberty as citizens of the Republic of Texas, not Mexico. This was their land. They must defend it to the last breath.

When he had dozed off to sleep, Santa Anna was convinced he held an unbeatable pat hand. Upon awakening, he found that Dame Fortune had silently removed one of his cards. At three o'clock on the morning of March 6, 1836, the moon was on the meridian of San Antonio de Bexar, and its altitude was nearly fifty degrees; the phase of the moon was eighty-eight percent of full. Despite all his fastidious planning, Santa Anna had failed to check the illumination of the moon in the pre-dawn hours of the preceding day.

Under a bright sky, Santa Anna cursed before ordering Juan to fetch General Amador. "Amador, you blithering fool! You did not tell me the moon would be so bright at this hour. We cannot achieve the element of surprise! Our men will be easy prey for their artillery, and I believe the enemy can sight their rifles."

"Your Excellency did not ask if the moon might be too bright, only if it would be in the sky through dawn."

"Very well. The assault order is not due for an hour. How bright will the moon be then?"

"It will be diminished somewhat. How much I cannot say."

Almonte, who had not shared Santa Anna's concern over a possible surprise move by Travis, became deeply concerned over the new development. Assault troops were being deployed to lie on cold ground until an attack order was given. The longer they lie on that cold ground, without blankets, he thought, the less effective they will be in battle. "Shall I rescind the deployment order?"

"No," snapped Santa Anna, "that would be bad for morale. Perhaps we can yet meet the schedule. I will wait until that cursed moon grows dim, or until some clouds come by to obscure it."

How ironic, Almonte thought, recalling Santa Anna's confidence that moonlight would minimize enemy advantages while providing enough light to scale the walls. Almonte desperately wanted the attack to begin on schedule, but when four o'clock arrived, the moon still shone brightly in a clear sky.

If Travis had stationed pickets outside the fort, they surely would have detected the Mexican soldiers. But the officers on watch, convinced the cease fire would not be broken at such an unlikely hour, did not scan the prairies around the fort. Those prairies were alive with hundreds of soldiers, crawling silently to temporary positions in arroyos and ditches, some within two hundred yards of the Alamo.

When four-thirty passed with no signal, Carlos cursed under his breath. His men were shivering on the cold ground, losing that physical and emotional edge of a few hours previous, when they had cheered their beloved leader whose name became "Santana" when shouted rapidly. At five o'clock, Almonte pleaded with Santa Anna to give the assault order. "Field commanders report their men in a restive, precarious condition," he said, "some in a state of frenzy, others fatigued and all cold, having lain on the ground for hours. It's an hour past time to attack. I implore you to give the order!"

"I will not be hasty," Santa Anna said, pacing the ground outside his tent where the band and buglers had been assembled. Peering again at the Alamo compound through his field glass, he watched Baugh stroll by the chapel. "The rebels may have been waiting for us ever since Travis had them shouting. Perhaps a spy told them we were assembling troops. You complain about our men waiting on the cold ground for an hour or so. The rebels have been waiting all night. Let them wait longer and become exhausted. It must grow darker before I expose our men to the open areas."

Minutes ticked by like hours for the Mexican soldiers, weary of gazing at the foreboding walls that lay ahead. Carlos and some other unit commanders were furious, but helpless. Why, Carlos thought, in the name of all saints, doesn't he give the assault order or permit us to withdraw? But some of the Mexican soldiers had indeed been worked into a frenzy by the rousing speeches and were over-primed to end this embarrassing siege that had taken its toll among their ranks. From the ditches west of the Alamo, came cries of *"¡Viva Santana! ¡Viva Mexico!"*

Captain Baugh, walking leisurely near the north wall, heard the shouting. As he started up a ladder, a sharp bugle call pierced the cold air. Santa Anna had finally given the assault order at five-thirty when, hearing the war cries, he had lost all hope to achieve the element of surprise. Baugh saw hundreds of Mexican soldiers clamoring about to form columns. He scrambled down the ladder, shouting, "Travis! The Mexicans are going to attack!"

Santa Anna's long delay proved costly for his men. Instead of catching the Texans deep in slumber, most of the Alamo defenders were already awakening when they heard the bugle call and Baugh's shouting in the plaza.

Travis dashed across the plaza to an artillery battery on the north wall. Watching the enemy lines form, he scanned the Alamo compound where riflemen scrambled to their positions on the walls, and artillerymen arranged powder and grapeshot.

At last, the long wait had ended. For a few more seconds, the prairies remained silent while men on both sides prepared for battle. In this electrifying atmosphere, Santa Anna broke the silence by ordering buglers to play the harrowing "Degüello," an ancient Moorish bugle call of no quarter. As Mexican assault forces began moving toward the walls, Travis paced back and forth, shouting to the riflemen. "Hold your fire! Ladder bearers first! Hold your fire!"

When advancing columns crossed that imaginary line into their range, the Texan riflemen commenced firing. Reverberating across the prairies, the artillery barrage from the Alamo shook the earth, as though it were engulfed by constant rolling thunder.

Corina leaped out of bed to watch from her balcony, saying one last prayer that Bowie might be spared. Bozita awoke seconds before her two young brothers, frightened and trembling, climbed into bed with her. She held them tightly, saying it would soon be over.

Travis placed his shotgun near the gun carriage and unsheathed his sword, using it as a pointer to direct artillerymen and riflemen's fire at the Mexican soldiers carrying the scaling ladders.

At first, the Mexican assault forces moved forward courageously, sustaining heavy losses as they tried desperately to reach the walls. Withering volleys of searing grapeshot slashed their ranks coupled with deadly fire from Crockett's men, most of whom had at least three loaded weapons beside them. Their rapid fire from the southeast area was devastating. Aiming for the chest or stomach at one hundred yards produced sure hits for these sharpshooters who could knock off a squirrel's head easily at that distance.

Scaling ladders lay useless on the ground. Texan fire had cut down all the original ladder bearers, plus those brave men who had replaced their fallen comrades. Some key Mexican officers, including

Colonel Duque, lay dead or mortally wounded. General Castrillón, replacing Duque, soon surmised the assault was in jeopardy of failing.

With men falling on either side of him, Carlos shouted for his unit to hit the ground. The Toluca Battalion lay pinned down alongside his position blasted with grapeshot and a hail of rifle fire from the smoke-shrouded walls. Carlos cursed the meager range of their obsolete British muskets. Their bayonets were also worthless in the open where they were such easy targets for the rebels firing from the walls.

Santa Anna turned to the buglers and band, ordering Degüello sounded repeatedly, and instructing the band to play marching songs. But those in the initial assault heard nothing but the deafening roar of artillery, the piercing cracks of rifle fire and the desperate screams of their fallen comrades, torn and mangled by scorching metal.

As he saw Mexican forces falling back on all sides, Travis was exultant. Cupping hands to his cheeks, he shouted to his cheering men on the north wall, "We gave 'em hell, men! Stay alert! They'll be back!" A few Texans had fallen during the first assault, but most had avoided enemy fire largely by keeping the Mexican soldiers at bay, beyond effective range of their muskets.

Santa Anna was frustrated, but undaunted. "Regroup!" he shouted to Castrillón. "I will order another assault!" Mexican forces moved again toward the dreaded walls, Degüello resounding across the prairies. Desperately, they fought closer to the compound. A few ladders were placed on walls, but each time a soldier ascended, he was blasted from the ladder by a Texan firing a pistol at point-blank range.

Several unit commanders, including Carlos, instructed their men to crawl until they were in range to fire their muskets at the Texan riflemen, who presented themselves as targets only at the instant they aimed and fired. Several riflemen fell on each wall, rendering those positions indefensible. There were no replacements. Though their ranks were thinned, the Alamo defenders continued to benefit enormously from their artillery, which time and again swept handfuls of attackers to the ground with searing blasts of grapeshot.

Santa Anna studied the pulsating battle through his field glass. Many of his units were firing from open ground with the swirling smoke and dust their only protection. Too many units were failing to charge the walls. They're cautious, when they must be bold, he concluded. "Why, Almonte, are they not charging?"

"The enemy fire is too intense from all directions. Perhaps we should concentrate forces at one point."

When the assault forces again fell back, Santa Anna became furious. He dispatched Juan to fetch Generals Amador and Ramirez y Sesma, and Almonte to bring Generals Cós and Castrillón. After they had rapidly assembled, Santa Anna spoke in sharp tones. "This battle will become a dishonorable catastrophe to haunt us forever unless we take the fort! The third assault must be decisive! Martín, you and Castrillón combine your forces to attack the north wall at the breach point. Amador will join you with the reserves. Joaquin, use your cavalrymen to prevent any of our soldiers from turning back. Use whatever means are necessary! Almonte will instruct the other commanders to deploy their forces also at the north wall. That is all, gentlemen. I will soon give the order!"

Juan was bewildered. At four o'clock he had expected a lightning strike followed by a quick victory. Instead, he had seen the normally stoic Almonte grow increasingly frustrated over Santa Anna's long delay of the attack order. Then, bitterly disappointed, he had watched his countrymen fall, killed or wounded by the intense enemy fire. Incredibly, the Alamo defenders had repulsed two fierce, well-coordinated assaults. They had forced Santa Anna to play all his cards by ordering the reserves into the third assault.

Reloading his shotgun, Travis experienced a glimmer of hope. Only a handful of Texans had fallen on the north wall where Bowie had said the compound was most vulnerable. If they could withstand still another assault, the Mexican soldiers surely would become demoralized. He scanned the garrison, finding most areas thinned by casualties. After blunting the first assault, the Alamo defenders had cheered in self-congratulation, but now they quietly attended to their weapons and back-up ammunition, sobered by the loss of friends who had fallen nearby. Pensive, they weighed what might lie ahead. Some, like Travis, believed they would demoralize the enemy by repulsing another assault, and a few thought the battle already stalemated. But Crockett and others, sensing the fanatical determination of the enemy, feared the worst was to come.

Santa Anna's mood improved after he took a few grains of opium in his tent. When Almonte informed him all attack units were ready, he adjusted his hat and marched briskly outside to make certain band, buglers, and standard bearers were properly assembled. With a flourish, he called for the third assault. A dense wave of humanity converged across the prairie and bore down on the north wall. Travis, watching the new strategy unfold, shouted for riflemen to converge from other areas, but firing had resumed and few heard his call.

In the Mexican attack units, body after body fell to be trampled by those charging onward, the band blaring and buglers sounding Deguëllo, no quarter, kill the enemy, every last one of them.

As they moved into musket range, Carlos spotted a tall Texan at an artillery battery on the north wall, waving a saber and shouting. Carlos steadied his musket, aimed carefully and fired. Shot in his forehead, Travis spun around, dropped his sword, and fell dead across a gun carriage.

Hundreds of cursing, frenzied soldiers reached the breach point on the north wall. As they poured through, the first group was ripped apart by a blast from a cannon atop the two-story barracks building. But others followed faster than artillery and rifle fire could repulse. Baugh, who had seen Travis fall, dashed through the center of the plaza, shouting, "They're inside the walls, fall back!" Musket fire cut him down before he reached the chapel.

Most Texan riflemen on the other walls were unaware the Mexicans had penetrated the plaza until it was too late. They were forced to fight in the open while a few of their comrades scrambled inside the chapel and barracks to reload their rifles and pistols. With Travis and Baugh dead, the command fell to Crockett, but he never knew it, caught in the frenetic close combat that engulfed the compound.

Isolated, the remaining Alamo defenders fought as Bowie had said they would, like wounded mountain lions. The certain knowledge of no quarter from the enemy drove them to supreme efforts. Without bayonets, the Texans used rifle butts as clubs, pistols and Bowie knives. But they were no match for the endless streams of Mexican soldiers, charging with levelled bayonets.

James Nowlin, a tall Irishman, fired his rifle into a Mexican soldier and clubbed another with his rifle butt before dying from a musket ball in the rib section, followed by a bayonet in the chest. Inside the chapel, Albert Martin, leader of the Gonzales volunteers, fired a pistol point-blank into the stomach of an attacker one instant before a Mexican officer almost decapitated him with a saber slash.

His ammunition spent, Antonio Fuentes grabbed a fallen Mexican musket to bayonet an onrushing attacker before two others crashed him to the ground where he was speared to death by their bayonets. By his side, lay one of the famous Bowie knives named after his old friend. Major Evans, torch in hand, estimated more than half of the Alamo defenders had fallen. He tried to reach the powder depot, but a hail of musket fire cut him down, the torch falling harmlessly to the ground.

Green Jameson fell dead across a cannon atop the long barracks, caught by a searing musket ball from close range. Bonham, Dickinson, and Esparza continued spraying death into the engulfing enemy by firing the twelve-pounders from atop the chapel until an alert Mexican commander ordered his men to climb the south wall where they gunned down the Texan artillerymen.

Carlos worked his way along the east side of the plaza when a pistol shot grazed his left upper arm. He barely felt the shot, and led his men on past the hospital, toward the chapel. Peering through dust and smoke, he saw a tall rebel in a coonskin cap, flailing away with his long rifle. Carlos dropped one with a musket shot and charged the tall rebel, trying to avoid his path of vision. Without appearing to see him, Crockett permitted Carlos to advance almost to where he could use his bayonet before he delivered a swift half-swing. Carlos reeled, and fell unconscious.

Vicious hand-to-hand fighting raged in the barracks, the chapel, and even the hospital. Few Mexican soldiers had pistols and rather than reload their muskets, they used their bayonets. Some of the last Texans to fall were fighting with emptied powder horns and pieces of furniture.

Bowie had awakened when Baugh's first shouts of warning resounded through the compound. For an hour, he had followed by sounds the ebb and flow of the battle, his spirits lifted by the widespread cheering after the first assault. When the firing had subsided a second time, he had felt a fleeting spark of hope. But he had dismissed that hope, recalling his estimate of Santa Anna's strength. When he had heard screams, cursing and a concentration of musket fire nearby, he knew the Mexicans had penetrated the plaza. Propped against the wall behind his bed, he waited with a pistol in each hand. Weak, but no longer weary, he anticipated the final combat of his long career. Suddenly, four Mexican soldiers barged into his room. When two lunged forward, Bowie fired point-blank into their stomachs, sending them sprawling to the floor. As he reached for his knives, the other two speared him. In a frenzy of unleashed frustration and hatred, they bayonetted him repeatedly and smashed his head against the wall with the butts of their muskets.

After reports from musket fire subsided, anguished cries of the wounded Alamo defenders were silenced by bayonets and swords as Santa Anna's order of no quarter was carried out. With the fort secured, His Excellency summoned Almonte and Juan to join his triumphant procession.

From north of the Alamo, Juan surveyed an eerie scene. Hundreds of Mexican soldiers lay on the cold ground, dead or twisting in pain. In despair, the wounded cried for help, but saw instead their beloved leader, with band playing and banners flowing, riding past them toward the foreboding walls they had tried so desperately to reach.

Chapter 10

AT the north wall, Santa Anna dismounted and walked into the compound. It was hardly possible to move without touching the body of a dead or wounded soldier. Blood was splattered everywhere, and Juan felt his stomach tighten as he viewed the carnage, his nostrils filled with the pungent odor of gunpowder and perspiration. Castrillón reported to Santa Anna with five prisoners, requesting that they be spared.

"We are not taking prisoners!" snapped Santa Anna. "Foreigners and traitors must die!"

Among the prisoners was an older man, whose right arm hung limp from a bloodstained shoulder. He stepped forward. "Kill me if you want more blood on your hands. I never seen Texas till last month. But this boy here," he said, placing his left arm around a slender, sandy-haired volunteer, "is only sixteen years old. He ain't no foreigner. He's from right here in Texas. No cause to kill him."

"Castrillón!" barked Santa Anna. "Execute these traitors now, or I will have you before a firing squad!"

Almonte turned away. Juan took one last glance at the young man's face before he lunged toward a wall as musket fire again pierced the early morning air. Juan vomited until his stomach was completely empty. He leaned against the wall, retching and trembling, until Almonte put his arm around his shoulder, leading him to a nearby well to wash his face.

Santa Anna commended General Amador and his reserves for piercing the Alamo defense at the crucial north wall. He assured General Cós that he had exonerated himself for the defeat in December. Then he toured the compound briskly, taking Ruiz to identify the bodies of Travis, Bowie, Crockett and Seguín. Santa Anna had assigned Ruiz the duty of disposing of all bodies, Mexican to be buried, Texan to be burned.

Ashen-faced and still trembling, Juan asked two officers if they knew the whereabouts of Captain Alvarez. One knew nothing; the other replied he had seen him inside the compound near the Alamo hospital. Searching the hospital, Juan found Dr. Pollard dead, along with all his comrades, but he couldn't find Carlos among the fallen Mexicans.

Walking outside, he swung to his left and found Carlos face down in the dust near the chapel. His mouth and arm were bleeding and a large bruise discolored one eye, but he was breathing. Juan pulled him from the ground, wiping the dust from his face, and called, "Doctor! Get a doctor!" When no one answered, he threw Carlos over his shoulder, carrying him through the maze of torn and twisted bodies to Almonte's carriage. He rushed Carlos to the garrison building near San Fernando Church where he knew doctors were available.

When the doctor saw Juan carrying Carlos over his shoulder, he directed him to a vacant bed, instructing him to lay the patient down gently. After a brief examination, the doctor rapidly began treatment. "I can stop the bleeding," he said, "but he took a terrible blow. There may be damage to the brain."

"What of his breathing?"

"It is about normal, but he may never awaken."

Juan swayed on his feet. The stench in the Alamo, the horror of the execution, and now Carlos before him, perhaps dying, were almost too much to bear. The hospital reeked of alcohol and chloroform. Leaning against a wall, Juan watched the doctor bandage Carlos' wounded arm. "How long can he live without awakening?"

"It is hard to say, but I would guess about forty-eight hours. He is weak from losing blood and needs nourishment and water, but if we forced him to drink, he would probably strangle to death."

"I am Lieutenant Calderón, assigned to His Excellency. If there is any change in his condition, will you please inform me at once?"

"You must understand," the doctor sighed, "that we are sadly understaffed, and little can be done for your comrade. Of course, you are welcome to visit from time to time, if you like."

"Thank you, doctor."

Under leaden skies Juan left the hospital to report to his original command post, expecting that Santa Anna would have returned. En route, he met Ruiz, who was shaking his head. "I never dreamed such bloodshed could occur," Ruiz said. "After the third charge, almost half of the Toluca Battalion lay dead or wounded. Colonel Morales reports heavy casualties in the battalions of San Luis, Ximenes and Matamoros. The rebels made a desperate stand."

"Were all the rebels killed?"

"Every single one. I toured the entire compound with Santa Anna, who wanted certain items and identities among the rebels."

After briefly savoring his victory, Santa Anna fell into a waspish mood, complaining to Almonte when Juan reported to the planning room, "Ruiz could not find the body of Seguin. I wanted that perfidious traitor dead and I wanted that 1824 tricolor. No one has found it. The only flag we have is a banner of the invaders from New Orleans."

"That flag will still be useful," Almonte said, "excellent propaganda to level against interfering Americans."

"True," said Santa Anna. "Attach it to my report to Tornel."

"Do you want an update on our casualties?" Almonte asked.

"No, I am reporting that seventy of our men were killed and three hundred wounded. Those figures should be accurate."

He is a liar or he is blind, Juan thought. There must be at least five hundred dead, and that many more critically wounded. He does not want to admit the valor of the enemy defense or the failure of his battle plan. We paid a high price for a fort with so few defenders.

Almonte announced that Mrs. Dickinson had been brought from the Alamo for interrogation. Escorted into the room and seated, she began to tremble. Santa Anna graciously insisted she have a cup of coffee and reassured her. "You have no cause to be concerned," he said. "I will not harm you in any way."

She stared, speechless, her trembling caused not by fear, but by a sudden urge to attack Santa Anna with a bronze candle holder on his desk. But as he walked away from her to a window, she relaxed, recognizing the futility of her situation and wanting only to be freed with her daughter as soon as possible.

"Now, Mrs. Dickinson, I'm sure you know I have a policy of mercy for non-combatants, even those aligned with the enemy. I am particularly helpful to those who are cooperative."

"I understand."

"I am interested in only a few details. First, what happened to Señor Seguin?"

"Captain Seguin rode out several days ago, or perhaps it was at night, on a mission for Colonel Travis."

"He was a courier?"

"More than that. I believe my husband said he was seeking reinforcements in the colonies. He's a friend of General Houston and may have tried to find him. That's all I know."

"Very well. Now, unfortunately, we have been unable to locate the 1824 Mexican tricolor. I saw it flying at sundown yesterday."

"So did I. Are you certain it was not flying this morning?"

"Positive."

"Then I have no idea where it is. There was a meeting last night, but my husband would say only that Colonel Travis made a strong speech."

"He did not mention the flag?"

"No."

"Can you recall more, anything at all, that your husband said about Travis' speech?"

"Only something about Travis drawing the line clearly for all the men to see."

"What line?"

"I don't know. My daughter was crying most of last night and I was busy with her."

"Very well. Calderón, see that Mrs. Dickinson and her daughter are well cared for. Do you have any requests?"

"Yes, I want to go home to Gonzales."

"But of course. Calderón, see that arrangements are made promptly."

Juan was puzzled. Why permit this strong-willed woman, who knew the size of the Mexican army, to go inform the enemy at Gonzales? After Mrs. Dickinson had left, he confronted Almonte with his concern. "I suspect," Almonte said, "that he intends to convince the colonists that their uprising is hopeless. If she tells what she has seen, and you know she will, it will spread fear."

"It will spread terror," Juan said.

"Are you still sick?"

"Yes, I am sick, sick of all this."

Almonte's sentiments lay somewhere between those of the idealistic young man standing before him, and those of the haughty, exultant dictator in the nearby planning room. He had protested the no quarter policy, but finally accepted it. He was no merciless conqueror, but he deeply resented the attitude of most Texan settlers, who had accepted generous grants of land, while refusing to acknowledge their benefactor.

Perhaps war required men to sacrifice principles, Almonte often thought, but he was a Mexican patriot who believed this was a war Mexico could ill afford to lose, and as a competent officer, he resolved to fulfill his duty. Yet, he once had been an idealistic young firebrand, and understanding Juan's strong convictions, he feared the young lieutenant might challenge His Excellency with disastrous results.

"You have performed your duties well," he said to Juan. "Your confinement is ended and you have earned three days of furlough. You need to rest and forget about war for a while."

"Thank you," Juan said. As he walked down the hall, he saw Señorita Arredondo requesting permission from Caro to see His Excellency. Santa Anna was surprised and delighted to receive a call from Corina since he had not forgotten the fascinating evenings with that lovely daughter of the prominent merchant. She was an admirer of Bowie, he recalled, which perhaps will no longer pose a problem with Bowie dead.

Corina came directly to the point. "I am here to inquire about Jim Bowie."

"He is dead."

"Are you certain?"

"Yes, your friend Ruiz identified him for me."

She winced, but maintained her composure. "In that case, I request permission to have him buried in the cemetery."

"I regret that I must deny your request. I have ordered the bodies of the enemy to be burned."

"Burned? You can't mean that."

"I have already issued the order to Ruiz."

"That's pagan. Won't you at least make an exception of Jim? He was a distinguished citizen of this community."

"I regret that I cannot. To make an exception of a prominent rebel leader would defeat the purpose of burning the bodies."

"Please, I beg of you."

"Ah, I recall a similar request to extend merciful terms of surrender to the traitors. My dear, I did just that before the battle, but they refused what would have saved their lives."

"I don't believe you! You raised a flag of massacre on a sacred place of worship. You had prisoners executed in cold blood, and don't deny it; I heard two officers discussing it less than ten minutes ago. You ordered an attack for a bloody battle on Sunday, of all days. Now, you burn the bodies of human beings, denying them a decent Christian burial. This is not war that you conduct — this is madness and blasphemy! May God have mercy on your wretched soul, and may God grant that I never see you again!" She walked briskly out of the room, sweeping past Caro before he could reach the door.

Santa Anna was shaken. No one had taken him apart verbally since his days as a young officer in trouble over gambling debts. After pacing the floor a few moments, he took three grains of opium before summoning Almonte and Juan.

"Where is Calderón?" he asked.

"He is ill," Almonte said. "Since he has worked diligently, and completed his assignment, I gave him three days of furlough."

"Very well, perhaps it is better that he is not here. He seems to question how I conduct my personal affairs."

"Not in any manner that has interfered with the performance of his duties or raised questions about his basic loyalty."

"You are always so tactful, Almonte. Now, I want you to be candid with me about the red flag on the church and the execution of those traitors in the mission. Do you believe these matters will cause serious problems?"

"Not within the army, for you and the Supreme Government have authority to set policy and we must carry it out. I worry, however, about civilians in the interior who are deeply religious and must believe this policy is fundamentally wrong."

"Yes, and they do not have to feed and clothe prisoners, either, and they do not have to face the cunning and deceit of these traitors, and — I am sorry, proceed."

"As for the colonists in Texas, I believe they will become fearful and discouraged when they learn all their countrymen perished here. Only the very courageous will contemplate further battle. Now, if you will permit me total candor?"

"Of course, proceed!"

"This so-called marriage, Your Excellency, has indeed caused some deep concern, not only among citizens of Bexar, but in the army as well. Many soldiers consider the enemy no better than coyotes and have no reservations about killing them unarmed. But they were married in the church and they respect those rights. Their talk at home about this incident might impair your political standing."

Santa Anna gazed out the window. The opium combined with Almonte's measured, if not reassuring, discussion of the issues concerning him had calmed his nerves. "Almonte, do you remember Señorita Arredondo?"

"Who could forget such a charming young woman?"

"Yes, but would you say that her views, as you recall them that night at the dinner table, would be representative of many people?"

"No, she is a highly intelligent person with strong moral convictions, a rare combination indeed. Her thinking also was clouded a bit by emotion, perhaps love, for this Bowie."

"Well, my little marriage ceremony was but a trifle. Why all the gossip? I have certain prerogatives as the commander-in-chief and president of the nation."

"I have no further comment."

"Very well. On the other matters, I consider morality and religion incompatible with the conduct of war. Those concerned about those subjects should be teachers or priests. I do not conduct war for their benefit. So long as I produce glorious victories such as I achieved today, the people of Mexico will continue supporting me as their president and military commander. Now, I want a meeting with the field officers."

Almonte wondered why he had been summoned to discuss such sensitive matters. Dispatching Caro with a call for the meeting, he walked outside to view the Alamo where teams sent by Ruiz were sorting bodies and gathering wood for the funeral pyres. At least two hundred Mexican wounded remained on the ground, awaiting medical attention. "One more such victory," Almonte murmured, "and we are ruined."

At the compound, Corina attempted to gain entrance to see Bowie one last time. Ruiz barred her path. "Corina, his body is so ravaged by disease and bayonets that you would be horrified. It will be better for you to remember him, as I will, at the Veramendi dinner table when our lives were carefree and pleasant." She walked slowly home, and later watched the fire from her balcony, weeping as clouds of smoke curled into the chill afternoon air.

Santa Anna's field officers were generally in a favorable mood. Losses had been heavy, including the popular Colonel Duque, but the frustrating siege had finally ended. The generals and colonels relaxed while Santa Anna stood at attention to address them. "This is a glorious victory! It will destroy the will of the rebels to fight and it will discourage potential invaders from the United States of the North. All of you have performed in a courageous manner that will earn proper recognition from the Supreme Government. Do what you will for three full days. Celebrate, let your men celebrate and savor the joy of our triumph. Then we will consider whatever further operations may be necessary."

Surveying the contented faces, Santa Anna relaxed. "Gentlemen, certain sensitive matters have come to my attention that would be in our best interest to discuss. You should be aware that my reputation must be protected so that we may fulfill our responsibility in this campaign and return home to prosper as heroes of the nation.

"To avoid unnecessary problems, it should be agreed that the personal conduct of the commander-in-chief is not a subject for speculation, especially not in any correspondence that might find its way into newspapers. So long as I command in a manner that produces victories for the Army of Operations and prosperity for those loyal to the Supreme Government, I see no reason why my personal conduct should be discussed. I suggest you assist me by discouraging such unhealthy gossip among your men.

"Now, the military policies set forth for this victory were discussed thoroughly and agreed upon by you. Therefore, I believe it essential to emphasize the accomplishments achieved here and refrain from discussing such inconsequential matters as our policy of no quarter. I trust there is agreement on my position? If not, speak up!"

Almonte marveled again at Santa Anna's rhetorical ability. His Excellency had mesmerized the officers with appeals to their vanity and sense of security. Another open argument over the no quarter policy seemed unlikely, and criticizing His Excellency to his face for his bogus marriage was too much for any of the officers to contemplate. They had been put on notice to sweep that affair under the rug and no one spoke out.

After they were dismissed, Santa Anna detained Almonte. "I appreciate your concern about these matters, and your forthright remarks before this meeting. But for the near future, it appears in the best interest of all concerned not to transmit those controversial items back into the interior where they would only create confusion. Diverting attention from our military campaign, they would reduce the public support to maintain these operations. Do you agree?"

"I suppose so," Almonte sighed.

Though Juan had slept only an hour during the night before the battle, he could not relax in the aftermath. He lay on his bed, eyes smarting from lack of sleep, and heard again the screams of his comrades, the thunderous roar of artillery, and the crack of endless musket fire. That vast field of writhing bodies stretched alongside lifeless forms flashed repeatedly in his mind, a horrifying mosaic, broken at the end by the sight of Carlos, unconscious, battered and helpless. At mid-afternoon, Juan, no longer trying to sleep, bathed, shaved and donned a clean uniform. When he returned to the hospital, he found it, as the doctor had predicted, overflowing. In his haste to cross the desert, Santa Anna had paid scant attention to medical personnel and supplies. Medicine was in short supply and bandages were being made from soiled strips of uniforms taken from dead soldiers.

Carlos remained in a coma. Juan opened a window near his bed and sat until nightfall when the doctor reassured him nothing had changed and nothing could be done. "Wait and pray," the doctor said. Leaving the hospital, Juan felt intense loneliness and despair. His whole world had been shaken severely by the recent events. Though he had been in San Antonio de Bexar only thirteen days, he felt much older that day.

In the darkness, Juan passed the cantina. He wanted to see Bozita, but was bone-weary and in no mood to quarrel with her. Yet, she would be the one thing of beauty to ease this long, terrible day. He walked quietly inside and seated himself near the door. The cantina was marked by contrasts. Some of the men, including Juan, appeared weary, or dazed, while at three tables, they were hoisting glasses with rousing toasts of *"¡Viva Santana!" "¡Viva Mexico!"*

Juan realized he had been on his feet about eighteen hours. No wonder he could scarcely hold up his head. It would be mescal tonight, not wine. When Bozita came to his table, her face was filled with concern, rather than her usual detachment.

"Are you all right?"

He nodded.

"Where is Carlos?"

"In a hospital. He was clubbed in the battle and is unconscious. The doctor has no idea whether he will survive."

"I am sorry. He is a good man."

"Yes, many good men fell today."

"I was told all the Texan fighters were killed."

"Yes, the last few were executed by order of His Excellency."

"Executed?"

"Yes, even a young boy who looked like my brother."

"So the blood-red banner carried the day. They even killed Jim Bowie, who was sick."

"There was no choice; he insisted on fighting from his bed. Most of the rebels fought like demons. Please, I do not wish to discuss the battle anymore. May I have a mescal?"

104

"Your face is drawn. Have you eaten today?"

"No."

"Then why not have a glass of wine? I will bring you some bread and cheese."

"I cannot eat, Bozita. Please bring a large glass of mescal."

"Very well."

When she returned, she placed the glass on the table, took his money, but lingered. "I am off work tomorrow. If you would like, we could have a picnic down the river."

Juan almost dropped his glass of mescal. "I'd love a picnic."

"Then have your mescal and go to bed. I do not want a weary companion on a picnic. I will be across the street at nine in the morning. Bring a carriage. Good night."

Though elated by Bozita's invitation, Juan was still unable to sleep after he crawled in bed. The battle and its aftermath kept coming to mind. Nothing can change what happened, he told himself. Pray for Carlos. Think of yourself and the future. Think of Bozita. So many conflicts. So many concerns. Finally, he fell asleep.

Chapter 11

IN the morning, Juan again borrowed Almonte's carriage and found Bozita awaiting him at nine o'clock with picnic basket in hand. She seemed younger and more beautiful than ever, her long dark hair freed from the severe swept-back style she usually wore. She caught up her flowing skirt as she ascended the carriage.

"How is Carlos?" she asked.

"There is no change this morning. If you like, we can light candles for him at San Fernando and then visit the hospital."

"Yes, let's do."

The church was crowded with people praying for the souls of loved ones lost or for the recovery of those wounded. At the hospital, the doctor saw Juan and shook his head. "No change," he said.

Bozita pulled the blanket a little higher over Carlos' chest and carefully brushed his hair from his forehead. "That is a terrible bruise, Juan. Is there nothing to be done?"

"Apparently not."

As they rode south on Calle de la Quinta, Bozita asked Juan if he had been to her favorite mission, San Jose. When he replied that he had not, she gave him directions. "Go east on Calle a la Nueva Villa across the river and aqueduct, then south on mission road. You will see things that you had no idea existed in this distant little province."

The crisp morning air was pleasant as they rode along mission road, in the shade of cottonwoods, pecans, live oaks, and willows, along with hackberry, mesquite, and *huisache* trees. On the winding San Antonio River, Juan saw gentle waterfalls, where fresh clear water splashed from limestone ledges. Reaching San Jose, he tied the horse outside the compound, and Bozita took his hand. "Close your eyes and walk with me."

She led him to the front of the chapel and said, "Now open." Before him stretched a facade of finely-carved stone statues depicting Our Lady of Guadalupe, San Jose, San Benedictine, San Augustine, San Dominic and San Francisco, all in recesses with conch-like canopies set around the thick wooden chapel doors.

"I had no idea such beauty existed here. Those figures rival the best I have seen in the City of Mexico. Who in the world sculpted them?"

"In a moment, I will tell you. First, answer a question: do you like my name?"

"I had never heard it before I met you."

"But do you like it?"

"I like you, very much."

"But do you like my name?"

"Frankly, no. It sounds harsh. I do not see you that way at all."

"Then, come with me around this side of the chapel."

At the south window of the baptistry, Juan marveled at the intricate mesh of stone carvings depicting roses. "Why, it is beautiful! Who is responsible for this fine art?"

"His name was Huizar, and this is the Rose Window, or Rosa's Window, named for his lost love. According to legend, he was a Spaniard who came here long ago to make a fortune so he could marry his Rosa. But she died, and he mourned for years, sculpting the figures of San Jose mission, including this window."

"Such a lovely legend. And such a lovely name, 'Rosa.'"

"Thank you, Juan. My name is Rosa. Rosa Elena Tristán. Does that not sound better to you?"

"Yes, but I do not understand."

"I made up the name 'Bozita' three years ago. I despise it, as I despise working in a cantina. I refused to use my true name in that wretched place."

"Why must you work there?"

"Three years ago, my father and mother were killed by Apaches on their way home from Laredo. To support myself and my two little brothers, and to pay taxes on some land my father owned, I needed to make some money. Nothing provided enough money for those needs except the cantina. I am the highest paid woman there, though it would break my father's heart if he knew. He came from Spain, and was a proud man. He met my mother here at San Jose; she was an Indian, a Coahuiltecan. He loved her and this mission, both beautiful things in a hostile wilderness. He named me after Huizar's Rosa, and I refused to desecrate the name or memory of my father when I went to work in the cantina."

"Was your father a rancher?"

"Yes, he had three tracts of land, two heavily mortgaged. I lost them within months of his death, but the other tract is mine. It is only three hundred acres, but I love this country, and just to own a small piece of it is an honor for me. But come," she said, guiding him to a spiral stairway of heavy oak, leading to the belfry. "This stairway is made of hand-hewn live oak logs, joined without nails or pegs, one of the many things I admire about San Jose mission."

At the top of the stairway, she led him through a window, and on-to the roof where they could see the landscape for miles around. A gentle breeze greeted them as they scanned the elaborate compound and the countryside beyond. Juan felt an invigorating new sense of belonging. He wondered if it came from Rosa, or the rolling coun-tryside, or the gradual relaxation of post-battle tension. Within San Jose compound, Juan could pick out retama, pomegranate, and moun-tain laurel. Near the abandoned living quarters of the priests, in-tricate vines of mustang grape curled around an arbor.

"This is a wonderful place, Rosa. The countryside is beautiful. And look how well that aqueduct system was designed. It is amazing that it could serve the city and all five missions."

"Father said this area was blessed by those wonderful springs since drought is an enemy worse than Indians for ranchers and farmers. Located north of the settlement, the springs feed the river with pure, cool drinking water, while the irrigation system was so dependable that most crops per acre were grown around this mission. No Spanish farmer could produce more corn, beans, squash, peppers, peaches or melons. At one time San Jose mission had fifteen hundred cattle and five thousand sheep and goats on a ranch that extended twenty-five miles from this compound."

"I confess I had no idea such a large operation had existed here. Who designed this compound?"

"Father Margil, a man my father considered a saint. They say he walked barefoot for years through the vast Indian lands to the south, establishing twenty-five missions before San Jose. He was a Fran-ciscan from Zacatecas. The Franciscans were priests, of course, but they were farmers, organizers, and engineers, as well."

As they descended the narrow stairway single file, Juan slipped. Rosa grabbed his arm to steady him, and suddenly, their bodies meshed. They both trembled, before she gently pulled away. "You need sandals, instead of boots," she laughed.

Inside the cavernous chapel, Juan stared at the high arched ceil-ing with its frescoed buttresses and long iron candle holders. They lighted candles near the elaborate five-step altar. Again, he felt a sense of belonging, of closeness to Rosa. He imagined them kneeling before a priest to be married, and rose reluctantly to his feet. As they left the chapel, Juan asked why the missions had ceased operation.

"Hostile Indians and terrible plagues," she said. "The Coahuiltecans could live with nature, in her harshest moments, but they were peaceful people. The Apaches ravaged their fields and pastures. My mother also told me plagues killed half the population over a period of about ten years."

They passed the huge stone granary, which could store five thou-sand bushels of corn, and strolled along the apartments built against the protective walls of the compound. Each of eighty-four apartments had a kitchen and a bedroom with stone shelves built into the walls and beds made of cedar and buffalo hide.

Leaving the compound, they rode to a portion of the aqueduct system that had caught Juan's eye from atop San Jose belfry. He held Rosa's hand as they descended the natural stone walkway across Piedras Creek where a clear, shallow stream was flowing. They climbed up the bank to the elevated canal, built fifteen feet above the bed of the creek. The trough was eight feet thick with three feet open for carrying water. "And this was constructed more than one hundred years ago?" he asked.

"Yes," she said, "and it will be here another hundred years."

She spread a blanket nearby for their picnic, and laid out bread, cheese, jelly and a bottle of wine. They shared a leisurely meal, chatting in the shade of tall pecan and oak trees, filled with thick twisting vines of wild grapes. "I dare you to taste one of these," she said, pulling down a cluster of small purple grapes.

He bit into one, and spat it out. "That is horrible, so bitter."

"Did you enjoy the jelly on your bread?"

"Of course, I ate two pieces."

"I made that jelly from these mustang grapes."

He laughed. "Well, Rosa Elena Tristán, you are full of surprises. If you can make such sweet jelly from those bitter grapes, I believe Bozita, that harsh woman of the cantina, can become the saint of the missions."

"You are teasing, but I like it. You seem more relaxed and happier away from the army."

"You make me happy, Rosa. Never before have I felt what I feel now."

"Juan, Juanito. You are far from home. You miss your family. Do not believe you can change who we are." When he tried to put his arm around her, she pulled away. "Please, do not spoil our day. Let's go down the river. There is more to see."

A dry norther was blowing as they rode to the lonely grounds of the mission named San Francisco de la Espada, Saint Francis of the Sword. It was a haunting compound with its low walls and buildings falling into ruins, yet somehow withstanding devastation. San Jose projected grandeur, but Espada reflected the hard times in which it had been active. Its modest chapel was a low parallelogram with a ceiling supported by heavy wood beams. Juan was surprised to find at least one hundred candles burning at the small altar. "Many of the older people around here will not pray anywhere else," Rosa said. "This is their church."

A lone scrub oak and a water well lay between the entrance of the chapel and priests' quarters, long abandoned. As they crossed the windswept compound, she pressed against him for warmth. He again felt the urge to kiss her, but she was quick to ascend the carriage.

"That is a lonely place," Juan said as they rode down the river. "You can almost feel the presence of forlorn souls who must have suffered there. So much time and toil to build these compounds, and now they are abandoned. I wonder how those buildings and walls were constructed."

"I will show you," Rosa said.

They were far down the river when she told him to stop. They walked within twenty yards of the river when Rosa pointed to a wide, shallow area. "Over there," she said, "is where tufa stones were taken from the river. They are a soft limestone, ideal for building since they can be molded into place, and then hardened under sunshine."

Juan sat down to remove his boots while she descended the final steps to the river. Suddenly, her scream pierced the late afternoon air, reverberating through the riverbed. She screamed repeatedly, as Juan scrambled down the ledge to reach her. He saw a limp hand protruding from the water, caught on a limb near the far bank of the river. Reaching Rosa, he held her, trying to console her, but she sobbed profusely, and refused to open her eyes. "Someone was murdered, as my parents were, and thrown into the river," she sobbed.

While he held her, Juan noticed three other bodies in the water, all in the blue and white uniforms of the Army of Operations. After what he had seen the day before, this sight could not affect him.

"Rosa, what you saw was a Mexican soldier. I heard Ruiz tell Santa Anna there was not space in the cemetery to bury all the dead. He said he would throw some of them in the river, and he probably had them carried this far so as not to spoil the drinking water in the settlement."

"It is horrible," she said. "Cannot we escape even one day from the war?"

She finally stopped crying and was trembling only slightly when he lifted her chin and kissed her. She held him tightly.

"I love you, Rosa."

"Please, Juan, do not say that."

"I fell in love with Bozita, but I love Rosa even more."

She kissed him tenderly, then pulled away. "We must start back," she said. "It will soon be dark."

Upon ascending the carriage, she donned her green cotton rebozo, a long wrap-around headpiece that also provided warmth for her neck and shoulders against the north wind that was whipping into their faces. She sat close by Juan as they rode quietly back along mission road to Bexar. The lights of the settlement glowed in the early evening as they rode toward the hospital.

Carlos' doctor greeted them with a wide smile. "He awakened about two hours ago. I believe he will recover."

"May we see him?" Juan asked.

"Yes, but please not for long. He is very weak."

110

As they approached, Carlos smiled. Juan held one hand and Rosa the other. "I knew the old farmer would be back," Juan laughed.

"We were almost out of candles," Rosa smiled.

"Some rebel gave me the worst headache I have ever had," Carlos said. "Lord, how it hurts! But the doctor says it will go away in time. I feel better now that I see you two together and happy."

"Carlos, you will be awarded the medal and a grant of land," Juan said. "You fought bravely."

"I told you before, my friend, that I want only to complete this campaign and return home to my family. I am thankful just to be alive." He held a damp cloth to his head. "Juan, have you not seen enough of war?"

"Yes," Juan said, "I have. I only wish I knew how to be relieved of duty without dishonor. Perhaps the enemy will cease hostilities, now that we have won this battle."

"I doubt it," Carlos said. "They fought with great skill and pride. If their garrison had been much larger, they would have held the Alamo."

"Santa Anna believes we have broken their will to fight," Juan said. "If they continue hostilities, he will destroy their colonies."

"It is such a waste," Carlos said. "There is so much land to be farmed and not enough farmers. Why must we kill each other?"

"When this campaign began," Juan said, "I believed we fought for the honor of Mexico and to secure this province to its rightful owner. I believe that to this day, but I hope Santa Anna will negotiate a settlement to avoid further bloodshed. With our strength, he might convince the enemy to accept a compromise."

"You are the diplomat," Carlos said. "But I told you before Santa Anna has no mercy in his heart. Do you not understand that now?"

Juan paused, gazing at the flickering candle beside Carlos' bed. "I suppose so," he said. "He is a vicious, vindictive man who will stop at nothing to fulfill his desires, personal or political."

Rosa, who had been listening intently, finally interrupted. "I believe both of you are talking in terms that could land you in trouble. Let no more be said tonight about the war."

"Agreed," Carlos smiled, "on the condition that you two have a quiet supper and enjoy the evening. My head hurts and it hurts more when I talk."

At Rosa's apartment, Juan saw a framed parchment copy of a statement by the Spanish explorer, Cabeza de Vaca, dated 1528 on the Coahuiltecan Indians: *"I believe these people see and hear better, and have keener senses than any other in the world. They are great in hunger, thirst, and cold, as if they were made for the endurance of these more than other men, by habit and nature."*

"You are justly proud of your heritage," Juan said. "That is quite a tribute."

"Mother's people were primitive, but resourceful. They lived on the sparse game and food they could find. When game was scarce, they ate things you would not touch—mesquite beans, cactus, lizards, even snakes and spiders."

Juan shuddered. "You are not helping my appetite."

"I'm proud of my heritage, Juan, but I know how people of your class feel about *mestizos*. I will not deceive myself. I am not of your class; I never will be. My heritage is a hopeless conflict of pure Spanish and pure Coahuiltecan, and neither culture accepts me."

"Rosa, I told you I love you. Do you not believe me?"

"A kiss is not love. I cannot accept love when I know we cannot be together past the brief time you stay in Bexar. But here come my brothers."

The boys were eleven and eight, sturdy children with wide, searching eyes. Juan played them a game of cards while Rosa prepared the meal—fried rabbit and squash, plus beans, peppers and bread, with wine for her and Juan while the boys had goat's milk. As she washed dishes, Juan slipped each boy a coin for candy, then Rosa came to put them to bed. She rejoined Juan at the table for coffee.

"It has been a wonderful day," he said. "I want you to know that. Though I hate this war, you have made me very happy."

"Juan," she sighed, "we perhaps should not see each other again. This only makes it harder for us to part."

"Rosa, that is the closest you have come to saying you care for me."

"If I ever say that, or admit it to myself, it would mean forever, and that cannot be."

He walked around the table and reached for her, but she eased away. "Please sit down," she said. "I have something to tell you." She stared into her cup of coffee, her face strained in the shadowy light. "I have tried every way I know to discourage you. I have tried to embarrass you, ignore you, shock you.

"You saw me first as fascinating 'Bozita' of the cantina and you wanted to possess me. If you had, you would have soon forgotten me. I knew this, but I do not sell my body, nor do I want a short romance, as many of these girls have done.

"I also knew that if you came to know 'Rosa,' you would feel perhaps more deeply. I could not resist today because I do care for you. But I have deceived you. You see me now as an unfortunate innocent girl, left without parents or resources and forced into a life she deplores. Your gallantry is aroused, and you would concede your wonderful life in our capital city to protect her."

Tears welled in Rosa's eyes, and Juan again rose from the table, but she admonished him to be seated. "Juan, I have deceived you. I could have sold the land and accepted work from people my father knew, the Navarros or the Seguins. But I was selfish, and wanted to keep the land. When I decided cantina work was the way to achieve my purpose, I went to see the owner. He is a large, powerful man who dominates everyone he deals with, and he told me coldly that the job was mine, but only if I slept with him that night. Instead of slapping his face, I sat there and thought again of my land. I asked him if I slept with him that one night, would I be left alone thereafter; he said that would be a bargain. I walked through the plaza that afternoon, thinking it over. No one had ever touched me before, but I could not bear the thought of losing the land I had roamed so often with my father. I met one of my father's old friends and asked him if that man could be trusted. With distaste, this friend did admit that his word in a bargain could be relied upon. By nightfall, I hated myself because I had resolved to go through with it and I returned to the cantina."

Juan tried to interrupt, but she raised her hand. "I have never told this to anyone before. I want you to hear it all. It was a horrible experience. I hated every minute of it, and I hated myself. The shame was so great, I could not confess it to a priest. I did not want to admit that it happened."

Juan was trembling. He rose and reached for his sword. "I will kill him," he said, "but slowly, so he will pay for your pain with his."

"Sit down, Juan. He is not worth killing. Please, sit down. I am not finished."

"The bargain was kept, and to ensure that I never again had to face such a proposition, I became the best dancer and barmaid in the cantina. So I have saved my land, but I have sinned beyond anything my parents could have imagined. I should have told you this last night, instead of tonight. I am sorry, so very sorry."

For a long moment, Juan sat in silence. He stared into the small, dancing shadows around the nearly spent candle. Soft sobs from across the table caused him to raise his head and he saw Rosa was holding her face in her hands. He walked slowly around the table and placed his arm gently on her shoulder. "Look at me, Rosa.

With tears streaming down her face, she looked up.

"I do not care what happened in the cantina; or whether you call yourself Bozita or Rosa; or whether your ancestors ate mesquite beans and rattlesnakes. I love you! I love you with all my heart and soul. Now, will you, once and for all, answer me: do you love me?"

Still sobbing, she flung her arms around his neck. "Juan, Juanito. I love you. I always will."

"And you will be my wife."

They retired to her bedroom where they made love far into the night.

Chapter 12

JUAN awoke to the sounds of Rosa preparing breakfast and her brothers playing outside. "Now," she said, "comes the real test. If you like my *menudo*, you are truly my beloved."

Juan had never enjoyed *menudo*, a thick stew built around tripe. It was not a dish he ate often and he preferred his food with less seasoning. Rosa luckily had not seasoned that *menudo* heavily and Juan downed a bowl without flinching. "It is delicious," he lied.

"The boys love it," she said. "If I am not here, they will stand by pots of *menudo* or beans to see they do not boil over."

"I am looking forward to when you no longer need to work," Juan said. "I will try to see Santa Anna today. I must have his permission to marry you."

"Juanito, is this right? I can wait until the campaign is completed."

"We are one," he said. "We should be married as soon as possible. It should not matter to His Excellency anyway."

"Be careful. If he is not in a pleasant mood, watch your temper."

Almonte was surprised to see Juan. "You have time remaining on your furlough; why are you here?"

"I wish to request permission of His Excellency to marry Rosa Elena Tristán, a citizen of this province."

"And who is she? I did not know of your interest in any woman other than that barmaid."

"They are one and the same. She does not use her true name out of respect for her family; her father was from Spain."

"Interesting. Are you quite certain you want to marry this girl?"

"I am positive, Colonel."

"I have no idea how His Excellency might react. I suggest you wait. Only a few minutes ago he received a report that the rebels have formally declared independence. Return in an hour and perhaps he will be in a more receptive mood."

Juan recalled the words of caution from Rosa and he respected Almonte's judgment. "Very well," he said. He went to see Carlos, who seemed in better condition, and told him of his intention to marry Rosa. "Do you approve, old farmer?"

"Of course, I approve. I knew you loved each other. But I must warn you, Santa Anna may refuse because of your family. If he does, be careful and hold your tongue. You may find another avenue."

"You are the third person to caution me today. I only lost my temper that one time and for a valid reason. I am not a fool."

"Of course you are no fool, but you are so set in your beliefs you often speak before weighing the consequences. In Santa Anna, you are dealing with one who reacts almost as abruptly. Do not lose all hope if he is not receptive today."

"I understand," Juan smiled. "I will speak with the even-tempered poise of Almonte, the graciousness of a priest, and the sagacity of an old farmer from Saltillo."

"For a young man so deeply involved in love and war, you have a fine sense of humor."

"Carlos, I've worried about so many things these past few days, I could only feel relieved when I awoke this morning. If I have to continue in the campaign to have Rosa, I will do so. I must tell you, though, it bothers me, the disregard Santa Anna has shown for human life."

"I am not surprised. By the way, Juan, the doctor told me this morning how I got to the hospital. You saved my life."

"If I ever have to do that again, I hope you will have lost some weight."

"Go see Santa Anna," Carlos smiled.

Almonte ushered Juan into Santa Anna's planning room where he found the president of Mexico in a pensive mood. Almonte remained in the room, prepared to intervene should Juan incur the wrath of their mercurial leader.

"Ah, Calderón," Santa Anna said, wheeling from the window. "Won't you have a seat? I have written your father about our victory. I informed him of your exemplary service, including your attention to the needs of Captain Alvarez, one of our most distinguished officers. Even though you were not in combat, I have ordered that you receive a medal of the Legion of Honor. I am certain your father will be most pleased."

"Thank you, Your Excellency."

"Colonel Almonte tells me that you request permission to marry."

"Yes, Your Excellency, her name is Rosa Elena Tristán, a citizen of Bexar."

"The name is not familiar. Who are her parents?"

"Her father was a Spaniard; her mother Coahuiltecan. They were killed by Apaches three years ago."

"And where has she been living since the death of her parents?"

"She has maintained a household, and is rearing her two younger brothers."

"Admirable. How old is she?"

"She is twenty."

"And how does she support herself and her brothers?"

For the first time in his life, Juan could not face a question squarely. Avoiding Santa Anna's eyes, he rose and walked to a window. Santa Anna realized Juan was evading him. "I asked you a question, Lieutenant!"

"In order to retain some land her father bequeathed," Juan sighed, "she has worked in a cantina."

"Has worked?"

"She is still working there," Juan said, "but will not do so after we are married."

"I see. Then this is the same girl you fought over before the battle?"

"Yes."

Santa Anna walked to where a map of the Texas province hung alongside the Alamo drawing. "I had believed," Santa Anna said, "that General Urrea's successful skirmishes and our decisive victory here would convince the rebel colonists their cause is hopeless. However, I now learn that foreigners are pouring across the Sabine River to support this independence movement. Instead of a quick victory, we face an arduous campaign, during the rainy season, to drive all these rebels from our land.

"Before I left our capital, I promised your father I would take special care of his beloved son. I have kept my promise by appointing you to my staff in order that you might learn military operations with a minimal risk of danger. I shall soon be back in the field, and you must keep that position. Though some of us may die, we still must fulfill our duty for the sake of our nation and our own honor. Surely, at this stage of the campaign, you see the wisdom of deferring plans to marry."

"I never sought favored treatment," Juan said, "nor do I seek it now. I love Rosa deeply, however, and want to be married with all dispatch. Are not requests for marriage routine between loyal citizens who have no criminal record?"

"I recognize your question is warranted, Lieutenant, but you must understand that this poses a serious problem for me. Though I did not discuss such personal considerations with your father, nonetheless, I feel a certain responsibility."

"But Your Excellency, I am of age. It is my decision!"

"Calderón, your family is one of the most prominent in the City of Mexico. You have a solemn responsibility to your family. Does your father know of this romance?"

"No."

116

"Then I have no choice but to deny your request at this time."

Juan bit his lip, thinking of Santa Anna's bogus marriage. That this man should deny me the opportunity to share my life with Rosa, he thought, is absurd. He started to speak to the point, but restrained himself by thinking again of Rosa.

Almonte, relieved to see Juan maintain control, was surprised to hear Santa Anna amiably resume the conversation. "Calderón, I said 'at this time.' I will strike a bargain with you. If your father approves, I will grant permission immediately. Otherwise, you must complete the campaign with the Army of Operations and be honorably discharged. At that time, I will have fulfilled my commitment and will no longer be a factor. Is that not fair?"

Juan thought of the delay. Even using the mail express to Mexico City, the exchange could take weeks. But Santa Anna had offered a bargain and apparently they would be in the Texas province throughout the spring.

"Your Excellency, I would appreciate the use of an express."

"There is one leaving for Copano this afternoon at four," Santa Anna said. "You are welcome to use it. Your letter will accompany some reports I am sending to the secretary of war and marine. They will arrive at the capital with all dispatch. Since this resolves the matter for the time being, you are dismissed."

Juan was unaccustomed to half a loaf. He had always been one to charge ahead for whatever he wanted, backing off only when completely stymied. Walking across the plaza, he felt lonely and disappointed. At her apartment, Rosa was waiting and embraced him before asking Santa Anna's response. She displayed only brief disappointment. "You will be with me, Juanito, for a few more days. Let us enjoy each and every minute. Do not ever let Santa Anna or your father prevent us from enjoying what is ours, now and when you return after the war. I must go to work, my love. Write your father, take a nap, and come for me at midnight."

Juan, recalling what Santa Anna had said, grudgingly admitted there was merit to the point about consulting his family. His father had been stern, but fair, and he had enjoyed every advantage that wealth and position could provide. Remember, he thought, Father is always direct and to the point. He wrote:

My Dear Father:

I trust this letter finds you well. As I wrote you recently, I continue to be in the best of health.

His Excellency informs me he has written you about the Army's victory here in Bexar. We may be leaving this settlement soon to pursue the campaign north and east of here.

Today, I requested permission of His Excellency to marry a citizen of San Antonio de Bexar, Rosa Elena Tristán, whom I love deeply. She is a mestizo, *but I hope you will understand that she is the only woman with whom I will ever be happy. I know you and Mother would learn to love her, for she is kind, compassionate and lovely. Her parents were killed a few years ago by Apaches and she has managed to run a well-organized household, rearing her two younger brothers.*

His Excellency said he would grant his permission should you approve. I beseech you, Father, to grant your permission. I should like to marry here, rather than at home, as Rosa is not familiar with the ways of our society, and a marriage there would be most difficult for her. After we are married, I will bring her to visit and we will probably settle there, near you, if that is agreeable.

Please give me your blessing, Father, and inform me soon. My fondest regards to Mother and all the family.

Juan

While Juan was signing the letter, Santa Anna paced the floor of his planning room, asking Almonte about Rosa. "Why does she use a false name in that cantina?"

"I have no idea."

"She is said to be a provocative dancer. She caused an altercation between Calderón and another officer. She has no parents, no standing in the community. A common barmaid, a wench, that is all she is. And what is your opinion, Almonte?"

"I do not know this woman."

"Have you no opinion at all? What of the evidence?"

"He seems to love her."

"What does he know of love? He has a fine family and high social standing. He can have the most beautiful woman he wants from a wealthy family in the City of Mexico. This is ridiculous! I have no choice but to write his father, and put this affair into perspective. Not one word of my letter, Almonte. When he comes to his senses, young Calderón will appreciate my concern for his family. But now he is blinded by that wench, and I have no intention of promoting his romantic nonsense."

"I have never known you to interfere in a personal matter such as this," Almonte said.

"And you have never known me to serve as father ad interim for a hot-blooded young aristocrat who ought to know better. I count his father among my most important political supporters." Santa Anna dipped a goose quill and began writing:

My Dear Señor Calderón:

I trust this letter finds you well and that you are in receipt of my previous communication detailing the success of our army here in Bexar and the exemplary service of your distinguished son.

Throughout this campaign, your son has impressed me with the dedication and loyalty you no doubt instilled in him. He is, indeed,

118

among my most valuable aides, and destined to prove himself of inestimable value to his beloved country.

However, a sensitive personal matter has arisen that I feel compelled to bring to your attention in the utmost confidence. Today, your son requested my permission to marry a mestizo barmaid of this settlement. This woman caused the only problem in which your son has been involved during this campaign, a serious altercation in a cantina where she dances in a manner described as "provocative." Because of these unusual circumstances, I deferred what otherwise would have been a routine request until such time as he might receive your permission.

It is with sadness in my heart that I bring this matter to your attention, but I felt it my responsibility to do so. You see, my friend, I have encountered this type of situation over the years in my numerous campaigns. A young soldier, far from home on his first campaign, encounters a provocative young wench with whom he becomes infatuated. He believes he has fallen in love because he has found temporary solace from that gnawing feeling of loneliness in a strange and distant land. I believe this to be the case with your son. Though I hesitate to write such things, I am certain you understand that with a wife of her background, his future would indeed be impaired.

Again, my friend, it is with a heavy heart that I pen these words, but I am relieved to have fulfilled my duty by giving you what I believe to be a true perspective of this situation. If I have erred, please forgive me.

As Santa Anna signed the letter, Almonte informed him another agent had arrived with news. "Sam Houston departed Washington-on-the-Brazos three days ago," the agent said. "At that time the enemy knew nothing of the Alamo battle and their convention was still in progress."

"Since Houston has departed," Santa Anna mused, "he will not become their president. How strange."

"Houston has been renamed commander-in-chief," the agent said. "He now has command over all rebels under arms in the province. There was talk that either David Burnet or Samuel Carson would be named interim president with Don Lorenzo de Zavala as vice-president."

"That devious traitor Zavala," Santa Anna snapped, "would maneuver himself into a high position. But he will rue the day he betrayed me for this dark treason against his native land. He will preside only briefly before he faces a firing squad. Proceed."

"We had expected the invading foreigners to gather at Washington-on-the-Brazos," the agent said, "but since Houston left, they must have another assembly point, probably Gonzales or Mina. There are new reports that foreigners from Alabama and Georgia have gathered on the coast, presumably to reinforce the rebels under Fannin at Goliad."

"Yes, I am aware of that," Santa Anna said. "General Urrea has that situation under control. It is Houston's plan of action that I must know."

"I have a word of caution to convey to Your Excellency, if I may."

"Proceed."

"Houston is no ordinary military commander. From many years of living with the Cherokees, he knows well the means of concealment and maneuvers to confuse those who would track him. We lost him this winter because he rode several miles down a rocky creek bed with two feet of water running through it. No one can track a man using such tactics."

"Perhaps not," Santa Anna said, "when he is traveling alone or in a small party. But when he musters an army, he can ill afford to waste time marching through creek beds."

"True, Your Excellency, but he will still use rivers and creeks as buffers between his army and yours. I have lived in this province for many years, and the Brazos and Colorado Rivers can be difficult, indeed, during the rainy season. This is true of all the creeks and the Guadalupe and the Nueces, and . . ."

"The Nueces," Santa Anna interrupted, "will be of no concern! We have established our positions north of the Nueces and there is absolutely no danger of the enemy driving us south of that river."

"Very well, Your Excellency," the agent sighed. "I only wish to point out that Houston will be an elusive adversary."

"Fair enough," Santa Anna said. "And since you believe he is heading for Gonzales or Mina, I order you to reconnoiter those settlements and report back to me."

After the agent departed, Santa Anna asked Almonte about the condition of their wounded. "It will be at least two weeks before most of those with healing wounds will be in condition to march."

"Two weeks!" Santa Anna snapped. "I would like to lead an assault on this so-called government now."

"Not on Houston?"

"I will dispose of him in due time. If all this talk about his cleverness is true, he will be difficult to engage in battle. I would rather destroy their government before it is recognized. Austin will not doubt seize upon this new legitimacy to further their cause with President Jackson. The rebels still lack organized military support from America, and so long as they do, their rabble army has no chance against mine.

"I've been thinking about Houston's alleged prowess. Perhaps I should divide our army to cover the north and west portions of the province. By flanking Houston, we can drive him into a trap."

"That might work," Almonte said, "but only if our right flank is secure. That means Fannin's army must be destroyed."

"Or contained," Santa Anna said. "Urrea can lay siege on that presidio at Goliad; he is quite adept at such operations. He is very resourceful, almost too resourceful."

"Why do you say that?"

Santa Anna paused. Instead of responding, he asked Almonte's opinion of Urrea's performance to date.

"Frankly, Your Excellency, I believe General Urrea is our best commander, besides yourself. He has proven himself most adept in all phases of military operations, and has a steadfast personality that generates respect among the men he commands."

"But Almonte, you must understand," Santa Anna said, "certain political considerations are involved here. As you know, my second in command, Filisola, is an Italian, who poses no political threat to me since Mexico would never bestow the presidency upon him. Urrea is quite another matter. As a former governor of the state of Durango, he has executive experience in government and a political base. As you pointed out, he has a certain flair which inspires men to follow his leadership. Furthermore, he has opposed me in the past, and I am convinced he remains a Federalist at heart. So let him savor his scattered victories, and even defeat Fannin, but he must not be allowed to defeat Houston or to capture the rebel government leaders. Those trophies must be mine."

"But if Urrea defeats Fannin, the entire coast will be open. That might prompt Houston to attack Urrea."

"An unpleasant possibility, but a valid point. I must conduct the campaign in such a manner to prevent Urrea from engaging Houston. If he defeats Fannin, I must guarantee he merely secures the southern coastal areas. After all, with accurate intelligence, I can always intercede into an area to engage Houston.

"Now with Urrea on the east, we need a force covering the left flank, perhaps under General Gaona. Let Ramirez y Sesma start the search for Houston. Finally, we should leave a nominal force here in Bexar under General Andrade. Study such a plan from a logistical standpoint, Almonte. When we flush out Mr. Houston, I want to lead the vanguard. Surely, the rebels will locate their capital in the interior of the province. This plan will give me the maximum opportunity to crush Houston's army and capture their political leaders as well."

Part II:

On The
Lost Plain

Chapter 13

JASON Gates could only speculate on the fate of the Alamo from his bed, having been confined to his room with pneumonia. From a window he had watched the thirty-two volunteers assemble under Albert Martin to march toward San Antonio. Tears of pride and anxiety had welled in his eyes when he saw several of his friends in the contingent wave to him as they marched past.

A few days later, volunteers were streaming into Gonzales. Twenty-eight additional volunteers attempted to reinforce the Alamo, but were driven back at the siege lines before they could learn if the Texans still held the fort. Eventually, Burleson arrived along with Neill and many other veterans of the December siege of Bexar. Most of the volunteers brought little more than a rifle, one change of clothing, and a few days of provisions. The settlers provided meat, corn, sugar and coffee. While all Texans were clad in civilian clothing of cotton or buckskin, a uniformed outfit of fifty-two volunteers from Kentucky marched into Gonzales under the command of Sidney Sherman. At thirty, this soldier of fortune had followed the sound of conflict and adventure to Texas. A commander of a state militia unit in Kentucky, he raised volunteers rapidly with the promise of land grants as pay for service. He sold his business, using the proceeds to equip and transport his unit of volunteers. In addition to their snappy uniforms, the Kentucky unit flew a white silk flag bearing a thinly-clad Miss Liberty, sword in hand. Inscribed on the flag was the battle slogan, "Liberty or Death."

Citizens of Gonzales gave the Kentuckians a hearty welcome. Even Ben Gates, an ardent Peace Party sympathizer, found his heart beating faster at the sight of such a well-drilled unit marching down the dusty street past his store. Ben had spent most of his life in Kentucky, and he was anxious to ask these men about friends and relatives there.

Of the three hundred and seventy-four men gathered at Gonzales, only the fifty-two from Kentucky had ever participated in formal drills or maneuvers. A few of the Texan volunteers had limited

125

combat experience against Indians or Mexican troops in which they fought under commanders they had elected.

On the first day that Jason had strength enough to walk, he went out to watch the volunteers gathering along the bank of the gentle Guadalupe River, its green waters welcomed by those who had filled their canteens last from the muddy Brazos. Most of these volunteers were new to Texas, eager for the arrival of the famous General Houston, and for word from the Alamo, as many expected to reinforce Travis. With ample provisions and weapons, there was nothing to do but wait. Some of the men occupied themselves with pitching horseshoes and target-shooting while others fished for perch and catfish from the Guadalupe or threw rocks at lazy turtles floating among the reeds.

Burleson, as temporary commander, imposed few restrictions on the men, other than to prohibit gander-pulling contests which the women of Gonzales had protested as grisly and inhumane. In those contests, men riding full speed on horseback attempted to pull the heads from unfortunate ganders tied to trees. Burleson also instructed Sherman and the other new commanders to caution their men about picking up wood. "Never pick up a piece of wood from the ground," he said. "Kick it over first. There may be a rattler under it, and north of here, there may be copperheads. At this time of year, snakes are awful feisty."

When he returned home that evening, Jason was confident he could ride the following day, at which time he would report to Burleson. He went to bed early, but woke at midnight to a heavy pounding on the front door. With pistol in hand, his father cautiously opened the door. A haggard, middle-aged man leaned in the doorway, his face drawn by misery and fatigue. His tattered trousers were blood stained from scratches by prickly pear and mesquite thorns.

"Please, sir, I need help," the man said. "My name is Rose, Moses Rose from Nacogdoches. I have a few dollars and I need a horse and provisions."

Ben invited Rose into the house. "Where in the world have you been?"

"I escaped from the Mexican seige lines. Now I'm hiding from Texas troops. I don't know how they will treat me if I get caught. I left the Alamo."

Jason had walked into the room. "What do you mean you left the Alamo?"

"I had to make a decision. I chose to live."

"How can you say that? There hasn't been a battle, has there?"

"There never was going to be a battle, son. There was going to be a massacre. There were thousands of Mexican troops spread all around the old mission. I've been fighting all my life, but it's been fights where I always had a chance."

126

Jason was furious. "How many other men deserted?" he demanded.

"I didn't desert, but there won't be anybody to back my story. You see, Travis assembled us in the garrison, and made a long speech about freedom and destiny, when all of a sudden he whipped out his sword, drew a line and asked the men to step across and join him if they were ready to die in the Alamo's defense. There were plenty of others who felt like me, but Bowie and Crockett and Bonham shamed them by hurrying right across that line. When they all finally crossed, they called me a coward, but Travis said it was my choice. I slipped through the Mexican lines that night, and before dawn, I heard cannons roaring for more than an hour, then the prairies fell silent. I guess that was the end."

"I know," Jason said, "some volunteers from Gonzales tried to join your garrison. And what about Fannin?"

"Thirty-two volunteers came from Gonzales, but no help from Fannin. Bonham came back from Goliad with word that Fannin would not reinforce the Alamo. Without Fannin, Travis told us there was no hope to defeat Santa Anna. You can say I'm a coward, but without a family or land in this country, I got nothing to die for."

"Crockett and his men didn't own land in Texas. They were there to fight for liberty."

"I told you, son, each man made his own decision. Mine was to leave. That's all I can say."

"I say you are a coward and a traitor."

Ben jerked his son back. "This man has suffered enough, Jason. Leave him alone. Go back to bed. You'll be no help to your cause in a weakened condition."

After buying a horse and provisions from Ben, Rose slipped away into the night. Jason crawled back into bed, thinking of the many friends he had lost in the Alamo. If Rose had told the truth, then all settlements north of San Antonio de Bexar were in jeopardy. "Lord help us," he whispered.

Ben walked into the room and placed a hand on Jason's shoulder. "I'm sorry, son. I'm sorry for all of us. Dickinson, Albert Martin, young Johnny Gaston — so many of our people are gone. Our town has been almost wiped out. Now, won't you help me prepare to evacuate?"

Jason sat up in the bed, brushing tears away. "No, Dad, and I want you to promise not to mention what this man told us. We should have official word before we do anything. We don't want to cause a panic."

On the following day, in an atmosphere heavy with uncertainty, two Tejano civilians arrived from San Antonio de Bexar to report that the Alamo had fallen. They also said a large Mexican force, perhaps two thousand strong, was en route under General Ramirez y Sesma.

127

Gonzales had paid dearly with the blood of her citizens, young and old, wealthy and poor. Cries of sorrow rang throughout households as new widows and their children learned the news. Furthermore, the startling report of Ramirez y Sesma's advance meant the settlement was in imminent danger. Jason feared panic would soon sweep the community. Hearing rumors that Houston was en route to Gonzales, he saddled up and rode out of town.

Less than three miles from Gonzales, Jason met Houston, who was accompanied by his longtime friend, George Hockley, and two volunteers from Washington-on-the-Brazos. Houston already had dispatched orders for Fannin to rendezvous at the Cibolo, a creek north of Bexar, for the purpose of reinforcing the Alamo. If this report from Jason were true, Fannin would be marching into a death trap with Santa Anna waiting at San Antonio, Ramirez y Sesma maneuvering to the east, and Urrea on his flank.

"I agree with your concern about panic at Gonzales," Houston told Jason, "but I must countermand my orders immediately." He dismounted and wrote orders for Fannin to retreat from Goliad northeast to Victoria there to await orders for a new rendezvous point. "Jason, this is a tough assignment. Are you up to riding hard and dodging musket fire?"

"I'm fine, General. Where should we rendezvous on my return?"

"I don't know. Somewhere between Gonzales and San Felipe. Now ride!"

As Jason dashed away toward Goliad, Hockley asked Houston what they could do to prevent panic from sweeping Gonzales. "I'll think of something," Houston said, spurring his horse into a gallop.

Just outside the settlement, Houston reined up. "George, you are now chief of staff of the Army of Texas. Go to that camp on the river and tell Burleson he is in command until I arrive. Tell him to make a strong speech about what sacrifices may be necessary, but that rumors about the Alamo or an enemy invasion must wait until scouts have verified them. Then find Deaf Smith and Henry Karnes. I'll want to talk to them in the settlement."

Hockley was puzzled. He had known Houston since he was a congressman, but never had he seen him change plans, bark orders and operate with such haste. The thirty-four-year-old Hockley tried to make sense of the fast-breaking events that had disrupted the few strategic plans that had been made. What if Jason couldn't find Fannin? What if Fannin were already under siege or defeated? He sighed, then spurred his horse toward the river.

When Houston rode into the town square, the Tejanos from Bexar were pouring out details of the Alamo disaster to a gathering of sobbing women and children. Amid the despair, Houston's imposing figure on his big horse was welcome indeed. With the two volunteers flanking him, Houston shouted in a booming voice, "Arrest those men

as spies! This is nothing more than a Mexican trick to spread panic!"
As the gathering turned to Houston, he pointed toward the
Guadalupe. "We already have a large army assembling! Do not be
afraid! We will soon meet the enemy!" And tipping his wide felt hat,
he rode toward the camp on the river. On the way, he met Deaf
Smith, considered by some to be the best scout among the Texans.

With many friends on both sides of the conflict, Smith had
remained neutral in the revolution until Mexican soldiers fired on him
when he attempted to return to his family at Bexar. That episode had
prompted him to join Burleson's force in the Texan siege of San
Antonio and he had recently reported to Gonzales. Though hard of
hearing, he was not deaf; some even said he had a peculiar ability to
hear distant sounds, particularly at night. Houston immediately
dispatched him to San Antonio to learn the true situation.

At the camp, Burleson prepared to make the requested speech to
the assembled troops. Though popular with his men, Burleson was not
an accomplished speaker. Besides, he thought, without accurate intelligence, what could he say about the enemy?

He strolled alone by the Guadalupe, its green waters graying in
the late afternoon. Oaks and willows cast long spidery shadows onto
the water. An air of quiet loneliness had settled over the camp, most of
the men silently cleaning weapons and preparing meals. They are
discouraged, he thought, but steadfast or they would have pulled out
with the first dreadful news of the fall of the Alamo.

"Assemble the garrison," he called to Hockley, turning back to
stand beside a large oak tree. When the men had gathered, he began.
"Men, you will soon be under the command of General Sam Houston,
commander-in-chief of the Army of Texas. Until he arrives, I remain
in command of this garrison and we will conduct ourselves in an
orderly manner.

"As you know, the enemy, with a force of two thousand, is
rumored to be on its way. These rumors have not been confirmed. If
our scouts confirm them, we will prepare ourselves for whatever
action may be necessary."

Some of the men whispered to their friends nearby. Fighting
against those odds would be suicide, with no fortification and only
two small cannons.

"I want to commend the many volunteers who have come from
the United States to aid our cause. The Lord willing, some other
rumors, good ones, will be confirmed that there are hundreds more
volunteers on the way." Applause and a few cheers followed that
statement.

Burleson continued in a forthright tone. "If you are captured,
Santa Anna has declared you will be put to the sword. You will never
survive as a prisoner in this war. Be prepared to fight to the death."
When no one responded to that harsh statement, Burleson wondered if

half of these men might desert during the night. But they were entitled to know the truth and he continued in calm, measured tones. "Men, right here at Gonzales, our noble cause of liberty was brought to bear. This is hallowed ground, the 'Lexington of Texas,' where a few patriots routed a much larger enemy force this past year. Those brave men refused to surrender their cannon to the enemy. 'Come and take it,' they said to the enemy, and I say, that if the enemy wants Gonzales, they can come and take us!" Whoops and cheers rose.

"Men, if what we hear is true, all our compatriots in the Alamo have perished, fighting for liberty. Thermopolae had her messenger of defeat; the Alamo had none! You men from the United States should be proud of David Crockett and all the volunteers who fought to the death alongside the Texans. Liberty is the tie that binds us together!"

Though Burleson had barely raised his stern voice, the men cheered wildly. One of Sherman's volunteers from Kentucky hoisted his rifle and yelled: "Let's go get 'em!"

"Hold your horses!" Burleson shouted. "Our course is to wait for accurate information on the enemy. General Houston will present the plan. Keep your weapons clean and your powder dry. Good night and God bless you."

Campfires were glowing when Houston stepped from the shadows and approached Burleson. "That was a fine speech, Ed. You ought to consider politics."

"You were here? Why didn't you make the speech?"

"Because I don't have anything to say. I'm waiting to hear from Deaf Smith."

Houston was weighing contingencies. He recalled that Burleson was from Mina, which could become a strategic staging area for a Mexican force, northwest of Gonzales.

"Were there any volunteers stationed at Mina when you left, Ed?"

"There was a unit of Austin's rangers, about twenty-two men under Judge Williamson."

Organized by Stephen F. Austin to protect colonists from Indian raids, the rangers were the most skillful fighters in Texas. As badly as Houston wanted those men in his army, he knew that if Santa Anna moved as rapidly into the interior as he had moved on San Antonio, the civilian population would suffer. He wrote orders to Williamson not to leave Mina until all civilians had been removed to safety. Then he posted guards in the Gonzales settlement to prevent looting. Houston believed the Alamo had fallen, but he wanted to buy every precious minute to make plans and maintain order.

Houston was approached by Moseley Baker of San Felipe, a thirty-three-year-old firebrand of the War Party. Baker, who had fought at Gonzales in October and during the Texan siege of Bexar, was a close friend of Travis'. He was not an admirer of Houston.

"General," he said, "I want to know why we're not marching to San Antonio de Bexar."

"Moseley, I'm not about to order any troops anywhere until I hear from Deaf Smith."

"General, my family is at San Felipe. This settlement and all those north of here are in utmost jeopardy. If we don't stop the Mexicans soon, they're going to overrun all of Texas. We have to stand and fight."

"Santa Anna has six thousand men under arms in Texas. We would be fools to try to contest him at this time."

"Why didn't Fannin reinforce Travis?"

"I'm not one to cry over spilt milk, Captain," he said slowly, "and I assume Colonel Fannin had logistical problems that could not be overcome. I ordered him to reinforce Travis, and you know that the General Council had undermined my authority; this is history. We must hope the new governmental authority will be respected by Fannin and all others."

Baker finally relaxed. "I'm sorry, Sam, these past few weeks have been hell. You know Buck Travis and I were close friends, fought together, drank together, and worked together for independence. It won't ever be the same in San Felipe without Buck. I know he's dead, and what hurts so much is I know he didn't have a chance. We forced the issue with Santa Anna and he's hitting us with three times more than we expected, and sooner. I know we can't attack at Bexar, but we must hold the line at the Guadalupe or the Colorado."

"Moseley, I don't know where we can hold the line. We need more troops, and we need to train what we have along the way. That won't be easy, particularly with the spring rains coming on. We must catch the enemy off guard, and that won't be easy either."

"What's your strategy?"

"I won't have a strategy until I hear from Deaf Smith. And I won't have a true estimate of our potential strength until I hear from Fannin."

After Baker left, Houston summoned Sherman. "I understand your men are trained militia," Houston said.

"Yes, they're ready to fight. Sooner the better."

"What did you see along the way?"

"Some settlers already fleeing their homes, others preparing to join your army. I would guess you are due at least three hundred volunteers in a matter of days."

"We may have only a matter of days to prepare for battle."

"Yes, I know, but I believe these men are each worth ten of the enemy. They are more genuinely motivated and they have more accurate weapons."

"I hope, Mr. Sherman, that you will not underestimate the enemy. The stories you heard about the fall skirmishes and Texan siege of Bexar were heartening to our cause, but the Mexicans had yet to put their best foot forward. Santa Anna is no Cós, nor is Urrea. These generals mean business and they know what they're doing. Plus the fact they have us outnumbered about six to one."

"You paint a bleak picture, General," Sherman said, puffing on a pipe. "We came to fight. We're ready."

"I appreciate your confidence and enthusiasm, Mr. Sherman," Houston said, "and I hope you will balance them with a little patience. We need additional troops, and we need time to prepare them for battle."

"I'm a newcomer to Texas," Sherman said, "but as I stated, we're anxious to engage the enemy. How do you plan to organize the army?"

Houston was unprepared for that question. He assumed Sherman was probing for a major command position. Though he didn't take to Sherman personally, he was still impressed, and from what he had heard, Sherman was an effective organizer. "I'll make some decisions along these lines in a day or so."

Later, Houston reviewed the list of officers at Gonzales and summoned Colonel James Clinton Neill. Like Houston, Neill had served under General Jackson in the War of 1812. And it was Neill who had commanded the remnant of the victorious Texan force at Bexar, the nucleus of the Alamo defenders. Though his tiny garrison had been underfed and without funds, its eighteen operational cannons had prompted Neill to write Governor Smith that he would engage one thousand of the enemy rather than surrender.

Neill had made two critical strategic decisions — to concentrate his small contingent in the Alamo, and later to refuse Houston's order to abandon the old mission. Houston would have considered this refusal as rank insubordination had not Bowie agreed with Neill. Still, Houston had not had a direct explanation from either and he was anxious to question Neill.

"James, won't you have a little nip with me?" Houston asked.

Neill had been braced for a fierce tongue-lashing. Surprised, he gladly accepted the cup of whiskey and stretched his long legs as Houston resumed. "I suppose you know, James, that all is probably lost at Bexar?"

"Yes."

"And I suppose you know I have been without a valid explanation of why you and Bowie insisted on disobeying my orders?"

"Very well," Neill said. "After so many of our people went home, and the hotheads left for Matamoros, I had only eighty effective men. But Sam, I had twenty-four pieces of artillery. Do you know what that's worth? Do you realize how much firepower that represents in a concentrated area? So we moved the eighteen operational cannons into the Alamo."

132

"James, you still had only eighty men. You knew they couldn't hold out under heavy siege."

"I had no means of transporting the artillery. Besides, there was enough activity to keep our hopes alive. Bowie came with a few men, then Travis brought his group, and there was talk of Fannin bringing three hundred men. But the deciding factors remained the number of artillery pieces and the fact we couldn't transport them from Bexar."

"All right, James. When you had to leave, why did you relinquish your command to Travis?"

"Sam, I had never known young Travis well, but I had heard he was one who didn't drink too much or get discouraged in adversity, a condition which, Lord knows, we had at Bexar. Bowie had been my friend and yours, but his despair over losing his family seemed worse at Bexar than elsewhere. He had taken to drinking hard, and had even turned some men loose from jail over Judge Seguin's bitter protest. Officers must respect the law, and set an example of discipline. Under the circumstances, Travis was the logical choice."

Houston placed his half-filled cup of whiskey on the table. "All right, James, thank you." After Neill had departed, Houston shuffled through the personnel lists again. One name kept returning, the one man he could entrust with the future of Texas should he be removed from the scene; it had to be Edward Burleson. He was the only one in this mixed bag who could command respect, who was a competent organizer, and who remained calm under pressure.

Houston reviewed the list once more, searching for deeper insight: Sherman was suave and assured, but lacked meaningful military experience; Neill was qualified, but with less command experience than Burleson; Baker was emotional, prone to snap judgments; Seguin was impressive, but Anglo support for him was doubtful. For the first time during that long day and night, Houston was encouraged. At least he had a strong nucleus of leadership. He summoned Burleson.

"Ed, we're going to organize these volunteers who want to be soldiers. We'll begin with one regiment. You'll command with the rank of colonel, and as such, be second in command of the army. I have veto power over your choice for lieutenant colonel, however. Organize the infantry how you want, letting volunteers elect company commanders, but get it done so we can start drills tomorrow."

Burleson had expected this assignment; he had thought through the same list as Houston. "What do you think of this dandy from Kentucky?" he asked.

"I don't like him, but that doesn't mean he's not qualified."

"He's too fancy for some men," Burleson said, "but a lot of them are impressed."

"Well," Houston smiled, "it might be good politics to have someone from outside Texas in a high command position. We expect hundreds more, and they would probably like to see newcomers recognized by us old warhorses."

"All right, Sherman it is; we'll make him lieutenant colonel under me."

"Neill should be commander of artillery," Houston said.

"Fine. What about cavalry?"

"Seguin might be the best choice," Houston said, "but I want to sleep on that, perhaps defer it until after we hear from Deaf Smith. I trust you have found farriers?"

"We have two with experience, who assure me they can keep horses shod and wagons repaired for an army three times our size."

"Take special care of them. Right now, I'd rather have two experienced farriers than ten cannons," Houston mused, "but don't tell Neill I said that."

It was late and both men were tired. Burleson yawned. "I'll have things moving tomorrow. We'll start drills and formal posting of guard duty."

"One other thing, Ed. Move the camp to the east side of the settlement in that open prairie. We can assemble and drill better there. If the enemy comes, I want the Guadalupe between them and us."

"We're not going to retreat, are we?"

"We may have to retreat, Ed. Remember, we know this country; they don't."

After Burleson departed, Houston lay on his blanket for an hour, unable to sleep. He had often prayed with the Cherokees to the Great Spirit, but with his return to Anglo life, he had neglected the Almighty. Now he found himself praying for guidance.

On the following day, more than a hundred additional volunteers reported to the new camp east of the settlement while a few civilians, accepting the Tejanos' reports from Bexar, departed for safety. That night it was quiet as the men, weary of drilling, turned in early.

Smith returned the next day. He had met Mrs. Dickinson en route from Bexar and escorted her to Gonzales where her report caused some panic. She did not know the size of the alleged enemy force advancing under Ramirez y Sesma, but she had heard a Mexican officer refer to it as *muy grande*, or very large.

Hearing the news, Houston swung into action, riding the streets, and calling for citizens to prepare to evacuate: "Join the army's march! Don't panic!"

He then negotiated with Ben Gates for provisions and ammunition from his store, a brief transaction since Ben was anxious to depart. "I'm more concerned about my son than this store," he said. "When will he return?"

"I expect Jason in another day or two, but we'll be in retreat. If you want to head for Nacogdoches, that might be wise. I'll be

134

corresponding with the Raguet family there and will send word about Jason."

Houston released from jail the bewildered Tejanos from Bexar, who thought they had provided a service by warning the settlement. Then he dashed to the camp, and without dismounting, called for Colonel Neill. "James, we can't transport the artillery. Dump those two cannons into the Guadalupe."

Neill was crestfallen. If there was one equalizer in this unequal contest, it was artillery. "Sam, can't we make a sacrifice and haul these cannons? I have grapeshot and canisters prepared."

"We're traveling light. Bring the ammunition, but dump the cannons in the river. That's an order!"

Houston rode by the campfires, calling for Burleson and Sherman. He barked brief instructions to prepare for a march to the northeast.

"To where?" Burleson asked.

"To the northeast," Houston replied.

"But it's almost dark," Sherman said.

"We're marching in one hour," Houston said. "After everything is packed and ready, have all the men assemble here."

Houston summoned Juan Seguin, who at twenty-nine had a reputation as a tough, resourceful commander, alternately daring and elusive. He was alive only because Travis had sent him from the Alamo to seek reinforcements. Houston also had summoned Deaf Smith and Henry Karnes, a twenty-three-year-old daredevil who had earned a reputation for cunning almost equal to Smith's. As sunset fell on the camp, the men met under a large oak tree.

Houston glanced about him to make certain no one was in hearing. "You three are to carry out secret missions. You will report directly to me and no one else. If I should be removed from the scene, Burleson will assume command of the army.

"Seguin, your primary responsibility is to protect our retreat. Keep your men between us and the enemy at all times. In addition, when you can, make sure enemy scouts don't learn our location and strength. Use whatever means are necessary. Find out as well all you can about enemy activity, but report only to me. Smith, you and Karnes, if anyone asks, will be cavalry officers. However, a sensitive scouting mission, or courier duty, may fall on one or both of you. Gentlemen, you are among the most trusted in this cause. Rumors, true or false, can tear this army apart. I'm not going to risk the fate of this republic on rumors or the emotional pleadings of firebrands. I'm going to base my decisions on accurate information and you gentlemen must provide it. Any questions?"

"With enemy strength so much greater than ours, I suggest we take another step," Seguin said. "The enemy will expect to reap supplies from abandoned settlements, such as this one. I believe we

135

should burn these settlements in their path. The enemy will find the land hostile for their needs."

Houston arose to gaze at Gonzales. How much work had gone into building that settlement, and how little its widows would have left to rebuild their shattered lives. But if the enemy learned of the Texan retreat, they might not even come this way. Houston realized he was rationalizing. Of course, Seguin is right, he thought, but Lord, to burn this town after what it has been through? He turned away.

"Put three of the army's baggage wagons at the disposal of civilians," he said to Seguin. "That's all we can possibly spare. We will delay the march until all civilians are evacuated. Put the torch to the town three hours after the march begins. Perhaps they won't see it."

Houston joined the men who were packing their belongings and weapons. Some were grumbling about the retreat while a few others were contemplating desertion. Texas settlers worried about their families, scattered throughout the province. Houston knew he should make a speech before leading the retreat, but his usual politician's zest for speech-making had vanished.

Before the troops assembled, Houston penned a report to James Collinsworth, chairman of the Military Committee of the convention, still in progress at Washington-on-the-Brazos: *"You may rest assured that I shall adopt and pursue such course of conduct as the present emergencies of the country require, and as the means placed at my disposal may enable me to do, for the defense of the country and the protection of its inhabitants."* Houston's penchant for ambiguity would confound friend and foe throughout the uncertain campaign he was preparing to launch.

He next wrote a long letter to his old friend and benefactor in Nacogdoches, Henry Raguet, estimating his force at almost five hundred, and recounting the Alamo battle from Mrs. Dickinson's report. He alluded to the loss of their mutual friend, Jim Bowie, and took a hard swipe at the General Council of the defunct provisional state government that *"has already cost us the lives of more than two hundred and thirty brave men. Had it not been for that we should have kept all the advantages which we had gained. We must repair our losses by prudence and valour. I have no doubt as to the issue of the contest. I am in good spirits, though not ardent!"*

In both letters Houston mentioned Fannin's failure to reinforce the Alamo. He would communicate with trusted friends about that disastrous decision, but continued to keep the subject out of camp talk or public debate.

When Seguin informed him the town was completely abandoned, Houston rode before a long column to join Burleson who awaited his order to start the march. Houston's decision was to retreat northeast to Burnham's Crossing on the Colorado River. He believed that any

Mexican advance to the west would move first to Mina, up the Colorado from Burnham's, while an enemy column moving centrally would come first to Gonzales. He told only Burleson, in the strictest confidence, of the retreat route. "If I should be removed from the picture, Ed, take them to San Felipe. By that time, most of the American volunteers en route could be melded into this force."

The men doused their campfires and lit torches. Houston could see many frightened faces among the civilians. The soldiers stood quietly at attention, gazing towards their commander, a towering figure mounted on his great stallion. Houston removed his hat and spoke in a strong, measured tone: "I know this is a bitter experience for you people of Gonzales, who must leave your beloved homes. Nothing is more sacred to a family than its home, built from the wonderful woods that abound here, filled by the nourishing crops you have worked so hard, and blessed by the Almighty. May God help us win this war so that you may return here in peace and tranquility. Men, we face an arduous campaign. Santa Anna has massacred all our compatriots in the Alamo, but they bought us precious time with their sacred blood. We have time to maneuver, to gain strength, to prepare ourselves for battle. They fought like Spartans, and so must we, but we must choose carefully the time and place of battle. Men, we must retreat, but we shall never surrender! I make you that pledge — we shall never surrender!" Finally, most of the men cheered, but only briefly. Houston waved his felt hat to the northeast and shouted the order to move out.

It was almost midnight when they heard explosions in the distance and saw a bright orange glow on the horizon. By then, the civilians were weary and reconciled to the loss of their settlement. So there was little reaction when word spread that their town had been put to the torch by the retreating Texans.

In that chill March night on the prairie, despair swept the women and children who had struggled, with husbands and fathers now dead, to build their homes and carve out a living in that small settlement founded by Green DeWitt. Regardless of the outcome of the war, they had already lost all that counted in their lives. "It's just as well DeWitt died last year," sighed one of the civilians. "Seeing the town burn again would have killed him."

A native of Kentucky, DeWitt had become a successful *empressario* in 1825, with a large land grant for a four-hundred-family colony he named for Rafael Gonzales, then governor of Coahuila and Texas. Rebuilt in 1827 after being burned by Indians, Gonzales had grown to a population of almost two thousand before DeWitt died. Houston learned later from Seguin that the loudest explosions in Gonzales, which had drawn the attention of the marching citizens and soldiers, had not been caused by gunpowder, but by barrels of whiskey.

Houston gave the order to halt the march for the remainder of the night and ordered heavy security posted between his position and the Guadalupe. During the pre-dawn hours, twenty-five men deserted. They fled to the north and east, and rumors went with them, touching off panic. The "Runaway Scrape" was soon in full progress, as Texan settlers evacuated with their hastily-gathered belongings, many without adequate means for hauling. Therefore women and children were required to trudge along, carrying whatever they could.

As Houston prepared to resume the march, Burleson brought news of the desertions. Sherman and Baker were not far behind. "This will happen again," snapped Baker. "No man worth his salt is going to follow you around, wandering across prairies with no plan of battle. I say it's time to make a stand."

"Moseley," Houston said, "there's a fine line between courage and stupidity."

"I'm in no mood for any of your two-bit philosophy. When and where are we going to make a stand?"

"We're better off without those men," Houston said. "If they're scared of a night march, they'd cut and run when the first enemy shot is fired. And I'll tell you, Moseley, why I'm not going to make battle plans in the middle of a prairie. For one thing, there's no enemy in sight and we're not prepared. Furthermore, if I had announced some grand battle plan yesterday, those deserters would be telling it every place they go. The enemy would soon hear it."

Baker stalked away, shaking his head. Sherman agreed with Baker, but remained silent, unwilling to risk his high command position in a quarrel with Houston. He wondered why Burleson seemed unperturbed over the desertions, and why Houston would make no strategic plans, but he chose to bide his time.

After Sherman and Baker had left Houston's campsite, Burleson sat down for a cup of coffee. "We can't afford to lose that many men every night, Sam."

"I know, Ed, I know. But we're going to have others desert to take care of their families. We can't blame them for that, and they'll probably return. The tougher problem is going to be morale, what with Moseley and the other firebrands clamoring for an immediate engagement. I'm not going to be stampeded, Ed. I'm not going to march this army into a death trap."

138

Chapter 14

WHILE Houston's army organized at Gonzales, Jason Gates spurred his horse down the Guadalupe River trail in search of Fannin. Instead, he found a small Mexican scouting party that forced him to deviate from his course and hide in a thicket of mesquite for almost an hour. He finally crossed the Guadalupe about thirty-five miles from Goliad, where he met a small group of settlers, dragging their belongings on rough sleds pulled by mules.

"Where are you from?" Jason asked.

An old settler by the lead mule tipped his hat. "We're from Agua Dulce, San Patricio and Refugio. The Mexicans have overrun all that country."

Jason held his breath. Those settlements were south of Goliad; perhaps Fannin was still holding out. "Any idea where Colonel Fannin may be?"

"Don't know," said the old settler. "We steered clear of Goliad 'cause we heard the Mexicans were there. All our country is gone, son. You may as well join us."

"I must go to Goliad," Jason said, "You people had better head toward San Felipe. The Alamo has fallen and the Mexican army will soon be at Gonzales."

"Lord help us," the settler said, hoisting his barefoot son onto the mule. "Let's get moving."

Late in the afternoon of March 14, Jason reined up in sight of Goliad. Fannin, if he were still in this area, would probably have remained in the large presidio, La Bahia, located on a hill east of the mission. Riding closer, he spotted a lookout on the northwest point of the huge presidio, a Texan waving at him. As he waved back, Jason heard the sharp crack of a musket shot and a copper ball whizzed past his right ear. Lowering his head, he spurred his horse toward the presidio, heard two more musket shots along the way, and dashed into the compound unharmed. Dismounting, he saw to his dismay that his horse had been crippled with a slashing thigh wound. One of the guards led the bleeding horse away and shot him.

Jason was escorted through several dimly-lighted rooms in the western wing of the compound to where Colonel Fannin maintained his headquarters. Jason had swallowed his intense dislike for this commander who had schemed for command of the Texas forces and then failed to reinforce the Alamo, because Fannin was needed, desperately, to build up Houston's little army. Jason presented the orders to Fannin.

"I hear the Mexicans gave you a warm welcome," Fannin smiled.

"A little too warm. I lost my horse."

"That's unfortunate. I'm afraid we have no replacements. This country is full of wild mustangs, but it is also full of Mexicans."

"Are you under siege?"

"No, only a few small units to harrass us. Nothing too serious."

"I suppose you know the Alamo has fallen?"

"Yes, we received word five days ago, just before receiving the order for the Cibolo rendezvous. I surmised Houston must have written it before learning of the Alamo's fall, so I remained here. I trust he is aware we did make an attempt to reinforce the Alamo garrison?"

Jason bit his lip and nodded as Fannin began reading the new orders. He looked up. "I cannot retreat at this time," he said. "There are too many men unaccounted for south of here."

"Sir, I suggest you consider the time. I encountered a Mexican scouting party near the Guadalupe. They could have a major force between yours and General Houston's any day."

"Perhaps, but those men are still unaccounted for."

"Some colonists from settlements to the south said the Mexicans had overrun that country."

"Some colonists? Surely, you don't think I would make a major strategic decision without information from my own scouts?"

"General Houston has already made the decision."

Fannin's face paled, and he pointed a trembling finger at Jason. "You, sir, are impertinent! An officer does not question the judgment of his superior. This order from General Houston states a withdrawal to Victoria should be commenced 'as soon as practicable.' Does it not occur to you that General Houston has the good sense to give me some discretion in determining the time of a withdrawal?"

Jason was no match for Fannin, who had seized on those four words to reject an immediate retreat. Jason suspected Fannin hoped some of his impulsive colleagues might have divided Urrea's forces, making the presidio at least a tenable defensive position, or at best for Fannin, a staging area for more volunteers expected by sea from the United States. If Fannin's force were beefed up rapidly, he might even try to move against Santa Anna himself.

In the shadows of the candle burning on Fannin's desk, Jason felt alone and out of place. He had no horse, money, nor provisions, but staying in this fortress was almost unbearable. He rose from his seat, requesting permission to be dismissed. Fannin blandly granted the request, adding a suggestion. "We have two fine outfits of volunteers from America, the New Orleans Greys and John Shackelford's group from Alabama. Why don't you join Shackelford's unit temporarily? After we move out, you might find a horse."

Jason reported to Shackelford, a doctor who was captain of the Alabama volunteers, nicknamed the "Red Rovers," because they all were uniformed in red jeans. If any rebel unit qualified as "perfidious foreigners from the United States of the North," this was such a group, armed from the Alabama state arsenal.

"Dr. Jack" took Jason under his arm with a hearty welcome. After Jason finished his evening meal, Dr. Jack offered to show him around the compound. They climbed to the lookout tower from where Jason had been hailed that afternoon and Dr. Jack pointed to the nearby San Antonio River. "You said Houston wants us to retreat to Victoria. I'm no general, but with this fort, that mission compound, plus adequate water and provisions, we have an area that could be held."

Jason viewed the landscape as dusk settled across the prairie of scattered mesquite and dry grass. "You mentioned provisions are low. That is critical should Urrea lay siege on this area."

"Provisions are low because we have no plan. Game and fish abound in this country. All you have to do is go after them. But because we've had no plan, we've let the Mexicans scare us from doing anything."

"I take it you don't have much confidence in Colonel Fannin?"

"He's a troubled, confused man. One faction of the provisional state government supported his plans for the capture of Matamoros, consolidation of various forces, and other moves, while the other faction continued to support Houston, who vanished for weeks to negotiate with the Indians. That kind of confusion will tear up any army, and most any man."

"It didn't tear up the defense of the Alamo."

"Don't get me wrong, son. I was one of the few officers who spoke out time and again for marching to Bexar. It was a group decision to turn back; you can't put the blame on Fannin."

"Did he speak out for continuing the march?"

"He was hesitant."

"And so all the brave warriors retired safely to Fort Defiance."

"I understand how you feel. I assure you I felt it was best to meet the main enemy force at Bexar, and I wouldn't have renamed this fort either."

"Fort Defiance isn't such a bad name, Doctor Shackelford. After all, Fannin has defied General Houston and the interests of Texan independence."

141

"Son, this is a confused situation. You want to win by swift action, but how can you, with no military organization or stable government? I won't defend Fannin's decisions, but I won't call him a coward either."

"Don't you think we increase our danger by staying in this fort without adequate provisions?"

"Yes, but Urrea doesn't have enough men to lay a full siege on this fortress. That would take half of Santa Anna's army and I suspect Santa Anna is more interested in destroying Houston's army."

"So does General Houston. That's why he needs Fannin's troops."

"But we still have two or three hundred men scattered to the south. I admit the rumors are discouraging, but I can't blame Colonel Fannin for wanting to verify them."

They walked down from the tower to the church, Our Lady of Loreto Chapel. It was a quiet, comforting sanctuary with thick walls and a high arched ceiling. At the two-tiered altar, several candles lighted a colorful mosaic of religious figures, and the statue of Our Lady of Loreto.

"Are you Catholic?" asked Dr. Jack.

"Yes and no," Jason replied. "Resident Texans were all Catholic until the declaration was signed, but I'm a Protestant at heart."

"So am I. Yet I love this chapel. Such an ornate well-designed place of worship, to be inside a fortress, intrigues me. They must have been a deeply religious people. The mission, only a stone's throw from here, also has an exquisite chapel. Can you imagine how impressive this must have been when this whole area was nothing but wilderness?"

"Doctor, you've fallen in love with this country."

"Let's say I appreciate human endeavor. That's why I opposed changing the name of this presidio. The Spaniards created this majestic structure — let the name and tradition remain."

They strolled into the vast open area between the chapel and barracks. Most of the four hundred men in La Bahia were preparing to sleep. Within the compound, a few dark green *anaqua* trees and some retamas broke the monotony of the level ground.

"Each corner of the fortress has an elevated platform," said Dr. Jack, "where you can mount artillery and post lookouts. The holes in these walls give perfect protection for riflemen. With all this space to store ammunition and provisions, this fort could be held against a force ten times its number."

Jason became more impressed with the sprawling compound as a fortification. It was far more defensible than the Alamo had been, despite all the efforts to fortify that old mission. Perhaps Dr. Jack is right, Jason thought. Perhaps Houston is moving hastily in ordering this fort abandoned. After all, if Urrea is not contained, he will sweep the entire coastal area before uniting with another Mexican force.

"What brought you here?" Jason asked.

"Oh, a combination of things," the fifty-year-old doctor answered. "My son, Temple, wanted to come to Texas, and the opportunity to try a new life in an open country was compelling. We plan to settle here after the war."

"You should see Gonzales then, and San Felipe and Nacogdoches. Since you're fond of the presidio and mission here, you would love San Antonio de Bexar as well."

"I want to see it all, to become a part of the new tradition, but still to preserve the past. A man dedicated to that idea is Stephen F. Austin. He inspected us upon our arrival at the coast, and impressed me as a man of high caliber and unquestioned integrity."

"No doubt about that," Jason said. "He has accomplished a great deal in the past twelve years, bringing settlers to Texas. Some of us felt he was tardy in taking on the Mexicans. However, looking back, I suppose he had good reason. He had worked so long with Mexican authorities that he honestly believed negotiations could prevent war."

Dr. Jack shrugged. "Who can say? Let me show you where to bed down."

Despite the massive walls of the south barracks, a cool damp breeze and a thick fog had drifted across the plains from the Gulf of Mexico, causing Jason to shiver under his thin blanket. Fatigue had set in, but he couldn't sleep. Finally, he walked outside the barracks and took a stroll through the eerie knee-high fog in the plaza. He walked to the chapel to pray for his family, and upon returning, saw an old man sitting by the door, puffing on a corncob pipe.

"Aren't you cold, sitting there?" Jason asked.

"I got me a warm-blooded companion here," the old man said, hoisting a jug of whiskey to his whiskered face. "Have a nip?"

"I guess a little won't hurt," Jason said, accepting the jug. The liquor burned his tongue, but he gulped it down without flinching. "You aren't wearing red jeans," he added, "so you're not from Alabama."

"I'm from Georgia," said the old man.

"What brought you here?"

"I ain't never had much, workin' for other folks, always in debt. My kids is grown, my wife died of malaria last year. When I learnt about all the land they was givin' away in Texas, I come first chance I got. Land is worth fightin' fer. If I had me some land, why I'd be contented as a turtle sunnin' on a log. If I don't git killed, I'm gonna have somethin' to show for my life."

The whiskey had relaxed Jason for the first time during that long, frustrating day. Wiping his mouth after his second drink, he laughed as the old man studied him. "You in trouble?" he asked Jason.

"No, just tired, and worried, I guess. I left my family at Gonzales. The Mexicans may be there by now, for all I know."

"Son, there's no sense in worryin'. You git like me and you're jest too darn old to worry. All I do is wonder when we're gonna fight. But I'll be ready when the time comes."

"So will I, but I can't help wondering if my family is safe. Sir, do you mind if I have just one more sip?"

"Go ahead."

Jason took a long, slow pull on the jug. Gazing across the plaza, he watched the fog thicken as though a cloud were descending into the compound. Warm, with his mind dulled, he soon fell asleep. The old man carried Jason into the barracks and laid him down for the night.

Jason awoke the next morning with his first hangover, but grateful for the sleep. The garrison continued its routine, as rumors abounded that Urrea's forces had wiped out the Texas contingents scattered to the south. The following day Colonel Albert C. Horton of Matagorda arrived with twenty-seven men, and enough oxen to transport the artillery and supplies.

Two days later, on March 18, an enemy force appeared on the opposite side of the San Antonio River. Men rushed to the artillery batteries and riflemen took their stations. Horton opened the attack, moving from the presidio toward the mission, as Texan rifle fire pierced the air. Horton, however, was badly outnumbered, and Dr. Jack raced to Fannin's command post. "Aren't you going to send him some help?"

Fannin was observing the action through a field glass. "Do you want to go?" he asked, without removing the glass from his eye.

"Yes."

"Then go."

Shackelford dashed down the western line of the presidio, shouting, "Rovers, follow me!" The Alabama contingent scrambled outside the fort, running toward the mission, Jason at their heels. As they neared the river, a cannonade from the presidio shook the earth. Though at a numerical advantage, the thundering of artillery put the Mexicans to flight.

Shackelford and Horton met near the river. "Fannin should have let us join the fight," Horton said. "He scared 'em off with the cannonade."

"I can't complain," Dr. Jack said. "We have no casualties."

"I guess you're right. Your men came flying down here so fast, it confused the enemy. I still would have liked to wipe out that bunch of . . . " Horton broke off, seeing Fannin approach, holding a crumpled piece of parchment.

"I have official word," Fannin said, clenching his fist. "Grant, King, Ward, all apparently lost. Gentlemen, prepare to march for Victoria. We leave first thing in the morning."

After packing that night, Jason sat down by the old man from Georgia. Another fog was rolling in from the coast, more dense than

144

on Jason's first night at La Bahia. "I don't like that fog," said the old man. "It's a bad omen."

"Don't tell me you believe in omens?"

"Call it omens or good sense. I never work or hunt in a fog. Might step on a moccasin or a bear trap."

"The country we'll cover tomorrow is mostly open plains. Besides, this fog will lift in the morning."

"Don't be so sure, son. This is heavy weather. Sometimes fog don't lift in weather like this."

Dr. Jack's son, Temple, joined them, excited about the move to Victoria and the rendezvous with Houston's army. "I've heard so much about General Houston," he said. "Dad told me Andrew Jackson thinks more of him than anyone who ever fought under him."

"I reckon Old Hickory likes Sam Houston 'cause Houston is one of his best political pals," the old man said.

Jason laughed. "In Texas, the military and politics go hand in hand. The best fighters get elected to the best political offices."

"Nothin' wrong with that," said the old man, "but if they ain't some good fighters around here, there ain't gonna be no political offices."

Jason and Temple laughed. They soon turned in for the night, leaving the old man to nip his corn whiskey as the heavy fog laid into the presidio.

The next day, the dense fog stayed almost waist-high as Jason joined the men for breakfast. Horton had already left to reconnoiter the trail. A large ambush could lie unseen in that fog, Jason thought, but anxious to leave, he considered the risk worth taking.

At the lower ford, a team pulling a cannon bogged down. Dr. Jack and several of the Rovers, with Jason, waded in to put their shoulders to the wheels, finally powering the gun carriage up the bank. Valuable time had been lost, but at least the fog was lifting. The march proceeded in a brisk, orderly fashion for about six miles, when Fannin called for a break to graze the oxen and horses. Dr. Jack approached Fannin. "Sir, I implore you to resume the march immediately. The Mexicans may be following and could surprise us with a cavalry attack. We have no cover or water."

"Doctor, calm down. You saw the enemy cut and run yesterday. They're not going to take us on."

"That was not Urrea's main force. We're about five miles from Coleto Creek. We must move now to reach its cover and water."

"These animals need to graze. We'll resume in an hour."

Dr. Jack returned to his men, shaking his head as he studied the map. "Jason, do you know any Spanish?"

"A little."

"According to this map, we're approaching the Plain de Perdido. What does 'perdido' mean?"

"It means lost."

The march had resumed for a few miles when Jason spotted an enemy cavalry force emerging from timber two miles west of Fannin's army. Coleto Creek lay ahead, perhaps a mile distant, and timber lay to Fannin's right and rear, but the army was caught on a barren, lonely plain without so much as a clump of brush to afford cover. Dr. Jack appeared at Fannin's side. "Colonel, we must make a run for the Coleto!"

"Horton should be able to open a path until . . ." Fannin's words trailed off as he watched the Mexican cavalry cut off the Texans' path to the creek. Hundreds of enemy infantry emerged from timber in all directions. Urrea had laid a trap and Fannin had marched right into it.

"Where in the devil is Horton?" Fannin shouted.

"Forget him," said Dr. Jack. "We must fight our way to the creek."

Rapidly scanning the plain around him, Fannin knew he must make a decision in a matter of seconds. "Form a square!" he shouted. "We fight here! Form a square!"

The Red Rovers and New Orleans Greys took the front line of the square. Other units manned the artillery batteries and riflemen took stations behind wagons and boxes, some lying prone on the ground. Fannin stood directly behind the right flank. "Hold your fire!" he shouted. "Hold your fire!"

It appeared as though the lost plain had become a giant amphitheater with the actors having carefully taken their places on center stage while a large audience was gathering quietly from all directions. The Mexican unit commanders, most of whom had never participated in a pitched battle, found it incredible that they were advancing, unchallenged, to within one hundred and fifty yards of Fannin's square. Jason and many of the other men were almost beside themselves to commence firing, but Fannin repeated his order. He knew precisely the effective range of the Mexican muskets and he wanted to lace them with a volley just outside that range, but close enough for every Texan shot to count. As the Mexicans approached to within one hundred yards, Fannin waved his saber downward. "Fire!" he shouted.

Clouds of smoke engulfed the plain as cannon and rifle fire tore into the advancing Mexican unit. The few Mexican soldiers who fought bravely forward were easy targets, although one charged within sixty yards of the square, took aim, and dropped Fannin with a painful thigh wound. A blast of grapeshot cut down that soldier as the Mexican attack force withdrew.

Dr. Jack dressed Fannin's wound. "How many do you think are out there, Doctor?" Fannin asked.

"Seven hundred or more. Has to be Urrea's main force."

146

"How many casualties have we sustained?"

"I'd guess twenty to twenty-five."

"Let's keep on fighting then. Maybe we can hold them at bay."

As Dr. Jack tied the bandage, he saw about three hundred Mexican cavalry forming to the rear. "Can you stand, Colonel?"

"Yes, I'll be all right." Gritting his teeth, Fannin pulled himself alongside a supply wagon. "Wheel those two cannons to the rear!" he shouted. "Load 'em with canisters and wait for my order to fire!"

Sabers drawn, the Mexican cavalry charged as Jason raced to the rear of the square, ducking under a wagon next to the old man from Georgia. Since the Mexican cavalry had no infantry support, Fannin allowed the enemy to advance within sixty yards, before he gave the order to fire. The two cannons, loaded with double canisters of musket balls, produced a withering spray of hot metal. Riflemen poured their volleys into the advancing cavalry, and the concentration of heavy fire sent scores of horses and riders tumbling to the ground, killed or wounded. The remainder retreated beyond range. Unknown to Fannin, Urrea himself had led that charge.

Jason slapped the old man on the back. "We're going to win this battle. We've got them on the run."

"Don't bet on it, son. Look over there, to the west."

Jason drew a long breath, seeing several hundred Mexican infantrymen crawling in the grass toward them. If Urrea had coordinated the cavalry charge with this infantry advance, the battle would have ended early in the afternoon. But with a few precious minutes to reload and regroup, the Texans repulsed the infantry attack. Several Mexicans landed deadly rounds in Fannin's impromptu square, but they were eventually shot or forced to retreat.

"I told you we were going to win this battle," Jason said, again slapping the old man on the back. But this time he did not respond. Jason rolled him over to find the old man badly wounded in the chest, gasping for breath.

"Don't worry. I'll fetch Dr. Jack." Jason scrambled up, but the old man stopped him.

"Hold on, son. I'm finished. If you git out of here write my oldest boy in Georgia. Here's a letter from him. I never learnt to read or write, but he can. He went to school for six whole years . . . Write him that I died fightin', and if they give land for my service, make sure my son knows about it. My children never had no land. They'd love to have some, I know. Will you do that fer me?"

"Sure I will, but you're going to be all right. I'll fetch Dr. Jack."

Jason vaulted over a gun carriage and returned with Dr. Jack to find the old man dead. Jason clutched the crumpled letter.

"You better take his pistol and rifle," said Dr. Jack. "They're no good to him anymore, and we need all the firepower we can get. I estimate we're outnumbered at least three to one."

The Texans dug in, but the Mexicans, after such heavy losses, were content with minor actions, firing from the grassy plain to avoid the Texans' concentrated volleys.

When all firing ceased at nightfall, Dr. Jack reported to Fannin casualties were seven killed, ten mortally wounded, and sixty seriously wounded, Fannin himself in that last category. Despite his painful wound, Fannin maintained his composure, and congratulated the officers. Later, he confided to Dr. Jack that their situation might be hopeless. "We can't hold here another day. We have no water."

"I know," said Dr. Jack. "Did you realize our cannons were too hot to fire again this afternoon? We needed water to sponge them."

Fannin stared dejectedly into the fire. "You were right about fighting to the Coleto. I put too much faith in Horton out front. I never thought they could cut us off. Could we transport the wounded to the Coleto, assuming we can fight our way there?"

"Some would die. How many I couldn't say. I'm afraid we're sealed in, unless Horton brings reinforcements from Victoria."

"That's unlikely. What do you think we should do?"

Dr. Jack gazed into the dwindling fire. "The doctor in me says surrender now for the sake of the wounded. The commander says fight our way out in the morning, when we can see."

"All right. I'll make the decision in the morning."

Jason drew guard duty until midnight, but found he couldn't sleep afterwards. He and Temple Shackleford buried the old man from Georgia, pausing at each false bugle call from the enemy camp. Those piercing calls continued throughout the night, the only sounds the men heard other than cries from their wounded comrades. Unable to sleep, many of the men dug trenches for the next day's combat.

Jason finally fell asleep about three hours before dawn, but was awakened by shouts to prepare for battle. The Mexican force had been increased during the night by five hundred troops from San Antonio de Bexar. In addition, Urrea's artillery had arrived. When the first cannonade whizzed over Fannin's camp, the psychological effect was profound. All hope for escape or victory vanished, but the determination to fight did not.

Fannin called a council of war after Dr. Jack reported he had seen the enemy raise a white flag, indicating a desire to parley. All but one officer opposed surrender at discretion.

"However," Fannin said, "I understand General Urrea is an honorable man, not cut from the Santa Anna cloth. It's possible we could obtain an honorable capitulation."

The officers considered this in silence. Finally, Dr. Jack spoke. "For the sake of the wounded, I will not oppose an honorable capitulation. But if terms cannot be agreed upon to guarantee the care of the wounded and the safety of all our men, I say let us fight to the death. Our graves are already dug in the trenches of this plain."

When no one responded, Fannin asked Major Wallace to write the articles for capitulation. Wallace prepared four articles with details for officer paroles and the transportation of American volunteers to Copano from where they could return to the United States. Fannin dispatched Wallace and two other officers who spoke Spanish to parley with the enemy.

Fannin's three officers met with two from Urrea's force, who indicated the Texan terms were acceptable. Then jut-jawed Urrea emerged on horseback to announce that no agreement would be valid unless negotiated between himself and the Texan commander whereupon Fannin limped out onto the plain. He conferred with Urrea and soon returned to camp, declaring an honorable capitulation had been agreed upon.

"Do you trust them?" Jason asked Dr. Jack, as Mexican officers walked through their square, inspecting weapons and equipment.

"Jason, we had to save our wounded. But I heard that Mexican colonel over there say, 'Well, gentlemen, in eight days, liberty and home.' That sounded reassuring."

Before proceeding to Victoria, Urrea ordered the Texan wounded transported in wagons to Goliad, while the prisoners marched under heavy guard. He then dispatched orders to Colonel Portilla, in command at Goliad, suggesting the healthy prisoners be put to work. Finally, he sent a report to Santa Anna, detailing his victory and that he expected to engage another contingent of rebels at Victoria.

The prisoners arrived at Goliad shortly before sundown and were ordered into the church. Exhausted, Jason slumped down by Temple to rest. The chapel was crowded, with little ventilation. The men had a few canteens of fresh water, but food was scarce. Fannin had surrendered on Sunday morning, March 20, exactly two weeks after the fall of the Alamo. Urrea could now move up the coast virtually at will. Santa Anna's right flank had been secured.

Chapter 15

AT Bexar, Santa Anna had lost his desire to search out Houston. He had received the startling news that his vice-president, Miguel Barragan, who was serving as president in his absence, had died. Though Barragan presumably died from natural causes, Santa Anna suspected foul play; the replacement was not of his liking.

In his planning room, Santa Anna conferred with his second in command, General Vicente Filisola. A portly man, expensively uniformed, Filisola had a long record of both Spanish and Mexican military service and he held a large land grant in East Texas, a special stake in ending hostilities.

Filisola outlined an elaborate plan to lure Houston's army into a trap near San Felipe de Austin. It called for bringing Gaona's force from the west into the central area to contain Houston, while Urrea's force guarded the coast. A third force, led by Santa Anna, would make the assault.

Since Filisola's plan was similar to Santa Anna's original plan, Almonte expected a warm response from His Excellency when Filisola concluded his presentation. But Santa Anna sat quietly behind his desk, reviewing a map of Texas. "I believe the war is already over. The Alamo victory and Fannin's defeat were decisive. Since I expect Houston to retreat beyond the Sabine, conceding Texas, I am considering a return to the capital."

"But Your Excellency," Filisola said, "Houston reportedly has gathered an army of about one thousand men. More foreigners from the United States of the North are en route to join him. If we do not strike soon, he may attack one of our forces in the field. In fact, Ramirez y Sesma is requesting reinforcements now."

"My dear Filisola, you have outlined a plan almost precisely as I had devised. It is sound, and if Houston pursues the war why cannot you lead the major force to victory?"

Filisola hesitated. If Santa Anna left him in command, he knew he would be expected to defeat Houston without Urrea's participation, not an easy task. "Your Excellency, what I say is not flattery, but fact. No one can inspire Mexican soldiers to fight as you can. This campaign needs to be brought to an early conclusion, so I implore you to lead our forces to a glorious victory."

"I will consider all circumstances before making my decision. Your remarks are most kind, General, and truly appreciated."

Juan had stood near the door, listening intently to each word. He sensed Almonte's concern over His Excellency's apparent indecision. Yet for more than two weeks, Juan had spent every off-duty moment with Rosa, so Santa Anna's indecision was more than agreeable to him. Each delay brought closer the time when he would receive his father's permission to marry.

When Filisola left, Santa Anna reviewed the orders he had written to Colonel Portilla at Goliad and to General Urrea at Victoria. "Have these delivered by express," he said. Juan glanced at the order to Portilla and gasped before Almonte ushered him out of the room.

"Can't someone prevent this?" Juan asked.

"I tried, but he is adamant."

"I can't deliver this order to a courier."

"Calderón, you will follow His Excellency's orders. If you are not careful, your conduct will land you in prison or before a firing squad. Orders are orders."

Returning to the planning room, Almonte found Santa Anna in a pensive mood. "Your Excellency, General Filisola found it incredible that you believe the war to be over."

"Yes, so incredible that he will immediately discuss this with all his colleagues. That talk will spread in the proper circles."

"You are not concerned?"

"No, I want that rumor to spread. If I return to the capital, I must take that position before the Supreme Government, so it will not appear I returned without securing this province."

"But isn't it more important to actually secure the province?"

"Timing, Almonte, is critical. I can see Bustamante's people maneuvering a thousand miles away. I believe he is out of the country, in Europe, but his schemers may seize this opportunity to bring him back to power. They will complain about the cost and duration of this campaign, or start rumors that the French or Spanish have plans to invade. Plots and intrigues will abound in the capital as the result of Barragan's untimely death."

While Almonte shared Santa Anna's concern, he believed Bustamante could return to power only if disaster struck Mexico during this campaign. The danger of a serious political reversal was far greater in abandoning an incomplete campaign than in leaving a figurehead to govern until Santa Anna returned as a victorious hero. Almonte searched for new reasons to continue the campaign, hoping His Excellency would see the folly of returning to Mexico City. He reminded Santa Anna that the dispatch about Barragan's death had been signed by two physicians friendly to Santa Anna, disproving the suspicion of foul play. "That no longer concerns me," Santa Anna said. "My concern is with Bustamante's people."

"Well, suppose, Your Excellency, that you returned to the capital. Filisola and Urrea cannot work well together. Houston might defeat one or the other, encouraging hundreds of foreigners to invade from the United States of the North. They could overwhelm our forces, which would be disastrous to the nation and to you."

Santa Anna did not respond. He stood by a window, gazing at the Alamo. "This is a difficult problem. I will reach a conclusion in a few days."

With Santa Anna in a reflective mood, Almonte decided to open another issue. "I have been corresponding with newspaper editors in the United States of the North. They know of our generosity toward non-combatants and our policy of freeing slaves. Your Excellency, these editors will remain favorable to our cause, if we maintain our humane policies."

"Of course, Almonte."

"Public opinion in America is divided over the question of acquiring Texas as another state. We must continue to exploit this division."

"And so we have agreed. What further need is there to discuss these matters?"

"Your Excellency, I believe it would be wise to countermand the order to Colonel Portilla at Goliad. That order might cause a reversal of the favorable impression we hold among important elements in America."

Santa Anna's eyes grew cold. "That order is unrelated to the policies you mentioned. I have no intention of changing it, nor will I discuss it any further. You are dismissed for the day, Colonel."

Meanwhile, following Urrea's order, Portilla prepared a work detail for the healthy prisoners at Goliad. They were to rebuild structures in the settlement and help slaughter longhorns gathered by the Mexican cavalry. Portilla was drawing up orders to implement these plans, when a courier arrived from San Antonio de Bexar with Santa Anna's orders.

Portilla read them while standing. He slumped into his chair, his face ashen and his hands trembling so badly that he dropped the orders to the floor. The surprised courier didn't know the nature of the orders. "Are you all right, Colonel?"

For a moment, Portilla sat, speechless. Finally, he retrieved the orders and placed them on the table. Staring at the courier, he asked unsteadily, "Are you sure, are you positive, these orders came from His Excellency?"

"Yes, Colonel, one of his aides gave me the envelope outside His Excellency's headquarters. As you can see, the envelope contains the official seal, and that appears to be his handwriting." The courier leaned slightly toward the table, trying to read what had so upset Portilla. "May I read those orders, Colonel, or would you explain the contents?"

"No," said Portilla. "You're dismissed."

It was early evening and refusing his supper, Portilla paced the dimly lit room. Two sets of orders lay on the table, those from Urrea, his longtime friend and commander and those from Santa Anna, commander-in-chief of the Army of Operations. Knowing he should honor those from the superior officer, Portilla sought some loophole by which he could honor Urrea's orders instead. As he thought of defying Santa Anna, his hands grew moist. He might lose more than rank; he might lose his life.

In the chapel, Dr. Jack and his men discussed the forthcoming journey across the Gulf of Mexico. Jason and many of the younger prisoners sang to the accompaniment of flutes, though Jason lacked the high spirits of the others. They had homes and families awaiting them, while he had received no word since leaving Gonzales. Late that Saturday night, he reviewed the week since Fannin surrendered on the Plain de Perdido. Imprisoned in the presidio, they had been easily guarded, and while their stomachs weren't too full, they generally had been well-treated by the Mexicans. Jason had searched for opportunities to escape, but security had been tight, and the volunteers from America, including seventy more captured at Copano, were content to wait for their ride home.

As daylight broke over the presidio on Palm Sunday, March 27, Mexican officers ordered the healthy prisoners, except for the doctors and those recently captured at Copano, to form three lines. They marched from the presidio in separate directions, ostensibly to pursue work details. Jason, marching beside Temple Shackelford, noticed the guard was extremely heavy on both sides of their line. They had marched almost a mile from the fort when Jason spotted a cavalry detachment, whose commanding officer was watching their movement through a field glass. "I smell a rat," Jason whispered to Temple. "This security is far too heavy for a work detail."

No sooner had Jason spoken than the officer in charge ordered a halt and shouted, *"Fuego!"* The guards turned and fired into the line of prisoners. "Jason, I'm hit!" screamed Temple, and when Jason grabbed him from behind, he felt warm blood gush onto his fingers. "Get out of here," Temple said, his dying words barely audible amid the musket fire and screaming prisoners.

Running more than a hundred yards, Jason twice heard musket balls zip by him. As the cavalry detachment swooped down from the hill on his left, he saw a handful of prisoners scrambling to the river and swimming across. That appeared to be the only avenue of escape, so he dashed the remaining distance to the river. Once across, he searched for other prisoners, but hearing Mexican voices nearby, he dived into a mesquite thicket.

He lay there, breathless and trembling from fear and the cold waters of the San Antonio River. Sporadic musket fire sounded several more minutes, and then was lost in the hoofbeats and shouting as the cavalry chased down the fleeing prisoners, killing them all. The wounded men back at the fort were executed as well, including Fannin, who was last to die. When informed of his fate, Fannin made a single laconic request about the disposition of his personal effects before being marched out to face a firing squad.

The seventy prisoners captured at Copano were spared since they were not under arms at the actual time of capture. Portilla had seized upon that legal loophole, and spared several others, including medical personnel, with the justification that they were needed to care for wounded Mexicans.

Jason hid in the thicket until nightfall. Shortly after dark, he began his journey north, following a cowpath, cut through the brush by wandering longhorns, until he came to a creek. Jason collapsed by the creek, gulping cool water from his cupped hands, and then relaxed, pondering his situation. Assuming Victoria had fallen into Urrea's hands, it seemed unlikely any settlements nearby would be under Texan control. Natural instincts called Jason toward home, Gonzales, but he reasoned that Houston probably had retreated down the Brazos. So, to rejoin Houston, he must chart a northeasterly course through the open country between Victoria and Gonzales towards San Felipe, a hundred miles away.

Jason had never been confronted by a journey without a horse, firearm, food, or even a canteen. Though he had a good sense of direction, he wished he had a map detailing all rivers and creeks; on a prairie without a canteen, water was a consideration equal to avoiding the enemy.

In pale moonlight, he resumed his journey. But after crossing the creek, he stepped within two feet of a long diamondback rattlesnake which probably would have struck had it been coiled. For a second, he was paralyzed by fear, but as the rattler coiled, Jason detoured briskly. For an hour, he traveled through the mesquite and brush, freezing for another heart-pounding moment at the call of a screech owl in the trees somewhere across a creek. With no further alarms, Jason collapsed exhausted under a scrub oak soon after midnight. Safely beyond range of Mexican search parties, he decided to wait and travel further in daylight. He fell asleep, ignoring the barking and howling coyotes, who pursued their prairie frolic throughout the pre-dawn hours.

About mid-morning, Jason was awakened by an approaching thunderstorm. A horned toad darted past him, responding to the sudden roaring from the sky. Though it soon drenched him, the storm blew over rapidly, yielding to bright sunshine. About noon he came upon a wide, shallow creek. Jason had gone without food for more than twenty-four hours, and his stomach gnawed with hunger. He spied some berries, but feared they might be poisonous, so instead hacked some leaves of prickly pear to the ground where he smashed them with his boots. He chewed the thick fiber and drank the bitter juice.

Later that afternoon he climbed a gentle hill, spying a house and corral about two miles distant. Letting out a loud whoop, he scrambled down the hill, running with renewed energy. Dashing to the porch, he stopped short, imagining how he looked in his dirty tattered buckskin. "They'll have to understand," he said, knocking on the door. When repeated knocking brought no response, he found the house abandoned.

There were no guns to be found, but there was food in the kitchen, and he ate two fried eggs with three thick slices of bread covered with sorghum molasses. Finishing his hearty meal, he walked outside to inspect the empty corral. As he closed the gate, he saw a large horse grazing in the high grass among some scrub oaks. Taking a frayed saddle blanket, bridle and reins from a nearby shed, Jason approached the old plowhorse and smiled ruefully as he bridled the gentle animal. "I bet you're not much faster than a mule, my friend, but I'm sure tired of walking."

Returning to the house, Jason filled a large cotton sack with bread and jars of molasses. Securing the sack to his belt, he mounted, and rode slowly to the north. It was peaceful on the prairie. He heard nothing more than the sounds of birds, dominated by sharp chirping of mockingbirds and melancholy calls of mourning doves and whippoorwills. Crossing the open country for days, Jason saw a few deer, longhorns, even a bear loping along. But although he savored the warmth of campfires, having found matches in the abandoned house, he yearned for meat to cook.

Approaching a shallow creek late one afternoon, he vowed not to build a campfire until he secured some game. With a handful of rocks in one pocket, and a thick oak limb as a club, he started stalking along the creekbed.

Hours later and with darkness approaching, Jason was resigned to returning empty-handed, and had started trudging toward the place he had tied his horse. Suddenly, he heard the croak of a bullfrog. Crouching, he crawled toward the spot where he guessed the frog to be. Peering through reeds, he spied the big bullfrog perched on the creekbank about fifteen feet away. He pulled the largest rock from his pocket, kissed it, and threw it as hard as he could. It hit the target, tumbling the bullfrog into the creek where Jason sloshed in pursuit, splashing water on both sides of the creekbed. Jason grabbed the stunned, struggling frog and killed it. Using the sharp edge of a rock, he prepared frog legs for his supper and enjoyed a satisfying meal, breaking the monotony of bread and molasses.

As he neared the Colorado River, Jason was jolted back to reality. He met a handful of fleeing settlers, fearful that Santa Anna was close behind. Though Jason assured them he planned to cross at Beason's Ferry, they insisted on going further downriver. Before parting ways, they gave him some dried beef, a welcome addition to his dwindling food supply.

Jason rode on into a dense, protected area of oak and pecan trees near a creek that fed the Colorado. He decided the place was safe enough for a nap before approaching Beason's Ferry under cover of darkness.

He was sound asleep under an oak tree when the point of a saber was poked in his side. Startled, he looked up at the Mexican officer standing over him. "Oh my God," he blurted, "they tracked me down."

"Who should want to track you down?" asked Juan Calderón, in crisp English, as he withdrew his saber.

Jason prepared to string out as many lies as he could to confuse his adversary. "I don't know. I guess I'm afraid some settlers might be after me for taking their food."

"Are you a soldier?"

"Do I look like a soldier?"

"Most of the rebels do not have uniforms. You could be a rebel soldier."

"I've been hunting, south of here. Some Indians took my guns and dogs, leaving me nothing. I found that old plowhorse roaming the prairie." Pointing to the plowhorse, Jason moved his right arm upward, exposing a number of cuts and scratches.

"That is all very interesting," Juan said, "but if you were a hunter you would be more careful with your hands and arms. You appear to be a fugitive. Were you at Goliad?"

Jason's throat became dry.

"You were at Goliad," Juan said. "I can see the terror in your eyes. You can relax. I will not harm you. You will be interested to know you have wandered to within two miles of the camp of General Santa Anna."

"Why should I trust you not to harm me? We trusted General Urrea and he turned out to be a murderer."

"It was not Urrea who ordered the massacre. It was Santa Anna. I saw the orders."

"Are you on his staff?"

"Yes. I also saw him order the execution of prisoners after the Battle of the Alamo."

"Many of my townspeople were there," Jason said. "I'm from Gonzales."

"They were most courageous," Juan said. "Those who came into the Alamo during the siege must have known the situation was hopeless."

"They thought Fannin would provide reinforcements. Do you know if Fannin was executed?"

"Yes, he was. However, the prisoners captured at Copano were spared by Colonel Portilla. Santa Anna was furious, but Colonel Almonte convinced him Portilla's decision would be sustained in a court-martial. Portilla also spared doctors, even though a Dr. Shackelford commanded a rebel group in the battle on the Plain de Perdido."

"Thank God. Dr. Jack is a fine man. His son was shot next to me when the massacre began. It was horrible."

"I suppose you would like to take this saber and run it through my body. I could not blame you. I am ashamed of this war, deeply ashamed. Santa Anna shames all of us by his inhumanity."

"Then why not disavow him as Zavala did? Why not join our cause?"

Juan recalled the horrifying moments after the Battle of the Alamo: the young Texan before his execution, the Mexican soldiers writhing in pain for hours without medical attention, and Santa Anna calmly dispatching orders for the mass murder at Goliad. "Had I not fallen in love with a girl in Bexar, I probably would have resigned my commission. I have sacrificed honor and principle in order to marry her."

"But why not join us? You would be free to marry her as soon as hostilities end."

"After what has happened, do you believe a Mexican officer from Santa Anna's staff would be welcome in a Texan camp? They would hang me from the nearest tree."

"I would help you. I know you would be welcome in Captain Seguin's company. They're all Tejanos from Bexar and thereabouts."

Jason kept the conversation alive as a ploy, hoping his adversary would be careless, but Juan maintained his distance and hadn't relinquished his grip on that long saber. Searching for other incentives, Jason recalled the last words of the old man from Georgia. "Not only would you have your wife in Bexar, you would be awarded a grant of land for service in the Texan army. The Seguins are prominent people in Bexar. You would receive the best land you could want."

"I appreciate your offer," Juan said. "I believe you are sincere, and perhaps I would be accepted in Seguin's company." As Juan paused, Jason held his breath. "But when I weigh the risk, the honest truth is I do not believe your army has a chance. Houston will soon be trapped. Our spies report that Houston has no artillery whatsoever, and that hundreds of settlers have deserted his army to protect their fleeing families. They believe Houston will retreat beyond the Sabine, leaving the entire Texas territory without a fight."

"I don't believe that," snapped Jason. "There were two cannons at Gonzales when I departed, and I know darn well General Houston is preparing to fight."

"Your countrymen are long on bravery, but short on numbers. If Houston decides to fight, his army will face the same fate as those at the Alamo and the Coleto. I must also say that if I defected, I would be signing my death warrant. Santa Anna hates no one more than Zavala. He regards his defection as a personal affront, and he will not be satisfied until he sees Zavala dead. He would view my defection likewise. I am not prepared to take that risk."

Jason knew the idea of defection had been a long shot, but it had at least diverted the young officer. I must rekindle the conversation, Jason thought. "Have you been to Gonzales?" he asked Juan.

"Yes. Santa Anna flew into a rage when we found one of our scouts hanging from an oak tree near the Guadalupe River. We had planned on securing provisions, but found the settlement burned to the ground. We found another scout late yesterday, also hanging from a tree with his throat slit. Both men had notes pinned to their coats that read simply, '*Recuerden el Alamo.*' Santa Anna has vowed vengeance on the guerrillas who, he says, are fighting outside the rules of warfare."

"His own throat should be slit ten times for what he's done."

"He has us searching carefully for these guerrillas. You would qualify merely by being in the path of our army."

"Well, I'm not a guerrilla. I'm a courier and . . ."

"You were about to say that you are a civilian courier who carries mail among settlements. You have wandered astray due to a storm, and if you are wise, you will head down the river at least three miles before crossing tonight in order not to be impeded by a segment of the Army of Operations . . . I must return to my camp."

Jason was dumfounded. "I . . . I don't know how to thank you."

"You have suffered enough. You should retreat past the Sabine to safety, but you will not. You will report to Houston and die with your countrymen. By the way, what is your name?"

"Jason Gates."

"I am Juan Calderón." They shook hands before Juan mounted his horse. Jason thought of the few expressions in Spanish that he could pronounce. "*¡Buena suerte!*" he called. The least I can do, he thought, is to wish him good luck.

"*¡Buena suerte!*" Juan returned the call as he rode away.

Jason rode downriver about three miles where he found a sturdy raft along the bank of the swirling river. Jason removed the last of his provisions, stuffing the bread under his belt, and wrapped the empty sack over the horse's head. Using two leafy branches to steer the raft across the river, he talked every minute to the old plowhorse, to keep him from leaping into the water. Then, he rode far into the night, until he had put all the distance he could between himself and the advancing army led by Santa Anna.

Chapter 16

WHEN he rode into San Felipe the following day shortly before sundown, he was crestfallen. He found the settlement burned to the ground, the ruins still smoldering near the Brazos River. Riding past the cemetery, he circled the two large plazas, but found no sign of life.

San Felipe had been the cultural and commercial center for Stephen F. Austin's prized colony, as well as a political meeting place, having been capital of the provisional state government. Its design had reflected Austin's careful planning and sound judgment. Now it was gone, as though a fiery hand had reached out of the earth and pulled it under. As Jason viewed the ruins, tears welled in his eyes. "Thank God," he said, "Mr. Austin isn't here to see this."

Whoever burned the settlement must be close at hand, Jason thought, as he rode slowly past some timber where the Arroyo Dulce Creek runs into the Brazos. From atop a hill, he saw a figure in buckskin across the river. "Captain Baker!" he shouted, waving his arm.

Moseley Baker recognized Jason and waved his hat. "We've destroyed every means of crossing for the Mexicans!" shouted Baker. "I'll come get you in a canoe!"

As Baker and one of his men paddled across the river, Jason spoke to the plowhorse for the final time. "Farewell, my old friend," he said, stroking his neck. "Stay out of these big rivers and you'll be all right."

Baker was only an acquaintance of Jason's, but as he stepped onto the river bank to greet Jason, he was a comrade-in-arms if one ever existed. Jason embraced him, then shook the other man's hand so hard he stepped back. "Son, you could wrestle a bear with that grip."

"Let's get going," Baker said. "The Mexicans may arrive any time."

As they paddled across the Brazos, Jason told Baker of his escape at Goliad. "You're one lucky man," Baker said. "First report we heard was all the men were killed. Yesterday, we heard some were spared and perhaps twenty-five escaped."

"Do you know if my family is all right?"

"They left Gonzales with us. Your dad said they were heading for Nacogdoches. That's the last I've seen or heard of 'em."

"I'm anxious to report to General Houston," Jason said. "Is his camp nearby?"

"You won't find him around here," Baker said, pulling the canoe onto the bank. "He and I have parted ways. When he said he would retreat again, Wylie Martin and I refused to keep our companies with him. I told him I was staying here, and Wylie took his men down the river to Old Fort."

Jason stared incredulously at Baker. How could he possibly expect to contest an army of one to three thousand with a company of no more than a hundred men? He assumed Baker must have had a fearful argument with Houston. But Jason was too hungry to worry about risking an argument with his benefactor. As they finished their meal, Baker poured another cup of coffee and opened the subject himself. "Son, aren't you interested in what I believe is going to happen?"

"Yes, sir."

"I'm not going to sit back and let the Mexicans ravage this land. I thought that by pulling out, I might bring Houston to his senses or, at least, attract enough men here to make a stand. Now, Houston and I do agree on the importance of keeping the Brazos between us and the enemy. So, I plan to stall the Mexican forces when they try to cross the river. Without bridges or rafts, they aren't going very far. Houston meanwhile is retreating northwest to the Hargrove Plantation."

"Why does he still retreat?"

"He says he won't fight without artillery, after ordering us to dump our only two cannons in the Guadalupe back at Gonzales! Then he says he has to gather and train more men, when he's losing men every day who don't think he'll fight. Sure, we need a trained army, but we just don't have time now for anything but fighting."

"Well, Captain Baker, there's merit in what you say, and I would like nothing better than getting a shot at Santa Anna, but my duty is to report back to General Houston. I hope you understand, sir." Jason needed a horse, and had seen several fine mounts grazing near Baker's camp. But he knew Baker had a short temper, and might be disinclined to help one of Houston's aides join the retreat.

"Son, your sense of duty is commendable, but I wish you would stay here. You're more than welcome to whatever provisions you need. We took supplies from the stores in San Felipe before burning the settlement."

"Captain Baker, you're a courageous man, doing what you believe is right, but I am assigned to General Houston."

Baker argued on. "But son, even Houston supports my plan more than he cares to admit. When Wylie and I refused to back down, he

161

actually wrote orders assigning us to our position. Sidney Sherman, with his fifty-two volunteers from Kentucky, also threatened to pull out. If Burleson hadn't stood firm for Houston, we would have had a new commanding general of the army."

Jason found Baker's story repugnant. While he and his comrades had fought a desperate battle and faced a firing squad, leaders in the Texan army were bickering and trying to oust their commander-in-chief. Gazing into the campfire, Jason reflected a moment. "Captain Baker, I said you're courageous. I meant that, sir. But you have implied that General Houston is a coward. To that I say you are wrong, and what you have done has hurt our cause."

Jason expected a tongue-lashing, but Baker became pensive. Several things had been haunting him, particularly Major Hockley's parting words. He had said, "Moseley, Sam doesn't take this personally. He understands how you feel." Baker tossed a twig into the fire. "Jason, do you know why Buck Travis and I were such good friends?"

Jason looked up, surprised. "No, sir."

"Because Buck struck hard for what he believed was right and condemned what he believed was wrong. I'm the same way. Since the Alamo, I've yearned to avenge Buck's death, and to stop the Mexicans from taking our settlements. My own family has already moved north. I'm sick of this. Sam, though, is calm, prudent. He's playing a game of concealment and delay, and maybe, just maybe, he'll be right. I pray for victory, no matter who commands. And young man, I didn't mean to imply Sam Houston is a coward. I know better than that."

"I believe you, Captain Baker. We have been under such pressure that it's been hard to think anything through. Colonel Travis had impossible odds against him at the Alamo and we were trapped on a plain without water or timber. I only hope our remaining forces will fight in a battle that can be won."

"Let's drink another cup of coffee to that," Baker said.

As Jason finished his coffee, he requested a horse which Baker approved. "They travel slowly," Baker said of Houston's army. "You can catch up with them tomorrow on the trail to the Hargrove Plantation."

"I can't thank you enough, Captain Baker."

"Forget it, son." As Jason chose a horse, Baker called after him. "Say, you can borrow my razor for a shave, if you like. I also have spare boots, shirts and pantaloons fresh out of a store across the river. They say that Molly Hargrove is prettier than a patch of bluebonnets. Why not get a good night's sleep and start first thing in the morning."

Jason accepted Baker's hospitality. He slept soundly through the night, and dashed away from camp at daybreak clean-shaven, in a brand new outfit, and riding a fast young stallion. Jason remembered

Molly Hargrove, an attractive young girl he had met at a ball in San Felipe two years ago. But surely the Hargrove family would have evacuated their plantation. No matter, Jason thought, it's invigorating enough to be clean, and to recall a more pleasant aspect of life before the war.

As he rode along, he crossed a fertile land, covered with wildflowers, bluebonnets, yellow buttercups and reddish-orange Indian blankets. He had paused to take a half-hearted long shot at a timber wolf, when he heard the sound of hoofbeats. A young rider reined up his exhausted horse. "Say, friend," Jason said, "you shouldn't ride that horse so hard. What's your hurry?"

"I have reports for General Houston. Important reports."

"Well, I'm a member of his staff," Jason said.

"I bring special news about artillery that will soon arrive for our army," the courier said.

"How much artillery?"

"Two cannons, a gift from the people of Cincinnati, Ohio. I know General Houston needs to know about them." Jason was holding his horse in pace with the courier's winded pony. The boy fidgeted at the slower speed, then chattered on. "I bet if Colonel Fannin had had those two cannons, he would have won that battle. Like General Houston says, you can't fight without artillery."

"Fannin had nine pieces of artillery."

"Really? Then he should have whipped those Mexicans."

"I believe his problem was lack of water and timber cover."

"Well, it was a terrible thing to execute all those men after they surrendered. You and I are lucky 'cause General Houston won't surrender and get us shot."

"I'm sure you're right about that," Jason said, straight-faced.

When they rode into Houston's camp, a guard recognized Jason. "Lord, I never expected to see you again. We heard almost all you people at Goliad were gunned down or sabered."

The young courier blushed. "I never dreamed you had been at Goliad, dressed like that, and saying you were on General Houston's staff," he said as Jason smiled and left in search of Houston.

It was late afternoon and the army had halted for the night. Jason found Houston, who gave him a warm handshake and slung his arm around his shoulders. "We had about given up on you, son. Welcome back. Though for a young man who has been through hell, you look like you're dressed for the fanciest ball in Texas. Where in the world did you fall upon an outfit like that?"

Jason had hoped he wouldn't have to mention Baker, at least not until he had time to feel out the situation. "From a store in San Felipe, General. Captain Baker took them before the settlement was burned."

Jason was relieved to see little reaction in Houston's tired face. He merely sighed before inquiring about Baker's condition.

"He's in high spirits, sir. He's determined to keep the enemy from crossing the Brazos."

"If he can keep the Mexicans from crossing the Brazos, he'll be doing the Lord's work. You appear ready to resume duty. Do you want to reconnoiter tomorrow?"

"Yes, sir."

"I don't anticipate enemy activity in this area," Houston said, pointing to an area on the map. "Go to the Hargrove Crossing, survey the area, and check out the plantation. No doubt the Hargrove family has abandoned the place. The house should be perfect for a headquarters, and we'll need their fields for training grounds. Lord knows, most of these volunteers need training. We're also going to eat better."

After leaving Houston's tent, Jason walked through the camp. He estimated there must be about eight hundred men there, most of them the worse for their wet, muddy march. Their morale was low, but it apparently had improved in the past few days, or so Hockley said, inviting Jason for a cup of coffee.

"How bad was the situation," Jason asked, "when Baker and Martin pulled out?"

"Critical," Hockley said. "It was like watching a herd of longhorns spooked up by lightning, but after Sam wore them down, things improved. The news from Goliad had its effect. The men know they're dead if they become prisoners. So they have accepted Sam's strict discipline, and know they're not going to a picnic at the Hargrove Plantation.

"Something else happened after the big blow-up. You know there's been an awful lot of sickness among troops and settlers. We came upon a poor woman, holding her five-year-old son in her arms. The boy had died from a fever. Sam asked her if we could bury the boy and she refused, saying her husband had been killed at the Alamo and this boy was all she had left in the world. Sam convinced her to let us bury the boy, and gave her a horse and enough money to get to Nacogdoches. When we gathered that night for supper, Sam made a short speech to all the officers. He said that we could continue bickering among ourselves and tear the army apart, or we could all pull together and prepare for battle. He said something like 'look what a terrible sacrifice that poor woman has made. If you want to wreak vengeance, act like soldiers. Those who want to leave, leave now!'

"I've never heard him make a speech quite like that. I suppose he was fed up with all the camp gossip about the retreat. We've had two or three men who might as well be agents for Santa Anna. All they do is stir up rumors, and I believe Sam is ready to put the wood to them, if they don't shut their mouths."

"What sort of rumors?"

"The usual, plus the Cherokee talk. Some say he thinks and acts like a Cherokee, keeps to himself too much, and most of all, won't call councils of war."

"Do you believe in councils of war?"

"No, and neither does Burleson, but he wants to be consulted. Burleson has stood by Sam, but he believes the field officers should have some say in devising strategy."

"Any late intelligence on Santa Anna?"

"Seguin returned to camp this afternoon. He says Santa Anna is moving down the Brazos, probably with Ramirez y Sesma, and is nearing San Felipe. He doesn't talk much, but I have a hunch Seguin has been really harrassing the enemy. He knows the country and he takes special pride in thwarting His Excellency."

"At least something sounds encouraging," Jason said, bidding Hockley goodbye.

Hockley returned to Houston, and found him furious. In the dispatch delivered by the anxious young courier, a letter from Burnet, president of the Republic of Texas, read simply, *"The enemy are laughing you to scorn. You must fight them. You must retreat no farther. The country expects you to fight. The salvation of the country depends on your doing so."*

"That old hog thief," Houston bellowed, "has no business telling me how to run the army. Why, he couldn't find his way out of a corral with the gate open."

As his anger subsided, however, Houston began to wonder if there were a connection between the camp talk and Burnet's letter. Houston had contended that Burnet's decision to move the seat of government to Harrisburg undermined public confidence, so perhaps Burnet simply was responding with an attack on his conduct of the war. "George, keep an ear close to the ground," Houston said. "I want to know if any of our men are causing us problems with Burnet."

Having relaxed, Houston sat down to pen a conciliatory letter to Burnet, praising him as "righteous." Houston wrote that he had kept the army together *"under most discouraging circumstances, and I hope a just and wise God, in whom I have always believed, will yet save Texas."* He made no mention of the retreat.

Houston also had received requests from Captains Baker and Martin for reinforcements. Hockley was encouraged to hear his commander order, "Send Martin one hundred fifty men and send fifty to Baker. Order them to be prepared to rejoin us if the Mexicans effect a major force crossing of the Brazos. I don't want them to be trapped."

Hockley told Houston a steamboat, the *Yellowstone*, would be available to use crossing the Brazos near the Hargrove Plantation. The army could train on the west bank and have the *Yellowstone* available for river transport whenever Houston chose to make his move. "Now," Houston said, "we have a strategic situation that begins to make sense. With Baker and Martin guarding the Brazos, Seguin and Deaf Smith scouting, I can rest a bit easier. I should have time to whip this army into shape, but will we have enough men?"

"After the reinforcements leave, we'll have less than six hundred effective men," Hockley said.

Houston stretched his long body beneath an oak tree, resting his head on a saddle. "Well, any way you cut it, George, we're still in much better condition. I wonder what Burnet will think when he receives my letter. He'll probably be furious, thinking his letter didn't bother me at all."

While Houston rested under the oak tree in his camp, Santa Anna barked orders to his men at San Felipe. First he directed artillery and small arms fire at Moseley Baker's camp, killing one Texan. Then after leading a fruitless search for means to cross the Brazos, he ordered his men to set up camp. "This is ridiculous," he said to Almonte. "First Gonzales, now San Felipe. No plunder for the army, and no provisions. This is bad for morale."

"It is obviously the policy of the enemy. We should engage General Houston at the earliest possible time."

"True! But where is he? He should be here, but that is only a small force across the river, nothing more than guerrillas. One scout says he is moving toward Harrisburg, another, that he is retreating beyond the Trinity, or even the Sabine. We are operating on rumors. I want facts. Send out more scouts."

"We have lost five of our best scouts and two are missing, Your Excellency. I am afraid the rebel guerrillas know this country much better than our scouts." Nevertheless, Almonte dispatched a few more scouts down the Brazos in search of rafts. He cautioned them that the enemy would increase as they neared the coast. He then returned to Santa Anna, who continued his complaints.

"You convinced me, Almonte, that I must lead the army to a final victory despite my concern for my political position. Do you realize how much time I am losing? And do you realize there is camp talk, among my own officers, criticizing the execution at Goliad?"

Santa Anna's only trophy from San Felipe was a charred copy of Travis' letter of February 24, appealing for help at the Alamo. After Almonte translated the contents, Santa Anna flung it to the ground. "Those who don't understand this war are fools. See how he wrote to 'all Americans in the world,' as if this were not an internal revolution. Such arrogance! The action taken at Goliad was entirely justified."

One of Santa Anna's agents had sent copies of recent newspaper articles in the United States about the Texas Revolution. After the Alamo and Goliad, most newspapers condemned Santa Anna for his "butchery." But Santa Anna's concern about the Goliad Massacre was not with Anglo public opinion, but with the negative reaction in his own army. Many of his officers were professional soldiers, including some from Europe, who believed in practical terms regarding treatment of prisoners. After Goliad, what would the Texans do to them, if they were captured? It was a chilling possibility to contemplate. These officers also understood the critical difference between a "capitulation," in which terms were agreed upon, and a "surrender at discretion," or unconditional surrender. Word had spread that Urrea and Fannin had agreed to a capitulation.

To calm his nerves, Santa Anna took a few grains of opium. "The policy at Goliad was not debatable. Portilla should have executed them all. The problem is that Urrea may have agreed to a capitulation. I simply assumed he accepted a surrender at discretion, which is all he was authorized to do."

"The concern of our men," Almonte said, "is actually more that the enemy, seeking vengeance, will not take prisoners."

"That is a cowardly concern," snapped Santa Anna. "If they are not prepared to die, they should not be in this army."

A courier arrived with mail from the capital. Santa Anna was relieved to learn that the news of his triumphs in Texas had strengthened his position. Though His Excellency's man had not been chosen ad interim president, Santa Anna was assured his own position would be even stronger when he returned with the Texas province secured to the nation. Among other letters, he found a reply from Señor Calderón:

> My Dear Antonio:
>
> We have marveled at the reports of your success in the present campaign. It appears to be more tedious than your triumph at Zacatecas, but perhaps more significant to the long-term interests of Mexico.
>
> I am deeply appreciative of your bringing to my attention the sensitive matter regarding my beloved son, Juan. I have informed him, in a separate letter, that I believe it unwise for him to marry during this campaign, and that if his desire has not changed after the campaign, that he bring this girl here to meet the family. Only then would I approve his marriage to a girl who, according to your description, might find it difficult to adjust to our way of life.
>
> With your many concerns and responsibilities, I hope that this matter has not imposed unduly upon your time. Señora Calderón joins me in sending our sincere wishes for victory and a safe return to the capital.

"An excellent letter from Señor Calderón," said Santa Anna, "and one less problem."

Outside His Excellency's canopied field tent, Captain Carlos Alvarez, returning from a fruitless search for rafts, sat down by the campfire. His friend, Juan Calderón, was sitting quietly across the fire with a crumpled piece of paper in his hand.

167

"Did you hear from Rosa?" Carlos asked.

"No, this is from my father. He will not approve of the marriage."

"Not at all?"

"He says I must wait until after the campaign is completed, then bring her to meet the family. He may as well have denied my request outright."

"What if you married her at Bexar after the campaign?"

"I do not know. You do not understand how strongly people of my class feel about these things. The blood lines are most important."

"Well, I defy anyone to find a girl more beautiful or one with more charm and strength of character."

"I know, but my class is of pure Spanish blood. In Mexico City, we are not supposed to marry *mestizos*. Besides, no one there even knows of the Coahuiltecan Indians, though that heritage is part of Rosa's strength."

"I am sorry, Juan. My fondest memories of Bexar are the times when I saw you two together and happy. I only hope there is some way you can become man and wife."

"I will find a way," Juan said. He had told no one, not even Carlos, about the enemy courier. Carlos was no admirer of Santa Anna, but he was a loyal soldier and might report Juan if he knew what he had done. The thought of defection again crossed Juan's troubled mind. His zest for war had waned in Bexar, and he prayed he would never again face a prisoner or potential prisoner, wanting no part of their death. He would fight when necessary, but only to protect himself in battle. Tossing his father's letter into the fire, he resolved to marry Rosa in Bexar.

"Do you think we will soon engage the enemy?" he asked Carlos.

"I would think so. This small force across the river must be there for a purpose. Their main army cannot be far away. It is just a matter of time until we close down on them."

"Do you feel better about the war?"

"The execution at Goliad will stain the honor of Mexico far into the future. But I do not see how the rebels have much of a chance. They cannot defeat us, when we outnumber them three or four to one. And if they should try to isolate General Urrea, we are near enough to reinforce him. So long as this force remains combined, the enemy cannot defeat us."

At a campfire nearby, a soldier spat out a bite of hard biscuit, and sighed. Every day, the same. Since leaving San Antonio, the army's diet had consisted of *carne seca*, dried beef, and *bizcochos*, double-baked corn biscuits. The soldiers had marched in mud, often at a turtle's pace as gun carriages and supply trains bogged down. They had anticipated new provisions at Gonzales and San Felipe, but found not a single slab of bacon or round of cheese. Days had been

168

demanding while nights were lonely, often with a cold rain to heighten their misery.

That night at San Felipe, a chill drizzle fell as dense fog settled along the Brazos. Surveying the dreary camp, Santa Anna returned to the warmth of his tent. "Almonte, we cannot struggle about this despicable country forever, searching for a ghost named Houston. I have a new thought. Notify our best scouts that I want to know the whereabouts of the rebel government leaders. If Houston thinks we are about to capture them, he will be drawn into a trap."

"I will execute your request as soon as the fog lifts."

"Execute it now! And send an express to Urrea! I want a full report on the conditions of Fannin's surrender."

Part III:

A Time To Temporize

Chapter 17

FOG shrouded the Texan camp the following morning, when Jason accepted an invitation for breakfast from Edward Burleson, anxious to learn about the Goliad Massacre. Jason in turn hoped to learn more about the attempted ouster of Houston. "I want to say, sir," Jason began, "that from what I hear, you saved the army from falling apart. I'm sure General Houston is grateful."

"No gratitude necessary," Burleson said. "I only did what I thought best for the army and our cause."

"I understand. But it seems that some of these people are after General Houston, no matter what he does."

"I've known Moseley Baker for years. Though he and Sam will never be friends, I'm convinced his argument was genuine. Wylie Martin is all right, too. Both will probably rejoin the army before we do battle.

"Sherman is a little harder to figure. He's ambitious and spoiling for battle, but at least he had the good sense to remain with the army when he realized Sam would maintain command. I've recommended to Sam that he form another regiment with Sherman as commander. I don't like him personally, but he knows how to organize units. Of course there are still a few soreheads who will make a noise about anything."

"Major Hockley mentioned this to me. Are these people in a position to threaten a change in command?"

"No, but I suspect politics is being played even now in this desperate military situation. A man named Perry starts most of the personal gossip that is getting back to the government leaders. My men are sick of it."

"How did you convince the rest of the men to stay with General Houston?"

"I told them that changing commanders at a drop of a hat is downright stupid. I told them that the lack of a unified command of our men under arms led to that disastrous attempt to invade Matamoros, which may well have caused the fall of the Alamo. They knew Sam opposed the Matamoros foolishness but didn't have the authority to prevent it."

"You really believe that with those troops Travis could have held?"

"He would have had a chance, either with that contingent, or with reinforcements from Fannin. Speaking of Fannin, I suppose you had the daylights scared out of you at Goliad?"

"Yes, sir, though it happened so fast I hardly knew what I was doing. I never suspected they would shoot us until seconds before it started. I learned from Captain Baker that Dr. Shackelford and some other medical people were spared, along with the new prisoners."

"We've had a few escapees from Goliad arrive ahead of you. There seems to be some confusion about the surrender. Do you believe Fannin reached a capitulation with Urrea?"

"Well, I never saw anything in writing. Dr. Shackelford said Fannin assured him and the other officers that an honorable capitulation had been reached. During the week we were held in Presidio La Bahia, the enemy let Colonel Fannin travel to the coast with a Mexican officer to find transportation for the American prisoners. I can't believe that would have happened unless terms had been agreed upon. I heard that Santa Anna himself ordered the execution, countermanding the capitulation."

As the fog lifted gently around their camp, Burleson drank the last of his coffee. "You know, son, I was more concerned about how my men would react to that massacre than I was about the fuss stirred up against Houston. Last December, I worked out a capitulation with General Cós at Bexar when at least a spirit of honor still existed between the opposing sides. I suspect Santa Anna forced Cós to renege on that capitulation, and he either forced Urrea to renege on a similar capitulation or rejected all humane alternatives after a surrender at discretion. In either case, this war has taken an ugly turn. We face an enemy that gives us no choice but to fight to the death. I worried that many of my men would desert, but most remain. Now, they have a new determination; otherwise, Texas is lost and they are all dead men."

"Is General Houston planning to trap Santa Anna?"

"I don't know. He consults no one about strategy. Sam may have gone too far in refusing to consult the experienced officers. We would feel better if we knew he had a basic strategy and would at least listen to our advice."

"Why doesn't he believe in councils of war?"

"Same reason I don't, I suppose. They usually produce bad decisions. Too much democracy will ruin an army. There's a crucial difference between a commander consulting his field officers while he controls the situation and throwing open a council of war to a deciding vote."

"I understand. Do you have any objection to training at the Hargrove Plantation?"

"None at all. I only hope we have time before going into battle. So many Texans think we can strap Santa Anna's army as easily as we whipped Cós. They can't realize that this enemy force is much larger and better trained than the conscripts they sent before."

Jason stood up and stretched. He looked over the rolling countryside, now almost clear of fog. "Thank you for the breakfast, sir. I must ride ahead to reconnoiter the plantation."

The fog gave way to a bright clear morning. Jason easily covered the few miles to the Hargrove Crossing where he was surprised to find the ferry across the Brazos still in operation. "Haven't you people heard the Mexican army is close at hand?" Jason asked the ferry operator.

"Some folks are more interested in growing cotton and corn than worrying about Mexican soldiers," said the whiskered old man.

"Are you telling me the Hargroves have not abandoned their plantation?"

"I sure am, son."

Jason hesitated. Should he return to inform Houston so he might make other plans? Perhaps the Hargroves would leave when told of the Mexican advance; if not, at least they would permit the army to use their fields.

Riding over open fields rimmed with timber, he approached the immense, stately Hargrove home. The mansion dominated a gentle hill, where live oaks and pecan trees sprawled in a vast lawn enclosed by low stone walls. Jason marveled at the long two-story house, built from sturdy pine, with towering fieldstone chimneys at each end. The radiant white structure with dark green shutters had wide porches, front and back, and a short stone chimney protruded from the kitchen. This house was the most impressive he had ever seen.

Stables, sheds, and quarters for servants and field hands stood in an orderly manner behind the back lawn. They were constructed of heavy logs with small windows to minimize danger in the event of an Indian raid.

Since Edgar Hargrove had been one of the few colonists who brought a substantial amount of capital to Texas, he had obtained more land than his original grant and bought slaves along the coast with the help of Bowie. He had also brought from Virginia the technology for growing and marketing vast amounts of cotton; thus he had become the wealthiest planter in the territory.

Two years before the Texas Revolution, his desire for expansion cost Hargrove his life. On a journey alone to the coast for more slaves, he was attacked and mortally wounded by a small band of marauding Karankawas. He had ridden into San Felipe where he died at the home of his friend, Judge Williamson.

His widow, Elizabeth, was left with vast holdings, but most of the capital had been invested. Her eldest child, Molly, was fifteen at the time of her father's death; Edgar, Jr., fourteen, and Garth, twelve. With the help of Williamson and Travis, her attorney, Elizabeth had soon learned the business, her first year of operation producing a profit almost equal to the best years of the past. Her second year was even better and she was now anxious to resume planting.

As Jason reined up to present himself, he saw Elizabeth Hargrove standing on the front porch, leaning gently against one of the spotless white columns. Jason guessed her to be about forty, a trim attractive woman, her brown hair swept back tightly. She would seem severe, he thought, except for her thoughtful blue eyes. Jason had met her daughter, Molly, at a ball in San Felipe not long after Hargrove's death.

Dismounting, Jason removed his hat. "Good morning, Mrs. Hargrove. I'm Lieutenant Jason Gates on a mission in behalf of General Houston."

"What is the purpose of your call, young man?"

"Santa Anna's army is on the other side of the Brazos. Since nearly all the settlers have moved north of the Trinity, General Houston assumed you had evacuated this plantation. He needs it for training the Army of Texas."

"I have no intention of abandoning this plantation."

"Well, ma'am, would you permit the army to use some of your land for training?"

Before her mother could answer, Molly walked onto the porch, greeting Jason. Moseley Baker had said she was pretty as a patch of bluebonnets. To Jason, she was prettier than all the bluebonnets in Texas. She had matured rapidly in two years. She had her mother's sparkling blue eyes and a warm, bright smile. Honey-brown hair flowed behind her softly rounded shoulders.

"I didn't know you two knew each other," Elizabeth said. "Are you a member of the Gates family in Gonzales?"

"Yes, Mrs. Hargrove. Your late husband did business with my dad on his way to and from San Antonio de Bexar."

"I see. Now, if General Houston needs land on which to train his army, I suggest he try elsewhere."

"Mrs. Hargrove, there isn't any other suitable land. We need to train seven hundred, perhaps one thousand men."

"Young man, you may tell General Houston that if he wants the land, he must deal directly with me."

Jason mounted, tipped his hat to Molly, and rode back .

"Mother, you were downright rude to Jason," Molly said.

"I was no such thing. You have no earthly idea what would be involved. We would lose our planting time, and they would want all our provisions. I won't have it."

176

"Jason and those other men have endured all kinds of hardship, protecting us. You didn't even offer him a cup of coffee."

"He looked to me as though he were dressed for a ball, rather than war. I doubt he has endured any hardship, running errands for Sam Houston, who has yet to fight in a single battle. I must admit Jason is a dashing young man; reminds me of Will Travis."

"You adored Will Travis, and Jason reminds you of him. Yet, you were so rude to him I was ashamed."

"Molly, I won't tolerate that kind of talk. There are matters involved in this war that you don't understand. I'm not going to sacrifice what your father paid so dearly for simply because Sam Houston wants his army to roam on our land."

When Jason reported his failure to Houston, the general sighed. "I should have guessed that if there was one bull-headed settler in Texas who wouldn't evacuate, it would be Elizabeth Hargrove." He changed from buckskin to his rumpled suit with frock coat, and smiled. "Lead the way, Lieutenant."

Houston had known the Hargroves casually since he had come to Texas, renewing an earlier acquaintance with Edgar, and he had admired Elizabeth's sound judgment and success following her husband's death. But he thought since she's refused to evacuate until now, practical arguments won't mean a thing to her.

Watching Houston and Jason approach, Elizabeth turned to Molly. "I want to speak to the general alone. I'm sure you won't mind entertaining young Gates."

Houston politely followed Elizabeth into the spacious mansion, through a wide central hallway, flanked by rooms with high ceilings, that led to the stairwell. Elizabeth had furnished the house with fine pieces of mahogany and walnut, including a pianoforte imported from London.

In the parlor, Houston leaned against a marble mantel awaiting Elizabeth's return with coffee. Seeing the many elaborate candle holders, he yearned to use this room after so many frustrating nights of trying to read or write in the erratic candlelight of a windblown tent. That sturdy pine desk and table would be perfect for his maps and papers, while the thick burgundy-colored drapes could be drawn for privacy. When Elizabeth returned, Houston decided to allow her to carry the conversation.

"Do you still prefer being addressed as 'Sam,' rather than 'Samuel'?" she asked.

"Yes, but if you prefer 'Samuel,' it's all right with me."

"I have a difficult time thinking of a general being addressed as 'Sam.' Since you don't mind, I will address you as 'Samuel.' "

"Have it your way."

"I might have been a bit harsh with your young aide, who came here dressed in Sunday clothes, requesting use of our land for your army. You must understand this is a critical time of year for planting. We have a large annual investment already made in slaves, livestock, and equipment."

"I want you to know, Elizabeth, that Jason's clothes were given to him after his own were practically reduced to rags. He's one of the few survivors of the massacre at Goliad."

She rose and walked to a window. "I'm sorry," she whispered. She stood there silently for a long moment, before turning to face Houston. "Samuel, Will Travis was our attorney. I knew nothing of law, but I certainly knew he was careful and considerate in explaining so much to me after Edgar's death. I have been distressed since learning what happened at the Alamo. I want to know why you sent him there, with so few men, and why you didn't help him."

"I suppose," Houston sighed, "I'll live with this until I die. I didn't send him to the Alamo; Governor Smith did. I was against defending that position, but Bowie and Travis insisted. I tried to get Fannin to reinforce them and, Lord knows, Travis tried, but to no avail. I couldn't help form the new government and gather troops in time to reinforce the Alamo garrison."

"I was in San Felipe when Will's letter of February 24 arrived, appealing for help. It was so typical of him to mingle high-flown language with practical details, and an assertion that the Lord was on his side. But I must say I was disappointed in the recent convention. I viewed it as the politicians insisting on another long meeting while Will, isolated with his small group, called for help in the face of a huge Mexican army."

"Elizabeth, we could only do what we thought best for our country. You had a great deal of respect for Travis. Bear in mind, some of these men with me have lost family and friends at the Alamo, Goliad and elsewhere. Sacrifices have been great. We all may be killed soon, but I shall not surrender our country to Santa Anna."

"Not long ago, Judge Williamson stopped by here with his rangers, heading west. I believed that between his force and yours, there was no danger to our land. What has happened?"

"I also respect Williamson and the rangers, but Lord, that's only a small Indian fighting outfit. Santa Anna has about six thousand men under arms in Texas. If I could keep all our men together, which I cannot, I would be lucky to have one thousand. That's why I desperately need time and a place for training. The souls of our lost compatriots cry for vengeance, and . . ."

"Don't make a speech, Samuel. I understand the situation perfectly well."

"Then, you will help us?"

"Yes, I will help, but I want a few things agreed upon. Can you complete your training in two weeks?"

"Yes."

178

"Then I will delay planting. In the house, you may have use of this parlor only; it's accessible to the front door. I will have this room cleared so you can move in your bedding and whatever else you desire."

"Please leave it as it is. I'll sleep outside in a tent. I don't want my men to think I take advantage of my rank for such comfort. However, use of this room for writing and planning will be most helpful."

"There is a sensitive matter that concerns me, Samuel. You have quite a reputation for drinking."

"That won't be a problem, Elizabeth. I've not been drunk once during this campaign, nor will I be."

"Nevertheless, I do not permit hard liquor in this household and I allow cigars only after the evening meal."

"It's your house."

"Do we have anything further to discuss?"

This woman would make quite a politician, Houston thought. She's resolute, but reasonable, a rare combination these days. "Elizabeth, I appreciate your cooperation. I'll sign a government note to repay you for anything we use or consume. I trust we will have access to the livestock, corn, and game on your land?"

"I knew that was coming. I suppose so. Those men can't whip the Mexican army without good food in their stomachs. Since I must rely on a government note for payment, I suppose we'd better get on with winning this war."

As Elizabeth and Houston walked to the door, they saw Jason and Molly chatting under an oak tree on the front lawn. "Samuel, I do not want any wartime romances on the Hargrove Plantation."

"Elizabeth, you drive a hard bargain, but on that point, the general pleads lack of jurisdiction."

For the first time during their conversation, Elizabeth smiled. She had devoted the two years since her husband's death to her children and to the plantation. Nothing had ever interfered until this agreement with Houston; she had not figured on Molly's falling in love as well.

Houston called to Jason and mounted. He tipped his hat to Elizabeth and Jason waved repeatedly to Molly as they rode away towards the ferry. Elizabeth returned to the parlor and sat down to write Rebecca Cummings, the girl who had been betrothed to Travis.

My Dear Rebecca:

Because of the enemy advance into our country, I suppose you may have departed your home at Mill Creek. I only hope this letter finds you and that you are well, wherever you may be.

I have hesitated to write, knowing my words cannot compensate in any manner for the loss of your beloved, but I pen them in the hope of providing some comfort in your mourning. During the first miserable days after my husband's death, I found solace in cherished memories of our most enjoyable times together. He lives in my heart today, as I'm sure Will lives in yours, and Will's heroic stand will live forever in the hearts of Texans who love their country.

I wanted you to know that today I agreed to permit the Texan army, under General Houston, to occupy our land for the purpose of training for battle. I will aid our cause as best I can with the fervent prayer that our forces will avenge the death of Will and his brave compatriots at the Alamo.

Will was more than our attorney, he was our dear friend, and I loved him as another son, for he was always kind and courteous to me. I shall always remember his unstinting idealism and chivalry. I admired his incomparable . . .

"Mother, must you carry on so about Will Travis?"

"Molly, how rude to be reading over my shoulder."

"I'm sorry, Mother, but you have been in a dreadful mood ever since we heard about the fall of the Alamo. Will Travis is gone. You should think about today, and the future."

"Perhaps you're right," she sighed, "but it's difficult for you to understand how I feel. Your father had never explained to me the legal and financial aspects of this plantation. There were many problems after his death that I was unable to grasp. Frankly, without the help of Will and Judge Williamson, I would have given up and returned to Virginia. By staying, I have preserved all that your father had developed, and you must know that I have a strong attachment to this land."

"Of course, Mother, so do the boys and I. We love this land. I only want you to help General Houston and try to forget what cannot be changed."

"I believe you're more concerned about his young aide, Jason, than about the general and his army."

Molly blushed and walked away.

Soon, Houston moved his army to the long line of timber between the Brazos and the main fields of the Hargrove Plantation. A wide creek flowed near the lower part of the camp with adequate water for all their needs. After the men had settled into their new camp, Houston summoned Burleson and Sherman. "Sidney, you are to organize the second regiment," Houston said. "I want it done today, so we can begin full drills tomorrow."

"I'll have it organized, General," Sherman said, "but I know nothing about your drill plans."

"I apologize, gentlemen. I wanted to see how much terrain we would have. Thanks to the generosity of Mrs. Hargrove, we have all the land we need. We can even drill with one long column on that wide field over there."

"Why drill a one-column advance?" Sherman asked. "We're going to be in a concealed attack situation or defending."

"Sidney, I want our men prepared to attack or defend in open terrain or from concealment. Now, remember the distance a unit can fire in unison is determined by the shortest range weapon in that unit. If a soldier has an old musket that won't fire accurately past eighty yards, then that unit must not fire until within eighty yards of the enemy. They must understand the importance of disciplined firing in combat."

"Sam, I'm not sure we can get these men under that kind of tight control," Burleson said.

"Ed, first you try. If they won't cooperate, I'll call them together. I trust you two agree this training is necessary?"

Burleson and Sherman nodded, but they anticipated serious complaints from their men. However, a stronger sense of resolve had settled into the Army of Texas and the field commanders encountered fewer complaints than expected. The first day of drills went well.

In his new planning room that afternoon, Houston was studying maps when the Hargrove boys asked permission to see him. Edgar resembled his late father, tall and thin with long black hair falling around his handsome face. Garth looked more like his mother. "We want to join your army, sir," Edgar said.

"Today, sir," echoed Garth.

"Have you gentlemen discussed this with your mother?"

"Well, no, sir," said Edgar, "but she would understand. We both can handle a rifle. Dad taught us."

Houston thought about this offer for a brief moment. Two more sharpshooters would certainly be welcome in the army, but they were just boys. Lord help him if their mother reacted as he expected she would. He glanced at some notes he had been making about provisions. "Right now I believe you men would be more valuable to the Republic of Texas in another capacity. Are you ready and willing to serve your country as best you can?"

They nodded eagerly.

"Splendid. I want you to organize the Civilian Food Corps. Since your mother has delayed planting, ask her permission to get field hands to assist you. Major Hockley will give you our daily requirements and you will be responsible for meeting those needs. We want buffalo meat, venison, turkey, all the stray longhorns you can round up, and squirrels or rabbits for stew. Also give Major Hockley an inventory of the hogs and corn available. You see, men, an army travels on its stomach. Unless you provide the Army of Texas with provisions, we won't be able to whip the enemy. Agreed?"

When the boys nodded, Houston shook their hands. "Gentlemen, report to Major Hockley." They made a sort of salute before scrambling out the door in search of Hockley.

At twilight, Houston rode through the camp on an informal inspection, pausing to chat with company commanders and foot soldiers. Fresh game was cooking, the savory smoke drifting among the live oaks and willows. The ration of corn had already been increased from one to two ears per day. Morale, Houston observed, was improving. Chirping crickets and croaking bullfrogs filled the air as darkness settled along the Brazos River bottom. Houston accepted an invitation to share a meal with Captain Seguin, just back from a scouting mission to the west. They were joined by Hendrick Arnold, a free Negro who was proving himself as a scout equal to Deaf Smith and Henry Karnes.

As the men ate roast beef and cornbread, a foot soldier at a nearby campfire swore furiously. "That's a new blister," he said, peeling off a boot. "The worst damned blister since Gonzales. 'March!' 'Quick Time!' 'Double Quick Time!' Hell, we were running. If old Sam wants us to run, he ought to give us hosses."

Seguin laughed. "I suppose, Sam, that the men are going to complain no matter what you do."

"I can live with that," Houston said. "Soldiers always complain. It's part of being a soldier."

"I can tell you, my men are far more cooperative," Seguin said. "But the first few days after the news of the Alamo were hell. Everyone had his own idea about how to run the war. The Goliad Massacre sobered them up. They know we have to pull together to avoid a disaster such as Fannin met."

"Apparently, when he started out," Houston said, "Fannin had no intelligence on Urrea's whereabouts. Are you two satisfied that our intelligence system is working?"

Arnold nodded. "I've ridden the perimeter of guards in all directions. The enemy shouldn't surprise us, especially since we're making it so difficult for them to learn our army's movement and strength."

"We're getting a big assist from the Brazos," Seguin said. "I'd wager anyone a new rifle that Santa Anna is furious, trying to find a way to cross. I believe only the devil would have designed such a feisty, treacherous river. The currents are vicious and there are strange, shifting sands along the banks, as dangerous as quicksand."

"We couldn't ask for a more effective buffer between us and Santa Anna," Houston said.

As they finished their meal, a guard rode up from the east, out of breath. "General Houston, there is a large party of Indians approaching, two or three hundred."

"How far away?" Houston asked.

"We challenged them at the main guard post on the east perimeter. Their chief agreed to wait there if he could speak to you. He called you his brother, 'The Raven.' "

Houston sighed. "That must be Chief Bowles. You two want to ride out with me?" Though his face remained impassive, Houston knew there was a serious problem at hand, possibly with the treaty negotiated less than two months previously with the Cherokees. With all those warriors accompanying him, Chief Bowles was not paying a social call. As they rode toward the east guard post, Houston asked Seguin if he thought Santa Anna might have influenced the chief. "I have no idea," Seguin said. "I can only say I would rather fight Santa Anna's entire army in the open than a few hundred Cherokees in these woods at night."

Beside a huge campfire, Chief Bowles awaited The Raven. When the old chief saw Houston was accompanied by two men, he designated two braves to flank him and directed the others to retire beyond the campsite. "My friend," Bowles said, "I have a heavy heart and weary body. I have traveled for all these many years in search of peace; yet, today, I find my people again in danger of losing their land."

"Chief, you know that our treaty was made in good faith. You know that I, your brother, will do all in my power to make certain the treaty is honored."

Bowles' weathered face remained expressionless as he poked with a long stick into the fire. "There will be no more fertile land filled with game. We will not move again. We will fight." The braves nodded as the old chief poked around the fire again, never changing expression. "Your enemy tells us to join them to keep our land. They say the white man has forced us from our land while they have kept their bargains. They say they do not want this land of ours. They say your new chiefs will take this land from us, if your people should win the war."

"Who among the enemy has told you these things?" Houston asked.

From a leather pouch in his lap, Chief Bowles produced two letters. He handed them to Houston, who could not read Spanish and so passed them to Seguin. One was signed by Santa Anna and a second, by General Filisola. Seguin assured Houston they were as Bowles had said, carefully worded so as not to threaten the chief, but with veiled references to Mexican military superiority that guaranteed victory over the small band of rebels and "perfidious foreigners."

They're clever, Houston thought. This puts Chief Bowles under tremendous pressure from his people. Our treaty has not been ratified, the enemy has the upper hand, and I am the only Texan leader they trust. If I should be killed or captured, they fear they would lose their land by having placed all their hopes on me.

Houston removed his hat, gesturing around the campfire. "We are all children of the same Great Spirit. We meet as brothers who love the land, who want to live in peace. You may assure your people, Great Chief, that The Raven will work in all ways that he can for your people to remain in peace on your land. In Texas there is room for all who want peace and a place to raise their families, free from war and the fear of invading armies. Our army will defeat the enemy in due time. Be patient, awaiting that day. Your people will never suffer at the hands of the army under my command. You have my solemn word."

Chief Bowles did not move. One of his warriors, who understood most of what Houston had said, seemed mildly reassured. The other brave had remained impassive throughout the discussion.

"Now," Houston said, "since we seem to have concluded the business at hand, I wonder if you gentlemen would excuse the chief and me for a few minutes? I need to inquire of him about personal matters regarding some of my friends in the tribe."

Houston and the old chief strolled between the campfire and the guard post. "I understand your concerns, old friend," Houston said in a voice barely above a whisper.

"And I know yours, Raven. You came to us before your enemy won these bloody battles. Had you not come, I am afraid my people would have supported your enemy. They believe you will soon be defeated and Santa Anna will punish all those who have not cooperated with him. General Filisola has a grant of land in this area, thus he will be a strong influence in the future, should your army be defeated. Our people hear talk that you will retreat beyond the Sabine, leaving this country to Santa Anna. I had to convince my people that we should hear from your lips that you intend to defeat your enemy and protect our treaty."

"Were they satisfied?"

"Yes, for the time being. I will be able to convince my people to stay neutral. But serious doubts have been raised over the treaty. What assurance can you give me?"

"I must admit that there are white men coming to Texas who have no desire to help the Cherokee. They would search for reasons to disregard the treaty. What I wanted to tell you privately is that if I lead our army to victory, I should become president of this new government. I would exert strong influence to see that the treaty is ratified, though I still could not guarantee it."

"I know your word is good, Raven, but I fear you have little chance of success in this war. I wish I could help, but that is out of the question."

"Have you replied to those letters?"

"No, I wanted first to seek your advice."

"I suggest you not reply for a few weeks. If we should lose the war, you can claim you didn't understand them. If we win the war, you've got a treaty that I will try my best to get ratified."

"Agreed," said the old chief. "Now tell me, how do you expect to defeat such a large army with your small force?"

"I don't know. I can only fight with the men I have, and hope my enemy makes a major error in judgment."

"I understand. Keep your head clear. Fortune may be on your side, but be prepared to move with the speed of the wind."

"I will. Farewell, old friend," Houston said, shaking the hand of one of the few people on earth he trusted completely.

Chapter 18

ON the following morning, Houston reviewed the infantry drills and was encouraged by the enthusiasm of the troops. In the planning room, Houston drew up a chart of organization for the cavalry, but could not think of a man qualified to be commander. "I'll start conducting cavalry drills myself," he said to Hockley. "Maybe we'll turn up the man we need."

Houston ordered an obstacle course prepared for cavalry drills. He had thirty willow limbs driven into a small field in a zig-zag pattern, each limb trimmed until its top, covered by a bandana, stood as high as the head of a mounted horseman. The object of the course was to land a saber slash on each limb below the bandana, without breaking stride.

Should have limited it to twenty limbs, Houston thought, after he dashed through the course with a seventy-five percent score. No other member of the cavalry could match him. "Some of these men don't know how to handle a horse properly," he said to Hockley, "and some don't have a horse worth handling. How many mounted men could we put in the field today?"

"Sixty."

"I mean prepared for combat, both the man and the horse."

"Then I would say no more than forty. About twenty of those horses are old and worn out."

"Have the Hargrove boys proved reliable?"

"No problems."

"Then ask them to find twenty fast horses in the next forty-eight hours."

"Sam, how in the devil are they going to do that?"

"We lack skilled cavalrymen, but we do have cowboys who know how to break wild mustangs. Get those boys to show our men where to find them."

Returning to the house, Houston stepped onto the sun-drenched porch as Elizabeth walked out the front door. "How is your army shaping up?" she asked.

"The infantry has no bayonets, the cavalry has no commander, and the artillery commander has no artillery. Other than those minor problems, I have the finest army on this side of the Brazos, assuming Santa Anna is still on the other side."

"Samuel, if that was meant as a joke, I don't think it's at all humorous."

"Elizabeth, it's the gospel truth," he said, walking past her to his planning room where Hockley joined him.

"Our two cannons are en route to Harrisburg," Hockley said. "They were on a ship from New Orleans with a Dr. Rice and his twin daughters. The people on board named those cannons the 'Twin Sisters.' It's rained again along the coast so it may be difficult getting them here."

"What size cannon?"

"Six pounders."

"They're not big sisters, but that's all right, George; heavy artillery slows us down. Those will be fine for maneuvering on a battlefield. Tell Neill we'll pull them in near Harrisburg. No sense taking a chance on their getting bogged down bringing them here."

Dr. Alexander Ewing and Dr. Anson Jones had requested permission to see Houston. Burnet had appointed Ewing chief surgeon for the Army of Texas, one of the few appointments Houston had heartily agreed upon. A handsome young Irishman, Ewing was one of the finest doctors in the territory. Jones had been appointed surgeon for the new second regiment under the command of Sidney Sherman. Houston was curious as to the purpose of their call. He had granted all their requests for medical supplies, rushed from Nacogdoches through his friends Henry Raguet and Adolphus Sterne.

Ewing came directly to the point. "General, we're here to request that you alter the training schedule."

"Alter?" Houston asked.

"I should have said 'reduce,' General. These men are being trained too hard."

"Part of the problem," Jones said, "is that we need a system to determine if a man is medically able to train, instead of leaving that decision to the man or his company commander."

"Gentlemen," Houston said, "I have not the vaguest idea what you're talking about. A man reports to duty, unless he's sick. If he's sick, he reports to you for treatment."

"We have forty-seven men," Ewing said, "who are too sick to train; they will not be ready for several days. We have another forty who are marginal."

"What does that mean?" Houston asked.

"It means we won't know for a day or two whether they will develop a serious fever," Ewing said. "These cases are not easy to diagnose or treat. Some start with measles, others with a mild fever.

They may recover in a few days, or they may become seriously ill." Ewing didn't want to admit that the sudden weather changes in Texas confounded his medical experience. Volunteers from America often couldn't tolerate those changes without developing a cough or mild fever. These cases worsened when men trained hard, worked up a sweat, then bathed in the cool water of the creek.

"Are any of these men going to die?" asked Houston.

"A few," Ewing said. "No one takes measles seriously, but this disease can have serious complications. We've lost three men, as well, to fevers that neither I nor Dr. Jones could diagnose."

Houston was nettled that Dr. Ewing had not brought this problem to his attention sooner. He had reviewed sick call lists daily, but had not suspected the serious nature of the illnesses. Reducing the training schedule was almost unthinkable, yet this problem was indeed serious if almost one hundred men were unfit for combat, one in eight of the entire army at the Hargrove Plantation.

"Gentlemen, I would rather have a small, combat-ready army than a larger one in less than top physical condition. Therefore, I will instruct the company commanders to have any man with measles report to you immediately, plus any man with a cough or signs of fever or fatigue. This should prevent those who are most vulnerable from wearing themselves down. Those who have the strength to train on schedule will continue to do so. Is that acceptable?"

"Yes, General, but please instruct the commanders to exercise diligence," Ewing said. "Some of these men are walking a fine line between health and serious illness."

"Doctor, we're all walking a fine line between life and death," Houston said.

After the doctors departed, Hockley handed a letter to Houston. "I intercepted this letter today. It's from that young lieutenant named Perry, to Robert Potter, secretary of the navy. So far as I can tell, this Perry is the last problem of any consequence remaining in camp."

Houston read the letter carefully. It was a long diatribe on Houston's alleged incompetence as commander-in-chief. It detailed Perry's theory which he implied was widely accepted that Houston would not engage the enemy and that a retreat beyond the Trinity was imminent.

"He may as well be an agent for Santa Anna," Houston said.

"I believe he's the source for President Burnet's rather scathing letters. You recall that Potter is a close ally of Burnet?"

"You bet I do. And did you know that Potter has secured funds for, of all things, four schooners? Our only artillery is coming as a gift from the people of Cincinnati, Ohio, and Burnet is buying ships. At any rate, I'm putting an end to this foolishness. Fetch Perry."

When the unsuspecting Perry arrived, Houston greeted him cordially. "Are you enjoying your tour of duty with this army?"

"Yes, sir."

"Have you been fed well?"

"Tolerably well. Better since arriving here, sir."

"Do you find a sense of discipline in this army?"

"At first, I admit that I was somewhat concerned. Yet of late there seems to be a higher sense of discipline."

"What about combat readiness?"

"Sir, I had my military training at West Point. Some of the training here is, well, a bit unorthodox."

"Have you ever been in combat?"

"No, sir."

"Well, I have. The training here is designed to prepare our men for the type of combat they can expect when we engage the enemy. Does that make sense?"

"Yes, sir."

"What single element in this army do you consider to be most important?"

"Why, they're all important. The infantry, cavalry and artillery should be closely coordinated."

"You're wrong, mister. If you had grasped our situation, you would know the infantry is most important, cavalry second, and artillery third. In a defensive position, we don't need cavalry at all. Didn't you know that?"

"Why, yes, sir, but the way you posed the question, I didn't want you to think I believe any one element is not important."

"Is this a land war?"

"Of course, sir."

"Can the enemy threaten our coast with warships?"

"No, sir."

"Then tell me why the Republic of Texas has purchased four schooners, before providing even basic artillery for the army."

"I . . . I can't answer that, sir."

"Sounds stupid, doesn't it?"

"I guess it does, sir."

"Then tell me why you, an officer in this army, are corresponding with the secretary of navy regarding our army's conduct?"

Perry was dumfounded. Had Potter informed on him? Or Burnet? He had not written him directly, but he assumed Potter had been in contact with Burnet regarding his reports on Houston. Hockley and Houston are incompetent, he thought, but they are honorable men; surely they hadn't monitored his mail. "I . . . I don't know what you're driving at, sir. I write to several people about many things."

"This is what I'm driving at," Houston said, brandishing the letter to Potter.

Perry turned pale. "I . . . I had no idea mail was under scrutiny," he said.

"Mister, so far as I'm concerned, this is treason. Do you understand what that means?"

Hockley had stood by the door, quietly enjoying Perry's mental torture. However, he was startled by the word "treason," fearing Houston might order Perry executed.

"Sir, I assure you I had no intention of aiding the enemy. Those were only impressions written to a friend."

"Mr. Potter is a cabinet officer in the new government. His influence with President Burnet and other officials is widely known, which you understood when you wrote him. Your so-called impressions were calculated to undermine the commander-in-chief of the army, during time of war. That's aiding the enemy, as I interpret military conduct, and mister, I am the one who interprets military conduct in this army."

Perry shuddered. "I . . . I mean I understand, but I . . ."

"How many times have you written Potter?"

"Three, perhaps four times, sir."

"With the same venom I've read in this letter?"

"Well, I don't know that . . ."

"The same or worse?" Houston's voice had grown progressively more demanding. "Answer yes or no!"

"Yes, sir."

Pointing his finger directly at Perry's head, Houston arose from his chair. "Your criticism of my conduct is unfounded, unjustified, self-serving, and above all, stupid. Isn't it?"

"Yes, sir," Perry gasped.

"I suspect you want to rectify your mistakes as soon as possible, don't you?"

"Yes, sir."

"Well, fine, but if I hear of one more word from your pen or one peep from your mouth that is outside military conduct, you, sir, will be brought to trial, after which you can choose whether you want to face a firing squad or to be hanged from the nearest oak tree. Is that clear?"

"Yes, sir."

"You're dismissed."

Hockley sighed. After Perry departed, he said, "Lord, Sam, I was afraid you were so worked up, you were going to have that boy executed."

"He's not worth shooting," Houston smiled, "and I wasn't nearly as worked up as he was. I just wanted to scare the daylights out of him."

"I suspect he'll be writing Potter that you have suddenly changed into a combination of Andy Jackson and George Washington."

It was late afternoon as Houston and Hockley walked onto the porch to observe the men retiring from drill fields to prepare for their evening meal. With a long-handled dipper, Houston took a swig of well water from a wooden bucket. "That's just what we don't need," he said, pointing to the western sky where a heavy bank of thunderheads was gathering.

"Probably no more than another little spring shower," Hockley said.

Houston walked from the porch onto the front lawn from where he could view the entire western horizon. An ominous silence fell across the woods west of the plantation as sounds of wildlife ceased with a final lonely call from a whippoorwill. Billowy white thunderheads, gentle in appearance, were gradually yielding to darker clouds laced with frequent streaks of lightning. No thunder could be heard since the storm was several miles distant.

From years of living outdoors with the Cherokees, Houston had developed a keen sense for changes in humidity and pressure. "It's too sultry, George. Way too sultry. There's more in those clouds than rain. We've only got a few minutes. Fetch Burleson, Sherman, Neill, Ewing and Jason. Hurry!"

Houston dashed into the house, finding Elizabeth overseeing the churning of butter while instructing Molly on baking a pecan pie. "Elizabeth, I must ask you to expand our agreement. We must bring the seriously ill men into your house. There's a storm coming."

"Don't you have tents that protect the bedridden?"

"Of course, but come here," he said, pulling her toward the back porch. A biting wind was sweeping across the plantation as the approaching clouds were rapidly reducing visibility. "For Heaven's sake, Samuel, bring all the sick to the house. We'll make do."

As Houston ran back to the front porch, Elizabeth told Molly to gather all spare blankets and quilts for the back porch where they soon began securing them between columns to protect against wind and rain.

Houston found Burleson and Sherman awaiting him, with Neill dashing across the lawn a few steps ahead of Ewing. Jason had also responded to Hockley's call, reining up near the porch.

Shouting above the howling wind, Houston barked orders. "Ed, you and Sidney muster two hundred men! Transport all the sick into the house, under supervision of Dr. Ewing! Tell your company commanders to secure their camps on high ground, under trees! Jason, find the Hargrove boys and get them into the house! Neill, make sure all kegs of gunpowder are placed in those sheds! George, muster the cavalry! Move the horses away from the creek to that heavy clump of timber over there! Tell the men to tie those horses with enough slack for them to pitch, otherwise they'll kill themselves! Get moving!"

Houston rode through the camp, shouting to the men. "Secure everything you can! Tie it down! Stay away from the creek!" As he rode along, his mount, frightened by rolling thunder and responding to the intense activity, began pitching hard. Houston permitted him to pitch briefly, then spurred him toward the creek where he found a barechested young volunteer, holding onto a willow tree with trembling hands. "Come on, son, it isn't safe here."

"I've been in a twister before, General. It's safer to be in a low place."

"I haven't seen a twister, son, and there may have been a cloudburst up this creek. A wall of water can kill you just as easy as a twister."

Small raindrops began falling, driven by the strong westerly wind. The storm had caught the young volunteer washing his shirt and the cold raindrops sent sharp chills along his bare chest and spine. "Please, General, leave me alone."

"Son, there's nothing wrong with being afraid. Look at me."

The youngster looked up at the demanding figure on his large horse. His only impression of Houston had been as the unswerving leader of the army, bellowing commands that could be heard across a field. But as the rain pelted him, he realized the calm, measured voice he heard was similar to that of his father. He recalled that terrifying day when a twister had struck their farm. His brother had failed to heed his father's advice and had been swept to his death while running across a field, instead of lying in a ditch.

"Come on, son, I'll take you to the house where Dr. Ewing needs your help."

After the youngster ascended behind Houston, he was barely able to reach around the commander's torso to secure himself as Houston reined from the creek and dashed toward the house.

Jason and the Hargrove boys preceded him by seconds. They reported to Dr. Ewing, who was supervising the placement of more serious cases in rooms with maximum protection. Some of the sick would have to ride out the storm on the porch as every foot of vacant space was being utilized.

"Here's the man you requested," Houston said to Ewing, who glanced at the barechested youngster, then looked to Houston.

"I don't recall," he said, before catching a wink from Houston. "Oh yes, the other orderly. Find you a shirt, young man, then report to me here."

As the youngster searched for a shirt, Ewing grasped Houston's arm. "Thank you, General. Thank you very much. Some of these men couldn't survive out there."

"Thank Mrs. Hargrove," Houston said. "It's her house."

Windswept torrents of rain soon pounded the area, preventing Houston from making another run through the camp. Brilliant jagged streaks of lightning slashed through the April sky, illuminating the countryside briefly between relentless torrents of rain. Sharp thunderclaps reverberated across the plantation, shaking the house.

With only a moment or two to spare, Burleson and Sherman had succeeded in supervising their men to prepare for the storm. In tents under trees on high ground, their troops huddled and prayed the wind and rain would soon subside. Those without tents shivered under wagons after arranging heavy equipment for whatever protection it might afford.

As Houston watched and listened from the back porch, Jason came to his side. "General, I'd call this a frog strangler."

"We can live with the rain," Houston said, cupping his right hand to his ear. He was the first person on the porch to discern a constant low roaring noise, resounding steadily past the sporadic deafening roar of thunderclaps.

A few steps away, Dr. Ewing was wrapping a blanket around a sick soldier when he heard that noise. "My God, that's a twister!" he shouted.

Before Houston could respond, Molly screamed. Terrified and sobbing, she tossed a towel to the floor and started to run upstairs. Elizabeth held her by the shoulders. "There's no place to hide, Molly. Help Dr. Ewing and pray."

"I want to go to my room," she sobbed. "Please, Mother."

Elizabeth held her quietly for a moment, until she stopped crying. "Now we must help Dr. Ewing."

Houston calmly held his hand to his ear for another moment before shaking his head. "That's not a twister, Jason. It's hail." Houston proceeded to walk rapidly through each room, reassuring the alarmed men.

Upon returning to the porch, he whispered to Jason. "I've been in hailstorms that were worse than twisters. I've seen hailstones the size of big peaches. They could kill our horses and all the livestock. Might even tear into tents and kill some men."

"For Heaven's sake, General. You just finished calming everybody down, and now you tell me that I think we're due some good luck."

"We'll know shortly," Houston said, peering into the awesome mosaic of twisting, windswept trees and driving torrents of rain, illuminated by brilliant flashes and streaks of lightning.

Jason had called the turn. Small hailstones soon crashed onto the plantation, but caused only minor damage. Nonetheless, that added terror from the sky prompted frothing horses to pitch even harder, and a few unprotected cattle and hogs were killed. The combination of protection from timber and tents or wagons was adequate for the men in their camp.

Grease lamps and candles could not withstand the swirling wind through the back porch, thus Ewing and his assistants had tended to the sick who were placed there by using what little light came through a kitchen window. As the storm finally subsided, Ewing shuddered at the thought of this scene having been the result of combat. He knew he could not have performed surgery under those conditions, nor even have dressed wounds properly.

Hockley reported to Houston that no men were injured seriously in the camp and the timber had protected the horses from the hail. Houston sighed, then smiled. As he watched the storm blow eastward, he slung an arm around Jason. "You know, son, that little old storm provided the best combat drill this army has had."

"Good Lord, General, why did you think of that?"

"I think about it all the time."

Chapter 19

DURING two uneventful days of limited activity on wet ground, the men grumbled about lack of dry firewood, settling for cold soup or stew with cornbread. Clear weather was drying the fields, but they had been soaked so thoroughly that Houston couldn't resume training until the third day after the storm. Riding again through the cavalry obstacle course, he found his proficiency reduced on ground that was slightly slick from remaining moisture. None of the other horsemen could match Houston, and he returned to his planning room still without a prospect for cavalry commander.

Hockley soon joined him with the word that an important visitor, Vice-President Lorenzo de Zavala, was due in camp late that afternoon. "I'm delighted Zavala is paying us a call," Houston said, "though I can't imagine why. He's taking a tremendous risk, traveling through country where Santa Anna could have advance units."

While preparing for Zavala's arrival, Houston approached Elizabeth. "You don't have to ask, Samuel. I have a guest room upstairs for the vice-president and I will expect you two for dinner."

"I'm grateful, Elizabeth. I hope this is not an imposition."

"Not really, Samuel. I must admit that I am rather anxious to meet Dr. Zavala. I have heard that he is a cultured gentlemen of the highest order, a rare person in this territory."

Houston didn't know whether to frown or smile. "I certainly wouldn't venture any advice about your dinner tonight since your cooking is superb. However, if there is a bottle of wine in the house, I suspect Dr. Zavala would enjoy some with his meal."

"Dr. Zavala, or General Houston?"

"Why, Elizabeth!"

"I'll see what might be available."

When Zavala arrived, Houston was surprised to see he had brought his son. "My son has insisted on joining the army," Zavala said. "He is an accomplished horseman, swordsman, and rifleman. He's too young to be a colonel and too old to be a lieutenant. May I suggest captain or major?"

"Major it is," Houston said, introducing them to Jason, who escorted young Zavala to the camp to meet Burleson and Sherman.

Three days of clear weather and constant attention had cured half of the sick men, who had returned to their units. Houston toured the training areas with Zavala, stressing that his only major frustration was the lack of a cavalry commander. As they stood talking on the front porch, Hockley joined them and shortly after Elizabeth emerged from the house. After introductions, she excused herself and Houston suggested they meet in the planning room. After they were seated, Houston produced a bottle of brandy. "Mrs. Hargrove doesn't permit hard liquor in this house. Brandy is not hard liquor, is it, Dr. Zavala?"

"It most certainly is not, General Houston."

While listening to Zavala describe trivial details of government operations, Hockley surmised his presence was causing the vice-president to be guarded, and he excused himself.

"All right, Lorenzo," Houston said the moment after Hockley departed, "you didn't come sloshing through the country to deliver your robust son to the army. Let's have it."

"Sam, I know the enemy troop strength as well as you. I understand the desperate military situation in which we find ourselves. I have studied the maps carefully. I offer no solution . . ."

"Lorenzo, for Heaven's sake, come to the point."

"Very well. The point is we also have a political crisis."

Had any other person in Texas said that to Houston, he would have spewed a curse and promptly reaffirmed his intention to ignore President Burnet. But he respected Zavala's judgment. "Burnet?" he asked.

"Yes," Zavala said, placing his glass on the table. "And Potter. With so many settlers suffering, and with the confusion and panic spreading, their venom against you is having a debilitating effect on remaining colonists."

"Why can't they understand that without troops, artillery, and training, we are not ready for battle?"

"I'm afraid nothing will satisfy them other than an immediate engagement."

"Engage the enemy when I'm sure to be killed or captured? So Burnet can run the war with Potter and his schooners launched against a non-existent enemy navy?"

"Sam, despite my worst personal misgivings, I have maintained a functional relationship with Burnet. He's vindictive, prone to making snap judgments, and highly sensitive to criticism."

"He's too thin-skinned; that's his problem."

"Perhaps, but I know of several bitter attacks made on you to influential people. In this desperate situation, unfortunately, they are listening."

196

"Who's listening?"

"Please, Sam, that's not the point. Four days ago, I became so concerned that I took the liberty of offering a compromise. I persuaded Burnet to hear me through and he finally agreed, but I assure you, this is a difficult proposition and one that you must honor."

"Now, you can't come riding in here expecting me to honor a deal you cut with Burnet without consulting me in advance."

"Time is running out. If you are forced to fight against odds similar to those at the Alamo, what are your chances?"

"You know what they are. That's why I have temporized, hoping Santa Anna will make a mistake. Burnet knows that."

"Sam, why not be a little more specific with him? Your recent letter infuriated him."

"It only takes one specific letter intercepted by the enemy, only one, to give Santa Anna that one bit of information he needs to force us into a battle we cannot win. I have no intention of specifying battle plans in written communication to anyone."

"That's what I expected you to say, and that's precisely why I persuaded Burnet to accept a compromise."

"Lorenzo, have they been using letters from a Lieutenant Perry?"

"Yes."

"There won't be any more from him. After a sudden burst of patriotism, he has pledged loyalty to me."

"That will help, I suppose, but the damage has been done. They not only say that you are reluctant to fight, they are using personal gossip, heavy drinking and such."

Houston cursed, slamming a stack of papers to the desk. "I suspected as much! You're barking up the wrong tree, Lorenzo. I regret you took the risk in coming here, but I will not deal with that damned old hog thief."

"That won't be necessary, Sam. Please hear me out. I discussed this whole situation in confidence with Rusk, who is certainly one of your allies. He agreed that something had to be done. So, I asked him to join the army as liaison to President Burnet, reporting what you and he believe should be reported, no more, no less. Burnet could hardly refuse since Rusk is the secretary of war."

Houston knew that pursuing a running political battle with Burnet would only reduce their slim chances of winning the war. He had returned to the window, watching campfires along the creekbed until, turning to face Zavala, he sighed. "All right, Lorenzo, I will cooperate with Rusk. I must admit you chose the only man in the government I believe would be an asset to our army."

"Rusk is mature for his age," Zavala said. "I have found him to be level-headed in government affairs. However, he is also anxious for combat. That may pose a problem, but you've dealt with that one all along."

"Moseley Baker and Wylie Martin refused to bring their companies here. Tom Rusk will be reasonable, I believe, when he sees how this army is progressing. Weather permitting, we'll have a reasonably well-disciplined army in another week. I wonder if there is any hope we might get some help from General Gaines, indirectly of course."

"We sent Carson, as secretary of state, to confer discreetly with General Gaines at Fort Jessup. American agreements with Mexico necessitate he remain in Louisiana. However, he is not unaware of our needs. He may soon grant furloughs for those men who might desire a better acquaintance with our country."

Houston smiled. "That might get us some volunteers who are combat-ready, for a change. I have something else in mind for General Gaines, should the need arise."

"For Heaven's sake, Sam, what is it? This is an extremely delicate area for President Jackson and the United States government."

"I'm sorry, Lorenzo, this involves a confidence I cannot break. It's one of a few long shots I plan to take, if necessary. Don't worry, I'm well aware of the precarious position President Jackson is in. I've read a few articles from newspapers back east that are favorable to Santa Anna; the undercurrent is the slavery question."

"If we win independence, do you believe the slavery issue will prevent us from attaining statehood?"

Houston took no position on the issue of slavery. He accepted the economic practice as a right of states, but he feared Texas would not easily be accepted into the United States because of the strident debate over the issue. "Yes," he said. "I believe we will be lucky to get recognition as a republic. Statehood will be much more difficult."

"Perhaps we can exploit the American fear of British and French influence re-emerging through their dealings with a new republic in need of financial assistance and further colonization, not necessarily American."

"Dr. Zavala, that's precisely the reason I want you on my team when I become president. It will take that kind of skillful diplomacy to negate opposition to Texas in the United States. Without it, we'll wither on the vine. We don't have the resources to develop a nation. It will be necessary to play the big powers against one another."

"Santa Anna, probably through Almonte, has been effectively exploiting the slavery issue. They had created considerable support with their policy of freeing slaves, declaring that their government stood for the freedom of mankind. However, they lost that advantage with the massacre at Goliad, which may ultimately cost them this province."

"I agree," Houston said, pouring another round of brandy. "If I could make a three-month speaking tour in the United States, talking about the Alamo and Goliad, I could raise five thousand volunteers. But we're sitting on a short fuse."

"I know, Sam, but take your time. I will continue to support your policy of temporizing. Each day that goes by turns the situation more our way. Think of the effects on Santa Anna's men. The rains must have taken a high toll in sickness. They must be bickering too about the conduct of the war. They are primed for making mistakes."

"That's the point of my strategy. The key ingredient I tell you in strict confidence." Houston walked again to a window. "As tough as these men are, as deeply as they crave vengeance, they're still outnumbered. They cannot possibly defeat an enemy force in open combat beyond two to one odds. If Santa Anna doesn't come to me, I will go after him, but only him, and only if there's a reasonable opportunity for victory."

"I had hoped you would want to engage only Santa Anna. To defeat another Mexican army, even that under Urrea, would in no manner be decisive."

"Precisely, Lorenzo. We've played long shots all through this revolution and this is the only route I can pursue to end the war in our favor."

Zavala relaxed, enjoying the brandy. He had feared Houston's intense dislike of Burnet would destroy his delicate arrangement. He understood Houston's reluctance to disclose strategy, and he only wished his political compatriots would accept the situation and stop calling for an immediate engagement. "I propose a toast, General, to your forthcoming victory."

Houston poured half a glass, pointing to his pocket watch on the table. "We have time for only this much," he said, "before getting dressed for dinner. I had rather cross swords with Burnet and Santa Anna together than incur the displeasure of our hostess."

Elizabeth and her children dressed in their finest for the dinner with Zavala as honored guest. She had carefully supervised preparation of the meal and her oldest slave, trained in Virginia as a waiter, served the steaming platter of smoked wild turkey, garnished with potatoes and onions. In addition, he served lye hominy, green beans, and biscuits with butter and honey. He poured white wine into the fine crystal goblets. Zavala's taste for exquisite meals had been honed in the best restaurants of Paris, Madrid, and Mexico City, but he found this hearty frontier meal savory after his day's journey.

"Dr. Zavala, I wonder if you have any late reports on the health of Stephen Austin?" Elizabeth asked.

"I believe he is improving, Mrs. Hargrove. The imprisonment he endured was debilitating, but Stephen appeared to have recovered before he left for the United States."

"I was surprised to learn," said Elizabeth, "that William H. Wharton was chosen as a commissioner to the United States, as well. From what little I understand about politics, I assumed he and Stephen were enemies."

Houston studied his plate, trying to think of a way to avoid another political discussion. But he was surprised to hear Zavala pursuing the conversation with obvious enthusiasm.

"Mrs. Hargrove," he said, "it's amazing how much wisdom and restraint our leaders have exercised. In this instance you mentioned, there were indeed serious differences between Stephen and Wharton. But the Texas leadership in their sound judgment named a third commissioner, Dr. Branch T. Archer, with the agreement of the other two. Dr. Archer is the unifying factor, and I am pleased to assure you that all three commissioners are working together, harmoniously, for our noble cause."

Houston winced. He's the honored guest, he thought, but he doesn't have to carry on like that.

"Why, that's marvelous, Dr. Zavala," Elizabeth said. "I never dreamed there were such delicate considerations in government business."

"I feel confident," Zavala said, turning to Houston, "that General Houston would agree there are outstanding Texan leaders, who are genuinely motivated, but who sometimes require a unifying factor to bring about cooperation."

"Yes, Dr. Zavala," Houston sighed. "You're quite right. However, I think it important for Mrs. Hargrove and her children to understand that three commissioners to the United States, serving with equal rank and responsibility, differ from army commanders with precise rank and responsibility. Wouldn't you agree, Dr. Zavala?"

"Of course, General," he nodded, proposing a toast to Texas independence. Houston joined the toast, biting his lip to avoid a chuckle.

As they lingered over pecan pie with coffee, Molly asked to be excused to help Dr. Ewing. She took a pot of soup to the back porch for the remaining patients, then slipped outside to meet Jason. She took his hands into hers. "It seems," she said, "like a year since we were alone."

"How long do we have?" he asked, glancing at a window of the dining room where sounds of laughter were barely audible.

"As long as Dr. Zavala will talk, Mother will listen. He started telling about his service in Europe and she was enthralled."

"How is General Houston's mood?"

"Just fine, Jason. To hear him and Dr. Zavala talk, the war will soon be over. Everyone was in such a pleasant humor, Mother even let me and the boys have a glass of wine."

What a perfect time, Jason thought, to approach Mrs. Hargrove for Molly's hand in marriage. He yearned to see Molly every minute of the day, but there were always other people present. He held her hand tightly as they strolled around the house to the front porch where Molly released his hand and moved silently to the tall white columns. She spoke across the shadowy porch. "I believe that you are about to say something to me, aren't you?"

Molly made it so easy for him, the words were out much more smoothly than he had dreamed he could make the proposal. She crossed the few steps between them and kissed him. For a long exhilarating moment, he held her to him before she pulled away, smiling, and glided back to the far end of the porch. "I knew this would happen," she said, "and I wish we could run away tonight."

"That's out of the question, but I will ask your mother for your hand, tonight, while she's in such fine spirits."

"Oh, Jason, it won't work. She'll say I'm too young, or that you may be killed next week. She won't listen. But maybe . . ."

"Maybe what?"

Molly's bright blue eyes twinkled. "Maybe General Houston could persuade her that we should be married. She respects him. He's our only hope."

"Molly, I don't think it's fair to ask General Houston."

" 'All's fair in love and war.' We're in both, Jason."

He thought of the times he had seen Houston explode when approached with an outlandish request. But if he had a choice, he had rather confront Houston than Mrs. Hargrove. "All right, Molly, but I want you with me. He's not going to accept this idea easily."

They stayed on the porch until they heard the dinner party breaking up. Zavala excused himself to retire, while Elizabeth went to the kitchen to supervise the cleaning up. Houston had gone into the parlor to review some reports when Jason and Molly knocked on his door. Standing before Houston, they lost some of their courage, as they could see he was tired and a bit irritable. Jason, trying to be casual, mentioned the beautiful sky outside, but was chopped off in mid-sentence by Houston. "Yes, I can see a beautiful sky out there, and I wonder why in the world you two are talking to me when you should be out under those stars."

"Well, General . . . sir," Jason stammered, "we have come to tell you . . . that we want to be married."

Houston grinned, reaching for the bottle of brandy. "That's more what I like to hear. Congratulations to you both. I know you will stay blissfully in love so long as you may live." Pouring three glasses, he proposed a toast to their forthcoming marriage. "You know," he said, savoring the warm aftertaste, "I almost said something to Elizabeth about you two acting like a pair of turtledoves. I guess she wanted you to surprise me, didn't she?"

When Jason bit his lip, hesitating to sally forth, Molly came to his rescue. "General Houston, Mother really respects you. I never thought she would cooperate with you as much as she has, but you persuaded her it was the right thing to do."

"Young lady, I appreciate the compliment, but you two are evading my question."

"General," Molly said, "you know Mother is a strong-willed person."

"If I had another brandy, I would say she is bull-headed, but I will accept 'strong-willed' for the moment."

"Well, because she is so strong-willed and because she thinks we are young and irresponsible, we knew we couldn't get her consent. Since you're so reasonable and persuasive, we decided you would be the only one to convince her that we should be married . . . tomorrow."

Houston winced, shaking his head. "You may as well ask me to dive into the Brazos River with a cannon tied to my back. I can't intrude into a family matter such as this."

Jason's face dropped, but Molly was undaunted. "General, a few moments ago you were delighted with what we told you. And you said you already knew we were in love, didn't you, sir?"

"Well, yes, young lady, but for Heaven's sake, I never dreamed you wanted me to convince your mother of the merits of your marriage, much less an immediate marriage."

"General," Molly pursued with tears in her eyes, "you're our only hope. If Jason should be killed in battle, I will go to my grave heartsick that I never knew him as my husband."

Houston sighed. He placed his glass on the table, and walked to a window overlooking the lawn bathed in pale moonlight. Molly's last statement had hit him hard. He recalled that Jason narrowly escaped death at Goliad, and how easily they might all lose their lives in a few days. "All right," he said. "I'll try."

Elizabeth had finished in the kitchen when she heard Molly's voice in the parlor. As she paused, Houston opened the door and she could see Molly holding Jason's hand while they bade the general goodnight. She hurried down the hall to confront them. "Samuel, this is too much! I've been as considerate and generous as I know how to be under the circumstances, but we agreed this parlor was designated for military purposes only. I am the head of this household, not you! My daughter had no permission to be up this late and certainly no permission to be with this young man. You have abused my household and I demand an explanation!"

Molly's face paled, and Jason wanted to dive through the nearest window. Houston, however, waved them out and took Elizabeth gently by the arm. "Now, now, Elizabeth, let's you and I have a little chat." He led her to a seat in the parlor, and smiled. "That was a wonderful meal you served tonight, absolutely superb."

"You said that an hour ago."

"Well, I just wanted you to know how much I appreciate the hospitality you extended to Dr. Zavala."

202

"That's kind of you, Samuel. He was very gracious and I thoroughly enjoyed the conversation. Now, I'm tired and it's late. I want to know why my daughter was in this room at this hour with Jason Gates."

"Elizabeth, do you mind if I have just this one glass of brandy?"

"Why, of course not, Samuel. I do appreciate the fact that you have not abused spirits since coming here. Your reputation is exaggerated."

"That's kind of you, Elizabeth. I appreciate that, and I want you to know how much I appreciate your cooperation."

"Your gallantry and manners are well established. Now, please, I want an explanation."

"Well," Houston said with a weak smile, "it seems as though I have been appointed Cupid."

"What are you talking about?"

"Elizabeth, now I'd like for you to be calm and reasonable about this. Is that a bargain?"

"What is it, Samuel?"

"Your daughter and Jason want to be married."

Startled, she sat upright in the chair, clasping her hands in her lap. "Why didn't they come to me?"

"Molly loves you dearly and Jason certainly respects you, but my dear Mrs. Hargrove, you are indeed a resolute individual. They're afraid of you."

She stood up and walked to the window, unable to meet Houston's eyes. She stood a moment, fighting off the desire to cry. "That hurt, Samuel," she said softly.

"I'm sorry, Elizabeth, I know this is a family matter, but they came to me because things have happened so fast. They're frightened about the war and Lord knows what else. These are difficult times."

"Samuel, she's just a child. She doesn't know a bale of cotton from a saddle blanket."

"Perhaps so, Elizabeth, but she is old enough to marry and she loves Jason."

"Love? Puppy love, perhaps. There hasn't been time for more."

"Love can develop suddenly. You can see it in their eyes."

Regaining her composure, she turned from the window to face Houston. "Would you marry Anna Raguet tomorrow?"

"That's an entirely different situation."

"It's entirely different because you would weigh the consequences more carefully than you have weighed them in the case of my daughter and your young aide."

"And well I should. I'm two decades older than Jason."

"You're one to lecture me on marriage, Samuel, having left not one, but two wives. And wasn't your problem with Eliza Allen in Tennessee due to a hasty marriage?"

Houston trembled. He had never discussed the breakup of his marriage to Eliza and he expected others to honor his feelings. "What I did in Tennessee was more in Eliza's best interests than mine. I will not discuss it further. That was an insensitive remark, Elizabeth, and I'm disappointed in you."

"Forgive me," she sighed. "I'm tired and terribly upset. I must admit Molly is somewhat mature for her age. She can cook and keep house. Those are not my real concerns."

"Jason?"

"No, of course not. Any mother would want him as a son-in-law, but be realistic, Samuel, instead of listening to their romantic nonsense. Jason could be killed next week, leaving Molly with a broken heart, and possibly a child with no father."

"Molly told me a few moments ago that if they were not married and Jason were killed, she would spend the rest of her life mourning for not having known him as her husband."

"Do you honestly believe she loves him that much?"

"After you chastised me so severely, I hesitate to comment," he smiled. "All I will say is she was looking me squarely in the eye when she said that. Your daughter wouldn't tell a fib, would she?"

"Samuel, I believe I would like just a small glass of brandy."

As Houston poured, his spirits lifted, recalling the forthright manner with which Molly Hargrove had confronted him. Relaying her thoughts to Elizabeth had proven more effective than he had anticipated.

"Elizabeth, I believe you have a situation similar to that described tonight by the distinguished Dr. Zavala. You must rise above personal concerns and exercise extraordinary statesmanship for the well-being of your noble family."

"This is no time to jest, Samuel." She sipped the brandy, pondering her objections. Fundamentally, she concluded, it's Molly's decision, not mine. "Very well," she sighed. "When do they want to be married?"

"Tomorrow."

"I suspected as much. There is no one available to perform the ceremony. Since we now live in a free republic, I have no intention of permitting a marriage by bond. I always viewed that particular custom as pagan."

Houston rubbed his chin, not having considered how the marriage was to be performed. With the exception of San Antonio de Bexar, priests were scarce in the Texas territory, thus, couples often lived together under their marriage by bond for extended periods of time before a priest finally arrived.

"Well, Elizabeth, I may have the solution. We have a parson with us in the army who can perform the ceremony."

"And what congregation does this parson represent?"

"Why, I don't believe he has a congregation. He's one of those circuit-riding parsons. But, believe me, he can read the Bible, says prayers better than . . ."

"That won't do. I won't permit that kind of marriage. I was married in a church and the least my daughter can have is a bona fide minister."

"Elizabeth, be reasonable. You know the Mexican government didn't permit Protestant congregations in Texas."

"I have attended services at McMahon's Chapel, Samuel, conducted by Brother Littleton Fowler, a Methodist missionary. I want him summoned to perform the ceremony."

"Elizabeth, do you know why that congregation, the only Protestant church in Texas, exists? It's practically in Louisiana. They've defied the Mexican authorities for two years, and I salute Brother Fowler's courage and dedication, but that's too darn far for anyone to travel from here. Besides, there may not be time."

"Military matters are not my concern, Samuel. I will not compromise on this point. Jason should be capable of traveling through the country between here and McMahon's Chapel, there being no enemy with which to contend."

"Elizabeth, I have refused all furlough requests, except for emergencies. I cannot send Jason on a mission to get himself married. Morale would suffer."

"Again, Samuel, the military situation is your concern. My decision is final."

"Very well," he sighed. "I'll see what can be worked out."

As Houston walked toward the front porch, he considered his next move. They'll have to understand this is the best bargain they're going to get. Smiling, he beckoned Molly and Jason to come into the house. Before he could speak, Molly embraced him and Jason shook his hand. "Now, hold your horses," he said. "You're going to be married, but it will take a few days."

They looked at each other, then Molly dashed into the parlor where she hugged her mother. Releasing Molly, Elizabeth pulled Jason to her for a hearty embrace, as Molly planted a fast kiss on Houston's cheek. "I knew you could do it, General," she whispered.

Houston smiled down at her. "Young lady, don't ever come telling me again about strong-willed people. I only hope Lieutenant Gates can hold his own with you."

"Well," Elizabeth said, brushing away tears, "you two certainly conjured up an unfair match. I could never withstand this overgrown Cupid."

As Elizabeth and Molly walked away arm in arm, Houston drew Jason aside to explain Elizabeth's insistence on bringing the Methodist missionary to the plantation "Jason, you know that only in extreme emergencies have I granted furloughs. Colonel Neill, however, has filed a request for more metal to make grapeshot, a priority request that must be filled at Nacogdoches by Raguet and Sterne. You will be the courier. Here's McMahon's Chapel on the map, east of Nacogdoches."

"General, that looks like about one hundred and fifty miles from here."

"I'm afraid that's right. I have no idea whether we'll be here when you return with Brother Fowler. If we have departed, go ahead and get married, but the following day I want you en route to rejoin the army. That's the best I can do for you."

"General, I don't know how to thank you."

"You'd better get some sleep so you can take advantage of this clear weather. It can't last much longer. Goodnight, son."

Chapter 20

JASON departed at daybreak. Houston missed breakfast with the Hargroves and Zavala, but he joined the vice-president as he bade farewell to Elizabeth. Walking across the lawn, Houston noticed that Zavala's complexion was sallow and that his eyes were sunken.

"Did you sleep well?"

"Of course," Zavala said. "I feel fine."

"You performed admirably at dinner last night, Doctor, but don't try it on me this morning. What's wrong?"

"Chest pains, Sam. Periodic, but persistent when they hit."

"Why don't you let Dr. Ewing or Dr. Jones examine you?"

"I know what they would say, and I don't want to hear it. They have no medicine to cure this condition."

"I'm sure riding through rough terrain is not the best treatment."

"You stick with law and the army, and I'll stay with medicine and government. Agreed?"

"But in the process, don't drive yourself to death."

Zavala mounted, tipping his hat. "By the way, from what I heard this morning from Miss Hargrove, if you confront Santa Anna as forthrightly as you did her mother, you will undoubtedly win the war."

"It's too early in the morning to talk about that," Houston smiled. "Have a safe journey."

"Farewell, my friend."

That afternoon Thomas Jefferson Rusk, the Texas secretary of war, rode into camp, leading twenty-seven new volunteers. Houston's men whooped and cheered at the sight of the popular, swashbuckling Rusk and his contingent of reinforcements. "There will be more here in a few days, General," Rusk said upon dismounting. "The pendulum of public sentiment is swinging our way."

"These men you brought," Houston said, "can they handle themselves?"

"They're not raw recruits. Some of General Gaines' troops have come on a sightseeing tour. Not as many as I had hoped, but at least they know how to drill and fire weapons."

207

"Are any of them qualified to be cavalry commander?"

"No," Rusk said, watching cavalrymen trying to master Houston's obstacle course. "And if you want someone who can whack all those limbs, he'd better be able to swing two sabers at once."

"I've given up on anyone mastering that course. I had decided to name Captain Karnes commander, but he's too valuable as a scout, almost as effective as Deaf Smith. Henry Millard is a fine infantry leader, but he's not that skilled on a horse. I have confidence in John Austin Wharton, but he's too important as adjutant general. The only other possibility is Captain Seguin. He, too, is a valuable scout, but I could make do with Smith and Karnes if Seguin were cavalry commander."

"Then why not Seguin?"

"I'm concerned about Seguin because of the distrust developing among Anglos for anyone with past Mexican connections, if only a Spanish name. It's worse since the Goliad Massacre. This isn't a problem with Burleson's men, but it's all these newcomers. They don't know that Seguin and his father were in the vanguard of this revolution before they even knew where Texas was. Tom, I've seen the same thing happen regarding Indians. Comanches and Apaches prey on settlers, so all settlers are against all Indians."

"Are you concerned about the safety of Seguin and his men?"

"No, no. They're integral to this army, so they're in no danger of physical harm. However, I don't believe all the cavalry would support Seguin, if I named him commander."

"I see now that this cavalry situation is a rather difficult problem."

"One of many," Houston said.

"I also know about this Anglo attitude toward Tejanos. Zavala has endured some unconscionable slurs recently, he of all people."

"Zavala has a tough hide. I'm more concerned about his health. He appears to be seriously ill."

"He's worked himself into a state of near exhaustion," Rusk said. "With so many settlers falling ill from exposure or fever, there hasn't been adequate medical care available. He's worked all night several times, and he bears too much personal burden for not saving every living soul."

"War takes its unholy toll," Houston said, "in every conceivable manner." Houston escorted Rusk to the planning room where he reached into the desk for a fresh bottle of brandy. After pouring two glasses, he sat back in his chair. "Let's get all the cards on the table, Tom. As I mentioned, Zavala was here. I know why you're here, and I accept it. My personal opinion of Burnet can be found at the bottom of the Gulf of Mexico, but that's not important. I suggest you and I meet privately at least once a day. At these meetings, I will keep you fully informed as to my plans. Frankly, though, the time and place of battle are important only to this army, not to Burnet. One captured courier or one deserter with sensitive information could give Santa Anna all he needs to wipe us out. Bear that in mind in any communication you send to Burnet or anyone else."

"Sam, I've thought about this every waking minute since Zavala proposed that I join you. I studied law under John C. Calhoun, and learned a few things about words and phrases. I'll be able to convince President Burnet that I'm fulfilling my mission without divulging strategic information to him. In a nutshell, I'll keep Burnet out of your hair."

"You're a man after my own heart."

"I'm only being realistic, Sam. The survival of Texas is dependent on this army. A second army could not be gathered and trained in time. The fighting capability of this army, then, is foremost in my thinking, and I will do all I can to enhance the opportunity for victory."

"I propose a toast to that," Houston smiled. "Since Zavala and I discussed this situation yesterday, I've done some reflecting. There's one other person who, I believe, should be brought into strategic planning. He has my complete confidence and deserves to be informed and consulted."

"Would that be Edward Burleson?"

"Any objection?"

"Absolutely none."

Houston summoned Burleson. As usual, he declined the offer of brandy. When told the purpose of the meeting, Burleson frowned. "I appreciate the confidence bestowed upon me," he said slowly, "but I believe both regimental commanders should be included in strategic planning."

Houston pounded the desk. "I don't trust Sidney Sherman!"

"Great Scott, Sam, he's a regimental commander," Burleson said, "What do you mean you don't trust him?"

"I don't question his loyalty, but I don't trust him to keep his mouth shut. He's an agitator."

"Sam," Burleson said, "things have calmed down since Sherman, Baker, and Martin stirred up the fuss. You've got to admit Sherman has proven himself to be an effective regimental commander."

"I'm sorry," Houston said, pulling a stack of maps from a drawer. "My decision is final. Let's get down to business." Houston spread the maps on a table, and pointed out how he had charted the movements of the various Mexican forces, using information gathered by Arnold, Karnes, Seguin and Deaf Smith.

Rusk marveled at the detailed reports. "Sam, you have so much more than we've been able to learn at Harrisburg."

"I couldn't ask for better scouts," Houston said, "and Seguin has been invaluable in harrassing Santa Anna's scouts. Overall, you might call this a 'rivers and streams strategy,' gentlemen. We keep water between ourselves and the enemy. Mother Nature has been on our side, plus we've taken steps to destroy crossings."

"Are you certain Gaona's movement has been that slow?" asked Burleson.

"Yes, Ed, it seems that he got lost. Remember, they don't know the terrain, and bad weather is worse for them than us. All that artillery they captured at the Alamo is worthless. They can't transport it."

Rusk worked his way carefully through maps and reports, savoring each word and set of figures. "Fascinating ... simply fascinating."

"Yes," Houston said, "but when you add up the figures, you still find us hopelessly outnumbered. Sure, I wanted to attack Ramirez y Sesma's force after the fall of the Alamo, and we probably would have defeated it, but what would we have won?"

"I still can see a case for engaging Urrea, if he remains isolated," Burleson said.

"It's too late for that, Ed," Houston replied. "Fannin's defeat was costly. Not only did we lose troops, but we let Urrea get too far up the coast. If we engaged him now, I'm convinced we would be flanked by Santa Anna."

"Sam, do you honestly believe Santa Anna doesn't know our location and strength?" asked Rusk.

"Let's say I have great confidence in our system of security."

Hockley interrupted, escorting Deaf Smith, who hesitated to speak.

"It's all right, Deaf, let's have your report," Houston said.

"General, you instructed me to report only to you, and this is, well, a rather unusual report."

"It's all right. Go ahead."

"I was down the Brazos the other night, trying to move in close on Santa Anna's camp. I ran onto one of their scouts. I captured him and asked him if he knew where their army was heading and he said he didn't. He did say the officers were clamoring for moving out 'cause the men were tired of the food, the weather, and the long campaign. When I asked him why they hadn't attacked the Texan army, he said Santa Anna didn't know where it was. I cut him loose. Then I told him I was sick of this war and disgusted with our army, and that you were retreating to the Trinity and maybe on to the Sabine. He and I had a little nip of his mescal before we went our separate ways."

"Good report," Houston said. "Get some rest, and head back down the Brazos tomorrow."

After Smith departed, Rusk broke into laughter. "Did he think of that on his own?"

210

"No," Houston smiled. "That was my doing. We've fed them several tidbits of misinformation. I've always thought there was a thespian in Deaf Smith. I bet that Mexican scout was in tears over his tale of disgust and despair."

"How do you expect Santa Anna to respond if he buys that pig in a poke about retreating to the Trinity?" asked Burleson.

"It might prompt him to divide his army further," Houston said, "to search us out. Or perhaps he will get careless as he moves toward the coast. At any rate, we should know something in a few days. Our only hope, gentlemen, is to trap Santa Anna. I can't win this war, but I'm going to give him every opportunity to lose it."

After the meeting broke up, Burleson returned to his regiment for the evening meal while Houston and Rusk stood on the front porch in the pleasant April twilight, awaiting summons for dinner at the Hargrove table.

"Have you thought through some contingency plans in the event we're defeated?" Rusk asked.

"I haven't had time to think about that unhappy prospect, but I intend to in the next few days. I trust the government has contingency plans?"

"Secret plans, but yes. If Harrisburg is threatened, Burnet and Zavala will go to Galveston. If all is lost, they will remove to New Orleans,"

"I can't argue with that."

During the following few days, Houston and Rusk drilled and ate with the men. They soon knew each company commander and scores of the men by their first names. While constantly stressing the importance of discipline, Houston provided new tactical problems each day to rekindle interest in maneuvers. Whether or not they could see him, the men learned to recognize Houston's resonant voice as he bellowed orders across the drill fields. "Keep that column straight!" "Tighten it up!" "Hold your fire!" "Hit the ground!" "Up, up!" "Quick time, march!" "Double quick time, march!" At forty-three, Houston was younger than almost half of the men, yet they had all begun referring to him affectionately as "Old Sam."

"Old?" Houston complained to Rusk. "Hell, I'm going to get married and raise a family after this war. I'm not old."

"I wouldn't worry about it," Rusk chuckled. "You have an army that's with you lock, stock and barrel, and they're primed for combat."

"I know they are," Houston said. "That column under Burleson marching over there would make Old Hickory himself want to lead them into battle."

"Who in the world is that man?" asked Rusk, pointing to a small figure on a fast horse running the obstacle course with astounding ease.

"I don't believe it," Houston said, shading his eyes. "He's going to whack every blasted one without breaking stride."

After the horseman deftly completed the course, he reined up near the porch and dismounted. "General Houston?" he called.

"I'm Houston."

"Mirabeau Buonaparte Lamar, reporting for duty."

"I still don't believe it," Houston whispered to Rusk. How in God's world, Houston asked himself, can that short, slender fellow ride a horse and swing a sword the way he does? "Come on up here," he called to Lamar.

After Rusk introduced himself, he said, "Lamar, you've been in Texas. Weren't you a friend of James Fannin?"

"Yes, I also hail from Georgia. I joined James in Texas after he wrote of all the opportunities here. I had returned to Georgia to settle my affairs, when I heard about the Alamo and Goliad. I have returned to avenge James' death and to fight for independence."

"What is your military experience?" asked Rusk.

"I have commanded militia."

"Any combat experience?" Houston asked.

"I have none, General."

Houston shook his head slightly, still disbelieving. "Where, may I ask, did you learn to ride and use a sword?"

"The academy at Eatonton had particularly fine instruction in horsemanship and fencing. When bored on my father's plantation, Fairfield, I practiced on my own cavalry course, remarkably similar to this one. If you have a fine horse, the rest is simply concentration. I suppose you have thirty or forty men who can romp through that course and I was actually about to suggest something more sophisticated."

"I believe General Houston considers that course adequate," Rusk said, restraining a chuckle.

"I suggest we have a drink," Houston said.

Lamar related his activities in Alabama, where he had been co-publisher of a newspaper, and Georgia where he had established a newspaper to support his friend, Governor George M. Troup. Lamar had won a seat in the Georgia state senate, but had lost a race for Congress. In addition to having written his states rights views in his newspapers, Lamar wrote poetry and painted.

Though Houston didn't agree with some of Lamar's views, he was impressed by the Georgian's crisp articulate manner of expressing them. Pouring a second drink, he leaned slightly toward Lamar. "Should we win independence, what immediate course of action do you believe should be pursued?"

"I believe Texas has a unique destiny as a republic," Lamar said. "These vast resources can be developed to support a formidable nation, free from the economic dictates of the northern states.

Further, it would be of utmost importance to secure the borders, providing stability, in order that more Anglo settlers, principally from the South, would find this territory attractive. To secure the borders, it would be necessary to drive all Indians from Texas."

Rusk winced, expecting Houston to explode. But the general merely toyed with his glass of brandy. "May I ask your views on President Jackson?"

For the first time during the conversation, Lamar wanted to sidestep a question. Finally, he sighed, facing Houston. "I'm well aware of your association with Andrew Jackson, General, but candor compels me to say that I am not one of his admirers."

"I appreciate your candor," Houston said.

That evening at dinner Houston listened quietly to the conversation between Elizabeth and Molly, who were preparing for the wedding. "I want two hundred pies baked," Molly said, "so that each soldier may have a generous serving with coffee or milk."

"She's gone through half a shed of pecans," Elizabeth said, "tieing down three field hands with the shelling. Since shelling slows preparation, dear, I promise you that I will bake enough custard pies to have an adequate supply." Stacks of pies had been placed on the back porch, and Dr. Ewing complained that his few remaining patients suffered more from a burning desire to taste the pies than from their ailments.

"Shouldn't Jason be here tomorrow?" Elizabeth asked Houston.

"He might have had problems with the weather. He should be here tomorrow or the next day."

Houston excused himself shortly after dinner, claiming he must attend to paper work. Instead, he strolled alone toward the army camp where several fires were still burning. He found his infantry commanders, Burleson and Sherman, discussing drill plans. As he accepted a cup of coffee, Houston asked them for an assessment of the combat readiness of their respective regiments.

"I have a few clerks and youngsters who don't fire their rifles so well," Burleson said, "but all in all, my men are ready."

"I have some who fire too well," Sherman said. "They're impatient for combat and frustrated with the controlled firing by columns. However, I believe they're finally accepting the idea that the army is more effective when disciplined. Are they ready? Yes, General, they're ready."

Houston moved on to the tent of his friend, Colonel Neill, who reported that his men "are anxious to get those two cannons from Cincinnati. They know all the maneuvers and understand their role in the army. Five of my men have combat experience in aiming, loading and reloading under intense bombardment. I'd still like some actual firing practice for the others, but I suppose it's not necessary."

"You're satisfied they're ready?"

"As ready as they'll ever be, Sam."

Houston walked toward the house. He appreciated the fact that Burleson, Sherman and Neill had avoided the obvious question about command of the cavalry, knowing that if Houston wanted advice, he would have requested it. In an engagement fought in open country, cavalry might be critical to success, yet he would leave things as they stood rather than risk a serious mistake. Not only did he have outstanding infantry commanders in Burleson and Sherman, he also had a strong backup in Henry Millard. He couldn't ask for a more dependable artillery commander than Neill, with Hockley as backup. But why oh why, he thought, has no clear-cut choice emerged for the cavalry?

Meeting people, Houston experienced certain initial impressions, or "gut feelings," as he termed them. He had been struck by adverse gut feelings during his initial conversation with Lamar. In the tenuous days following the fall of the Alamo, Houston had indeed disciplined himself rigidly to assess men for crucial responsibilities. He had accepted Sherman, despite personal misgivings, and he had forgiven Moseley Baker and Wylie Martin, whose actions had been insubordination at least. Lamar, Houston thought, is a product of the southern plantation aristocracy, a remarkable man with a keen intellect. His skilled horsemanship had firmly convinced Rusk that he's qualified to be cavalry commander. But the dashing Georgian had triggered Houston's deepest concerns for the future of Texas since he had leadership written all over him. How strong, Houston thought, are his political views? For instance, how would his attitude toward Indians affect the treaty with the Cherokees? Lamar, like most other Texan leaders, had been captivated by the vision of establishing a new republic, but Houston knew the citizens of Texas could not finance a permanent, well-disciplined army to secure the borders of their vast territory. Lamar, he thought, was naive at best, and at worst, could be a counterproductive factor following the revolution. He would oppose annexation, and if Texas were to become a state, he would be in the vanguard of those clamoring for a separate nation composed of Southern states.

Lamar posed a more immediate problem. Houston knew that if he didn't name him cavalry commander, his heretofore productive relationship with Rusk would be strained. A strong cavalry commander was the final building block needed to solidify the organization of the army. Rusk had said he was more concerned over that problem than he was over Houston's retreat. And Rusk, Houston reminded himself, has been his steadfast ally in the government, along with Zavala.

Houston weighed carefully his impression of Lamar, discounting his political ، views. He recalled vividly the skilled horseman conquering his obstacle course before walking gingerly toward him and Rusk with that dignity and bearing peculiar to the southern aristocracy. Lamar used three and four-syllable words as naturally as Deaf Smith spoke blunt frontier language.

Lamar impressed Rusk, an articulate attorney from South Carolina, but would he rub tough frontiersmen the wrong way? To turn over the cavalry command to a newcomer with no combat experience could cause morale problems, not to mention the possibility that this polished horseman and fencer might find combat entirely different from dashing through an obstacle course. Houston poured a glass of brandy, concluding he would do exactly what he had told Rusk — sleep on the decision.

After breakfast, Rusk followed Houston into his planning room, eager to learn of his decision. However, Hockley was standing by and Houston refused to discuss any matters with Rusk until he had finished conferring with Hockley. "George," he said, "make sure each commander reads these orders today and understands his place in the sequence. If any of them have comments or complaints, I want them today. I don't want any confusion or delay when the time comes to pursue the enemy."

After Hockley departed to distribute the evacuation plans, Rusk sat down with a cup of coffee. "I know little of logistics, but I certainly appreciate fine horsemanship. It was all I could do to restrain myself at breakfast from asking if you have arrived at a decision."

"I have. The decision is to temporize."

Rusk was exasperated. "But why?"

"Tom, you and Lamar are products of a way of life that provokes envy among most of the men in this army. You were fortunate to have been born into wealth, but you've also advanced yourselves admirably. You're born leaders."

"Sam, what the devil are you driving at?"

"You recognized leadership ability in Lamar immediately, but the men will not, partly because he's a wealthy, well-dressed newcomer, perhaps an opportunist. But more importantly to me, he has no combat experience. Veterans don't want to go into battle under a man who might panic under fire. It's only natural."

Rusk slowly shook his head. "Sam, we've discussed the ironies of this war. Travis, a fine horseman, became commander of a fortress where cavalry was not a factor. Fannin, with a separate artillery command, fought Urrea on an open plain where foot soldiers were most important. You have the finest horseman I've ever seen available for cavalry commander, and you just admitted that you also recognized his leadership ability. Isn't it time to gamble a little bit?"

"You glossed over the key point. Travis earned quite a reputation by leading that raid on Anahuac, ill-advised though it may have been, and he won Austin's admiration by capturing all those Mexican horses during our siege of Bexar. Many of the men in the

215

Alamo didn't like him personally, couldn't have cared less about his horsemanship, but they respected his record of courage under fire. Fannin had participated bravely in numerous engagements. My major concern in regard to Lamar is lack of experience in battle."

"Travis never would have built a reputation without the Anahuac raid. Each man must have an opportunity to prove himself."

"Travis was elected to the leadership of the Anahuac raid by a handful of volunteers. If I threw this open to election, Henry Karnes would win, not Lamar. Karnes would be adequate, but he's more valuable as a scout."

"But Sam, this is an opportunity to complete a strong team of commanders. You're issuing contingency orders for moving out, yet you have no commander for the cavalry. Don't you think that with a strong cavalry unit, Fannin could have fought his way to Coleto Creek?"

"I'm not in the business of second guessing what has happened. I simply would not feel comfortable with Lamar as commander of cavalry."

Placing his coffee cup on the table with trembling hands, Rusk frowned at Houston. "Why don't you admit you don't feel comfortable with Lamar at all?"

Houston looked Rusk squarely in the eye, pointing a forefinger at him. "You're out of line, mister. I don't give a damn what you write about me or Lamar to that old hog thief Burnet. But don't you ever say, or imply, again to me that my decisions are not based on what I believe to be the best interests of the army. Is that clear?"

Rusk took one long look at Houston before storming out of the room. Walking toward his tent, he planned a blistering letter to Burnet, with a separate letter to Zavala to inform the vice-president that he would keep the bargain but would assume no responsibility for success in view of Houston's failure to organize the army properly. Before he reached his tent, Burleson hailed him. "I suppose I forget to compliment folks when they deserve it," Burleson said. "You and Sam have done wonders working together. I never dreamed this army could shape up so well, so fast. And I wanted to say the evacuation plan shows the best attention to logistical detail I've ever seen."

"General Houston prepared that by himself," Rusk said.

"At any rate, I hope the political leaders down on the coast appreciate what has been accomplished."

"Ed, are you comfortable with the army not having a cavalry commander?"

"Well, it would be better to have a cavalry commander, but under the circumstances, I don't know who it might be."

"Have you seen this new man from Georgia, Lamar?"

"Yes, handles a horse real well."

"Why not him for commander?"

"I heard he's never been in battle."

Rusk chose to discount that remark by Houston's staunch ally. Instead he sought out Sidney Sherman, who was certainly no one to apologize for Houston.

"I had a long talk with Lamar," Sherman said. "He's an engaging fellow and quite a horseman. As far as cavalry commander is concerned, I'm new to Texas myself and hesitate to make a recommendation. Bear in mind, I brought an organized unit from Kentucky where I had been a militia commander. Therefore, my designation for major command responsibility caused no problems with the men. But these veterans and old settlers might not approve of a brand new man from Georgia."

"Aren't you concerned that we may go into battle without a cavalry commander?"

"Well, I've been more concerned with molding these infantry volunteers into a disciplined fighting unit. I assumed the cavalry might eventually be placed under me or Burleson. Perhaps you or Houston could lead the cavalry into battle, if necessary."

Rusk walked slowly away, shaking his head. I may as well talk to Colonel Neill, he told himself. He's a friend of Houston, but an army veteran if one ever lived. He'll speak to the point.

"Naturally, I've spent most of my time working with the men assigned to artillery," Neill said. "I've watched a few cavalry drills and those men seem to know what they're doing. I'm not worried about how they will perform in battle."

"Colonel, don't you think it would be wise to have a commander of cavalry?"

"I think it would be wise to have twenty-five artillery pieces and three thousand foot soldiers."

"Have you met Mirabeau B. Lamar?"

"I have."

"Don't you think he's capable of commanding the cavalry?"

"I don't know what he's capable of doing. It's none of my business."

"If you were commander-in-chief, would you consider him for commander of cavalry?"

From Rusk's first question, Neill had suspected he might be dragged into a controversy. Now he knew it, and didn't like it. "Look, Tom, I've stayed out of Sam's way as best I could. I figured he's had more problems to contend with than I could imagine. All the commanders have made do with much less than they need. I assumed he had his reasons for not selecting a cavalry commander. Now, I'll say this about Lamar. He could become either a first class commander, or a real trouble-maker. Or he might cut and run when the shooting starts. To answer your question, if I were commander-in-chief, I'd take a close look at Lamar before I sent him on a detail to fetch firewood."

As a light rain began falling, Rusk returned to his tent where he wrote a long, bland letter to Burnet, reaffirming his previous correspondence about progress of the army's training and overall preparation to meet the enemy. Then, he returned to Houston's planning room, finding the commander-in-chief talking to Hockley. After the aide departed, Rusk told Houston, "I've returned to fetch my hat, and to apologize for my intemperate remarks."

"Forget it," Houston said. "I may name him yet. If you hadn't flown off the handle, you'd have realized I said my decision was to temporize. When you get past forty, Tom, you learn to temporize about all sorts of things."

Chapter 21

LATER that morning, Elizabeth came to see Houston. "I'm concerned about Jason, Samuel. Suppose his horse has become lame. Suppose Brother Fowler is ill. Can't you send one of your scouts to find them?"

"For Heaven's sake, Elizabeth, I told you last night I expect him today or tomorrow. For one who was apprehensive about this marriage, you seem mighty eager."

"Don't start that teasing. Of course, I'm eager. I want the marriage performed before the army leaves. Aren't you preparing to leave?"

"When I receive the proper information."

"Samuel, you can't leave before the ceremony. I've decided you should give Molly away in marriage. She admires you as she did her father."

"Elizabeth, I can't do that. Look at these tattered clothes. My only change is buckskin."

"I've already taken care of that. I've let out Edgar's finest gray frock coat with black trim. I saved that along with the vest, tie and trousers. You will be elegant, Samuel."

"Elizabeth, I'm warning you. If and when I receive certain information, we're pulling out immediately."

"Then I suggest you find Jason, Samuel. I shall never forgive you if you leave before the ceremony."

Hockley had been standing inside the door, amused by the conversation. After Elizabeth departed, he chuckled, asking Houston if a scout should be dispatched in search of Jason and Fowler.

"Between that woman and Santa Anna, I'm fighting a two-front war," Houston said. "If they don't arrive before dawn tomorrow, I suppose we'll have to send a search party. Still no word from Deaf Smith or Arnold?"

"Not yet."

"Are the commanders satisfied with the evacuation plan?"

"They're prepared."

Late that afternoon, Houston stood on the front porch viewing the drills. Even with the ground somewhat slick, Lamar dashed through the obstacle course again, slashing each limb with precisely enough swing to make another perfect score. Some of the other horsemen cheered as he completed the course. Lamar waved at Houston, who returned the gesture with a tip of his hat. Having deferred the cavalry commander decision, Houston was eager to see the marriage performed and anxious for new intelligence regarding Santa Anna.

Peering through the timber past the north field, Houston saw a figure approaching on horseback. "Oh, no," he murmured, "it's Jason without Brother Fowler." But as the rider came into view, he breathed a sigh of relief. Fowler was seated behind Jason, his arms wrapped tightly around the young courier.

Houston shouted for Elizabeth and Molly, who came running, their hands and arms covered with flour. Molly flung her arms around Jason, kissing him long and hard.

Littleton Fowler, the Methodist pastor, was a tall, stately man dressed in black suit, vest and tie. He had brought his only change, a suit of clothes almost identical to those he wore. "Brother Fowler," Elizabeth said, extending her hand, "it was good of you to come."

"Pardon our delay, Mrs. Hargrove. Two nights ago, my horse stepped on a copperhead and we had to dispose of him. I recall your attending services at McMahon's Chapel, and I am delighted to be here. I certainly couldn't refuse young Gates' offer to perform the first marriage ceremony under the Republic of Texas."

After they walked inside, Houston proposed a toast. "Samuel," Elizabeth said in a measured tone, "I have coffee prepared and I don't think this is any time for Jason to be nipping spirits. I have made considerable plans to ensure the ceremony will be performed in three hours."

Hockley marveled at the fastidious planning Elizabeth outlined. "Mrs. Hargrove," he said, smiling at her and Houston sitting on a couch, "you and the general are both excellent planners. I have only one suggestion for the celebration — that you and the general lead the Virginia Reel."

"George, that's impossible," Houston said. "Dr. Ewing still has a few patients on the back porch. Besides, with only two women, we can't form lines for the Virginia Reel."

"I'm having the patients moved to inside rooms," Hockley said, "with the approval of Dr. Ewing and Mrs. Hargrove. You two can lead off with some sprightly dance."

"Samuel, I haven't danced in years. I don't know that I could manage."

"You'll manage, Elizabeth," Houston said.

Hockley told the commanders to assemble their men for the evening meal, and to invite all of them to the wedding celebration where pie would be served. For most of the men, a fresh piece of pie was a savory inducement to attend, since they had not had any pastry since leaving Gonzales a month ago. As Jason and Molly walked onto the front porch alone, he showed her the ring he had bought at Nacogdoches, with the help of Houston's friend, Henry Raguet. Raguet had told Jason that his family had returned to Kentucky, his father holding little hope for Texas achieving independence.

Clutching the ring, Molly said she regretted Jason's parents and sister could not be with them. "I was disappointed not to find them at Nacogdoches," Jason said, "but relieved to learn they were all well. Dad never believed in this war. It didn't surprise me that he went back to Kentucky."

"You won't hold that against him?"

"No. I want us to win the war so they can return to Gonzales where we can live. We're going to rebuild that settlement."

"We've had so little time together, Jason. That's the first you've said about living in Gonzales."

"It's my home, Molly. I know that country and I can make a decent living for us."

"I'm sure, deep down, I knew that would be your desire. I just hadn't thought of leaving this plantation, Mother, and the boys. I suppose you've considered Mother's accepting you as head of the household, if we chose to live here?"

"I respect your mother a great deal, Molly. But, no matter how hard we might try to make it work, we couldn't be happy living here. Your mother will always be head of this household. If she thought it wise for us to live here, she would have mentioned it the night she agreed to the marriage. In fact, she might have made it a condition. She's a forthright person."

"She thinks the world of you, Jason."

"Well, I'd like to believe that," he smiled. "But after hearing those wedding plans she outlined a while ago, I just want to make sure I meet her schedule."

Molly laughed. Strolling in soft twilight with Jason, the war seemed unreal. She was the happy and carefree girl who had caught Jason's eye at the ball in San Felipe almost two years ago. "Oh, Jason, after the war, just as soon as it's over, let's go to a ball in San Felipe."

"I thought I told you," Jason said. "San Felipe was burned to the ground. There's nothing left."

She lowered her head. "Perhaps you told me. I suppose I didn't want to believe it. Let's not talk about the war. What did you think of Mother's recruiting General Houston to give me away in marriage?"

"I wanted to ask General Houston to be my best man, but I never had a chance."

"Who will you ask?"

"Colonel Burleson."

"Are your clothes ready?"

"Yes, I'll be wearing that fancy outfit that Captain Baker gave me."

"Was there any problem convincing Brother Fowler to come?"

"No, he just sat me down, looked me straight in the eye, and said marriage is the most important decision a person makes and he always wanted to be certain the couple was ready for it. When he asked if parents on either side were pushing us into marriage, I told him how you had persuaded General Houston to speak to your mother. He laughed, and said he supposed we must be dead serious about our marriage."

When Molly went upstairs to dress, Jason found Burleson, who promptly agreed to serve as best man. Then Jason returned to the house and met Elizabeth who beckoned him into a small sewing room. "I am curious to know who you chose for best man," she said.

"Colonel Burleson."

Elizabeth frowned. "It's your decision, of course, but I had hoped you might ask Colonel Sherman. He's the only officer with a uniform."

"Colonel Burleson is my friend; I hardly know Colonel Sherman. Besides, Colonel Burleson has already accepted."

"In that case, the only solution is to ask Colonel Sherman to lend his uniform to Colonel Burleson. Certainly he would understand that we want to have the most elegant marriage ceremony possible, and some sacrifices must be made because of the press for time."

"Mrs. Hargrove, I don't know how to explain this to you, but I just can't ask that of Colonel Sherman."

"Not even for Molly's sake?"

"Molly didn't ask me about the best man's clothes. Colonel Burleson said his pantaloons are a bit worn, but they're clean. I'm sure he will be dressed in an acceptable manner."

"I see no reason not to attempt to have an elegant ceremony. If you won't ask Colonel Sherman, then why not have Samuel ask him?"

Jason gritted his teeth, rubbing his hands slowly in his lap. "Mrs. Hargrove, I . . . ."

"Won't you please address me as 'Elizabeth'?"

"I believe I'd better call you 'Mrs. Hargrove.' Ma'am, you must understand General Houston might be embarrassed by your request, not to mention Colonels Burleson and Sherman."

"Samuel certainly wasn't embarrassed to confront me in your behalf. This is a minor request, but important, since so many sacrifices are being made for this marriage."

"Mrs. Hargrove, I'm at a loss. May I return in ten minutes?"

"Very well, Jason."

Instinctively, Jason knew he must avoid Houston's being embarrassed by a rebuff from Sherman, particularly if others were

222

present. And what of Burleson? He was proud of his own clothes and had once remarked that Sherman paid more attention to his uniform than to his men. Jason checked his watch. I have five minutes, he told himself, and I bet she's sitting by a clock. I suppose I'll have to wade into this mess, myself. Passing by Houston's planning room, he found it unoccupied. On the desk was one of Houston's ever-present bottles of brandy, and Jason took a drink alone for the first time in his life.

Hockley and Seguin walked into the room, and were surprised to find the bridegroom there alone, still wearing the soiled clothes from his journey, less than an hour before the ceremony was scheduled to begin. Hockley, always amiable and understanding, put his arm around Jason, suspecting a spat between Jason and Molly. Before Jason could speak, Seguin raised a hand. "All I want to know is if the marriage is still going to take place in an hour?"

"Yes, sir, it is," Jason said.

"Then, I must leave at once to prepare myself and make certain my men are clean-shaven. I suspect Mrs. Hargrove will conduct a more precise inspection tonight than General Houston has ever contemplated."

Hockley chuckled and Jason smiled weakly as Seguin left.

"All right, son," Hockley said. "What is it?"

Jason blurted out the details. Hockley burst into laughter, visualizing the sequence of Elizabeth confronting Houston; Houston exploding, but finally relenting; then Burleson and Sherman exploding, with no telling the outcome. "You might be married by dawn," Hockley said, wiping tears from his eyes.

Jason poured himself another glass of brandy. The warm liquid deadened some of the tension, but his face remained pale and grim. "Dad gummit, Major, she's being downright unreasonable. I'm afraid Colonel Burleson will refuse to be my best man."

"I'm sorry, son, I couldn't help laughing about how that woman expects prize bulls in a tiny corral to defer to one another."

"My time has run out, Major Hockley. I don't know what to do."

Hockley took the glass from Jason's hand. "No more of that. You get cleaned up and dressed. I'll work on this problem."

Hockley's first concern was keeping a straight face. As much as he would enjoy seeing the sequence carried out, he had to agree with Jason that ill feeling might be rekindled between Houston and Sherman. He found Elizabeth sewing with one eye on the old mahogany clock on the wall directly in front of her.

"Mrs. Hargrove, may I join you for a moment?"

"Only for a moment, Major. Jason is overdue here to discuss an important detail for the ceremony."

"Did I understand Jason correctly when he said you wanted Colonel Sherman to lend his uniform to Colonel Burleson?"

"You understood him correctly, Major."

"Well, Mrs. Hargrove, Colonel Burleson is a proud gentleman, and perhaps somewhat sensitive. Though they may be a bit frayed, he's mighty proud of his frock coat and pantaloons. I'm afraid he would be insulted if asked to change clothes. That's like telling him his clothes are not good enough for the occasion."

"Why, that's sheer nonsense, Major. Surely, Colonel Burleson will appreciate the dignity a fine uniform will lend to the ceremony."

"Mrs. Hargrove, Colonel Sherman is also a proud gentleman. I venture to say he covets his uniform more than anything in the world. Also Colonel Burleson and Colonel Sherman are not exactly close friends."

"Then why not have General Houston confront them together?"

"This is not a military matter. They would resent the presence of another gentleman telling them what to do."

She tossed the garment aside. "Fiddlesticks, Major Hockley. If all you're going to do is whine about this matter, I will ask the gentlemen myself. Fetch them, immediately."

"All right," he sighed. "I'll bring them to the planning room . . . er, I mean your parlor. One favor, please?"

"What is it?"

"Please be gracious with these gentlemen."

"I will be gracious and I will be direct at the same time. Now hurry, Major!"

While Hockley rounded up the two regimental commanders, Elizabeth changed into her dress for the ceremony. Molly would wear her mother's light blue wedding dress, while Elizabeth had chosen a darker blue velvet dress with a flowing floor-length skirt and a tight-fitting bodice. Her lovely brown hair was swept back behind her ears, and she looked stunning to Burleson and Sherman when she greeted them in her parlor.

"My, you two are certainly handsome," she said. Hockley poured himself and Sherman a glass of brandy, while she and Burleson declined. "I find it interesting that you two are equal in rank, and about equal in physical stature."

Burleson assumed he had been summoned early to rehearse his role for the ceremony. Sherman had no idea why he had been invited, but he enjoyed being in the company of Mrs. Hargrove. "It's almost as if there were no war, being here tonight," he said. "Your home is lovely, and you are such a gracious hostess."

"That's kind of you, Colonel. Hasn't General Houston had you here before?"

"No."

"That's dreadful. Let me take you on a tour," she said, offering her arm. As they strolled through the house, Sherman was impressed by the fine paintings and ornate furniture, and delighted with such attention after weeks of sleeping in a tent and trudging through dust and mud. "It's a pity," Elizabeth said, feeling the fabric of Sherman's coat, "that all the officers don't have such fine clothing. This is a beautiful uniform."

"Why, thank you very much. When I left Kentucky, I never dreamed I would be the only officer with a uniform, but I'm not about to stop wearing it. I'm most proud of it."

"And well you should be, Colonel."

While Elizabeth and Sherman chatted in the living room, Hockley poured himself another glass of brandy. A servant brought coffee for Burleson, who checked his pocket watch. "Where is the preacher?" he asked Hockley.

"He'll be here in about fifteen minutes. Things are shaping up well, but Mrs. Hargrove wanted to discuss one last little item. Before she returns, I just wanted to ask if you're a close friend of Jason's?"

"Of course I am. I wouldn't be best man if I weren't."

"Would you be willing to sacrifice for him?"

"Of course."

"Even if it involved a personal matter of pride?"

"What the deuce are you driving at?"

"Oh, I was just thinking that some people of high principle find it difficult to make a sacrifice over a personal matter of pride. Sounds silly, but I've seen it happen."

"I've never turned down a friend who needed help."

"That's admirable, Ed."

As Elizabeth and Sherman returned to the parlor, Burleson was again checking his watch. "Gentlemen," Elizabeth said, "we only have a few minutes before Brother Fowler will be here. There was one small request that I wanted to make of you two. You've been so gallant and thoughtful, I hate to impose upon you, and I know that you may not feel obliged . . ." her voice trailed off.

"Please, Mrs. Hargrove," Sherman said, "I'm sure Colonel Burleson and I would be honored to fulfill any request we can."

"Of course, Mrs. Hargrove," Burleson said.

"Well, since Colonel Burleson is best man, and since Colonel Sherman has a beautiful and distinguished uniform, I wondered if I might prevail upon you gentlemen to exchange clothing? Just for the ceremony, of course."

Burleson was thunderstruck, and Sherman stared at the wall, speechless. Standing near the door, Hockley restrained laughter by biting his lower lip. She better not stop now, he thought.

"Colonel Sherman, you're such a highly-cultured man, surely you appreciate what added dignity your distinguished uniform would lend to this ceremony, the most important event of my daughter's life. And you, Colonel Burleson, would be so handsome in a fine uniform that you certainly deserve, but which fate has denied you. Gentlemen, the hour is late. I trust this meets with your approval?"

225

Burleson was gazing at the floor, so Elizabeth trained her eyes on Sherman's tense, flushed face. "I . . . I suppose so; that is, if Colonel Burleson finds this acceptable."

Burleson remained at a loss for words, staring at a rug in the center of the parlor. Finally, he nodded his head slowly.

"Thank you, gentlemen. You are gentlemen in the truest, finest sense of the word. Major, help me close the drapes so they can change here. We're running a bit short on time." When Elizabeth had departed, Hockley closed the door and it took two glasses of brandy for him to keep a straight face while the grim, silent regimental commanders peeled to their long-handle underwear. These prize bulls, he thought, hardly had time to paw sand.

Hockley rejoined Elizabeth in the large living room where the ceremony would be held. "I must admit that you were right about their being a bit sensitive, Major," she said. "I could feel all along they were jealous of one another. We were playing a game, and I didn't enjoy having to put on so."

"Mrs. Hargrove, if you ever tire of plantation life, you might consider going on stage."

Jason raced into the room, out of breath from dashing down the stairs. "Mrs. Hargrove, I saw horses hitched outside that belong to Colonels Burleson and Sherman. What's happening?"

"They're exchanging clothes. Everything is on schedule. Run on back and brush your hair, and will you please call me 'Elizabeth'?"

"Yes," he said, tucking his shirt into his trousers, "but Miz, er Elizabeth, are you sure they aren't upset?"

"They're gracious gentlemen, aren't they, Major?"

"Nothing to worry about, Jason."

Not one word had been spoken by Burleson or Sherman as they exchanged their clothes. Walking through the door, Burleson said stiffly, "Colonel, I'll meet you in the parlor immediately after the ceremony."

"You won't find me tardy," Sherman said, looking over the loose cotton pantaloons and frayed frock coat he had traded for his elegant dark blue uniform. Upon seeing them, Houston suspected there was more at hand than a casual agreement between the two proud commanders. Burleson twisted slightly, trying to adjust his muscular body to the tight, form-fitting uniform. "I believe you should shorten your stride a bit, Ed," Houston smiled, "but I must say Sidney's uniform really does something for you."

"I feel like I'm stuffed into the bore of a cannon," Burleson said.

"Now, now, both of you gentlemen look elegant," Houston said.

"For the first time in my life," Sherman said, "I prefer not being called a gentlemen."

Houston chuckled, not daring to ask why they had exchanged clothes. He walked to the living room where he found Elizabeth with

Brother Fowler, directing her servants in last-minute chores. "Samuel," she smiled, "you are absolutely stunning. You look as though you were prepared to step onto the floor of the United States Senate as the most distinguished senator in America."

"I suspect that you hornswoggled Sidney out of his uniform, so don't butter me up to exchange these clothes. I love this coat. Would you consider selling it to me?"

"Certainly not. Nothing Edgar owned will ever be sold. However, since he admired you, and since I understand you have plans to be married, I am giving you the coat."

"Brother Fowler," Houston smiled, "would you consider it blasphemous if I kissed the mother of the bride?"

"Not at this moment."

Houston kissed Elizabeth gently on the cheek. Blushing, she excused herself to check on Molly and her brothers. She found Molly almost dressed, eagerly awaiting the ceremony. "You're not nervous?" asked Elizabeth.

"Just a little, Mother. I haven't had time to be nervous."

"When you hear me start the organ music, walk slowly down the stairs. General Houston will escort you from there to the living room. That's all you have to do."

"I know. That's the third time you've told me. Are you nervous?"

"Certainly not. Everything is going fine."

Under the elaborate chandelier in the spacious living room, Brother Fowler, Bible in hand, awaited the bride and groom. Around him were most of the senior officers of the army, plus friends of Jason from Gonzales and San Felipe. Jason and Burleson walked slowly toward Brother Fowler as organ music filled the house. Edgar and Garth Hargrove stood by the organ, waiting to escort their mother.

As she descended the stairs, Molly was a picture of youthful beauty and grace in her mother's long, pale blue wedding dress of silk brocade. Houston escorted her into the living room, and Elizabeth, flanked by her sons, joined the ceremony. Brother Fowler was alternately stern and gentle in his reading of the ceremony. As Molly and Jason exchanged vows, Houston recalled his marriage to Eliza Allen in Tennessee and the misery that had ensued. It won't happen to these two, he thought. One can feel their love vibrating throughout this room.

Elizabeth also recalled her marriage to Edgar and a wedding celebration that Richmond society had found incomparable. Now, she felt she had done her best for Molly in this wilderness where life was so uncertain. All their hopes for the future rested in the hands of those assembled around her. God protect them, she prayed, and God protect my son-in-law.

When the ceremony ended, Jason kissed the bride amid the soldiers' whoops. Elizabeth thanked Brother Fowler, and turned to

Houston. "Samuel, you appear so solemn. It's time to celebrate. Remember, you insisted that we lead the dancing."

As she and Houston walked arm-in-arm toward the back porch, Sherman eased near Burleson, who had remained standing stiffly at attention. "Colonel," Sherman said, "I suggest we retire to the parlor."

"Lead the way," Burleson said, as the fiddlers on the back porch began tuning up.

Jason and Molly lingered in the living room, receiving congratulations, then joined the rest on the back porch where Houston and Elizabeth were preparing to lead off the dancing. Houston chose "Red Wing," a bouncy tune that was his favorite, and he and Elizabeth glided swiftly around the huge back porch together. Jason, also a fine dancer, preferred slower music, and so requested a waltz. As he and Molly danced, the men became pensive, thinking of home and loved ones. In each other's arms, Jason and Molly thought only of themselves. When Houston returned from escorting Elizabeth to the kitchen, and saw the graceful couple, mesmerized in their dancing, he instructed the two fiddlers to play that waltz again.

Servants began carrying urns of coffee and stacks of pie to the tables outside. When the music ceased, Elizabeth stood on the steps and announced, "Gentlemen, before we enjoy our food, Brother Fowler will say the blessing."

Brother Fowler raised his right hand, and looked up to the stars. "Oh Lord, we beseech thee to guide us, your humble servants. Grant us courage and strength as we seek the freedom to worship Thee as we choose. Lord, we seek freedom to till the soil and raise our families, safe in their homes, free from the horror of war and the bondage of tyranny. Hear us, dear God, and bless these men that they may fight bravely for Thee and for this bountiful land. The souls of the brave men murdered at Goliad on the Sabbath cry out for vengeance. The voices of my friend, Brother Travis, and his courageous compatriots who fell on the Sabbath at the Alamo can be heard, calling on us to avenge, to carry our banner to victory over the forces of the tyrant. Please, Lord, we beseech Thee, let them not have died in vain." He paused, bowing his head and lowering his arms. "And now let us partake of what You have bestowed upon us. We ask Thy blessing on this food for the nourishment of our bodies that we may serve Thee. Amen."

A rejoinder of "Amens" was heard throughout the gathering. Lines formed for pie, coffee, and milk as the fiddlers resumed their music on the porch. Sipping a cup of coffee, heavily spiked with brandy, Houston whispered to Rusk, "Now, if your friend Lamar could speak like that parson, I'd name him cavalry commander."

"If the Lord listens to that parson the way our men did, the parson ought to be commander-in-chief."

228

"I'll drink to that," Houston smiled.

Elizabeth brought Brother Fowler a piece of pie and coffee. They sat on the end of the porch, away from the fiddlers' piercing music.

"I didn't know that you were a friend of Will Travis."

"In a way. I thought he would make a brilliant preacher as far as delivering sermons, but his personal life was a problem. When I knew him, he had begun to indulge himself."

"I find that difficult to believe. He never once displayed a problem with spirits, nor did I ever hear talk of his indulging himself anywhere near the point of intoxication."

"It's true that he was careful with alcohol; but I must say, I was somewhat concerned when he admitted affairs with five women in one month, and . . ."

"That's quite enough, Brother Fowler. I know Will also gambled a bit, which might have upset you, but he was a high-spirited young man. I'm afraid you may expect too much of people. During the time we knew him, he was a gentleman of the highest order."

"Please don't misunderstand what I said, Mrs. Hargrove. Will's resolute, high-spirited personality was admirable. I merely stated that one cannot be a minister and conduct his personal life as Will had been prone to do."

"Well, we must not argue. I'm gratified to know that Will never had a problem with alcohol. I hope it doesn't upset you that I have permitted spirits to be served in the house?"

"I suppose people will insist on spirits for such occasions."

"However, I have enforced a strict rule on the army, including General Houston, that no hard liquor is permitted in this house."

"That's certainly a step in the right direction, Mrs. Hargrove."

Houston interrupted their conversation to tell Elizabeth that two young men, friends of Jason, had a gift for her outside the porch. She walked arm-in-arm between Houston and Fowler to the steps. The two young soldiers introduced themselves, and one stepped forward. "I'm from New York, and he's from Massachusetts. Since we're the farthest from home, we were chosen to represent our unit in presenting a gift to you. Mrs. Hargrove, we want you to know we consider your plantation more than a training ground. It's been like home."

Looking into the happy faces of the young soldiers, Elizabeth saddened. They're just boys, she thought. They didn't look a day older than Edgar.

"We wanted to find something fancy," the youngster said, "but we couldn't. We had to do the best we could."

"It's the thought that counts, young man. I'm sure that whatever you have brought will be most appreciated."

Pulling a large crock urn between them, the young soldiers came up onto the back porch. "What is it?" Elizabeth asked.

"It's eggnog, ma'am," the youngster said, "for you, your family, and your guests."

"Eggnog? What's in it?" she asked.

"Why, it's just plain eggnog, Miz Hargrove. Made from an old recipe. The whiskey came from Kentucky."

"Not bad," Houston said, tasting a few drops on his finger.

Elizabeth frowned. "Samuel, Brother Fowler and I were just discussing . . ."

"Mrs. Hargrove," Fowler interrupted with a smile, "wouldn't you say these young men are high-spirited and resolute, somewhat in the mold of our departed friend, Brother Travis?"

"Why, I . . . I suppose so, Brother Fowler. Thank you, young men, you're very kind. Since General Houston approves of your eggnog, it must have special quality."

As the young soldiers scrambled down the steps to report to their friends, Houston smiled, taking another taste of the eggnog. "Elizabeth, there's not enough whiskey in this batch to harm a fly."

"Flies don't drink it by the cupful, Samuel. Since my rule is being altered, will you see that no one in this house becomes intoxicated?"

"A few may get tipsy, Elizabeth, but I'll make sure no one gets drunk."

Elizabeth and Molly were much in demand on the dance floor with Sherman, back in uniform, Hockley, Lamar and Rusk their most persistent partners. Jason was about to seek a dance with Molly when Seguin found him near the kitchen. "This is for you, Jason," Seguin said, handing him a long sword with an ornate silver handle. "It's an old Spanish saber that my father once said has the finest silver handle in the world."

"Why, I can't accept that, Captain. It's part of your family."

"To refuse my gift would be an insult."

"Thank you, Captain," Jason said, holding the blade in both hands, marveling at its balance. "I'll take good care of it."

"You'd better. You may need it any day."

Jason sought Houston to show him the saber and thank him again for the gold watch Houston had given him earlier. "It's a fine blade," Houston said. "Seguin has honored you with this gift. Don't let him down."

"You mean in battle?"

"I mean as a friend."

They watched as Sherman swirled around the dance floor with Elizabeth while Lamar led Molly, who hadn't missed a dance throughout more than an hour since the wedding ceremony. "General," Jason said quietly, "I need your advice."

"Sure."

"Well, General, I knew Molly would want to dance tonight, but it's getting kinda late."

"Why, it's not ten o'clock, Jason," Houston said. "I paid those fiddlers from Sherman's regiment to play until midnight."

"I was just thinking that I'd like to be alone with my wife, and I wanted to know if you thought it proper for me to ask her to leave?"

Houston chuckled, slinging his arm around his young aide. "Son, if I'd just married that lovely young lady, I wouldn't be standing around, asking for advice."

As Molly completed the dance with Lamar, who bowed graciously, Jason took her arm, and gently led her away. "It's time to leave," he said. "There will be other dances." She hesitated a moment as the fiddlers started playing one of her favorites, "Lorena," a slow, haunting ballad.

"This one last dance with you, please, my darling."

When the music ended, she kissed him on the cheek. "It was a perfect wedding. Let me say goodnight to Mother and General Houston."

The young couple went up the stairs as the fiddlers struck up a rousing rendition of "Turkey in the Straw," an old favorite that prompted more toasts and stomping. "When I was a child," Molly laughed, "I dreamed of a serenade of soft guitar music on my wedding night."

Jason smiled, shaking his head. "That sounds more like a pack of hound dogs baying at the moon."

"It's the prettiest music in the world," she said, as he carried her to their room.

Chapter 22

DOWNSTAIRS, Brother Fowler excused himself for the evening. Weary of dancing, Elizabeth declined another request from Sherman. She sought Houston, who continued to make requests of the fiddlers. "Samuel, I'd like some quiet and fresh air, if you would care to escort me to the front porch."

As they walked alone onto the front porch, Elizabeth heard an unfamiliar song with disquieting lyrics. "Samuel, you didn't request that risqué number? It must have come from a saloon in New Orleans."

"Elizabeth, that song is popular all over the United States. That's 'Will You Come to the Bower?' by Thomas Moore. Those lyrics aren't so suggestive."

"Well, I hope Brother Fowler has fallen asleep."

"You're tired, Elizabeth. Let me fetch you a cup of your eggnog."

"I can't stand the taste or smell of eggnog," she sighed, "however, I did appreciate so much the gesture of those young men. They must be terribly lonely during these long days and nights so far from their homes."

"Loneliness is the constant companion of a soldier, Elizabeth. Despair is his real enemy."

"Why, how poetic, Samuel. You so rarely display such a depth of feeling for your men."

"I'm not supposed to share grief or joy with any of the men. These men expect their commander to be above all that, thinking and planning for the entire army."

"You made an exception in the case of my son-in-law."

"Thanks to you and me, my dear Mrs. Hargrove, I believe this whole affair worked for the benefit of Lieutenant Gates, and for the morale of the entire army. That is, with the possible exception of Colonels Burleson and Sherman," he smiled.

"Well stated, again, General Houston. I believe I might enjoy a small glass of brandy if you would care to bring me one. I seem to be relaxing a bit."

232

When he returned, she was leaning against a column, gazing across the fields. "Samuel, I want you to know how much I appreciate the admirable manner in which your men conducted themselves tonight. I'm proud of you, and I'm confident your army will be successful. You should become a man of means following the war."

"I've never aspired to wealth."

"Well, perhaps wealth itself isn't that important, but you will need some property to fulfill your political aspirations. I assume you will become president of the Republic of Texas."

"I intend to seek that office."

"And beyond?"

"I would steer toward annexation into the United States."

"After which you will become a senator, and perhaps even president of the United States."

"I must admit, I would seek the office, if I had the opportunity."

"I hope you will indeed become president of the United States, fulfilling your highest aspiration."

"I have never said that was my highest aspiration."

"What could be more important?"

"Several years ago, I walked away from my wife and my responsibility as governor of Tennessee. I turned my back on Anglo society, rejoining the Cherokees as a member of the tribe. I took to heavy drinking, and soon didn't have a dollar to my name. One night, by a quiet campfire in an open prairie, Chief Bowles sat me down for a talk. He said that I had run away to find myself, but that I had remained lost. 'You must return to your people,' he said. 'You are blessed with a rare opportunity to obtain the most valuable of all possessions, wisdom. You must sow carefully the fields of knowledge and understanding. Then, my brother, you will reap wisdom, which is more precious than wealth or power. Your destiny is to lead your people; but without wisdom, the sun of life, you will remain in despair.' Elizabeth, I cannot describe how I felt that night, other than to say I know what a preacher means when he says he has a calling."

"How reflective, Samuel. Edgar once said that a man can't chart a wise course for the future unless he truly understands where he has been. I must say your personal background is a bit unorthodox. I suppose I have never quite understood it."

"You know," he said with a twinkle in his soft, blue eyes, "neither have I."

They chatted for a few more minutes, enjoying the brandy and fresh air, before Elizabeth excused herself to mingle with the guests. As midnight approached, Houston was about to retire when he saw Deaf Smith and Hendrick Arnold hitching their weary horses. Houston led them to his planning room where the exhausted scouts slumped on the couch, accepting the brandy Houston brought with a pot of coffee and a custard pie. As they cleaned the pie plate, Smith gulped down his second cup of coffee and thanked Houston. "I feel alive again, General. I could go three days without eating if I knew I had a tasty pie waiting on the fourth day."

"All right, Deaf, what does it look like?"

"Their system of security is improved a bit, General. They got more scouts, and them scouts are moving farther in advance of their armies. And I know this for sure. They're moving toward the coast."

"All armies?"

"Santa Anna is moving between the Brazos and San Bernard Rivers. I'd guess he's got about three thousand men. Urrea is coming up the coast. They must have a rendezvous point. My guess is that it will be on the San Bernard, near Columbia."

"What about Urrea's strength?" Houston asked, making notes.

"I was trying to get near enough to Urrea's camp near Brazoria to make an accurate count," Arnold said, "when I was captured. All these years I've lived as a black man, under the threat of slavery. But when they hauled me into their camp, I was plenty glad to rely on this black skin. I told them I was a runaway slave, trying to find my way to some friends in Refugio. All the while I was talking, I was counting their units as best I could. They told me they had garrisoned Victoria, Goliad, and Refugio so I was safe to travel that country. When I left I had to travel south, past their southern guard posts, before turning west and moving up the San Bernard. Then I cut north to return."

"What's your estimate of Urrea's strength?"

"No more than a thousand, General," Arnold said.

"Are you sure?" Houston asked.

"I'm sure."

Houston glanced at the clock on the wall. "Can you men make do on six hours of sleep?" They nodded. "Then report here at daybreak. Not a word of this to anyone."

After Smith and Arnold departed, Houston sat alone for a half hour, pondering the few options available to him, now that one conclusion could be safely drawn — Santa Anna still didn't know the location of his army. What course would Old Hickory choose under these circumstances? Sometimes, Houston recalled, when all the intelligence and speculation only created more confusion, Old Hickory would calmly play a hunch. Houston had a course of action in mind, but recalling his tenuous relationship with Burnet he decided to confide in Rusk.

Houston met Elizabeth leaving the kitchen. Most of the men had retired to their camps for a night's sleep, their stomachs full and their heads dulled from singing and drinking on the lawn. Houston requested a pot of coffee, which she gave him. "That's the last of the coffee, Samuel," she said.

"It was a wonderful evening, Elizabeth. Congratulations. I'll see you in the morning."

234

Houston found Rusk talking to Hockley over the last of the egg-nog. "I'd like to meet with you for a few minutes, Tom."

"Do you need me, Sam?" asked Hockley.

"No, have a good night's rest. I'll need you at daybreak in the planning room."

After they walked into the planning room, Houston replaced Rusk's small china cup of cool eggnog with a large tin cup of steaming black coffee. "You look a bit tipsy," Houston said.

Rusk was nettled at the fatherly admonition. "I certainly am not tipsy," he said. "Tired, perhaps, but not tipsy."

Houston beckoned to Rusk to pull his chair closer to the desk. He showed him the latest information from the scouts and Rusk studied the map time and again, perplexed. "Sam, why is Santa Anna moving away from us?"

"He still doesn't know our location. If he thinks we're retreating beyond the Trinity, he may plan to rendezvous with Urrea and sweep northeast along the coast. His plan well may be to wipe out all settlements near the coast, particularly Harrisburg, if he knows the seat of government has been moved there."

"No matter what plan he's pursuing," Rusk said, "if they mass their forces, we are hopelessly outnumbered."

"That's always been the case. According to Arnold, Urrea has garrisoned Victoria, Goliad, and Refugio. That spreads his force a little thin. Santa Anna garrisoned San Antonio and probably left a force in the San Felipe area. If he were to divide his force again, say to pillage various settlements or to try to track us down, then we might have a chance.

"Now, as I see it, we have only three courses of action worth considering. One, we can stay here, take a defensive position in the timber, and wait for them to come to us. Two, we can retreat beyond the Trinity to buy time to recruit and train more volunteers. Three, we can head for the coast and pray Santa Anna will make a mistake."

"Half these men would desert if you ordered a retreat beyond the Trinity. They're spoiling for a fight."

"I know, though logically that's probably the wisest course of action. That's why I believe Santa Anna is convinced we're retreating. Zavala told me he has a morbid hatred of the United States, and would believe we're retreating to a point where United States volunteers could bolster our army. Do you believe the men would accept a policy of remaining here?"

"Perhaps," Rusk said, "if they were convinced a battle was imminent. Santa Anna would learn of this location, sooner or later."

"Correct," Houston said. "And we would probably be outnumbered by at least three to one. We could protect ourselves for some time with the Brazos as a buffer, but once they crossed, it would be the Alamo all over again."

"Then, it's move to the coast."

"Yes, move toward the coast, and maneuver for position."

With a goose quill, Houston traced a course through the labyrinth of rivers, creeks and bayous down the Brazos to the Gulf of Mexico. "Consider, Tom, that Santa Anna's success has been built on the element of surprise with superior logistical tactics and fast strikes in battle. He led an army to San Antonio faster than any of us believed it could be done. 'The Eagle' has been swooping through open country, where it's easy to see and easy to move. But the country on that map is not for eagles; it's for alligators and water moccasins."

Taking another long look at the map, Rusk raised his cup in a toast. "I suspect a raven can operate in that country. When do we start?"

"In the morning. We'll travel this route, so Moseley Baker and Wylie Martin can rejoin the army. Then, after we secure those two cannons from Cincinnati, we'll be ready to meet the enemy."

"It's a shame we don't have more artillery," Rusk said.

"That doesn't concern me. If this strategy has any merit, we can't carry much artillery. It's too hard to transport over that terrain."

"I have a good feeling about this strategy."

"So do I," Houston said. "A hunch is always worth something."

"It's more than a hunch with me," Rusk said. "Zavala told me a number of things about Santa Anna — that he's brilliant, but nervous and high-strung, prone to tear off rapidly on a sudden impulse. He's bound to be frustrated, trying to operate in country that defies speed and maneuverability. He should be primed for making a mistake."

"Probably so, but the odds are still heavily against us. If we could catch Santa Anna with fifteen hundred men, I believe we could whip him. I wouldn't have said that two weeks ago."

"Well, Sam," Rusk said, "whatever you do, don't engage him on a Sunday. I hadn't thought of it until tonight when that parson pointed out the Alamo battle and Goliad Massacre both occurred on a Sunday."

"Not only that," Houston said. "but Fannin surrendered on a Sunday."

"Are you superstitious, Sam?"

"Not at all. I'll fight him anytime, anywhere," Houston smiled, "so long as the conditions are favorable for our side."

Houston was bone-weary when he lay down to sleep. He had made the decision and Rusk concurred, but he knew the odds for victory were no better than one in five. Finally, he fell asleep, awakening in time to prepare for his first scheduled meeting.

Jason was sleeping blissfully in Molly's arms when he was awakened by a loud voice and a heavy knock on the door. "General Sam wants you in his planning room. Pronto!" Jason struck a match to light a candle. He scrambled into his clothes, and Molly asked when he would return. "I don't know," he said, kissing her on the cheek. "It must be something important, meeting at this hour."

As each man reported to the planning room, Houston checked his name on a list. Bleary-eyed, Hockley eased through the door and poured himself a cup of coffee. Within minutes, Deaf Smith and Arnold arrived together. Seguin soon joined them, followed by Karnes. Dashing down the stairs, as he stuffed his shirt in his trousers, Jason completed the gathering.

"Gentlemen," Houston said, unveiling a large map, "you have drawn the most daring and difficult assignment. Today, the army moves toward the coast." He outlined the route he had chosen between the Brazos and San Jacinto Rivers to Harrisburg. "This is our country, not the enemy's. We intend to keep it that way, the good Lord willing, through the ability, dedication and valor of you gentlemen. You are the vanguard of the Army of Texas, the only means by which it will ultimately achieve victory. You are the best scouts in the army.

"You must hold your spirits high and your heads close to the ground," Houston continued. "Be swift, yet careful; daring, yet cautious; imaginative, yet prudent. You must be prepared to cross rivers, creeks, bayous, swamps and marshes in daylight or darkness, without being detected. Smith, Arnold, and Karnes will take these advanced positions to determine the strength and movements of the enemy forces," he said, pointing to enemy positions charted on the map. "Seguin, move your men to this point and fan out. Gates, maneuver between these two points, working with Seguin, and relay the information to me with all dispatch. Gentlemen, the destiny of Texas rests on your shoulders. Any questions?"

The men were speechless. They had been to numerous briefing sessions conducted by Houston, but none in which he exhorted them beyond the tasks at hand. "Very well, gentlemen," Houston said, checking the clock nearby. "I expect you to saddle up in thirty minutes."

As they departed silently, Hockley poured Houston a cup of coffee. "You sounded as though you were sending them into a life or death struggle. They're stirred up, excited."

"No sense stirring up men until they need it," Houston said. "Now, fetch Burleson, Sherman and Neill."

"What about Rusk?"

"Let him sleep."

When the three commanders had assembled, Houston outlined the route he had chosen. "And we'll finally secure those two cannons for you, Neill."

Neill smiled, but Sherman's face was grim. "You're moving the army toward Harrisburg. Where and when do you plan to engage the enemy?"

"Sidney, I don't know. By the time we reach that area, I should have fresh information on enemy movements. I'm not going to make any commitments now."

Sherman was disappointed, as he had been spoiling for a battle since arriving in Gonzales. He had assumed Houston would not leave the plantation without a specific plan of attack, preferably a direct confrontation with Santa Anna. As Houston reviewed details, Sherman considered challenging this plan, but he hesitated. Burleson had not raised an objection, nor shown any concern. Neill was pleased that he would soon have those two cannons from Cincinnati under his control. Hockley was a Houston man and would never object openly to anything Houston said. Sherman decided it was hopeless to start an argument with Houston now over fundamental strategy.

"Then let's take advantage of this fine weather," Houston concluded, "and move out with all dispatch."

Burleson had not spoken to Sherman since after the wedding ceremony. As they walked past the front porch, Burleson detained Sherman. "You've got something stuck in your craw, Sidney; let's have it."

"It's none of your business, Colonel."

"Now, look, if you're still upset over what happened last night, you ought to know I had not talked with Mrs. Hargrove before she strapped it on us."

Sherman sighed. "She certainly strapped it on us, didn't she? No, I hold no grudge over that. Just a little wounded pride."

"Then what is it?"

"I don't want to create dissension. Forget it."

"Sidney, I know you well enough to see you were upset in that meeting. Are you opposed to Sam's plan?"

"That plan is no plan."

"Sidney, we lost a man of rare insight when Jim Bowie fell at the Alamo. He once told me that the difference between Houston and most military leaders is that Houston has raw courage, tempered with prudence. He said most of us hunt, while Houston hunts and traps. That takes time and patience."

"But why doesn't he tell us how he intends to trap Santa Anna? We may be marching into a trap ourselves."

"That's not my concern. I've never heard of a military operation this size with more guards and scouts. We're not going to be trapped."

"All right, Ed, you haven't convinced me as to the merit of Houston's strategy, whatever it may be. But you have convinced me that you have so much confidence in him I'm wasting my breath."

"I suggest you convince your men we will soon be engaging the enemy. Plans won't be discussed since security must remain tight."

"I'm not going to carry water for Houston until I'm convinced we're heading into battle."

238

As the commanders left the house, Jason embraced Elizabeth and walked, with his arm around Molly's waist, to saddle his horse. "At the end of each day," Molly said, "in the soft quiet moments, think of me. Think of the joy and love we share, and you will feel close to me, no matter where you are." Jason kissed her one last time, and rode away, waving until he disappeared in the woods.

From the front porch, Houston and Elizabeth watched Molly walk past them with her head high and eyes clear. Once in her room, she fell on the bed in tears.

"Your men seem anxious to leave, Samuel," said Elizabeth. "Was the hospitality that bad?"

"You heard those 'Amens' last night to Brother Fowler's call to arms."

"That was Brother Fowler's only opportunity to express himself in a patriotic manner. I thought it was quite appropriate."

"Well, it saved me from having to make a speech to the men."

"You've been quite a politician these past few days," Elizabeth said, "and I must say it's been enjoyable. We're going to miss you and all the activity."

"Not nearly so much as Molly will miss Jason."

"I don't want to talk about that, Samuel. I have no idea how she will adjust."

"She'll adjust."

"I suppose I shouldn't ask, but was it absolutely necessary to send Jason ahead on a dangerous mission?"

"Yes, Elizabeth. I bent a rule for Jason to fetch the parson, but I won't break a rule to protect him or anyone else. He's a valuable courier, perhaps the best in the army. At any rate, he won't be in nearly the danger that the scouts will soon encounter."

"You're welcome to leave the sick soldiers here, Samuel. We can provide adequate care in the house as well as a private room for a doctor."

"Thank you, Elizabeth, but it's too risky for them and you. Since the enemy executed our wounded at Goliad, no soldier is safe here. And if the enemy discovered our men here, or any evidence of our army having been here, you might be in considerable danger. My evacuation plan reflects what the Cherokees taught me when breaking camp — leave the land as you found it."

"That's very thoughtful of you, Samuel."

"It's the least we can do after all you've done for us."

Hockley hailed his commander. "In twenty minutes, we'll be ready to load your belongings and pack your papers." Houston excused himself to make certain he left Elizabeth's parlor as he found it. He made one exception.

After waving good-bye to Houston, Elizabeth walked into the parlor to find her husband's elegant frock coat laying on the couch

neatly brushed and folded with a note pinned to a lapel, addressed
to her in Houston's distinctive hand:

> *My Dear Elizabeth: I could not bear to take this fine coat into the
> swamps and marshes that lie ahead, not to mention the uncertainty of
> my life. If I should survive, please send it to me, in care of Henry Raguet
> at Nacogdoches. If I should die, I bequeath it to the fortunate man who
> some day will fill your life with the joy and companionship you so
> richly deserve. I bid you a fond farewell. Samuel.*

Part IV:

The Raven vs. The Eagle

Chapter 23

FROM their respite at the Hargrove Plantation, Houston's army soon returned to the visible reality of war and the Runaway Scrape. Household belongings were strewn along the road to Harrisburg and the most chilling reminders were the hastily-dug graves for those who had not survived the physical demands or disease. Jason relayed messages to Houston from Moseley Baker and Wylie Martin; Baker had reluctantly agreed to rejoin Houston, while Martin chose to escort a large group of terrified settlers, mostly women and children, in their flight to the north.

Picking up the two cannons, Houston dispatched Seguin to confirm Deaf Smith's hunch that Santa Anna planned to strike at Harrisburg. Though Neill was delighted to have the Twin Sisters, they proved to be both a blessing and a burden. All the men felt reassured with artillery support, but they found transporting the cannons slowed the army considerably. Recent rains had made the dark Brazos bottomland heavy with deep mud, requiring strenuous pulling and tugging to keep the gun carriages rolling. Houston often dismounted to assist the cursing artillerymen as they fought through the endless bogs and creekbeds.

Along with mud and rain, the men fought swarms of gnats, flies and fever-bearing mosquitoes, a new enemy that Dr. Ewing feared more than Mexican muskets. His sick list soon doubled, but most of those men had to continue marching, since there was room only for the worst cases in the baggage and ammunition wagons. Measles and whooping cough spread rapidly, and Dr. Ewing had no antidote, except to remind Houston to exempt those afflicted from extra duty.

Houston designated the cavalry under temporary command of Sherman, a decision that astounded Rusk. If Houston must temporize, Rusk thought, why not place the cavalry under Burleson, his more trusted regimental commander? Houston's reply to Rusk was simply that "Sherman is a finer horseman than Burleson."

Meanwhile, frustrated by the failure to locate the Texan army, Santa Anna had led a lightning strike on Harrisburg in an attempt to capture leaders of the rebel government. Texan scouts provided a last-minute warning, and Burnet and Zavala escaped to Galveston. Burning the settlement, Santa Anna set up camp later that afternoon between Harrisburg and the tiny settlement of New Washington near Galveston Bay.

"I have put their so-called government to flight and their army is retreating," Santa Anna told Almonte. "If transportation by sea is available, I shall soon return to the capital."

An express arrived from San Antonio de Bexar after a stop to secure a dispatch from General Urrea. Almonte brought the message to His Excellency, who was shaving. "At last," said Santa Anna, "I will learn about Fannin's surrender. What does he say?"

"He states that he accepted a surrender at discretion. If Fannin thought there were terms, it must have been caused by a mistake in interpretation between the two languages."

"Splendid. Urrea is a political enemy, but his word can be relied upon. Spread the word among our officers."

"Perhaps you had better read this dispatch. There is more than that comment about the executions at Goliad."

Santa Anna continued shaving. "Just tell me what he says."

Almonte sighed, searching for tactful language. "Your Excellency, General Urrea expresses some concern that the executions were carried out, that they have had an adverse effect on his campaign. He describes in detail warm receptions he once received from Anglo colonists, some providing supplies for his army, a few offering to defect. But now, he states, since the executions, his army is viewed as . . . as . . . ."

"As what?"

"As part of a gang of murderers. He requests that humane treatment be extended in the future to prisoners."

Santa Anna wheeled from the mirror, flinging the towel from his shoulders. "His campaign? Aid from the colonists? Mercy for rebels? I am afraid the Federalist heart of Señor José Urrea is beating again. It was a mistake ever to grant him a high position of command. What more does the distinguished Federalist have to say?"

"He urges an immediate attack on Houston, which he is prepared to lead."

"That is ridiculous. I will not honor his request with an answer. Let him have his Anglo colonists for the duration of the campaign. Then they will be driven from this territory."

The courier also had brought personal mail and Juan Calderón and Carlos Alvarez read their letters around a campfire. Carlos was happy to learn from his wife, Estella, that their five children were all in fine health, helping her work the farm near Saltillo. *"Please,"* her letter ended, *"let this be your final military campaign, my darling. We all miss you so much."*

244

Reading his letter from Rosa, Juan suddenly let out a whoop. "Say, old farmer," he said, slapping Carlos on the back, "I am going to be a father."

"Why, that is wonderful," Carlos grinned. After two rounds of wine, Juan reread the letter carefully:

Dearest Juan:

This war has brought sorrow to our land, but it can never take from me the blessing of love you have bestowed, and now the blessing of our child, my dearest. The doctor says I am fine, so you must not worry. Bring yourself safely through this war and return to me. Each day I pray at San Fernando for your safety and on Sunday I pray at San Jose where I first knew that our love had the strength to survive. Praying is no longer permitted in the Alamo chapel, desecrated as it was by bloodshed. Legends are forming about the Alamo, the most recent being that General Andrade's men were chased by ghosts with flaming swords. My brothers say a bolt of lightning struck the Alamo, which would account for the swords, but the men came into the cantina, trembling and vowing never to return. General Andrade was furious, and forbade us from serving them. Many of your comrades who fell at the Alamo remain in hospitals; so many have died from their wounds or fever. There is little else to report. I pray this letter finds you and Carlos well and in good spirits. Carry my love with you, dearest, and know that I pray with all my heart for your safe return. You are my life.

Rosa

Juan yearned to be in San Antonio with Rosa. Why couldn't their commanders force the issue with the rebels? How much longer must they wander through swamps and marshes, burning small settlements in minor actions that any sergeant could lead? He decided to approach Almonte with a request for a furlough.

"The answer is 'no' if the purpose of the furlough is to marry that girl in Bexar," Almonte said. "His Excellency has pledged to your father that he will not permit that marriage while you are under his command."

"But Colonel, she has written me that she bears my child."

"That is your responsibility, Lieutenant. This war cannot last much longer. There will be ample time to marry her before your child is born, should that be your decision."

Almonte struck Juan as cold and indifferent until Juan noticed him quietly stroking his chin. "Come here please, Captain Alvarez," Almonte said to Carlos. "Can you two be trusted with information of the utmost secrecy?" When they nodded, he continued. "You are close friends and have a special place in the scheme of things: you, Captain, as a courageous hero of the Alamo victory, and you, Calderón, as the son of a prominent political ally of His Excellency. We have a report from New Washington that a German vessel may be available to transport His Excellency to Copano where one of our ships would take him on to Veracruz. From there he will travel overland to the capital. I shall need to appoint a select guard for His Excellency to escort him to the capital. I see no reason why you two should not be appointed. I will confer with you tomorrow."

Back by the campfire, Juan refused Carlos' offer of more wine. Though he despised Santa Anna, he would take the special duty if it would shorten the time until he could rejoin Rosa. But once home in the capital, his parents might devise new barriers against his marriage. If he refused the special duty, he would serve under Castrillón and Almonte, an appealing prospect. Their leadership and Urrea's brilliance should soon rout the elusive rebels. Also, with Santa Anna out of the way, Castrillón might permit him to marry Rosa at once.

"How do you feel about this, old farmer?"

"I have a responsibility to the men I command," Carlos said. "I vowed to see this campaign through to completion. I also believe that Castrillón and Urrea will not commit atrocities such as occurred at Bexar and Goliad. I assume that would also be the case with Filisola."

"I agree and shall remain," Juan said, sipping coffee. "I hope His Excellency does retire to the capital. He has brought dishonor on us and destruction upon this land."

The following day, as he rode into New Washington, Santa Anna was in a jovial mood. The German captain negotiated an agreement, and Santa Anna ordered his considerable baggage packed for loading on the schooner that afternoon. Before loading could commence, however, an armed schooner, one of four Texas warships equipped at Galveston, swept down in an attack on the German vessel. German sailors swam to shore as their burning ship sank in Galveston Bay. Houston had cursed the decision to purchase warships, but it was one of Potter's sleek schooners that prevented Houston's prey from escaping the one trap that could force him into a decisive battle.

Santa Anna was furious. Directing his artillery piece at the enemy vessel, he sent cannon shots splashing near the Texan warship, but it sped out of range, unscathed. "Bring me those maps," he snapped to Almonte. "I will punish these rebels so they shall never forget. Strip this wretched settlement, then put it to the torch. Prepare to return along our original route. I may decide to destroy Anahuac, up the coast, then over to Nacogdoches, and . . ."

"Your Excellency," Almonte interjected, "should we not first rendezvous with Filisola?"

"We have en route five hundred reinforcements. That will make our force sufficient for any contingency. We depart this cursed place in the morning."

Carlos was disheartened to see again yet another town swirling rapidly into smoke. "At least," he sighed to Juan, "we did not get our hopes up over a journey to the capital."

246

"I wish Santa Anna had left," Juan said. "He is in no frame of mind to command in a responsible manner."

While Juan and Carlos ate a quiet evening meal near the smoldering remains of New Washington, Jason and Seguin were drying out after a day of scouting near Harrisburg. They relaxed by their meager campfire near a shallow, muddy creek. Seguin had removed his boots and socks, stretching the damp socks across a willow branch he held over the coals. "Lord," he said, "I'll be glad to get back to Bexar. This land is wet all the time."

"I'm afraid this mud has detained the army. I thought it would be here by now, but I suppose it's even slower moving with settlers hanging close for protection."

"With Deaf Smith, Karnes and Arnold searching for Santa Anna, we should soon have some news. When we locate him, the settlers and sick soldiers will have to leave."

Within minutes, they heard the advance of Houston's army. When the general arrived, he was disappointed to find no word from the scouts led by Deaf Smith. Houston received a bundle of dry logs from Harrisburg and a warm fire blazed for those fortunate few in the general's camp. Shortly before midnight, Smith and Karnes, caked in mud, rode into camp with a Mexican courier they had captured. Houston summoned Zavala's son, who translated the dispatches, including one from Santa Anna to Filisola, requesting five hundred men, and revealing Santa Anna's position at New Washington.

"I wonder," Houston said, "why he needs five hundred more men? This might be a ruse to deceive us."

"This man knows more than he's telling," Smith said. "Karnes and I captured two others who didn't know anything, but all three of 'em are mighty upset. I don't think this is a ruse."

Having listened quietly to Zavala's translation, Seguin beckoned Houston aside into the darkness behind a nearby ammunition wagon. "Suppose you and I conduct a private interrogation. Young Zavala is quite learned, but I have another idea," he said, patting the Bowie knife at his hip.

"In a few minutes," Houston said.

Returning to the campfire, Houston slung his arms around Smith and Karnes. "You fellows have had quite a day and night. Wonderful work, men, but tomorrow's another long day. There's fresh cornbread and rabbit stew waiting for you at Burleson's camp. All you men are dismissed for a night's rest. Captain Seguin will see to the prisoner," he said, disappearing in his tent. After they dispersed, Houston rejoined Seguin, waiting with the prisoner near the smoldering campfire.

"He's been to Santa Anna's camp," Houston said. "He knows approximately how many men he has at New Washington. That's the vital information."

Unsheathing his Bowie knife, Seguin asked, "¿Cuantos soldados tiene Santana?"

"Setientos y cincuenta, mas o menos."

"He says about seven hundred and fifty."

"I don't believe that," Houston said.

"Nor do I," Seguin said, placing the knife point against the belt of the frightened courier.

"¡Hombre, no me diga mentira!"

The courier recoiled, holding his bound wrists to his face. "Es verdad, Valgame Dios, es verdad."

"He swears it's true," Seguin said.

Houston shook his head in disbelief. "Why in God's world would he be leading a smaller force than ours?"

Seguin pushed his knife closer. "¿Porque Santana no tiene mas soldados?"

"No se . . . Tal vez he querido ir muy en sequida por esta ciudad que he tenido el gubierno de Tejas . . . Tres dias pasado, Santana dice que 'vamos para matar el cabrón Zavala.'"

"That makes sense," Seguin said. "He says Santa Anna decided to move rapidly to Harrisburg to kill his old enemy Zavala."

"All right," Houston said. "Give this man some food and have a watch kept over him tonight. Not a word of this to anyone, Seguin."

Houston's hands were trembling as he sat down by the fire with the incredible knowledge that he commanded an army larger than Santa Anna's only a few miles away. Assuming the intelligence was correct, Dame Fortune had suddenly dealt Houston a favorable hand. If he could soon force Santa Anna into battle, the odds for victory were in his favor.

Hendrick Arnold rode into camp, reporting that after Santa Anna had swept Harrisburg and moved to New Washington, he had attempted sea passage only to be thwarted by the Texan warship. Rusk, who had joined Houston, couldn't resist reminding the general of his earlier reaction on learning of Potter's warships.

"Remind me," Houston chuckled, "not to call Burnet an old hog thief again, unless he's an opponent in a political campaign."

Houston, Rusk, and Arnold then reviewed the more detailed maps of the territory between Harrisburg and New Washington. "Santa Anna may be planning to take Lynch's Ferry and head for Anahuac," Houston said, "or he might aim for Vince's Bridge and move away from the coast. At any rate, we're heading for that position," he said, pointing to where Buffalo Bayou joins the San Jacinto River. "From there, we can control both the ferry and Vince's Bridge."

"Were you near enough to make an accurate estimate of their strength?" Rusk asked Arnold.

"I was close enough, but they were in their tents. I can say that it wasn't a large force; certainly not more than eight hundred."

248

"What about artillery?" asked Houston.

"They have only one cannon, medium-sized, somewhere between a nine and twelve-pounder."

"And what about this terrain?" Houston asked.

"About what you see on the map, only worse. There's a nasty marsh to the east, along the river. If you arrive first and take the position you want, the enemy would be forced to attack across this open plain, or defend from a dangerous position, with marshes and swamps around them."

"Arnold, are you certain the enemy has only one artillery piece?" Houston asked.

"I'm positive, General."

"Not a word of this to anyone," Houston said.

After Arnold departed, Rusk looked at Houston. "You must tell the men something."

"Of course. I'll tell them we're going to meet the enemy. If word gets around we might have the drop on Santa Anna, Sidney Sherman and Moseley Baker will be beating the drums to engage the enemy before we're ready. My major concern is to establish that position on the San Jacinto before Santa Anna returns. If he escapes this water-locked trap, we lose all our advantages. We'll be open to a flank attack from the enemy reinforcements."

Hockley walked into the tent, smiling his congratulations. "I hear we've found Santa Anna not a stone's throw away."

"The war's not over, George," Houston said. "We have a little time to attempt the fastest maneuver this army can manage. Tell Dr. Ewing to leave the sick outside Harrisburg, in a concealed camp under guard. I want only able-bodied men mustered tomorrow at daybreak. We're making a forced march for that position marked on the map. Now, fetch Burleson, Sherman, and Neill."

On the morning of Tuesday, April 19, Houston and Rusk ate a pre-dawn breakfast beside their campfire. At daybreak, a light mist began falling as Hockley reported on the muster.

"Do you feel like an able-bodied soldier today?" asked Hockley.

"That I do, George."

"Then, counting yourself, we have seven hundred and eighty-three effective men prepared to march."

Houston was elated by the report. He was taking to battle a force slightly larger than Santa Anna reportedly possessed, and he had two artillery pieces to Santa Anna's one. Houston summoned Arnold, Karnes and Smith. "Gentlemen, I want you to know your work has been superb. Today, you know the route and our objective, and you understand, perhaps better than anyone, what accurate information means to the outcome of this campaign. Don't fail."

After the army assembled, Houston mounted and rode slowly before the line as though conducting an inspection. Reining up before the men, he removed his black felt hat. He sensed the men's anticipation and anxiety that had grown as rumors spread that the enemy was close at hand. They were spoiling for a fight, and they wanted to know what their leader proposed to do. Camp talk had revived backing Sherman for commander-in-chief, should Houston fail to engage the enemy promptly.

To sharpen their anticipation, Houston paused a long moment, in the gentle mist. "Men," he bellowed, "we depart now to meet the enemy, led by General Santa Anna himself!" They responded with piercing cheers and war whoops, hoisting their rifles in the air.

"You are the only means of saving our beloved country! Each of you must draw on every ounce of energy, courage and dedication that you possess — and more! The sacrifices you have made, the privations you have endured, will not be in vain. The men who died at the Alamo and Goliad cry out for vengeance! Are you ready?" Houston shouted, drawing a long round of yelling, stomping, and rifle-waving.

"Search for inner strength and trust in God! Victory will be ours!" The men shouted again as Houston unsheathed his saber, pointing in the direction of New Washington. "Our battle cry shall be, 'Remember the Alamo!'" he shouted and the cheering soldiers of Texas, clad in soiled, mud-caked clothing of buckskin and cotton, stepped forward smartly toward the Plain of San Jacinto.

Even Moseley Baker, Houston's most caustic critic, was inspired by the brief speech and he urged his men to keep pace. Sherman and Lamar, caught in the exhilaration of the moment, were still disappointed that Houston had not divulged a precise plan. Sherman concluded that Santa Anna was en route to an area that made an engagement mandatory, but wondered if they would attack or await the enemy.

Houston was pleased to find the weather clearing and scouting reports indicated Santa Anna would not reach the desired position ahead of him. Houston ordered that there would be no breaks for meals until the position was reached. When darkness fell, the men were bone-weary and wracked by hunger, but Houston alternately cajoled and harangued them to continue the march. It was almost midnight when Houston realized he had driven the men to the point of exhaustion. He called for five hours of rest. After eating, the men fell asleep to the incessant croaking of bullfrogs and buzzing of mosquitoes.

Before dawn, Houston ordered the march to resume without breakfast. When the army reached a grove of oak trees draped with Spanish moss, it was almost daybreak. Deploying scouts and guards, Houston sent a cavalry unit to chase down some stray longhorns to provide a hearty breakfast. That the cavalry performed smartly, after twenty-four hours of wading and swimming across creeks and bayous, was a source of surprise and strength to Houston. He reviewed the drenched foot soldiers and the snarling artillerymen under Neill, as they tugged and twisted to position the cannons on the soft ground in front of the oak grove. Most of the men smiled at Houston as they tended to their duties, grateful to have crossed Buffalo Bayou on an old ferry boat rather than swimming the dank, muddy water.

From the Texan position, Lynch's Ferry lay two miles to the east, on the left flank. On the right flank, about eight miles up the bayou to the west, lay Vince's Bridge. The road from New Washington, eight miles away, would carry Santa Anna directly into the path of the Texans.

Assuming an advance Mexican party would be on the road, Houston granted Sherman's request to ride out with a few volunteers to reconnoiter. Sherman soon returned to camp, having slain three of the enemy, sending three others scurrying back to their main unit. Sherman's contingent sustained no casualties.

Within an hour after returning from the skirmish, Sherman captured a flatboat of supplies that Almonte had dispatched from New Washington. Since the boat held mostly flour and coffee, Sherman's popularity with the men rose dramatically.

In the Mexican main force, news of the rebel attack on his advance unit startled Santa Anna. "The enemy is coming!" he shouted, directing Castrillón forward with a hundred dragoons. Checking his map, Santa Anna estimated he was four miles from Lynch's Ferry. "If the rebels have more than a line of skirmishers," he told Almonte, "they may contest us before we reach the ferry."

As Santa Anna approached the Plain of San Jacinto, he had worked himself into a near frenzy. He led a column of picked cavalry, prepared to engage the enemy.

Sherman had become a close friend of Lamar and they shared a large slice of freshly broiled steak as Sherman poured out his plan for meeting Santa Anna. "I will take a cavalry contingent to that ridge. The Mexicans will believe they're facing a small force that they can easily defeat. When Santa Anna commits all their forces to the ridge, our infantry will attack with artillery support."

"It certainly makes sense, Sidney. Of course, Houston must approve."

"Not necessarily, my friend. If Houston approves of the cavalry skirmish, he won't have any choice but to contest the enemy once the skirmish becomes a general engagement."

"You're taking quite a risk."

"It's time to take risks. Houston has no plan. He calls no councils of war, while the enemy marches on us. Won't you join me?"

"Houston thinks more like a Cherokee than a Southern gentleman," Lamar said. "Sidney, I see no reason why I shouldn't lend my support to you on the field of battle."

On Wednesday, April 20, Houston was unprepared for a general engagement. The men needed to rest and to make certain their weapons were functional, and he wanted to gain a thorough knowledge of the terrain. Yet, he was acutely aware of camp psychology. Sherman's exploits had made the Kentuckian the man of the hour. An electrifying excitement had engulfed the camp as the Texans anticipated the imminent arrival of Santa Anna with his force. So when Sherman requested a brief skirmish to determine enemy strength and their will to fight, Houston knew a denial would rekindle the heated charges that he was reluctant to engage the enemy.

"All right, Sidney," Houston said, "but I'm not prepared for a general engagement. Bear that in mind."

Soon Santa Anna arrived on the plain, and trained his field glass on the grove of oak trees near Buffalo Bayou. Noting the two cannons, he counted only about one hundred rebels. "They're not deceiving me," he said to Almonte. "There must be more. Bring up the cannon. We'll find out what's in those trees." Santa Anna directed cavalry and dragoons near the ridge, with a company of skirmishers positioned in the trees near the center of the plain. Then he ordered the buglers to sound the "Deguëllo," no quarter.

Sherman had called for volunteers, accepting only experienced horsemen. Rusk impulsively joined them, upon hearing the bugle call.

"Don't be foolhardy, Tom," Houston said. "This is a half-baked scheme Sidney has come up with. I don't guarantee support."

Rusk's hand was trembling as he shoved a pistol in his belt. "I'm going to kill that bastard Santa Anna."

But before they could depart, the Mexican cannon fired, the ball slashing into the trees above the soldiers' heads. "Use grapeshot, you fool!" Santa Anna shouted. "And move the cannon closer!"

Castrillón rode to Santa Anna's side. "They are preparing to respond. Please, Your Excellency, do not expose yourself to gunfire. Do not lose a war we have already won." Cursing, Santa Anna reined around to follow Castrillón to a position of safety.

Neill's men returned the enemy fire, wounding one of the Mexican artillerymen. Neill shouted words of encouragement to his men, helping them reload and sponge down the cannons with buckets of water from Buffalo Bayou. His batteries had fired another round when Neill was struck in the hip by a jagged piece of metal from an enemy blast of grapeshot. He spun around, dropping his torch, and crumpled to the ground. One of his men helped Dr. Ewing drag him to safety.

When Sherman and his cavalry volunteers neared the ridge, they found the enemy more than willing to fight. Rusk felt a musket ball whiz by his ear and saw a Mexican cavalryman aim a pistol at him. He ducked, only to see another enemy horseman bearing down on him, saber in hand. His horse pitched, and he dropped his pistol. Trapped between two enemy cavalrymen, he wavered and then saw Lamar charge one of them. "This way!" Lamar yelled, pointing to an open path. He and Rusk dashed to safety.

Houston and Burleson were watching the action from the right flank of the main Texas position. Cursing repeatedly, Houston saw confusion envelop Sherman's men. Learning from Dr. Ewing that Neill had been seriously wounded, he came to a decision. "I've had enough of this foolishness, Ed. Get two of your companies out there to protect a retreat."

As the Texans retreated, Walter Lane, a teen-aged volunteer, was knocked off his horse by an enemy dragoon who swung around to drive his lance home. When he saw Lane hit the ground, Lamar reined about and charged the dragoon, killing him with a pistol shot fired at full stride. Lane leaped behind Lamar and they rode into the cheering camp.

There were several bystanders within earshot when Sherman dismounted near Houston. Furious, Houston pointed a finger at Sherman's ashen face. "Damn you, Sidney, you almost caused a general engagement in violation of my orders! This army has lost the best artillery commander there ever was, all because you had to try to stir up a battle. You told me you would take a handful of men. You took at least sixty. I've made some serious mistakes in my life, but none worse than accepting you as a commander!"

Sherman stared at the ground, confused and embarrassed. The enemy had responded more forthrightly than he had anticipated. His eager volunteers were in trouble before he could either silence the Mexican artillery battery or repulse their cavalry. "I regret that Neill was wounded," Sherman said, "but you should have dispatched more troops early in the engagement."

"That was no engagement, mister, that was a skirmish. It was a damned poor performance on your part, and you're lucky to be alive. You wanted to find out if they're willing to fight. Now you know. You're dismissed!"

As Sherman walked briskly away, Houston sought out Deaf Smith and Karnes, who were cooking their evening meal. "Gentlemen," Houston said, after accepting their invitation to join them, "did you see the horsemanship of that fellow Lamar?" They nodded, and Houston continued. "Karnes, I always thought you and I were strong in the saddle, until today. I hate to bow to newcomers, but I must say that man from Georgia knows what he's doing."

"Anybody with a little courage and a fast mount could have pulled the trick that saved Rusk," Karnes said, "but I never saw anybody react the way he did, saving that young feller. Most folks can't shoot a pistol like that standing still on solid ground."

"Men will follow Lamar," Smith said. "He wears fancy clothes, and quotes poetry, but he's a brave man."

"Well," Houston said, "I believe you two have convinced me. Colonel Sherman has too much responsibility, leading a regiment of volunteers in addition to the cavalry. So I'll bet a jug of whiskey you can convince the cavalry to elect Lamar as their leader."

Karnes knew he had been passed over as cavalry commander because of his scouting duties. But now that the army no longer needed long-range scouting, he had hoped the command might come his way. Smith, though, preferred operating in his own way, detached from the internal politics of the army. "I believe you're right, General," Smith said. Karnes had no choice but to concur.

"Please keep my name out of this, gentlemen," Houston said. "No sense ruffling feathers."

Finishing his meal, Houston walked to the makeshift field hospital to inquire about Neill. "I've stopped the bleeding," Dr. Ewing whispered to Houston. "He's suffered a great deal of pain, but I expect he will survive. That young fellow Trask, though, is still unconscious. I'm afraid he's not going to make it."

"Can Neill be removed?" asked Houston.

"Yes, if there's some place nearby."

"Fetch young Zavala," Houston said to an orderly.

Major Zavala reported that their family home, a large two-story structure with long porches, was indeed available for a hospital.

"Major, will you please escort Dr. Ewing there by raft and help establish a hospital?"

"Yes, General."

"Tell your father he can bill me for rent."

As Ewing prepared to remove Neill, Houston saw his old friend had managed a faint smile. "Colonel," Houston said, clasping Neill's forearm, "you had those Twin Sisters spraying like a double-barreled shotgun. Don't worry about our artillerymen. You've taught them well."

Neill winced, fighting pain. "They respect George Hockley. Will you name him?"

"He'll be the one," Houston said, releasing Neill's arm.

When Houston returned to his tent, he found Rusk still visibly shaken from his close brush with death. Houston poured a drink of whiskey and handed it to him.

"Mr. Secretary," Houston said, "I believed a distinguished cabinet officer of our sovereign nation knew better than to present himself without proper credentials before representatives of a hostile power."

"That's not a damn bit funny, Sam," Rusk said, wiping dust from his cheek. "Thank God that daredevil from Georgia was there."

Hockley joined them, reporting that all scouts and guards were properly deployed.

"George, I'm naming you artillery commander," Houston said.

"Nobody can take Neill's place," Hockley replied. "I'll do the best I can."

Word came that Lamar requested a meeting with the general. "By all means," Houston said.

Lamar strode into the tent dressed immaculately in the black frock coat and tight red vest that he had worn that afternoon in combat. "General," Lamar said crisply, "the nature of my call touches on sensitive matters."

Rusk and Hockley prepared to leave, but Houston motioned them to remain seated. "Mr. Lamar," Houston said, "is the purpose of your call a military matter?"

"Yes, General."

"Well, any military matter certainly can be discussed in the presence of the secretary of war and the commander of the artillery."

"Congratulations, sir," Lamar said to Hockley.

"Proceed, Mr. Lamar," Houston said.

"General," Lamar said, "I understand that regrettable confusion has been created in the past by the practice of enlisted men electing their officers. I want to assure you that I know I am a relative newcomer, and that I don't seek rank or special privilege."

"I have recognized those virtues in you, sir," Houston said.

"Well, General, this is an awkward situation, but I want it clear that in no manner have I instigated what has developed."

"Your word is certainly accepted among gentlemen, sir. Proceed."

"General, the fact of the matter is that some of the men, that is, most of the cavalrymen, have demonstrated by their votes that they want me to be their commander."

"Why, that's marvelous, Mr. Lamar," Houston said. "I believe those men recognize in you the leadership and bravery they expect from a commander when they go into battle. You should be proud."

"I am proud," Lamar said, "but I was concerned that you would believe I had manipulated them for personal gain."

"Mr. Lamar, you'll find that there are times when enlisted men respond to the needs of a situation with more wisdom than those at the command level. I believe I should address you, henceforth, as Colonel Lamar," Houston said. He shook Lamar's hand and offered him a drink.

"I might permit myself one," he said. "This is a special occasion for me."

"George, if you'll draw up the orders designating yourself and Colonel Lamar to your respective commands, I'll sign them now. By the way, Colonel Lamar, since you're a personal friend of Colonel Sherman, I believe it appropriate that you inform him of your new command."

"That's fine, General," Lamar said, sipping his drink.

255

After Hockley and Lamar departed, Houston produced a fresh pot of coffee. "You'd better get some rest, Tom. I assume you agree with the decisions?"

"You know I agree, but I didn't expect you to accept Lamar so graciously. You surprise me sometimes."

"With a major problem at hand and only a few contingencies," Houston said, filling his cup with hot coffee, "there is no time for squabbles. Good night, Tom."

Pouring over the map, Houston recalled serving as a young lieutenant under General Jackson. Old Hickory had put his arm on Houston's shoulder and advised him to "always choose the time and place of battle. Try to utilize weather conditions. Don't fight unless you know the terrain. Then put yourself in the boots of the enemy commander. If you can figure out what he's thinking, you'll find a way to defeat him, even though he has a larger force."

Between three and four tomorrow afternoon is the ideal time for attack, thought Houston. The sun will be in the eyes of the enemy, if there is a sun. If there's cloudy weather, I'll attack anyway. To wait is to invite enemy reinforcements. If it's raining, though, I can't risk an attack. The small arms might malfunction and artillery moves too slowly across wet terrain.

Using the latest scouting reports, Houston carefully recorded the enemy positions on his map. Since Santa Anna had deployed cavalry to the Mexican left flank, Houston would send his cavalry against that position. The main attack force of infantry would march across the plain with the two cannons front and center of their line. If all the pieces came together for Houston, the enemy would be trying to calibrate artillery and sight muskets while squinting into the sun. Discipline will be essential, Houston thought, lest they break our ranks with their first volley.

Houston worried that the afternoon skirmish had demoralized his men. On the other hand, Houston thought, Santa Anna may well see that skirmish as evidence of our inability to mount a major attack, particularly if he underestimates the size of my force. The prospect of capturing Santa Anna was indeed encouraging. Santa Anna had taken a position that was open only to the west, on the Mexican left flank. If Houston contained that enemy flank, Santa Anna could retreat only into the marshes and swamps behind and to his right. "I'll catch him in camp, or in that marsh," Houston whispered to himself. This attack will put "the Eagle" to the test, thought Houston, laying aside the map.

Satisfied with his plan of attack, Houston turned to the unsavory contingency of defeat. He poured another cup of coffee, recalling how the War Party had scoffed at Austin's caution, as friction mounted toward hostilities. What was Austin's political standing now, and what would his standing be in the event of this army's defeat? Could he rally the Texans if Houston were killed? As president of the republic, Burnet would be the logical choice to rally the country, but Houston truly believed him incapable of effective political leadership under the crisis he contemplated.

Houston also held Zavala in high esteem, but the intellectual leader of the revolution was in failing health. "Then it must be Stephen Austin," Houston murmured. Without this army and with most settlers in flight, where would Austin turn for help? Houston dipped his goose quill twice, but words wouldn't come. Finally, he walked outside the tent, passing through the oak grove where camp-fires were smoldering into small beds of orange and gray coals. A brisk breeze from the Gulf of Mexico swept across the San Jacinto Plain, a favorable omen for Houston that night, since he knew weapons and powder would be dry, barring a sudden shower.

Returning to his tent, Houston remained quietly confident that victory was close at hand. Yet he had a solemn responsibility to provide whatever insurance he might for the preservation of Texas, should his army be defeated.

In the dim candlelight of his tent, Houston paused a moment in reflective thought, and at last dipped the goose quill and addressed three envelopes with the identical caption: "To be delivered only in the event of my death or capture. (signed) Sam Houston." He ad-dressed envelopes to President Andrew Jackson, Stephen F. Austin, and General Edmund Gaines.

> *Mr. President, My dear General Jackson:*
>
> *As you must know, I am removed from the scene. Texans are now in peril, not only of losing their liberty and property, but of their very lives. I implore you, sir, to inform the world of their despair and to consider whatever measures you deem necessary to alleviate their plight.*
>
> *Enclosed is a true and accurate roster of those massacred at Goliad by order of General Santa Anna, the president of Mexico. You will find bona fide Texas citizens, including Colonel James Walker Fannin, among those murdered. Though some question remains, I am informed that an honorable capitulation was reached seven days prior to the massacre. In any case, no war policy of any sovereign nation should ever be allowed to supersede the fundamental laws of God and humanity. Therefore, the bar of American public opinion, and sub-sequently a court of justice, should be brought to bear on Santa Anna.*
>
> *I further submit, sir, that treaties between the United States and Mexico do not condone such atrocities. If barbarism is permitted to run rampant across this land, it may soon engulf the entire continent. Santa Anna also has attempted to instigate insurrection among Indians of this territory against Anglo settlers. In separate communication, I am in-forming General Gaines of this situation.*
>
> *My removal requires the formulation of alternatives for rallying the cause of Texas to the purpose we have long contemplated. In my*

judgment, the only individual capable of effective long-term leadership is Stephen Austin, who is now, or soon should be, in Washington, D.C. in behalf of our cause. Austin is an honorable man upon whose counsel and discretion you may rely. Farewell, my dear friend and commander, may God guide you in the matter at hand.

Dear Stephen:

With all my will and strength, I have endeavored to save our beloved Texas, but I have failed. Whatever differences we may have had in the past must be forgotten in the present desperate situation. The colonies are at the mercy of a tyrant whose bloodthirsty act at Goliad should awaken and alarm all free men who value their liberty. I have communicated to President Jackson my conviction that you are the only individual who can be entrusted with the responsibility of regrouping the people of Texas to pursue the struggle. Many of these colonists came to Texas under your guidance, and they never would have taken up arms without your sanction.

I cannot recommend how best to sidestep Burnet, but his abrasive, short-sighted attitude is certainly not conducive to building confidence in the government. Perhaps if you organize and lead a new army to victory, your leadership would provide the answer, since an election would be called for president after hostilities are ended. I regret to inform you that our trusted friend, Zavala, is in failing health. If Burleson and Rusk should have survived, I recommend them highly for the exemplary service they have rendered their country. Burleson can be trusted as a steadfast, prudent military leader. Though young, Rusk is maturing rapidly, displaying a rare blend of political acumen with courage under fire on the battlefield.

The bearer of this letter is a survivor of the Goliad Massacre about which he can give you further details. Since he is also my most trusted courier, you may find it desirable to use him in communicating with President Jackson. I urge you to seek a meeting with the President with all dispatch. I bid you farewell, Stephen, with admiration for your devotion to Texas and with every good wish and Godspeed for saving our beloved country.

General Gaines, Dear Edmund:

I trust this letter finds you in the vicinity of Fort Jessup where you may render essential service to settlers fleeing Texas. Sir, I pray that your sense of moral justice, bolstered by legal sanction from possible treaty violations committed by the Mexican invaders, will hasten your intervention to protect the lives and property of these innocent victims.

May I suggest, sir, that you consult immediately with Chief Bowles, who will confirm that agents in behalf of Generals Santa Anna and Filisola have been attempting to incite the Cherokees into conflict against Texans. May I further suggest that the atrocity committed at Goliad represents wanton immorality, outside the bounds of all accepted codes of warfare among civilized people. Appropriate documents are enclosed for your perusal.

I pen these words, sir, with the fervent plea of one who trusts in God and believes his countrymen will secure this precious land for the colonists who have toiled and sacrificed so diligently here. The bearer

258

of this letter will carry an appropriate communication to President Jackson after leaving your presence. He is most trustworthy should you also deem it desirable to communicate with the President.

Lastly, Houston penned a note to Anna Raguet at Nacogdoches:

My Dear Anna:
Misfortune has befallen me, my love. The bearer of this letter will provide you with details. Please know that I have cherished those wonderful memories of times together, when our world was peaceful, filled with music and laughter.

Houston became maudlin, recalling the leisurely times he had been a guest in the gracious Raguet home. How lovely Anna had appeared when he had first come to call, and how lovely she appeared in his thoughts that night in his tent near Buffalo Bayou. His thoughts were interrupted by Hockley, who reported the changing of the guard and no enemy activity. Dashing a "Thine, Sam" at the end of his note to Anna, Houston placed it into an envelope and asked Hockley to fetch Jason.

"Jason," Houston said, pouring two cups of coffee, "I am entrusting you with what might be an extremely important secret mission. First, I must tell you something no one else knows at this time, something you must not divulge to anyone — not even Rusk, Burleson, or Hockley. No one, do you understand?"

"Yes, sir."

"Unless a rainstorm blows in, we're going to attack the enemy tomorrow afternoon." Houston was puzzled to find little reaction on Jason's face. "Son, aren't you surprised, or excited?"

"Well, General, you said during a drill at the plantation, you would launch a well-coordinated attack on the enemy unless they outnumbered us by two to one. And you said you wanted the element of surprise, or at least an attack that prevented them from full adjustment. I thought that meant you wouldn't give them long to fortify their position, or be reinforced. I guessed you would attack tomorrow, at dawn."

Houston smiled, recalling that though Sherman had heard those same points several times, they apparently hadn't registered. "All right," he continued, stretching a map toward Jason. "How would you assemble the line of attack?"

"I would assemble the infantry to advance straight across the plain with a cannon on each flank. I would deploy the cavalry on our right flank to contain their cavalry and prevent an escape by Vince's Bridge or the road to New Washington."

"Did you learn all that at the plantation?"

"Most of it. When I was at Goliad, Dr. Jack explained some strategy to me, similar to yours."

259

"Well, you're close to my plan, Jason. Only major difference in deployment is I want our artillery pieces in the center to concentrate firepower into their breastworks. It's essential that we penetrate rapidly; otherwise, we'll lose too many men on the plain. As to timing, dawn was a reasonable guess, but I want our men well rested. That was a hell of a march they endured to reach this position. And I'm praying for clear weather tomorrow afternoon so the sun will be falling into the enemy camp."

"You can trust me, General. I won't breath a word until you issue the order. I can't wait to tear into that enemy camp."

"Jason, I've chosen you, because I trust you to carry out an assignment that could spell the difference in the future of Texas. Unfortunately, this assignment requires that you evacuate to Zavala's house tonight for maximum safety, should the enemy attack first and defeat our army."

"But if the enemy doesn't attack, couldn't I return before you attack tomorrow afternoon?"

"No, I want you to remain there and see what transpires," Houston said, handing Jason the waterproof buckskin packet containing the letters. "If we're victorious, destroy these contents immediately. If we're defeated, deliver them with all dispatch."

Disappointed, Jason started to protest. He recalled his sorrow and helplessness when Moses Rose told him at Gonzales that the Alamo had fallen. He remembered his horror when Temple Shackelford fell bleeding into his arms at Goliad. He thought of the long, lonely journey across the wilderness. "General, I've never dodged an assignment, nor failed to fulfill my duty, but, sir, I want a crack at the enemy tomorrow more than you might imagine."

"Jason, each man in the army wants a crack at the enemy tomorrow."

"But sir, I was at Goliad, and . . ."

"There are several survivors from Goliad in this army, and there are relatives of men who fell in the Alamo. Lord help Santa Anna if any of them reach him before we can stop them. Son, I chose you for this assignment because you are my most reliable courier. Believe me, if those letters need to be delivered, they must be delivered without fail! You have no idea how important they might become for you, your family, the Hargroves and all of Texas."

"General Houston, I've learned a great deal from you about the military and other matters, including how you bargain or compromise to make sure things work out. Now I want to bargain with you, sir, if I may."

"You may try."

"If I agree to spend the night at Dr. Zavala's house and not return to camp until three o'clock tomorrow afternoon, that would protect the packet from enemy capture. If I station myself tomorrow afternoon inside the marsh, on the road to Lynch's Ferry, I can view our attack without exposing myself to enemy fire. I promise not to come within three hundred yards of the enemy. That should be a safe distance. Sir, I believe this to be a reasonable compromise."

Smart as a whip, Houston thought. After pouring more coffee, he pointed to the map and asked, "What are you going to do after we ascend the ridge?"

"If I see the tide of battle obviously going our way, I would consider the bargain filled, and myself free to participate."

Houston reflected for a moment, studying the map. "All right, Jason, that's reasonable. But I must insist you not expose yourself to enemy fire or participate unless we have penetrated the breastworks. Only then will the tide of battle be certain. Further, you must destroy the contents of that packet, without reading a word, before you take a single solitary risk. Is that a bargain?"

"Yes, sir," Jason smiled.

"Now," Houston said, "listen carefully. If we're defeated, go to the Hargrove Plantation. Stay only long enough to inform them, and urge your bullheaded mother-in-law to evacuate immediately to Nacogdoches. Deliver those letters, no matter what she does. After you've delivered the letters, there may be other duties at your most distant destination. You will serve a countryman whose name you know well. I believe that covers it. Any questions?"

"No, sir, but don't worry, General; we're going to win that battle tomorrow."

"Since you're going to Zavala's, tell Colonel Neill that Major Hockley has the artillerymen in fine shape."

"I'll do that, sir. Good night."

For the first time since he had assumed command of the army at Gonzales, Houston felt as though he could enjoy a full night's rest. After instructing Hockley not to have him awakened at reveille, he prayed for clear weather and fell asleep.

261

Chapter 24

A crisp dry norther blew in during the night, dropping the temperature below forty degrees. Houston awoke from more than nine hours of deep sleep. Under a gray cloudy sky, he ate a hearty breakfast, then summoned Deaf Smith. "What do you make of this weather?"

"No rain today," Smith said.

"What about sunshine?"

"It's a late dry norther, General. Sometimes they clear up, and sometimes they don't."

"I know that, Deaf, but how do you feel about this one?"

"I'd bet it will clear up by noon."

After seeing Smith off toward Vince's Bridge, Houston walked through the camp, chatting with the men whose spirits seemed high. As he returned to his tent, he was startled to see Smith lashing his horse on both sides, tearing toward camp at full speed. Smith dismounted, out of breath, and before he could speak, Houston took him into the tent where they could meet alone.

"General, several hundred Mexican troops have crossed Vince's Bridge. They'll be along this way within an hour."

No, Houston thought, no, no, no. He cursed, spat on the ground, and shook his finger at Smith. "I thought Arnold was stationed where he could watch that bridge."

"He was, General. He must have been captured or killed."

"That damn bridge is only eight miles away. I should have put several scouts on it. It's not your fault, Deaf; I'm sorry I lost my temper."

"I thought I was going to lose my hide. I almost rode right into 'em. Since I hadn't heard from Arnold, I figured there was no danger between here and the bridge."

Crestfallen, Houston concentrated on this possibly fatal development. Several hundred, Smith had reported. But Smith had had little time for a careful estimate. There could be a thousand or more veteran troops under Filisola or Urrea, in which case he must take a defensive posture. But perhaps these troops are the reinforcements Santa Anna requested. If Santa Anna had taken the precautionary measure of sending two couriers by separate routes, then Filisola might have sent the five hundred reinforcements.

Several men had seen Smith whipping his horse into camp. They were milling around Houston's tent, trying to learn what had happened. Houston knew he must respond rapidly, lest the camp fall into disarray. My choices, he thought, are narrow and dangerous. I could scramble an attack on Santa Anna before his reinforcements arrive. But I would be wide open to a flank attack from the west by those reinforcements. The wise decision probably is to assume a defensive position in the trees. Or, I could stay with my original plan. But how in hell can I maintain morale among these men until mid-afternoon?

"Deaf," he said, "the morale of our men is critical at this point. When the enemy reinforcements appear, I want you to walk among the men. Let them think that these are some of the same Mexican troops you saw yesterday during the skirmish. Tell them this is an old trick Santa Anna has used for years to discourage his enemies."

"I just can't believe Arnold got careless," Smith said.

"Forget about that. Will you do what I asked?"

"All right, General. I won't have any trouble keeping a straight face today about anything."

When the Mexican reinforcements began marching across the western perimeter of the plain toward Santa Anna's camp, Smith carried out Houston's request. Most of the men believed the story. Rusk and Sherman, however, suspected a ruse, recognizing new standards and the epaulets of a general leading the column. Through his field glass, Burleson recognized none other than Cós, his adversary at Bexar who had pledged never to return to Texas. Burleson also surmised a ruse, but remained silent, hoping for a crack at Cós. As the lines disappeared over the ridge into Santa Anna's camp, Houston summoned Smith. "Take a handful of volunteers and destroy Vince's Bridge," Houston said. "There will be no more reinforcements."

"General, they control the road to New Washington. Vince's Bridge is the only way out for us if we have to retreat."

"I can read maps. I said destroy that damned bridge. That's an order!"

When Smith returned from his mission, Arnold was riding behind, holding tightly to Smith's chest as the veteran scout reined up at Houston's tent. "Arnold, you didn't pull that old yarn on them about being a runaway slave?" Houston asked.

"No, General, I didn't have time to think or speak. I was riding on the other side of Vince's Bridge, when I spotted their advance guard. Just after I rode across the bridge, my horse pulled up lame. I let him go and climbed a big oak tree filled with Spanish moss. It was a fine hiding place."

"Then you saw them close at hand?" Houston asked.

"They marched right by that tree. I thought they would never stop coming. Every now and then one of 'em would look around, and I just held my breath."

"Were you able to count?" Smith asked.

"Not very well. I'd estimate four to five hundred. They marched in irregular formation, trudging along with their heads down. Most of them were weary. Must have made a long march."

"Gentlemen, get some rest. You've had enough excitement for a while. And please, not one word of this around camp."

His confidence somewhat restored, Houston walked alone to the edge of Buffalo Bayou, studying the new odds of attacking a superior force or remaining in their strong defensive position, awaiting an enemy attack. With the bridge destroyed, there could be no retreat.

If the enemy reinforcements were weary, though, they couldn't be in top fighting condition today, Houston mused. Tomorrow would be quite another matter. Convinced his original attack plan remained basically sound, Houston turned his concern to the officers. They had been clamoring for an engagement for weeks. He would test their mettle.

As Houston walked toward his tent, he met Rusk and Hockley. "I'd like to speak to you a moment, Sam," Rusk said.

"George," Houston said, "fetch the field officers for a meeting here in thirty minutes. All right, Tom, what is it?"

Rusk was tense as he walked into Houston's tent. He had talked to Burleson and Sherman about the advisability of an attack, and recalling Houston's abhorrence of councils of war, he had decided to confront Houston alone. Before he could complete a sentence, Houston interrupted. "Save your breath, Tom, and relax. The council of war begins in thirty minutes."

Puzzled, Rusk deemed it wise to take more pulses before the officers assembled for the meeting. Since Houston was in no mood to discuss strategy with him, he excused himself to search out Lamar and others. When the eight officers gathered before Houston at noon, he opened the meeting with a brief statement. "Gentlemen, the purpose of this council of war is to explore the alternatives available to us as we prepare to defeat the enemy and capture Santa Anna."

The enemy reinforcements and yesterday's harrowing skirmish had tempered the zest for attack in Rusk and Sherman. When approached by Rusk, both Burleson and Lamar had been noncommittal. Of the other officers, only Henry Millard came to the meeting with a fierce resolve that the Texans should attack.

Rusk asked to be recognized as the first speaker. "It seems to me, General, that we have a favorable position with protective timber from which we can repulse enemy attacks coming across the plain. To expose ourselves in open combat, against a superior force, seems

264

hazardous, particularly since we have no bayonets and the Mexicans do."

"I further believe that our meager artillery would be more effective from a defensive position. We could concentrate grapeshot into their columns. Whereas, if we attack, our small cannons would have to be transported across open ground to within musket range of their breastworks.

"If we should attack and our cavalry were contained, our infantry column would be exposed to a flanking movement, perhaps driving us into the swamp near the river. Santa Anna won't take prisoners, and we don't want to be trapped in a swamp where defense or retreat would be impossible. All things considered, I believe the wise and prudent course of action is to fortify our position and await an enemy attack."

Burleson searched vainly for some clue from Houston's impassive face as the general recognized Millard. "I don't have nearly the combat experience of some of you gentlemen," Millard said, "but I firmly believe the time has come for battle. My men are cocked and primed to attack the enemy. They will be restless and dispirited, if we don't attack. But there can be no stand-off. We must be successful on the first charge, or they'll cut us to shreds. If we don't attack, they may soon receive substantial reinforcements, making our position indefensible. We all know we aren't going to be reinforced. I say it's time to attack."

Houston glanced at Lamar, expecting the firebrand from Georgia to support Millard, but Lamar remained silent. Then Sherman rose to speak. "I must agree with the distinguished secretary of war," Sherman said. "When you carefully review the terrain, you find that we not only have a favorable defensive position, but it's one that can withstand an assault from a force much larger than ours. It affords us maximum concealment and protection, while fighting in open combat exposes us to potential disaster in a matter of minutes. Since we cannot expect reinforcements, we have all the more reason to stay with the strong defensive position."

Only two officers had been truly undecided when they entered the council of war, Burleson and Lysander Wells, one of Sherman's Kentucky volunteers. Burleson had reviewed the strategic situation carefully before the meeting and found himself in a quandary. Emotionally, he was prepared to fight, and his dander was up after seeing Cós, his old adversary. But Burleson had a cautious side. He wanted to have the upper hand, and he found no upper hand in the present situation. As the twenty-five-year-old Wells had listened to Millard, his adrenalin had begun flowing for an attack. He had wanted to speak out in support of Millard, but hesitated.

As Sherman sat down, Houston scanned the faces of his officers. Burleson assumed Houston then would present his position, but the general merely put the question to a vote: whether to attack today or await the enemy.

Houston called for a verbal vote. "Await," Rusk said. Sherman made the same response, but Lamar hesitated. The new cavalry commander believed an immediate attack was warranted, and he had been disappointed to hear Sherman's opposition. Since Houston had failed to express an opinion, the general must be undecided on the question, he thought. To oppose the secretary of war and his friend, Sherman, a regimental commander, might be foolhardy. This council of war is not going to vote for an attack, so why should I play the role of a sore thumb? "Await," Lamar said.

Millard hoped to stem the tide with his loud vote of "attack," but Burleson, assuming Rusk reflected Houston's sentiment, cancelled Millard's vote. Sherman frowned when his protegé, Wells, called out a snappy vote for "attack," but the remaining two men preferred to wait.

Houston recorded the votes without expressing an opinion, six to two in favor of defending their position. Houston paused, checking his watch. "Gentlemen, I'm not certain your votes reflect the sentiment of the men you command or the realities of the strategic situation. I suggest we reconvene here at two-thirty this afternoon."

If Houston's resolve needed bolstering, it came when he saw outside a clear, blue sky. Walking among the men, he chatted with company commanders wherever he found them. He saw his longtime critic, Captain Moseley Baker, sitting down to a meal of beef, cornbread, and coffee. "Do you have an extra plate?" Houston asked. The captain pointed casually to a tin plate and cup nearby. "Moseley, you old warhorse, you've called me everything under the sun for not engaging the enemy. Now that they're perched over there across that ridge, what do you think?"

Baker spat a bite of stringy beef into the fire. "You know what I think. I haven't changed my mind since the fall of the Alamo. Neither have my men. I know that was some sort of foolishness Deaf Smith pulled this morning, and I don't care. We can whip them anyway. Sooner the better."

"Have you talked to your men about taking prisoners?"

"We're not taking prisoners. Santa Anna had no quarter bugle calls played yesterday. My men know what that means."

"We're not going to be guilty of atrocities."

"Look, Sam, this whole damned war has been a case of our fighting with short sticks. Now, don't come winging in here, telling me how to control my men. They haven't been paid since they joined up. They're sick of being hounded by disease, lack of clothing, loneliness, and disgust over not fighting the enemy. They're mean, mad as hornets. They want vengeance, and when they tear into the enemy, they're gonna kill every damned one of them they can. My

266

question to you is when are you going to stop pussyfooting around and tend to the business at hand?"

"You refused the combat training at the plantation. I will not lead this army into battle without a strong sense of military discipline, and that includes taking prisoners. That's final!"

Baker washed down a bite of cornbread with a long swig of coffee. For the first time since he began his running feud with Houston, he sensed the general was genuinely seeking his help. "What are you driving at, Sam?"

"Give me your word that you will convince your men to take prisoners, and we'll pay Santa Anna a visit."

"When?"

"Today."

"That's a bargain!"

Houston found Seguin sitting alone in his camp, cleaning a pistol. "Captain, what is the feeling of your men?"

"They will fight here or over the ridge."

"What's your preference?"

Seguin was weary of uncertainty. Yet, he knew Houston wouldn't be soliciting opinions from company commanders unless he had other ideas in mind. "I believe we can catch them flatfooted with an immediate attack. That is my preference, General."

"Thank you, Captain," Houston said, slapping Seguin on the shoulder.

Houston worked his way throughout the camp, increasingly convinced that the foot soldiers were prepared for battle. The backbone of the army is secure, he thought, motioning Hockley aside near the Twin Sisters.

"How long would it take your artillerymen to prepare for moving out?"

"No longer than thirty minutes."

"How soft is the open ground?"

"We could move the cannons on it, but why are you asking? The council voted to hold this position."

"My opinion of councils of war has been reaffirmed. Be at the meeting at two-thirty, George."

Houston sought out Lamar, whose vote in the council of war had disappointed him. He found him under an oak tree, reading a book. "You don't seem too worried about the enemy," Houston said.

"Since the meeting, I considered it unlikely that we would engage the enemy today. I enjoy reading, particularly material about Texas. Did you know this river was named in memory of Saint Hyacinth, the anglicized form of San Jacinto, traced to ancient Greek mythology with Apollo having . . ."

"Colonel Lamar, I have no time for history lessons. I want your honest, confidential evaluation of the fighting condition and attitude of your men. At the moment, I'm more concerned about Santa Anna than Apollo."

"Very well. A few of the cavalrymen were unsettled, discouraged you might say, after the skirmish yesterday. My own evaluation is that was caused by a failure to conduct an organized, forthright attack."

"Then, it's your opinion the cavalry is prepared to attack, if convinced the battle plan is sound."

"That's an accurate statement, General."

"And I trust that also reflects your sentiment?"

"That's correct, sir."

"I hope that you will be at a stopping place in your book at two-thirty."

Sensing Houston had no interest in continuing the conversation, Lamar pursued a concern he had felt when the general had adjourned the council of war. "General, may I make a pointed comment?"

"No time better than now."

"After the meeting, I thought that you preferred to attack. I couldn't understand why you remained silent while Rusk and the others argued against an attack. Further, I now suspect you will order an attack when we meet at two-thirty."

"Colonel, do you recall my remarks about the wisdom of the cavalrymen in choosing you as their commander?"

"Certainly."

"Apply those remarks to the situation at hand and you have your answer."

"But if you planned to go directly to the men, why call a council of war for the field officers?"

"This is the most important decision I've had to make in my life. I wasn't about to miss evaluating all aspects, as best I know how."

"But you're going against the council, including Rusk, Burleson and Sherman. This is indeed unorthodox."

"That may be true, Colonel, but I believe this decision to be wise, and beyond that, imperative."

Rumors spread throughout the camp that an attack order was forthcoming. Sherman considered openly challenging Houston for disregarding the council of war, but fell silent when his friend Lamar supported the attack. Moseley Baker scoffed at Rusk's reluctance, suggesting "the secretary of war should be renamed the secretary of wait." Burleson quietly prepared his regiment for battle.

As they walked into Houston's tent, Rusk and Sherman were resigned to the general's decision, though Rusk remained upset that Houston had not brought him into his confidence. Houston came directly to the point. "Gentlemen, viewing all considerations carefully, I believe we must attack the enemy with all dispatch. In one hour, at three-thirty, assemble your men." Houston charted the line of attack, starting with Sherman's regiment, then Burleson's regiment and the four companies under Millard's command. In front of the center of the infantry line, Hockley was designated to assemble thirty artillerymen to move out with the Twin Sisters. To the far right of the infantry line, Lamar was assigned with his sixty cavalrymen.

"Sidney," Houston said, "if your men can work their way into this line of timber, you should surprise the enemy's right flank, forcing them to divert their attention. We will move the major infantry column over the ridge, straight at their camp. Don't get too far ahead of us, or you'll be outnumbered in close combat.

"Colonel Lamar, you must keep our right flank secure. If you can move ahead, uncontested, you should create confusion by drawing the attention of their left flank.

"Burleson and Millard, keep your men in a disciplined advance while Hockley's men are pulling our cannons, keeping pace, and gentlemen, the pace will be brisk. I will lead the main assault directly at their breastworks.

"We will hit them when the sun is falling into their camp. Remember, the enemy has only one cannon, and their muskets are short-range British models. We should be able to withstand a few short volleys before we penetrate their breastworks. From there, it's close combat.

"Now, the Mexicans have bayonets, which we do not have. So we must hit them hard and fast, before they can organize a bayonet attack. Make every rifle shot count. Don't waste a pistol shot outside the breastworks, unless they contest us in the open. For each Mexican soldier killed before we arrive in their camp, a bayonet becomes available.

"Despite my faith in the company commanders, I suspect it will be difficult to contain the men once inside the breastworks. Stress the responsibility they have in conducting this attack. We must take prisoners and, gentlemen, here is the location of the prisoner we want most." Houston pointed to where Santa Anna's tent lay charted on the map. "If you have to shoot him, or hit him with a rifle or whatever, for God's sake, try not to kill him. Any questions?"

"Where will the reserves be stationed?" asked Hockley.

"There will be no reserves," Houston said.

As the field officers departed Houston's tent, the general placed his arm on Rusk's shoulder. "I feel like a fool," Rusk said.

"You know, Tom, I didn't feel like a damn genius when Deaf Smith reported those enemy reinforcements a few hours ago. I appreciate the fact that you and Sherman didn't bring that up."

"How could we? You had the most reliable scout in the army claiming those were troops he had seen yesterday. I can't speak for Sherman, but the only reason I voted to wait was because I knew we were outnumbered by a substantial margin."

269

"I regret that you were embarrassed, Tom, but I had to make sure the men were not discouraged by the fear of a superior enemy force. I was running out of time."

"I can understand that, but why didn't you bring me into your confidence?"

"The simple truth is I wanted honest evaluations which would not have been forthcoming had I first presented my views to you or anyone else. I wanted to evaluate the opinions of the field officers, company officers and their men, all at one time, and I couldn't follow Deaf Smith around, lest I destroy the ruse."

Rusk shook his head. "Is this the way you play politics?"

"Only when necessary," Houston smiled. "Democracy may be our form of government, but too much democracy will ruin an army. I had to make the decision my own way."

"Well, I've got to admit, it's an exciting plan of attack. But you're taking a tremendous risk in leading the main infantry advance where you'll be an easy target. You ought to follow Sherman, or perhaps Lamar."

"That main line must hold together. That's where I belong."

While the Texans cleaned their weapons and filled powder horns, Santa Anna entertained Generals Castrillón and Cós, and Colonel Almonte, in his tent.

"I am upset about Filisola," Santa Anna said, as Almonte poured wine. "My order to him for reinforcements stated specifically that they were to be picked men. Now, Martín, you tell me these men are mostly raw recruits, deficient in instruction."

"Unfortunately, that is the case," Cós said. "Filisola reasoned that these men were young and healthy, thus better prepared to make a forced march."

"And does that distinguished general expect them to be better prepared for battle?" Santa Anna asked.

"He did not expect a rebel force in this area. His scouting reports had Houston in retreat toward the Trinity."

"We are not certain Houston is commanding this force," Almonte said, "but we estimate it is comprised of perhaps five hundred men."

"We must forget about Filisola," Santa Anna said. "Because of these circumstances, I will grant your request, Martin. You may permit these exhausted recruits to rest themselves today and tonight. We will attack tomorrow."

"Your Excellency," Castrillón said, "I would recommend another skirmish this afternoon to draw the enemy from their concealment. Perhaps we could then make a more precise estimate of their strength."

"A waste of time," Santa Anna said. "They ran like dogs yesterday. They will not reveal their strength today. It will be necessary to attack their position, driving them into that bayou. I

270

doubt they have five hundred men, but even if that estimate is valid, we can defeat them with a forthright attack. Their cannons have such meager range they cannot be fired accurately more than once before we overrun their camp with a cavalry charge, supported by infantry. My only concern is to see that our men are rested, in top fighting condition. Other than guards, permit all men to rest the remainder of the day. Give them full rations and require the cavalry to water their horses."

"Even if our men must seek water beyond the perimeters of the guard stations?" asked Castrillón.

"Of course," Santa Anna said. "This band of disorganized rebels could not possibly mount an effective attack on our position."

"At what time should we prepare to attack tomorrow?" asked Almonte.

"I want to reflect on that," said Santa Anna, finishing his glass of wine. "I need some rest myself. If you gentlemen will excuse me, I wish to enjoy a nice long nap before dinner."

Santa Anna had given little thought to a battle plan. He despised the terrain and settlements in this area, so foreign to his homeland and San Antonio de Bexar. He sensed the morale of his men had faltered since leaving Bexar, but he was proud of their fighting spirit in the skirmish. If only the cursed rebels had not prevented his return to the capital. That thought sent him to his silver pill box from which he drew five grains of opium. He soon relaxed, preparing to sleep.

Not far from Santa Anna's tent, Castrillón sat down beside a campfire to drink coffee with Carlos and Juan. "We should be leaving here after tomorrow," he said.

"Does that mean we will attack tomorrow?" asked Carlos.

"You know," Castrillón smiled, "of His Excellency's penchant for secrecy and surprise. He will not disclose the battle plan until he feels it absolutely necessary, but he has said we will attack tomorrow."

"After this battle, will the campaign be over?" Juan asked.

"We are not certain," said Castrillón. "Let us say the Army of Operations will have completed its primary mission, that of defeating most of the rebels under arms. Beyond that, the army will have to search out whatever remnants of rebels can be found to the north, besides maintaining strong garrisons at Bexar and Goliad."

"Suppose," Juan said, thinking of Rosa, "that you were commander of this army, General Castrillón. Would you, sir, permit officers and men to choose their place of occupation duty after hostilities are over?"

"I had not considered that," said Castrillón. "I suppose that under such circumstances, it might be acceptable. I suspect most of the men would prefer Bexar. However, I would have to consider the reason for the request."

Carlos, who thought only of returning to his family and farm near Saltillo, asked Castrillón if he would consider permitting combat veterans to return to their homeland, since hundreds of new recruits had poured into Texas.

"Of course, I would consider that, Captain, and you would head the list, having fought bravely and having suffered a severe wound. The duty of occupying this country should fall upon those who wish to remain and upon new recruits without families."

"General," Juan pursued, "assuming I had a personal reason for desiring duty in Bexar, could that be valid for assignment there?"

"That would depend upon the reason."

"Let us suppose I want to marry a girl there, and settle in that community."

"That might be valid," Castrillón smiled.

Castrillón stood beside the campfire to view the surroundings. Most cavalrymen had taken their horses to water behind the camp, and all the weary men brought by Cós were asleep. Many of the other soldiers had stacked their muskets and retired, sleeping or idling away the time playing cards. No guards were stationed beyond the ridge, which concealed the Texan camp from theirs. The Mexican breast-works consisted of fairly even piles of unused saddles and empty boxes that had contained provisions or ammunition. There was no other protection.

When he sat down again, Castrillón sighed. "Your desires reflect the sentiment of this army. You want to leave this swamp-ridden country to the snakes, alligators, and mosquitoes. You want to return to the country you love."

"And to the people," Carlos said.

"Of course," said Castrillón. "No wonder this part of Texas was never settled by our people. It may as well be in Louisiana."

Chapter 25

AT three-thirty, seven hundred eighty-three members of the Army of Texas assembled in battle formation. Other than Sherman's uniformed Kentucky volunteers, the soldiers were dressed in tattered jeans and mud-caked buckskin. This army was, indeed, a mixed bag. Though dominated by Anglos, Seguin commanded a company of nineteen tough Tejanos, and there were two free Negroes, the brilliant scout Hendrick Arnold and Dick the Drummer.

One hundred and seventeen of these men owned land in Texas, and ten of the fifty-nine signers of the declaration of independence were there, led by Houston and Rusk. The Box family had given four members to the army, which had solid colonists, such as Baker and Burleson, along with many cursing, hard-drinking adventurers with no education or property — some of whom couldn't write their names. There were intellectuals such as Lamar and Robert Kleberg, who held a doctor-of-law degree from a European university. Another of the men reputedly had been a close friend of the late English poet, Lord Byron.

Most of these men had ventured into Texas in search of a new life, running away from failure or misfortune in America. Their loyalties had been divided during the tedious, demoralizing days following the fall of the Alamo. They had lived from moment to moment, day by day, hoping and praying for an opportunity to turn the tide of war. Now, they were united for this one desperate attempt for a decisive victory.

Before mounting, Burleson stuck two pistols into his belt and secured a Bowie knife in his scabbard. Sherman, Millard and Hockley stood silently by their men, awaiting Houston's order. Lamar, leaning forward slightly in the saddle, had challenged his men to keep pace, once he began the attack on the enemy's left flank. With his right hand, he unsheathed his saber, while his left hand rested on his saddle horn.

In his tent, Houston tucked his cotton pantaloons into his heavy boots, then buttoned his black vest over a soiled, sweat-stained shirt.

273

Donning his frayed black frock coat, he recalled Moseley Baker's remark about "pussyfooting around." He and Rusk had already made brief speeches. There would be no more.

Houston mounted his horse and cantered before the long thin line, checking briefly for any flaws in the formation. There were no rousing songs to be played, no Lone Star banner to be unfurled. Instead, the three fifers could agree on only one song, "Will You Come to the Bower?", that saucy tune that raised eyebrows among refined ladies of the land. A few tattered banners had been preserved, but only Sherman's white silk flag was prominent in the afternoon breeze. Reining up before the center of the line, Houston bellowed: "Trail arms, forward march!" With a flourish, he waved his black felt hat at Lamar and reined around to canter ahead of the marching soldiers.

As the line moved forward, most of the men found their hands trembling, not from fear but from anticipation. "Remember the Alamo!" shouted the left flank, and "Remember Goliad!" called the men in the center. Seguin promptly yelled to his men: *"¡Recuerden El Alamo! Recuerden La Bahia!"*

The fifers began the bouncy tune, backed by Dick the Drummer. Houston motioned them to quiet the music, hoping to maintain some element of surprise until they reached the ridge. Despite Moseley Baker's stern warning, one of his men tied his red bandana around his rifle, hoisting it as a defiant flag of no quarter.

As Houston galloped toward the ridge, he saw that Lamar's cavalry would soon be in position to contest the enemy. Riding back to the line, he shouted: "Quick Time, March!" As the brisk pace began, Millard saw portions of his four companies were falling out of line. "Tighten it up!" he called. Mounted on a big roan, Burleson cantered before his men, waving them onward.

Riding toward the far left of the line, Houston saw Sherman leading his men into timber without drawing enemy fire. With Lamar's advance yet to draw enemy fire, Houston again increased the pace of the infantry. Galloping before the center of the line, he bellowed: "Double-Quick Time, March!"

In the Mexican camp, Castrillón was chatting with Carlos and Juan when a sharp bugle call from their right flank pierced the air. Sherman's men had been detected, but no shots were heard. Instead, Castrillón heard strange music from over the ridge, and the unmistakable sound of drumbeats. Dashing toward the hill, he saw a few rebels in the timber to his right and heard the word "Alamo" shouted several times from beyond the ridge where he had heard the music. "My God," he said, "the rebels are attacking."

Racing back to the breastworks, he shouted orders to Carlos and Juan to join him at the artillery battery. He barked orders to Captain Delgado to man the cannon. As Castrillón squinted into the bright sunlight, gunfire erupted on his left where Lamar's charge was being contested by a handful of dragoons. Castrillón shouted orders for all units to consolidate with troops behind the breastworks.

Almonte burst inside Santa Anna's tent to awaken His Excellency. Startled by the incredible news, Santa Anna ran from his tent to cracks of gunfire and the confusion of cursing, shouting soldiers. Deadened by the effects of alcohol, opium and sleep, Santa Anna was slow to respond. Shading his eyes, he peered through dust and smoke at the main Texan advance crossing the ridge. He began shouting orders for nearby units to advance beyond the breastworks to contest the rebels, thus countermanding Castrillón's previous orders. When he finally focussed clearly upon the advancing Texans, screaming their battle cries, the "Eagle" took flight. Seizing the reins of a cavalryman's unused horse, he mounted and galloped away to the west, seeking a path of safety toward Vince's Bridge.

Though widespread confusion engulfed their camp, many Mexican soldiers attempted to make stands, principally under the direction of Castrillón. Cós had also disappeared, leaving the reinforcements temporarily without leadership. Those soldiers within earshot of Castrillón followed his orders, protecting the cannon and defending the breastworks. Some had worked their way forward, obeying Santa Anna's orders, unable to hear subsequent orders, as gunfire and shouting intensified across the plain.

Castrillón had the artillery aimed directly at the center of the main Texan advance, but the first blast of grapeshot was calibrated too high, failing to drop a single Texan. The next shot, accompanied by musket fire, dropped several Texans, including Moseley Baker, who collapsed with a slashing leg wound. Houston's horse fell wounded, throwing the general to the ground. He rose immediately to accept the horse of a junior officer. "Hold your fire!" Houston shouted repeatedly along the Texan line, advancing to within about sixty yards of the breastworks. At that point he knew the Texan firepower could be brought to bear with utmost accuracy and effectiveness.

Houston was preparing to order his line to fire when another volley of Mexican artillery and musket fire shrouded the breastworks in smoke, masking the enemy position for a few seconds. "Wheel them into place!" he shouted to Hockley, whose artillerymen had not breathed without cursing since they had begun dragging the gun carriages across the plain. Within seconds, Hockley had the Twin Sisters loaded with grapeshot.

As smoke cleared along the breastworks, Houston ordered the line to kneel and aim. Two of Hockley's men stood with lighted torches, prepared to fire the fuses for the cannons. Houston knew he had but an instant to make the initial volley count before the Mexican defenders could reload. "Fire!" he bellowed.

From close range, the double blast of grapeshot shattered holes in the breastworks as rifle fire cut down several Mexican defenders,

275

including two of Delgado's artillerymen near Castrillón. The brave general stood his ground, ordering another round to be fired from the lone Mexican cannon. As Houston's men reloaded, Castrillón directed the soldiers around him to fire at Houston.

When the Mexican cannon roared again, the grapeshot spewed forth at Houston in the center of the Texan column. He felt a burning sensation in his right ankle as his horse tumbled to the ground. Hockley pulled Houston to his feet, and waved a horseman nearby to relinquish his mount. A musket ball had shattered Houston's ankle, filling his boot with blood.

Remounting, Houston saw that most of the Texans crouched on the ground had reloaded their rifles. I must, he thought, pour this next volley into the enemy camp, then charge before they can reload. Hockley had barely managed to have the cannons reloaded when Houston unsheathed his saber and shouted "Fire!" That second volley from the main Texan line was deadly, knocking out the artillery battery. Castrillón fell dead across the steaming cannon, while Carlos sustained a rifle wound in his chest. Juan's life was spared only because he was reaching for a keg of powder on the ground when the volley crashed into their position. More than half of the Mexican defenders near the breastworks lay dead or wounded.

An instant after Houston's second volley, Lamar's cavalry charge broke through scattered enemy resistance to the far right of Houston's column. Cascading over debris and fallen bodies, Lamar dashed into the Mexican camp. From Houston's left, Sherman and Seguin drove the Mexican right flank into retreat and disarray. Sensing the main Mexican defense was crumbling, Houston ordered the infantry line to charge.

Through dust and smoke, Juan tried to reach Carlos, but Lamar's horse crashed into him, smashing him to the ground unconscious. Lamar waved his men toward the center of the camp where he saw Houston's men tumbling through the breastworks. With Castrillón dead, the Mexican defense collapsed.

Vaulting over bodies, the Texans poured into the Mexican camp, preventing any consolidation of enemy troops. Sherman's attack on the enemy right flank had prevented Almonte from assuming control of the bewildered reinforcements. Shouting and cursing, the Texans rained death throughout the enemy camp, using rifles, sabers, Bowie knives, pistols and captured bayonets.

Dazed by the intense pain from his wound, Houston rode through the Mexican camp searching for Santa Anna. Finding His Excellency's tent unoccupied, he peered around the camp which was consumed by smoke and dust. Spotting Burleson, he shouted for him to start taking prisoners, but Burleson was already pursuing some frenzied members of his regiment, who, flushed with victory, were wreaking vengeance on helpless Mexican soldiers. Trapped in a swamp, many died while protesting "No Alamo!" and "No Bahia!" With the help of a few company commanders, Burleson finally halted the carnage.

Rusk and Seguin saved many lives among small scattered groups of Mexicans before Almonte offered a surrender in behalf of several hundred confused soldiers. Rusk accepted the surrender, gathering about one hundred Texans to serve as guards. Less than twenty minutes after the first Texan volley had been fired, the enemy camp was secured.

Houston rode throughout the Mexican camp, searching vainly for Santa Anna. Finding Lamar, he ordered him to lead a search party far beyond the battlefield in an attempt to capture Santa Anna and General Cós. Organized retreat had been impossible for the Mexicans, but some had managed to escape through the mud of nearby swamps and marshes. However, most of those were killed or captured in the twilight aftermath of the Battle of San Jacinto.

Houston reined toward his camp, his vision failing as he rode slowly across the plain. His ankle wound and the failure to capture Santa Anna had drained his energy, isolating him at the very moment his men were cheering and hoisting their rifles in tributes to "Old Sam."

Riding up alongside him, Burleson flung one of his pistols in the direction of their camp in a rare gesture of exultant victory. But as the normally composed commander viewed Houston's bloodstained trousers, he spurred his horse ahead, to search out Dr. Ewing. Ewing led them to a large oak tree under which he spread a blanket. After he and Burleson helped Houston dismount, Ewing soon had the wound cleaned and was wrapping it tightly. "How long did you ride with this wound?"

"Not long."

"You won't be riding or walking for quite some time. I'll have a crutch made, and I want you to promise you won't try to walk on this foot."

"I promise not to put this foot on the ground," Houston winced, and asked for whiskey to ease the pain. Ewing pulled a bottle from his hip pocket, and gave his patient one strong swig. As the doctor walked away, Houston smiled weakly at Burleson. "You know, Ed, Dr. Alexander Wray Ewing isn't so smart, after all. He didn't forbid me to ride."

"We'll do the riding."

"You better ride fast, if Lamar can't find Santa Anna. Don't talk this around camp, but if he's escaped, he'll soon return with three thousand men. Pick your best men and cover all the area you can around Vince's Bridge and the road to New Washington."

"It's almost dark, Sam. I doubt they could find a thing now. If Santa Anna escaped on horseback, he's long gone."

Houston's vision blurred again as he tried to shift his bandaged foot. "It is almost dark, isn't it, Ed? Then try first thing in the morning." His voice trailed off as the general slumped into an uneasy sleep.

True to his bargain with Houston, Jason had followed slowly behind Sherman's advance, carefully remaining outside range of enemy fire. After he had heard intense firing beyond the ridge, he galloped to where he could view the main infantry line pouring through the breastworks. When Lamar and Sherman executed their flanking maneuvers, he knew the battle was won.

He had guessed Stephen F. Austin was to have received one of the letters in the packet, and he couldn't resist at least learning the names of the other potential recipients. When he opened the packet and read "President Andrew Jackson" on the first envelope he gasped and rapidly shredded all the letters. Tossing the scraps of paper into the air, he shouted a war whoop and galloped down the slope toward the Mexican right flank. Seeing him, Seguin motioned Jason to join his company searching through the timber and a nearby marsh. After they brought three prisoners to an open area, Jason departed to find Houston. Hockley told him the general had sustained a painful wound and had retired to the Texan camp, whereupon Jason joined the search for Santa Anna.

When twilight fell, Lamar gave up the search, dismissing the men for their evening meal. Jason was too excited to eat. He thought only of returning to the plantation and perhaps taking Molly to Kentucky to visit his family. He rode alone through the Mexican camp, viewing hundreds of blood-drenched men, dead or dying on the ground.

Dismounting, he crossed to the lone Mexican artillery battery where the courageous Castrillón lay lifeless across the cannon, his comrades strewn around him in the dust and debris. A body moved slowly, and Jason aimed his pistol at the head of the fallen Mexican. Realizing the gesture had been harmless, he crouched by the dazed Mexican, lying face down in the dirt. Squinting at Jason, the wounded man asked for water, in a strained voice that Jason recognized as vaguely familiar. Jason considered leaving the fallen Mexican to his fate. He knew he had heard that voice, but where? Perhaps, he thought, this man was one of the guards who had cracked down on him at Goliad.

Turning to walk away, Jason recalled Brother Fowler's stern words. The parson had been firm in his conviction that the Lord was on the side of the Texans, but he had reminded Jason repeatedly that Christian charity could not be ignored, even in war. Jason spat upon the ground, and kicked a powder horn aside. "This is for you, Brother Fowler," he murmured, returning to the fallen form. He held his canteen to Juan's eager lips. Slowly reviving, Juan thought at first he was in the Alamo again, as his nostrils filled with the lingering odors of gunpowder. He saw Jason as Almonte, attending to his sickness after viewing that carnage. Then as Jason bathed dust and gunpowder from Juan's face, he recognized him as the one who had spared his life during his odyssey from Goliad.

Juan's head was still pounding from the crashing blow by Lamar's horse. Bewildered, he gazed around him, before turning to Jason. "I once helped you. Help me find my friend."

In the darkening twilight, Jason pulled Juan to his feet. Together they worked their way through the bodies lying about the battery. Juan found Carlos crumpled face down across a box of ammunition. He rolled him over to check for breathing, but the farmer from Saltillo had died instantly from the same Texan volley that felled Castrillón. "Oh, no," Juan cried, sobbing on Carlos' chest. "No, no."

Jason stood by for several minutes, before grasping Juan gently by the shoulder. "We'd better be getting out of here," he said. As Juan stood up slowly, Jason motioned him towards the prisoner camp.

They walked slowly, and Jason expressed again his gratitude for Juan's sparing his life. Juan, however, did not respond. He was preoccupied by Carlos' death and the shattering defeat of their army had overwhelmed him. He had been seething with frustration since departing Bexar, yearning for Rosa who was now carrying his child, and loathing Santa Anna's arrogance and disdain. Bitterness consumed him as he viewed the death and debris around him.

When they reached the Mexican prisoner camp, Juan found Almonte. The colonel had attempted to rally resistance, but unable to mount a stand, he had surrendered. He welcomed Juan with a smile and handshake, having thought him to be dead. Jason lingered nearby, chatting with one of his friends who had drawn guard duty.

"What of His Excellency?" Juan asked Almonte.

"He departed early in the battle."

"Departed? What do you mean?"

"It was a difficult situation. He chose to escape before the enemy enveloped our camp."

Juan's eyes grew cold. "Lieutenant Gates," he called. Jason joined Juan and Almonte in the dim light of a nearby campfire. "You once made me an offer that you would help me join your side, under Seguin. Does that offer still stand?"

Startled, Jason couldn't respond for a moment. To him, the war had been won, and to permit a defection now would be tantamount to freeing a prisoner. For the first time during his association with Juan, Almonte was speechless. After Jason had gazed down at his boots for a moment, he faced Juan. "I'm not sure. Conditions have changed."

"You mean that you are free and I am not? That your offer was only to save your life?"

Jason was ashamed to admit to himself that his offer had been nothing more than a ruse. Now that he had the upper hand, he must

279

honor the offer. "If that be your firm decision, I'll speak to Captain Seguin tonight. This might require approval from General Houston himself."

Almonte winced, shaking his head in disbelief. "I must insist," he said, "on a private conversation with Lieutenant Calderón. Please excuse us for a few moments."

Jason had made a commitment, but he hoped Juan would change his mind. Jason doubted that Seguin or Houston would be in a mood to accept a Mexican defector seeking an easy route to freedom.

Almonte placed his arm on Juan's shoulder, leading him toward an oak tree. "You have been through another difficult experience," he said, "and you need time to reflect. I suggest you at least sleep on this decision."

"My decision is firm, Colonel."

"Have you thought of your family? Have you thought of the disgrace this would cast on their name, as well as yours? Have you no sense of responsibility to the Supreme Government and the honor of our nation? You have served on the staff of His Excellency. You have a responsibility to him."

"To him? So long as he represents Mexico, he casts dishonor on our nation. What did General Castrillón die for today? And my friend Carlos, and all the others? So he could steal away like a common coward?"

"You are young and short-sighted. You fail to understand the difficulty of the situation today. His Excellency made a wise decision in escaping. He will return in a few days with more troops than these rebels can possibly withstand. He will secure this land for Mexico, in due time."

"I have no stomach to serve him another day, nor to live under his rule."

"What makes you think these rebels would accept you? They hate us. Did you not hear their cries for vengeance? Did you not see their wanton murder? There is no compassion in their hearts. I implore you to sleep on this decision. His Excellency will soon return to lead another triumph."

"I appreciate what you have done for me in the past, Colonel, but my decision is final. Farewell."

They found Seguin sitting by a campfire with two of his men, passing around a bottle of whiskey in celebration. "Why bring a prisoner here?" Seguin asked.

"Captain," Jason asked, "could you take a few minutes to discuss a pressing matter with this prisoner and me?"

Seguin motioned his men away, making room for the visitors. After being introduced to Juan, Seguin hesitated before offering him a drink. Juan accepted a small portion of whiskey, enjoying the warmth of the strong liquid.

"This man spared my life," Jason said, "during my journey from Goliad to rejoin the army. He could have killed me, or taken me prisoner. I had offered then to present him to you, if he should desire to defect from Santa Anna. He now desires to defect and join your company."

Three swigs of whiskey had mellowed Seguin's mood. Defectors had crossed both ways during the early stages of the revolution, and some Anglos reportedly had been helping Santa Anna in the San Jacinto vicinity in the past few days. Yet, hatred had been building between the two armies for weeks, and accepting an enemy soldier, fresh off the battlefield, wasn't exactly Seguin's idea of a victory celebration.

"Can't we sleep on this?" he asked.

"I'm afraid not," Jason replied. "His intentions are already known in the Mexican prisoner camp."

"You've rapidly crawled out on a limb," Seguin said to Juan. "So far as I know, General Houston has no policy on such matters."

"General Houston listens to you," Jason said. "If you're willing to accept him in your company, I'm confident he would concur."

"My company is composed of Tejanos, principally from San Antonio de Bexar. These men chose to oppose Santa Anna when the odds appeared hopeless. I'm afraid they would not take kindly to accepting one of Santa Anna's men after the defeat of that wretched tyrant."

"I know I am asking more than I should," Juan said, "but I came to Texas from the City of Mexico without previous military experience. I was chosen to serve on Santa Anna's staff because of my father's political support for His Excellency. I have grown ashamed of Santa Anna's personal and military conduct. Besides, I have my own special reason for wanting to join your company. I had never seen the province of Texas, but I fell in love with San Antonio de Bexar and with one of her citizens, Rosa Elena Tristán."

"Why, I knew her father well," Seguin smiled. "Little Rosa will make you a fine wife, if you'll take her out of that cantina."

"I will work night and day to support our family, including her brothers."

"Ah," Seguin said, pouring Juan a larger portion of whiskey, "affairs of the heart must often take priority over military considerations. I suppose I had better speak to General Houston about this. Jason, have a drink; you're always too serious, and keep the swamp crawlers away from my camp until I return."

After more than two hours of fitful sleep, Houston awakened to cheers and laughter resounding through the camp. Though the pain from his wound had subsided, he was unable to savor the victory. Lamar had reported that he had scoured the road to New Washington and the area around Vince's Bridge without finding a trace of Santa

Anna. Houston was chatting with Hockley when Seguin came to talk to him about Juan. "Fine with me," Houston said. "If you want to accept him, he's your responsibility."

Seguin returned to his camp and put his arm on Juan's shoulder. "You've found a friend in Jason, and you'll find a few more among the Anglos. But life won't be easy for you in Texas. You are a Mexican who served with Santa Anna at the Alamo. You'll be a marked man. I'm convinced you're sincere and will become a valuable citizen of Bexar, but you must understand what you are undertaking."

"I understand, Captain, and I am counting on your support in Bexar."

"Very well," Seguin said. "My men have been through a few surprises these past few weeks. I have no intention of foisting you into their midst as an officer of this company. I will assemble them now, and I suggest you tell them exactly what you have told me."

Seguin gathered his company of Tejanos. Manuel Flores, first sergeant, called the roll, and Juan presented his case. Juan and Jason were excused while the company debated acceptance of the young lieutenant. They knew Juan was acceptable to Seguin or their resolute commander wouldn't have brought him before them. A few expressed reservations, but the majority moved to accept him. When Seguin called for an open vote, the issue was easily in Juan's favor.

Congratulating Juan, Seguin said the first order of business was to find him a change of clothing. "I've got a change of buckskin," Jason said. "That ought to do for now."

Revelry in the camp had heightened. Some Texan guards discovered Santa Anna's large supply of wine, including two cases of champagne, and twelve thousand dollars in silver, an unexpected bonus. Rusk reported that find to Houston, with estimates of other items seized. In his exuberance, Rusk had failed to report the casualties until Houston interrupted him to ask.

"Sam, you won't believe this. We killed more than six hundred Mexicans and took about that many prisoners. We're still counting. On our side, we had only nine killed or mortally wounded and thirty others seriously wounded."

Propped against a saddle, Houston smiled weakly. "What about Moseley Baker and James Neill?"

"Dr. Ewing says both will recover."

Houston beckoned Burleson to join him and Rusk. "Gentlemen," Houston said, "you two have been my closest associates during this campaign. We may as well face reality. If Santa Anna returns with the forces under Filisola or Urrea or both, we will be in a precarious situation, to say the least. I'm now a commanding general in name only. If we face further combat, I will choose one of you to lead the army, the other to be second in command. I trust that you will cooperate with one another."

Houston's words jolted Rusk. Burleson, however, had anticipated this as the hours went by with no word on Santa Anna. Sensing Houston needed rest, Rusk suggested he and Burleson join the celebration, lest the men suspect a high-level strategy session was in progress to meet some new challenge.

After they departed, Houston listened to the prolonged celebration. They've earned this ten times over, he thought, but he wondered how Santa Anna had escaped through his advancing units. The one chance, he thought, the only real chance that he had to win the war, had slipped through his fingers. Exhausted, Houston again experienced a commander's particular brand of loneliness when confronted by uncertainty.

Before daybreak, Burleson was shaking some of his men awake to organize another search party. James Sylvester and Joel Robison were slow to respond, feeling the effects of the night's merriment. Burleson considered those two his best "bird dogs," followed closely by Joseph Vermillion and David Cole, who were cunning, if not quite so persistent. "Hurry up with breakfast," Burleson told them. "As soon as you can see, head for Vince's Bridge. Search carefully. Bring back every stray Mexican you can find."

Santa Anna had avoided Lamar's cavalry attack by seconds, dashing toward Vince's Bridge. He found it destroyed, and when his mount refused to enter the bayou, he had swum across, continuing his journey on foot. On the other side of the bayou, he had discovered an abandoned house in which he found cotton work clothes that fit him fairly well. So he discarded his uniform for a civilian disguise, planning to travel on foot to join his comrades under arms.

At mid-morning, Santa Anna was walking gingerly through high grass when he heard voices behind him. He crouched in the grass, hoping they had not seen him, but Sylvester, Robison, Vermillion and Cole came riding up. When the four-member detail saw the tired, thin figure in soiled cotton clothes, they scoffed at him.

"He ain't worth taking in," Cole said. "He ain't even a soldier."

"He could be a medical orderly or something," Robison said. "I say we take him in."

"I tell you he ain't got nothing to do with their army," Cole said. "He ain't nothing but a field hand."

"Orders from Colonel Burleson," Sylvester said, "were to bring in every stray Mexican. This is the only one we've found. The colonel won't like it if we don't bring in one or two."

"If we don't take him in," Robison said, "we may have to stay out all day. There's food and whiskey in camp. I say let's take this field hand into camp and present him as a prisoner."

Cole shook his head. "All right, but I think we're going to look like a bunch of drunk hoot owls, parading this skinny, unarmed man into our camp as a prisoner."

"Well, don't hold a gun to him," Sylvester said. "He looks harmless enough, anyway."

Since the Napoleon of the West didn't understand English, he was spared the demeaning remarks of Burleson's search party. Guessing they had accepted his civilian clothing, he believed they might set him free. But his heart sank when they told him to mount behind the lead rider. Heading back to camp, they held a leisurely pace, hoping to capture a uniformed soldier to bolster their meager morning's catch. Vermillion became hungry, so they stopped for lunch. Santa Anna accepted the dried beef, and water from Cole's canteen.

"You know," Cole said, "if we capture a real Mexican soldier, we ought to let this poor devil go. I tell you we're gonna be the laughing-stock of the camp, if we drag him in."

"And I tell you," Sylvester said, "that I was half asleep this morning, before we left camp, but I heard Colonel Burleson say to bring in every stray Mexican. I consider that an order. Besides, look at his hands. They're smooth, with neat fingernails. He's more likely a medical orderly than a field hand."

When they finally headed toward the prisoner camp, Sylvester and Robison were surprised to see some of the Mexican prisoners pointing at their slender captive. They were startled to hear calls of *"¡El Presidente!"* coming from the camp. When he heard the calls, Santa Anna winced. He had hoped this unlikely little band of tattered rebels couldn't understand Spanish and would deposit him with Almonte, who was trying calmly to quiet the prisoners.

"My God," Sylvester whispered to Robison. "Could this be the big one himself?"

Lorenzo de Zavala's son was chatting with Jason when the detail halted near the prisoner camp. As they prepared to dismount, Zavala said, "You have captured Santa Anna. I suggest that you take him before General Houston."

Burleson had been gratified that morning by the capture of General Cós, but Houston's sobering observation of the night before had tempered his enthusiasm. He was elated to learn his search party had brought the prize of all prizes. Excitement swept the Texan camp. But instead of another celebration, hundreds of irate, vengeful men who yearned to see Santa Anna hanging from a tree began to talk about lynching the Mexican leader.

When Hockley told Houston of the capture, the general smiled briefly. "George, bring him here under heavy guard. Fetch Burleson, Sherman, Rusk, Lamar, Seguin and Deaf Smith. Dead, Santa Anna means nothing to us. Alive, he means everything."

Houston lay under a huge live oak tree filled with Spanish moss only a stone's throw from Buffalo Bayou. When Santa Anna was brought before him, Houston motioned for him to take a seat on an empty ammunition box next to Dr. Ewing. Deaf Smith sat on a stump to Houston's left, rifle in hand. The various commanders formed a line of protection around Santa Anna, who saw a few men approaching with coils of rope in their hands. "Shoot the bastard!" yelled a swarthy Texan from Moseley Baker's company.

"Let's let things simmer down a bit, gentlemen," Houston told his commanders.

Santa Anna had recognized young Zavala. He offered a handshake, but Zavala refused. Zavala, who would interpret for Houston, had a loathing for Santa Anna more intense than that of his father. Zavala informed Houston that Santa Anna requested Colonel Almonte be permitted to serve as interpreter for him. Houston promptly granted the request.

When Almonte arrived, the danger to Santa Anna was subsiding. Though disgruntled and disappointed, the men clamoring for an immediate execution had no stomach for taking issue with their victorious commanding general. They hoped instead that Houston would order a court-martial, confident that Lamar and Rusk would be among those to demand the death penalty for the executions Santa Anna had ordered at Goliad.

For weeks, Houston had looked forward to this negotiation with Santa Anna. He had no intention of executing him, but Santa Anna must not know that. To Houston, the only agreement worth reaching was an end to hostilities throughout Texas. And the only way to achieve that was to trust Santa Anna's subordinate commanders to fulfill the terms of a retreat order while the Texans held His Excellency hostage.

The men exchanged formal greetings. Then Santa Anna asked for opium. After taking five grains, he relaxed, presuming Houston might be reasonable in reaching an agreement. After all, he still had four thousand troops under arms in Texas, at least four times more than this rebel commander, with his small army concentrated in a defenseless position. But he was nettled to hear Almonte translate Houston's first question. Houston asked why the men at Goliad were murdered after a capitulation had been reached between Fannin and Urrea.

He answered that he had never been informed of a capitulation, that Urrea contended Fannin surrendered at discretion, and that as commander-in-chief of the army, he was obligated to carry out the policy of the Supreme Government.

When Houston replied that "a dictator is the government," Santa Anna shrugged. He added that Houston must understand that if Urrea had informed him a capitulation had been reached, he never would have ordered the executions at Goliad. Santa Anna became concerned by the grim expression on Houston's face. He proposed that an agreement be reached between the two countries, implying he would support recognition by Mexico of the Republic of Texas.

"Tell him I do not possess the power to negotiate a treaty," Houston said. "That must come later, through the elected authorities of our government."

Hearing Houston's reply, Santa Anna knew he must now bargain for his life. Young Zavala relayed his offer: "In exchange for setting me free to return to my capital, I would agree to support recognition of your new government with a boundary at the Nueces River."

Houston decided his prisoner had practiced such control over military and governmental affairs that he no longer could understand the distinction. Otherwise, Houston thought, he must think I'm a damned fool to consider setting him free on a loose bargain like that.

Lamar, Rusk and Zavala frowned, hoping Houston would order a court-martial. Burleson and Seguin sensed Houston was about to place his chips on the table. Houston looked directly at Santa Anna. "If you will order your subordinate commanders, specifically General Filisola, to remove all your troops beyond the Rio Grande, I will try to see that your life is spared, so that formal treaties may be negotiated between our two governments."

Hearing Almonte's interpretation, Santa Anna frowned and folded his arms across his chest. Humiliated and defeated, but acutely aware of the hard bargain Houston was driving, he asked for a few moments to deliberate. They walked a few steps away, and Santa Anna whispered to Almonte, "Do you believe Houston would have me executed?"

"I doubt it," Almonte replied, "but he has a serious wound. I overheard his doctor say that he will be moved to New Orleans for treatment when possible."

"If he were removed from the scene, who would command?"

"Rusk, Burleson or Lamar."

"Could any of them control this unruly mob?"

"I cannot say, Your Excellency. It seems that these men respond only to Houston."

"I see. Almonte, our people will never accept the Rio Bravo as a border. If I order Filisola to retreat beyond the Bravo, he may interpret that as meaning I will ultimately concede all that territory. But if Filisola resumes hostilities, these rebels will execute me."

"I would not concern myself with Filisola. He will obey your orders. Urrea will have no choice but to follow."

"Yes, you are right about Filisola. The only point in question is the distance of the retreat. I cannot order a retreat past the Nueces."

"Your Excellency, the lack of staging areas along the Nueces makes a retreat beyond the Bravo logical. Concern yourself with protecting your life, and worry at a later time about negotiations regarding boundaries."

Granting the logic of Almonte's observation about the Nueces, Santa Anna still considered that to be a symbolic point of negotiation.

286

He accepted Houston's proposal but he would order removal of all Mexican troops in Texas only south of the Nueces.

Houston shook his head. "Beyond the Rio Grande."

Santa Anna sighed, looking at Almonte. "I have no choice."

When Santa Anna nodded to the Texan commander, Houston called for Hockley to bring writing materials, with Zavala remaining close at hand to translate each word carefully. Houston reviewed the order word by word with Zavala, then ordered it sealed and handed to Deaf Smith for delivery to Filisola. Then, Houston ordered a heavy guard placed around Santa Anna, who was quietly escorted through the grove of oak trees.

As he walked past Juan, Almonte paused. "You should rejoice, Calderón; His Excellency has capitulated. But the day will come when you regret your decision." But Juan was thinking only of Rosa. He imagined kneeling beside her before a priest in the beautiful San Jose chapel. Seguin joined him smiling. "I'm told that I'm to be promoted to lieutenant colonel, in charge of Bexar, following the retreat of General Andrade. I don't suppose that news will upset you."

Hockley found Jason. "The general wants you to leave in the morning to find Wylie Martin. Spread the word that the war's over and the settlers can return. Here's some letters he wants you to deliver to the Raguets and to Sterne in Nacogdoches."

"Then what, Major?"

"Son, he didn't give me any more instructions. If I were you, I'd take a few days of furlough."

Jason wanted to whoop and yell. He saw himself riding across the fields of the Hargrove Plantation, dismounting, and running into Molly's arms.

Late afternoon shadows descended over the camp as a large group of Texans slowly gathered around Houston. Pulling the crutch under his arm, he was assisted to his feet by Hockley and Seguin, and limped a few steps toward the bayou where he viewed the peaceful plains. "Now, gentlemen, the bugles are silent. Let the word spread throughout our land and throughout the world that the Republic of Texas has truly been born. Let the people come home and plant the fields. We're free to build this great land of ours."

EPILOGUE

Following the Battle of San Jacinto, the Republic of Texas endured almost 10 years, sustaining economic and military problems, before Texas became a state in the U.S. on December 29, 1845.

Or, as some would point out, until the Republic of Texas flag was lowered for the final time on February 18, 1846.

Sam Houston was the most prominent figure, serving two terms as president of the republic and later as a U.S. Senator and governor of Texas.

For years frustrated Mexican leaders wouldn't accept the loss of Texas, mounting an occasional threat, but they couldn't conquer Texas, which became much stronger as a state in the U.S.

The Texas situation prompted the U.S. - Mexican War, resulting in the U.S. acquiring vast amounts of western territory including California.

Acknowledgments

Through months of gathering research and conducting interviews, I often felt more like a coordinator than a writer. But without guidance and help from many people, I couldn't have compiled the research or gained the insight necessary to write this book.

My special thanks to Mrs. J. B. Golden of Austin, a retired librarian of the Texas State Library, who was invaluable in organizing research while pulling together fascinating and informative material from various libraries.

Of particular help in providing guidance were T. R. Fehrenbach of San Antonio, author of historical books on Texas and Mexico, and Richard Santos, also of San Antonio, author of "Santa Anna's Campaign Against Texas" and former archivist for Bexar County.

I'm grateful to C. J. Long, curator of the Alamo, for his assistance and to Sister Gertrude of San Antonio, archivist of the Catholic Chancery, for the insight and historical materials she provided. Thanks also to Sue Flanagan, director of the Sam Houston Museum in Huntsville, author of "Sam Houston's Texas" and other books.

Among many libraries utilized, I'm most grateful to the Texas State Library, Austin Public Library, and the J. Frank Dobie Library and the Latin American Collection, both at the University of Texas at Austin.

Many thanks to the staff people at the historical sites I visited with notepad in hand, including the Alamo and other missions, particularly San Jose and Espada, and the Institute of Texan Cultures, all in San Antonio; and to those helpful people at Fannin State Park, Goliad, Gonzales, San Felipe, the San Jacinto Battleground and Washington-on-the-Brazos.

Special thanks to the staffs at the Spanish Governor's Palace in San Antonio and the French Legation in Austin since those sites were studied in considerable detail in order to be used as models for fictional locations in the book.

Alan Kiplinger, Department of Astronomy, University of Texas at Austin, provided sun conditions at the Battle of San Jacinto; and referred me to the U. S. Naval Observatory in Washington, D. C. and the Royal Greenwich Observatory in Sussex, England which provided precise information on the moon condition at the Battle of the Alamo.

I'm grateful to family members, including my mother, Samantha Schadegg of San Antonio, who edited much of the manuscript; my brother, Albert Knaggs, also of San Antonio, for assistance in studying the missions; and to cousins Bill Knaggs and Mrs. Joe Teel, both of San Antonio . . . and to my children, Lisa, Ryan, Bart and David, for their help and understanding . . . to friends and acquaintances who helped along the way — Al and Lin Adams, Jimmy Banks, Ed Clark, Ann Fears Crawford, editor of Santa Anna's memoirs; Bill Gainer, Mrs. Carolyn Hart, Jack Lawler, Louis Mecey, Vickie Motley, Mike Quinn, Pat Robbins, Helen Soto, and Sheila Wilkes, all of Austin; Alfredo Cardenas of Alice; Ed Garza of San Antonio; Minon Slayton of Navasota; Senator John Tower; Mrs. H. H. Vollentine of Gonzales; and Juan Zorilla of Ciudad Victoria, Mexico.

And my special thanks to Mills Cox of Houston, a key supporter of the restoration of Washington-on-the-Brazos, for encouraging me to write this book.

John R. Knaggs   Austin, Texas